All were obsessed with the black-haired voluptuous beauty and passionate spirit of the woman they knew only as

RAVEN

SIR ROGER PENSCOTT the cunning intriguer whose ruthless will to power made him first the master, then the deadly adversary, of the woman called Raven . . .

JAMES GREGORY—the corrupt captain who dreamed of the wealth and lascivious pleasure that would be his when he captured the woman called Raven . . .

ARMIDE—the sensuous mulatto wench, wise in the ways of voodoo, whose hunger for Jason Brand and seething jealousy made her plot the downfall of the woman called Raven . . .

JASON BRAND—the bold, lusty Scot who loved only the high seas and the dangers of a pirate's life. Women he had aplenty, but none could hold him long—until he came to know the haunting charms of the woman called Raven . . .

From the wild rain forests of the Caribbean to the gracious country estates of England . . . from America's vast frontier to the turbulent waters of the Atlantic . . . this panoramic novel sweeps the globe in a tidal wave of intrigue and romance.

RAVEN

Shana Carrol

A JOVE/HBJ BOOK

First Jove/HBJ edition published February 1978

Library of Congress Catalog Card Number: 77-80710

Printed in the United States of America

Jove/HBJ books are published by Jove Publications, Inc.
(Harcourt Brace Jovanovich)
757 Third Avenue, New York, N.Y. 10017

Prologue

Today is December 4, 1740. Bitter winter has come, even to this Carolina. A chill wind warns with icy breath, Abide. Abide . . .

I rejoice in this month of languid hours, for it has afforded me an opportunity, long awaited, to play the scribe and trace the moments of my days. I shall tell of tears—many—and laughter—abundant. To me has been given the heady excitement of battle and danger. I have known the fullness of loss and the emptiness of triumph, thrilled to the exquisite torment of love and the burning fires of passion.

Times, places and names now vie, one with the other, caught on a ragged precipice of dimming memory. I would not lose any of them: the kind, nor the cruel. Let parchment be their salvation.

Sing me a song that's never been sung
And a tale that's never been told—
Of pirates bold and a Raven's gold
And life upon the Blue-O.

I'll sing you a song, my own little dear
Of a love both harsh and true.
In a pirate's haven, met the Rogue his Raven,
And they lived upon the Blue-O,
And merrily on the Blue.

PART I

Chapter I

Marie Celeste Ravenne sighed with lazy contentment, leaned back against a huge chunk of driftwood and gazed across the sparkling sea. Far to the northeast lay Cuba, an island she had never seen. Squinting and trying to imagine the wonders of La Havana, she curled her toes into the sand in order not to be carried away by dreams. A gull screamed and she looked up and half-consciously reached for a shell to pitch at the intruder. The black and white gull banked to the left and disappeared beyond the headland.

Alone again with her thoughts, Marie appeared but a waif tossed upon the shore, lonely and lost. Black hair, damp from sea spray, fell in shoulder-length waves around a lighthearted young woman's face. A streak of dirt soiled a slightly puggish nose that accentuated the tomboy look left by cutoff men's breeches and altered cotton shirt. Both knees—and an elbow as well—were scraped, in contrast to the bronze tone of flesh that glowed with health imparted by the fierce Caribbean sun. Barely parted full lips and the soft line of swelling breasts under the thin, bloused shirt were infallible indicators of her sensuality.

Contemplation erased the impish look, left behind the more serious countenance of a young woman, out of which stared liquid gray eyes slitted against the noon sun. She had traveled in solitude from La Cachette, and if her father, Jean Ravenne, discovered she had left without telling him . . . How he disliked her wandering off alone, without Tomás to keep her company. She squirmed, dug rounded bottom deeper into the sand and fit her toes back into the series of round notches in the blazing white beach. The impish look returned and she giggled with the sure knowledge of the dearly loved, who know exactly which rules may be broken with impunity.

"Oh, father," she would say with a small, crooked, sweetly devious smile calculated to melt his heart, "Whatever is there to worry about? What could possibly happen to me? You yourself have said there is no danger."

She could hear his answer and sighed in resignation. So much fuss about a tiny trip around Mysteré. After all, she would travel much farther one day. How wonderful to be as free as one could be! Sometimes she couldn't understand her father. One moment he averred she was as free as Pia had been, the next he ringed her about with a thousand constraints.

Mysteré! The beginning. A tranquil jewel in the shimmering sea. Place it a short hundred leagues south of the western end of Cuba, a long hundred north of the eastern tip of Honduras, which is to say almost exactly halfway between the two. There, from the Mysterioso Bank, a shallow, submerged reef in the midst of the azure Caribbean, spring many tiny islands, most forgotten or ignored.

No longer than five miles, nor broader than three at the widest point, an unnamed island lay like a teardrop falling toward the morning sun. It was here the crew of the battered sloop Raventazón dropped anchor in 1692. Sick of a life of buccaneering and seeking haven, the hopeful arrivals named the small but well-protected harbour Voûte Paix, or as it would be said in English, Peace Bay. The name was apt, for the isle was uninhabited and there was, indeed, peace to be found.

The island itself they called Mysteré, a name chosen by my mother in honor of an uncommonly accurate representation of a human face on a cliff readily visible from the southern approaches to the island. Whether this sculpture was hewn by human hands or the elements, we never knew. In any case, Mysteré suited the tiny band's needs. Of native foods there were plenty, as of cattle and feral hogs, no doubt left there to grow wild by earlier callers.

A colony of respectable citizens, their crimes buried in the past, had been established by 1695. I was born in April of the same, an event sadly followed by my mother's death some eight months later, on the last day of the year. Notwithstanding this grief, our colony throve, as may be discovered in my father's journal, which I was lucky enough to find some years ago. Suffice it to say we numbered ninety-three by 1712, among us not a few women, a half-dozen children my own age and even babes in arms. Our population included an additional hundred and fifty slaves, not counting their issue.

Mysteré had become self-sufficient. A bustling town, La Cachette, grew up around Voûte Paix. Spread inland on a small, fertile plain were plantations which supplied most of the food we ate and tobacco for trading with smugglers and, occasionally, pirates (my father's old ties kept us safe from attack). Meat, tobacco and rum were exchanged for such manufactures as civilization could best supply. In addition, though of this little was said when the slender threads of Spanish authority touched our shore, we were in occasional receipt of luxuries originally destined for others' hands.

My years on Mysteré were uneventful for the main part. I took for granted our emerald isle surrounded by the deep, throbbing blue of the Caribbean, for we lived at peace with as much of the world as we could see. I remember hardly more than happy days and quiet nights, broken only by occasional storms which broke over Mysteré and left the air clean and vibrant. I remember studying my lessons, playing games on land and aboard the sailing vessels that visited us, running and swimming and riding on horseback. I remember the taste of fruit, the warmth of sun on my back and legs, the gentle tug of sea breeze through my hair. I remember a state of innocence in which the days flew by without note.

11

Innocence came to an abrupt end on a bright July day in the year 1712. . . .

She glanced at the sun. There was more than enough time to get back before sunset, when, in daily pilgrimage, father and daughter visited wife's and mother's grave. Marie often wondered about the daily climb up the mountain to the flowered glade where Pia Ravenne lay. Why the ritual was so important to her father was an unfathomable mystery to a child. She had questioned the trip but once, only to receive a hurt stare in answer. A tear had run from his eye. Never before had she seen such a troubling display of emotion, and from that day she suffered the climb and stood in reverent silence while Jean kneeled by the ivory cross over the white stone slab and prayed for the woman he had loved and would never forget, the woman Marie had never remembered.

Pia Marie Ravenne
Born 1672–Died December 31, 1695

On a clear day Marie could look from the back door of their house and, if the riot of vines had been cleared recently, see the little white marker high on the slope. Pia Ravenne, in death, overlooked the slumbering village of La Cachette, the middle plantations where the tobacco grew and the fruit- and grain-laden fields sloping up the flanks of the mountain. Sometimes the lofty emerald height was concealed by a cloudy shadow as gray and fathomless as Marie's eyes. Often, as she gazed up the long trail to the clearing, Marie wondered if the dead could see through the mist, if Pia watched her daughter, standing below and looking up.

Whether or not Pia watched, Jean did, with trepidation and sometimes fear, for Marie resembled her mother more and more with each passing day. How the daughter reminded him of the mother, especially when she tossed her raven-black curls! The ebullience of spirit, the headstrong will, the ravishing beauty that

12

drove men to excess. How incomparably fortunate he had been! Pia was a woman to choose one man and one man only. Would Marie mirror her mother in this respect too? He hoped so, yet dreaded the day she would leave him.

The years passed and Jean became less and less able to separate daughter from mother, past from present. Secretly at first, then openly, he took to filling large wooden mugs with palm wine and wandering aside to sit beneath the low sweeping branches of an ancient ycao tree. There, nearly hidden from sight, he drank to assuage the bitter loss.

The older Marie grew, the more often such episodes occurred and the greater was Jean's pain. With greater and greater frequency, he retired to the quiet, haunted realm at the base of the ycao, leaving Marie at liberty to explore the island that was her home. This day she had coaxed a mare from the corral and, ignoring Tomás, the mestizo servant, rode off in reckless exploration. Why not? Father was brooding with the last of his wine.

The day was warm, balmy and ripe for adventure. Marie was young and full of life and energy, free as the gulls and carefree as the wind. One day soon, her father had threatened, she would have to act her age, wear gowns and assume a woman's responsibilities. Seventeen was, after all, past the age for marriage. Until that day came, Marie had decided, she'd better have as much fun as possible, not only for herself, but for her mother, who would never laugh or love again, who lay beneath the mist and spongelike loam high on the mountainside. No matter what Jean would have said about that, Marie imagined that Pia watched with approval, taking sad joy in her daughter's escapades.

The trip around the island was always a pleasant adventure. The pony, a small, barrel-chested brown mare, climbed the steep rise out of La Cachette, dipped back down to the shore a half-mile north and followed the long curve of open, sandy beach along the western side of Mysteré. Here on the lee side of the island, the water lay calm and gentle, not at all like a vast sea. Horse and

13

rider plodded along the water-packed smooth sand, stopping from time to time to inspect a shell or piece of driftwood, carefully avoiding the purple-jeweled air-bags and streaming tentacles of Portuguese men-of-war washed up during the night before. By eleven in the morning they had reached Point de las Pleurs, the point of tears at the northwestern tip of Mystéré, where currents swirled around the huge, water-sculpted boulders.

A half-hour later, after Marie fell off one of the boulders and received a thorough and frightening drenching, they started down the eastern side of the island. Here, on the windward beaches, the Caribbean took on a new aspect as the sea, driven by the easterly trades, sent streaming combers to beat on the rocky, boulder-strewn shore. A hundred yards south of the point, she stopped to rest and dig for shells in a shallow cove. Now, rested, Marie sprang up as the pony started to nibble at a low-hanging branch of a stunted, gnarled tree sprouting from a pile of rocks heaped near the shore.

"Aiae!" she yelled, throwing up her hands in alarm, gray eyes glinting with the fiery inheritance of her Spanish mother. *"Caballo loco!* Would you torment yourself with the venom of the mancanilla? Even the fish have more sense!"

The startled mare bolted from the tree and galloped down the coast, leaving the exasperated girl to heave a parting shout of disgust. "Stupid horse! To eat poisoned apples? I should rather walk home than ride on your back. I am glad to be rid of you. Tomás was right!"

The mare disappeared around a boulder and Marie slumped dejectedly against the driftwood log. The long walk home promised to be more adventure than she had anticipated. Now Jean would surely miss her, and as usual, assume the worst. She pouted. He worried to excess. "Well, let him worry, then," she said petulantly, immediately regretting the words. That was no way for a daughter to talk. Even if she didn't understand his unreasoning fear, he was her father and deserved respect and love. He didn't like her to wander the whole

14

island unescorted? Very well. If she went over the mountain, she could say she'd only been visiting Pia's grave. This will take some clever talking, she mused.

A small red fruit from the mancanilla dropped into the water. Marie sighed, got to her feet and started for home, following the mare's zigzag path along the increasingly rocky coast until she came to the beginnings of a trail leading upward and hence over the mountain. That the trail had been used by wild dogs and feral hogs was evident from the multitude of old tracks, but Marie determined to follow it anyway in order to avoid the longer walk around the southeastern belly of the island.

The first hundred yards bent slowly upward. Once under the trees, the offshore breeze was cut and an eerie, howling wail floated down from the summit ahead. Wild dogs. Marie gritted her teeth and wished she'd brought along one of the big flintlock pistols. She could shoot as well as any man and frequently went hunting with her father or Tomás.

The unearthly chorus plummeted past like some tangible substance and lost itself among the breakers below. Grimly, she determined to continue rather than wander around the island in a runaway horse's footsteps and face her friends' laughter as she trudged through town. After all, there was little real danger: such animals generally preferred to be left alone and usually avoided humans. Still, there were gruesome tales of shredded remains and gnawed bones found along solitary trails. "I shall not be afraid," she said aloud, brushing back the raven-black tresses. "A stick will have to do." Armed with a dead but stout branch, she continued.

By the time she'd scrambled up three quarters of the rock-littered and forested slope, Marie began to think better of the whole escapade. She might have been home, sitting down to a hearty noonday meal and not listening to a hungry stomach growl at every step. A tree ahead promised relief, though, and the dogs had stopped their unearthly din. She wiped the sweat from her eyes and persevered another thirty yards. Now, if only there were no boars . . .

Stopping under a caremite tree whose branches were extravagantly laden with clumps of plumlike fruits, she stripped off the baggy shirt and gathered a dozen of the ripest. A rock painted with bright orange moss served as a table. In rapid succession, Marie gorged on the pleasant fruits, relishing each bite all the more for the strenuous exertion of the long hike. Soon the sweet milky juices flowing from the fruit's oddly colored black meat covered her chin and dripped down her naked chest and breasts. Finishing the last of the delicious feast, she dried off, using the shirt for a towel, and sank back onto the ground to close her eyes and luxuriate in the warmth of the sun. Somewhere nearby a *grillon,* as her Spanish friends called the huge crickets, sang a sleepy song. A small green parrot landed on a limb above and preened, chuckling to himself before attacking one of the barely ripened plums. Half-dreaming, Marie's hands moved unconsciously to her breasts and she shuddered as her thoughts turned to more forbidden fruits. Someday, soon perhaps, Marie Ravenne would take a man. What would it be like to be loved like that?

One of the women in La Cachette, Nina by name, had gotten drunk one night. Taking Marie in tow, she explained the duties of lovers, graphically describing every function and pleasure of each partner in a most explicit fashion. The imagery evoked was exciting, but somehow sullied. From her words, Marie could not picture Nina being loved. "But I *shall* be," Marie vowed. "None shall have me but to whom I first give myself. He will be my own true love, my only heart." Romantic notions tumbled through her mind, evoking image upon image. "We will have a magnificent plantation. Or even a castle. The sun will fill our room with gay and golden light and sweet birds will sing and flowers fill the air with perfume. Together, we will do what Nina said . . ."

But what would it be like? The human body, male or female, held no mysteries for an island girl of the early

16

eighteenth century. Talk was cheap, coarse, and ribald jokes were common.

Only two weeks ago, at a party to celebrate the return of one of Mysteré's ships, she had found herself alone with Guy St. Martin. Together, she and Guy walked down the beach until Guy pointed to the water. "Turtle!" he whispered. "Let's get him."

Two bodies, lithe and firm and young, hit the water as one. When they reached the spot where the turtle had been spotted, it was gone. "Race you back," Guy shouted, starting for shore.

Marie followed, swimming smoothly, catching up but not being able to forge ahead. Laughing, hand in hand, they stumbled through the surf and flopped onto the beach. For a moment they lay still, breathing heavily. When Marie sat up, it was to see Guy lying on his back, staring at her with a strange look in his eyes.

Both wore light cotton breeches, Marie a cotton shirt as well, which had become nearly transparent when wet. Under his gaze, Marie felt her breasts tighten, could not help but look down to the rising ridge between Guy's legs. Bewitched, thrilled and not a little frightened, she did not stop him as his hand reached out to touch her breasts, then open the clinging shirt. She, too, could not resist placing her hand on him and running her fingers over his outlined manhood.

Was this to be it, then? Gently, Guy pulled her atop him and their lips met. Her breasts, exposed, pressed against his chest, and their fever, youthful, wanting, hungering, grew.

Then fear! Marie struggled, shoved herself away from him and, angry at her own cowardice, lapsed into silence. Eventually, her distemper subsided, replaced by awkward embarrassment. Not knowing what to say or how to say it. Not daring to look in his eyes. An empty feeling, as if she'd done something wrong, perhaps, even though her body felt so alive and right. Trying to act naturally, Marie rose and walked into the water, rinsed off the sand and then stood on the beach, waiting. A

17

moment later, Guy joined her. Hand in hand, silently, they walked back to the party.

What would happen the next time? There was to be another party that night. Would Guy be her own true love? Would they walk down the beach again? Her eyes squinted and she tried to imagine what would follow.

A rolling crescendo sounded deep in the distance. She sat up, alert and breathing raggedly, the fantasy broken. Thunder? The sky above was devoid of clouds, a shining azure shield as far as the eye could see. But thunder? Yes, there it was again. A storm to the far south? The only way to tell was to reach the summit.

Marie jumped up and began to run, donning the shirt without breaking stride. Many a night she had lain awake during a storm and seen the lightning jab incandescent lances into the peak and upper slopes. Frightening from a distance, she knew it would be far worse this close: she had to cross the summit and be well down the other side before the storm broke.

Cedar gave way to a host of stunted coffee bushes planted by old Juan, the crazy Spanish outcast, a few years earlier. There the underbrush had been cleared away and the going was easier. A hundred yards further along and she emerged from the coffee onto the cleared top of the mountain. Resembling a monk's shaved head, the lofty height was covered with rock and, in places, a windswept carpet of undulating grasses mirroring the ocean far below. She would have enjoyed the vista had there not been a sooty, gray-black column of smoke funneling upward from the south.

The thunder sounded again, faint at first, then louder, with a brief lull in the wavering easterly breeze. Marie cried out and raced across the open ground. A line of cedars blocked the view, but her mother's gravesite, lower down the mountain, would be clear. There was a lofty, stalwart old palm she could climb. Already the frond-laden top was visible above the lesser growth. The mountain sloped down and Marie rushed along, scrambling to avoid rock and shrub, tree and crevass. A moment later she reached the clearing. Quickly, she skinned up the first ten feet of the ringed trunk. . . .

La Cachette was burning! The low-country plantations, crops and houses, burning! The tobacco lands, the middle ground, burning! Three galleons squatted in the ruined harbor. Puffs of black smoke ripped from the side of one craft, followed by a slow, rolling explosion. A sloop running for the open sea appeared to crumple: masts toppled and fell, followed by a flash of fire. Of the four vessels at anchor in Voûte Paix when Marie had left that morning, the sloop was the last. The other three were already reduced to tortured wreckage.

Figures scurried about the shore, a tide of men sweeping inland, moving up with the ground, running and marching through the yet unburned fields and plantations. Now she could make out the faint crackling of guns. New fires sprang up. Mysteré was under attack. But why? Had pirates unknown to Jean taken to the sea? Probably not, especially in such fine ships. No. English or French privateers? No, of course not, for as a breeze kicked up in the harbor, Spanish flags became visible. But Mysteré had an agreement with the Spanish commander in La Havana. Each year they paid and swore allegiance to Spain, in return for which they were supposed to be left alone. The attack did not make sense, yet La Cachette was burning, the ships were sunk, the plantations were afire. And all by Spanish hands. Why? Why?

Frightened, utterly so. Down the palm tree, past the low fence surrounding the grave and the engraved white marker. Running now, calfhide slippers sure on the worn, oft-used path. Below, glistening with the sweat of fearful haste, running slaves take shape as they approach in a mad dash for the hills and safety. White mortar walls, pristine from a distance, tucked under the dark blotchy browns of thatched roofs. There is no joy now. Only panic. The fields are smoldering. A thatched roof explodes in a gout of new flame. Smoke curls in great clouds. Distant cries sound through the roar of flame, punctuated by gunfire. Father!

Running! All the boys are jealous because none is as

fleet as Marie. Her hair, jet black, trails in the wind like the past streaking out of time, from which the fugitive heart can never flee fast enough. Do not look back, whispers the wind. Turn aside, girl. Run to the hills! Do not look back. What can a young woman do? Run! Run to sorrow!

A figure ahead burst from the undergrowth. Eyes wide with horror bulged from the copper-colored flesh of a mestizo. "Tomás!" Marie called.

The servant caught her arm. "Come with me. We hide."

"What is it? What has happened?"

Tomás jerked her off balance, hauled her up the slope. Marie tore free. "No! Tomás, what happened?"

"Murcia," the mestizo hissed. "Murcia come. He burn. Kill. Captain Solia, the cayman-faced. He come, too."

"But Father said there was nothing to fear."

"Murcia! Mur . . . ciiia!!" The terror-stricken servant howled and ran off alone, unwilling to remain close by any longer.

"Where is Father?" Marie screamed, but the mestizo disappeared into the trees. Marie turned, saw flames dance atop the roof of their house. The dried palmetto thatch went up in a great coughing roar, devoured at once. Marie was crying now, crying as she ran. Down to the high fields. Men were setting them afire, swinging torches through the grain in wide arcs. Gleeful Spaniards in soot-covered doublets and breeches. Peaked helmets gleamed atop some of the heads, cloth caps atop others. They hooted and called to one another, pointing at the girl. Three gave chase.

"Father!!" she screamed to the house's burning interior. No answer. Someone was behind her. Clawed hands reached. Marie leaped away and two Spaniards collided, the one without the helmet catching the worst of it. He groaned and sank unconscious to the ground.

Marie ran, looking over her shoulder. The helmeted Spaniard shook his senses clear and gave chase. A third rounded the house and cut across her path, but she proved quick enough, ducked under his arms and ran like the wind toward La Cachette, eyes searching frantically for her father.

Corpses. Horror contorted her face into a mask of disbelief. Neighbors, men and women she had known. Slaves. Always the old, those of no use to anyone.

Breathless, weary, exhausted. Gasping for air, mouth thick with fear and mucus. Did her pursuers still follow? No matter. Other Spaniard dogs stopped to gawk. She passed before they could react, for most were caught in a frenzy of looting.

The middle lands and fertile low-country plantations were in ruins. Death had reaped a bitter harvest there. She could no longer bear the stench of burning flesh, could barely stomach the smoldering oven that had been La Cachette. There were men ahead on the beach, prisoners huddled about a longboat, bunched together and resembling so many leaves waiting for a scattering wind.

"Father!!"

Jean Ravenne turned, his face still handsome despite harsh years and worse treatment during the last hour. Tall, angular, stooped by an excess of grief. Sullen eyes lit with newfound fear. Marie rushed to him through the throng, though he cried out for her to escape.

An arm engulfed her, spun her around. Knocked to the sand, Marie struggled as a pair of gasping pursuers sought to examine their newly won treasure. Obscene laughter filled her ears, defeated the roar of flames and cannon. A huge boulderlike figure leaned down and Marie screamed at the sight of the hideous, mottled face with which mothers frightened their children into good behavior. Captain Solia, the feared! The blotches gave a reptilian cast to his flesh.

"Quiet, woman," he growled in a voice that sounded as if it came from a throat filled with rocks. His massive paw ripped apart her blouse. Marie squirmed against the rough hands pinning her to the moist earth. "Magnificent!" he said, his eyes sparkling coldly. He touched one breast, then the other. Callus-hardened fingers

21

traced a line to the top of her breeches, deftly probed the softness below. A horrible grin split his face. "You and me. We will talk later, eh, *corazón*?"

"Animal!" Marie's father bolted from his fellow prisoners, lunged across the sand. With the strength of madness, Marié twisted from her captors' grasp, saw Jean, heard the sharp crack of a pistol and screamed as Jean Ravenne stopped in his tracks, stumbled forward and crumpled to the sand. An immaculately dressed Spanish don stepped to the fore, wiped away the traces of gunpowder from his fingers.

Marie scrambled to her father's side. "Papa? No, oh, please, no!"

Jean Ravenne opened his eyes, blinked away the pain. "Dear Marie. I . . . am . . . sorry . . ." His brow knotted, then relaxed. He looked past Marie's shoulder. His killer stood nearby, a lazy smile drifting across his face. "Murcia," the dying man muttered.

The nobleman laughed, bowed slightly. "Don Juan Francisco García y Murcia. He who teaches lessons to insolent Frenchmen. And their women. She will be mine. First."

"Murcia," Jean sneered. "He who steals women and butchers children." He spat blood at the Spaniard's feet. "Forever more they will call you butcher. . . . The butcher of Mysteré. Men will spit when they hear your name."

The nobleman scowled. Jean coughed, gripped Marie's hand and pulled her close. Life fleeing, he whispered one word and died. Marie buried her face against his neck.

Brutal hands tore her from his side, denied her even the briefest of farewells and dragged her to where the other choice women of the island waited to be taken aboard a galleon bound for Barranquilla, the center of Murcia's power along the northern coast of South America.

The afternoon waned and the women were given water and loaves of stale bread. No man touched them, but only because the order had come from Murcia himself. As the night passed, they lay huddled on the beach, listening to the screams of the new victims as they were found. Spaniards came from the remains of La Cachette, carrying bloody booty paid for with their victims' lives.

When dawn came and before the wind shifted offshore, the women were herded aboard the flagship of the tiny fleet. Marie hardly noticed the ship's motion when it eventually set sail, nor did she hear the keening sorrow of the unfortunates who had seen whole families destroyed and could no longer bear the torment in silence. She noted not the passing of the days and nights, only sat benumbed in one corner of the dungeonlike hold.

Three days out they ran into an early storm. The hurricane came from the southeast and tossed the awkward galleons about like so much flotsam. Still Marie sat in her corner, holding onto a piece of line, scarcely caring when the ship cast her against the heavy timbers and left her battered and bruised.

The winds increased. Main- and foremast split, left the deck a jumble of rope and gear. The ship broached, lay on its beam. Tortured wood shrieked and split. A huge wave picked up the galleon, slammed it into a trough and broke it like a toy. Marie was in the water. Amid the cries of the drowning her father's fading whisper gave her the strength to cling tightly to a hatch cover. Later, by sheer luck she managed to gain a seat aboard an already crowded and half-swamped longboat.

Two days later Marie was one of the few left alive when an English vessel, only half its mainmast still standing, hove to and rescued the half-dead survivors. Hauled aboard, she was dried out, fed warm gruel, given new clothes and a hammock. By the time they reached the straits of Florida, she had recovered enough strength to walk the deck. There, she caught the eye of the captain who, because of her great beauty, resolved to keep her and install her in his household.

Sun, wind and the passage of time. Creak of line and hiss of wave. Boundless track of deep waters, cold and clean and pure. No matter how horror strewn the past, the young are strong and soon discover that life goes on. Days passed as in a dream. When the *Glorianna*, captained by Lord Roger Penscott, came at last to anchored rest in the great Pool of London, it was the spirit voice of Jean Ravenne repeating a final entreaty that bolstered Marie's courage as, in Lord Penscott's entourage, she traversed the teeming, vulgar streets of London and rode the choppy waters of the Thames to a strange new life.

Her father's voice echoed still. In her mind's eye Marie Ravenne watched from afar as she bent close to hear Jean say, with the conviction of impending death, one single word: "Live!"

Chapter II

"Ravenne!" The shrill bellow reverberated down the long hall of the servants' quarters.

"Ravenne!" Stern footsteps underlined the repeated word, emphasized each syllable.

"Ravenne!" The strident voice promised angry punishment. All the doors along the hall save one stood open. Penscott Hall's personnel had scurried to their posts half an hour past, long before the sun rose.

Master Servant Thrush's spare frame was rigid with indignation. The low-hanging, stiffened skirts of his coat flapped and fluttered like the wings of his namesake. A beakish nose protruding from a heavily powdered face completed the vision. He slapped a short length of cane against one spindly shank and hurried toward the single remaining closed door.

Dragged from a nightmare of death and ocean storms by the master servant's vocal talons, Marie glanced with dismay at the faint predawn glow softening the room's single window. The narrow bed along the opposite wall lay mussed and empty. Arabella had purposefully stolen out without waking her, that Marie might incur Thrush's wrath on this of all days. At twenty, a year older than Marie, Arabella possessed no little animosity toward her roommate, the newest upstairs servant in the house. There could be no doubt. Arabella was jealous because Marie had been advanced to an undeservedly exalted position. That the upstart child refused obeisance to her elder, in fact tended to look down her nose at or even ignore Arabella, served to further infuriate her. Worst, since coming to Penscott Hall some two years earlier, the French bitch, as Arabella was fond of calling Marie to one and all, had blossomed into a thoroughly enchanting young woman whose nymphlike

25

beauty the chunkier servant girl could never hope to match.

If three reasons were not enough, another more heinous could be found. Not a single roister in the Penscott household and holdings had been refused Arabella's favors, a romp in the stables, a rump offered in the privacy of one of the manor's multitudinous closets. In contrast, Marie scorned such behavior and, though well beyond the age for bedding, adamantly refused to permit the least caress. Above all else, Arabella hated Marie's virginity and imagined that the "sweet mistress of Mysteré," another favorite epithet, disapproved of her roommate's promiscuity.

The truth, were it known, was far different. Marie's reclusiveness was a result of several factors, none understood by Arabella or any of the others. Born and raised French, English was still a tongue with which she felt uncomfortable. Born and raised Roman Catholic, the Protestants still seemed heretical. Born and raised a child of love and freedom on an island of peace, hate and servitude in a vicious and violent England were beyond her understanding or ability to assimilate.

Forced to live in an alien society, Marie's thoughts ever ranged to the past. There, protected by a blanket of shyness, she took refuge in a dream world of warm and wondrous memory which in turn spawned dreams for a similar future. There was hope. Marie Ravenne would not remain in England forever, surrounded by vicious, pale louts. Time and again she remembered the night on the beach with Guy. Guy was dead—she'd seen him, blood-drenched on the sand—but another, a wildly passionate hero, would one day appear at Penscott Hall to rescue her. Together, they would return to the Caribbean and live in a castle on a marvelous plantation. Sunlight would drench their bedroom, and they would live for love. . . .

Once, before she knew better and on a night when the loneliness was too great to bear any longer, Marie confided in Arabella. The older girl listened intently, then laughed outright in derision. Stunned, Marie stammered something about "only a dream" and fled the room, followed by a torrent of caustic jests, soon taken up by the rest of the servants. From that night Marie's only recourse was to keep silent counsel, work as diligently as possible and dream in solitude, for she was yet too inexperienced to wage battle against such odds.

The door to her room flew open. Thrush, rouged cheeks streaked with sweat and eyes glaring, pointed a long, furious finger. "Unspeakable behavior!"

Marie clutched the cotton nightshift to conceal her nakedness. "I'm sorry, Master Thrush. Arabella promised to wake me. Instead, she—"

"Enough! I will listen to no excuses. You will be punished later. Were it not that Lord Penscott wishes to see you this moment, it's a good caning you'd get."

"I'm terribly—"

"Silence!" Bony fingers pinched the flesh of her arm. "The king," he hissed importantly. "Our new sovereign graces us on the morrow and the little mistress lies abed? Perhaps our great French lady disapproves?"

"Of course not, Master Thrush," Marie managed, wincing with pain.

"Of course not. Of course not," he mimicked. "Worse and worse. Lovely." His tone darkened and his face flushed. "Insolent French pig. Your disrespect will be punished." He loosed his hold and a reddening bruise flowered against the whiteness.

"I meant no disrespect, sir," Marie vowed, vigorously rubbing her arm.

"Silence!" Marie yelped as the cane cracked sharply against her taut buttocks, naked beneath the shift. "Get dressed and to the library. Do not keep m'lord waiting, or I'll see you in the scullery, to serve with the blackguards." Coat wings fluttering around spindly stocking-wrapped legs, he strutted down the hall, a diminishing picture of authority in the frame of the open door.

Marie watched ruefully, then closed the door and slipped out of her sleeping chemise. "That Arabella!" she said aloud, rubbing her behind and peering over her shoulder at the line of scarlet. "She's no better than any of the others, from the grand ladies on down. I should have known her generosity but a stinking trick." Marie rummaged through a small stack of neatly folded clothes. "I've early duties myself, love," she mimicked. "Besides, we'll all be up before dawn tomorrow. I'll wake you as I leave. . . ." She returned to her own voice. "I should have known. She's jealous, is all. Jealous and petty."

The house would be a beehive of activity today, she mused, already depressed. Master Thrush would keep an ever watchful eye and his cane would be handy, ready to inflict quick punishment for the slow or bungling servant. The king was coming and there were a thousand things undone. A new thought sprang to mind. All the commotion could work in her favor. If she hurried through her tasks there might well be an opportunity to steal some time with her one true friend in all the household, Behan, the tutor.

"Ill started, ends well," she muttered hopefully, rubbing the welt on her hips. A simple working dress slipped over her head. An apron followed, tied tightly in the back. Long black tresses, uncut for the past three years, were piled beneath the traditional servant's cap. Losing as little time as possible, Marie hurried through the house, down the long halls to the library. Lord Penscott himself, Duke of Brentlynn, answered the knock. Marie adjusted cap and apron, patted her cheeks and finally entered, uneasily noticing how the huge portrait of Lord Blythmoor Penscott glared from the south wall, the graying pigment of impassive features repeated in the grizzled countenance of the current duke.

The trappings of wealth were commonplace in Penscott Hall, but the library, because it was the center from which Lord Penscott ruled, was held in awe by Marie and the other servants. Here was the inner sanctum of authority, entered only rarely and then by one fully conscious of the importance of the summons that haled one before the master. A massive bookcase lined the north wall. Amidst the books, especially carved niches held exquisitely wrought figurines and priceless vases of gold and jade and mother-of-pearl. Great velvet swags hung with gold tassels adorned the wide leaded-glass windows overlooking the formal gardens outside. A massive globe tracked with paths of silver wire to indicate the *Glorianna*'s journeys dominated the center of the east wall between the windows.

This was the first time in months she had actually faced her master. The lord of the manor wore a morning coat of olive velvet. The buckles on his slippers were broad bands of pounded gold. His head, bald from a combination of age and years beneath a wig, was wrapped in a brocaded turban. Gwendolyn, the newly acquired Lady Penscott and some twenty years his junior, had aged him more than Marie thought possible.

"Shut the door, child." He spoke in French, gently and with no trace of irritation. Marie complied and approached the desk of carved walnut. The huge article of furniture dwarfed Lord Penscott's compact frame as he sat and stared at her without speaking for a long moment. "You are such a delicate creature," he sighed. "Like a rare, fragile carving. It was that quality—that and your French, of course—that prompted me to separate you from your bedraggled companions. A bit over two years, wasn't it?" He raised an inquisitive eyebrow.

Marie nodded, not wishing to risk a reply. Four or five times a year the duke sent Thrush for her. Then followed a short, one-sided conversation, with him doing most of the talking and Marie answering in subdued monosyllables. He seemed to be studying her, marking what progress she made. Not at all unkindly, he inquired of her health, asked if she found her duties suitable and even, once, if she was happy. The occasional interviews mystified Marie, for she could discern no reason for them beyond a patronizing interest in a piece of property. At the same time she knew there must be a deeper purpose, for it was common knowledge Lord Penscott did nothing without an end in mind. Furthermore, of all the servants, none other received the somewhat secretive attention of the master.

Lord Penscott waited in vain for an answer, hoping as always that for once she would dare respond, that she had indeed and at last become woman enough to face him without fear. Evidently, not yet. He sighed inwardly, envying Behan the pleasure of her quick tongue and reportedly rare intelligence. Perhaps a little nudge in the right direction would help. A suitable gown, makeup and a decent coif would accentuate her figure and do wonders for those soft, gray eyes that, were they bolder, would reduce a man to a quivering mass of jelly. And still a virgin, so his spies averred. A useful commodity, virginity, especially in one so beautiful. But one to be handled carefully. Adroitly. When the time was ripe, she'd blossom. And then? For a brief moment he allowed himself the luxury of imagining the girl abed. By God! but she'd be marvelous to behold. And to play teacher to such lithe beauty! Smooth skin, firm breasts, not a sagging muscle . . . She'd learn quickly, no doubt.

Too quickly, aging flanks whispered dolefully. Difficult enough to rise to the occasion with Gwendolyn from time to time, and she but a year past thirty. However in heaven's name would he handle a nineteen-year-old? Better to sit back and watch and plan and dream. Lord Roger Penscott had had his day with nineteen-year-olds. To each was given only so much, to each was meted out a share and no more. Abruptly, his mood changed. He chuckled, poured a goblet of port, his second of the morning. "Of course it was two years ago. Who should know better, eh?" He rose, walked behind her and circled back to the great chair. "So my wife has grown fond of you, eh?"

"I don't know, sir," Marie responded shyly.

"Well, she has. I have heard it said Marie Celeste Ravenne is the one she prefers above all others."

"M'lady is gracious," Marie answered dutifully.

Lord Penscott's countenance darkened. "Most gracious," he echoed.

A soft knock sounded at the door. Lord Penscott sighed, bade the intruder enter. Thrush stepped into the room, carefully avoided looking at Marie. "A message from your son, m'lord. I thought you'd want to see it immediately.

The nobleman broke the seal on a parchment, read quickly. "Good, Thrush. Edmond's arrival with the king's entourage has been confirmed. I expect he'll reside with us for the time being. See he's well taken care of. The guest room above the sculpture gallery should do, I suspect."

"Begging m'lord's pardon, but Captain Gregory—"

"—will have to be moved."

"Yes, m'lord." Thrush bowed to the inevitable and backed through the door, casting an eye in Marie's direction. The girl had no business there, and if the duke had no sense of propriety, Thrush did. Such things, in his estimation, were best kept to night and back rooms, not the library.

The door closed and Marie relaxed slightly. "Where were we?" Lord Penscott asked. "Ah, yes. The graciousness of my wife. But enough of that."

"As you wish, m'lord," Marie answered, embarrassed.

"You know we entertain tomorrow," he went on, reverting to French. "There will be many here who speak French only. I shall need ears—more than are available, I'm afraid."

"Of course, m'lord."

"Good." He paused. "I've arranged for a gown for you."

"M'lord," she gasped, taken aback. "A gown, m'lord?"

A hint of a smile crossed Penscott's face. "You hear correctly," he said, obviously enjoying her reaction. "You'll have to wait on my wife, of course, but no serving food or drinks, you hear? Mingle. Be a little mysterious, but be careful to pretend you don't understand French. When they've left, we'll speak again."

So here was the surprise for this visit. A gown! "As you wish, m'lord," Marie answered, trying to hide her excitement.

"I do. You will be rewarded, by the way. If there is anything you want? Perhaps a little extra time off to spend with Behan?" Marie reddened. Her English lessons were supposed to have stopped a year ago. "He tells me you're an apt pupil. Perhaps a word to Thrush would help. Well, we'll see. That will be all then."

"Yes, m'lord." Curtsying deeply, Marie backed toward the door. Lord Penscott knew she was still spending time with the elderly tutor and wasn't at all angry. Two surprises! Each time they met he impressed her with some hitherto unknown bit of knowledge. . . .

"Ah, yes, my dear. One more thing."

"M'lord?" Marie jumped, startled.

"We've much to accomplish today. If you'd wake my wife and get her started?"

"Of course, m'lord."

"While you're at it, please request Captain Gregory to join me at tea in the garden."

Marie's eyes widened and she swallowed. A third surprise? "Sir?"

Lord Penscott looked up from the paper he was reading. "You heard me, woman. Please do as I ask and quickly." His surprisingly clear, light hazel eyes betrayed no emotion, gazed guilelessly into hers. The moment passed and Marie thought a trace of cold amusement flitted across the nobleman's face before he went back to the paper in dismissal.

Quickly Marie closed the doors and started up the stairs. Lord Penscott was far too deep for a simple maid. Everyone else in the house knew Lady Gwendolyn had been bedding Captain Gregory for the last week but rumor had it that her husband didn't know, and would be furious if he found out. Marie herself had stayed away from the lovers as much as possible, not wanting to become embroiled in conspiracies against his lordship.

Gown forgotten, she paused on the stairs, seeking some excuse to tarry. With luck, the captain would have returned to his own rooms. Penscott Hall was large enough to offer hope. The stately, two-story mansion shaped like the letter H stood a quarter mile from the Thames. The crossbar comprised a spacious gallery below and a superb receiving hall above. South of the bar, between the wings, lay the chapel and Lord Penscott's garden facing the Thames, upon which he loved to gaze. The east wing consisted of servants' quarters at one end and the plethora of offices necessary for the functioning of Penscott's estate at the other. Above were a warren of sitting and bedrooms, galleries and parlors.

In the west wing, the state bedroom occupied the front, facing the river. Running back, or north, were sitting rooms and the intimate dining room where the duke and duchess took their meals, accompanied by what few close friends had joined them for the occasion. At the far northern end was Lady Gwendolyn's boudoir, with views to west and north, where the forest began.

Ascending up the grandiose stairway leading to m'lady's bedchamber, Marie passed beneath stately landscapes where noble demigods, in a world circumscribed by gilded frames, cavorted in sensual disarray on lawns marred by no more than signatures of unfamiliar Venetian masters. Secure in their unchanging excesses, nymphs and satyrs danced before the unseeing eyes of marble statuary posted on the landing.

She could procrastinate only so long. Marie neared the end of the corridor and paused at the door, still hesitant. The hour was too early to disturb the mistress. Perhaps . . . She pressed an ear against the panel, hoping for a clue. Suddenly the door opened, and with a yelp of surprise the girl plunged into a decidedly masculine embrace. "Ha! And what have we here? Woodsprite? Mischievous imp?"

Marie struggled to extricate herself from the gentleman's exploring hands. "No. Not a woodsprite. A mermaid or siren, I believe," he continued, laughing.

Marie straightened her cap and with embarrassed haste, darted past Captain Gregory and into the room, only to be halted by Gwendolyn Penscott's angry glare. Her lord's lady was sitting up in bed, bare shoulders visible above the quilt held over her breasts. "What is the meaning of this, Marie? Spying?"

"Beggin' your pardon, ma'am. No. I meant no harm. I was listening only to see if you were awake. Truly."

"I believe her, Gwen," the captain said, pulling thoughtfully on his upper lip. "The girl has no reason to lie." He chuckled. "But then, I've always been prey to young beauties with quick tongues." Captain Gregory laughed again, clearly enjoying a number of meanings known only to himself.

Marie, confused, blushed and backed away from the bed, only to run into the officer, who reached to slap her on the rump. "Be off with you, shameless rooster," Gwendolyn ordered him, "and take your coat. I fear your conduct and my weakness may well give us rue this sunrise."

The captain bowed courteously, took his coat from the chair. "Captain Gregory?" Marie said.

"Yes, girl? What is it?"

"Lord Penscott . . . that is, the duke . . ." She couldn't go on.

Gregory raised his eyes. "Out with it, girl," he said, voice flat and dangerous.

"Lord Penscott wished to see you in the garden. For tea. He instructed me to tell you, should I happen . . . that is, should I *happen* to see you," she finished lamely, wishing she were far away.

The mariner glanced at Gwendolyn. His eyes betrayed panic for a brief second but he recovered quickly, assumed the pose of cocky, self-assured lover, bowed once quickly and left.

Gwendolyn sighed and dropped the cover. Marie walked to the window and tied back the curtains. Sunlight cast a luminous sheen on the parqueted floor. Gwendolyn stood naked in the dazzling wafer of amber light seeming to emanate from underfoot. Hands high overhead, her body tightened as she stretched and yawned. Marie watched from the corner of one eye. Only twelve years separated the two women, yet that span was enough to hold a lifetime. Lady Gwendolyn had once been a ravishing woman. Two marriages and seven children later, at thirty-one, her beauty had faded, though there was still a great deal for a man to reckon with. Widely spaced eyes crinkled wickedly at the corners and gazed out from under a high, regal forehead and arched, thin lines of plucked eyebrows. Irises deep brown as chocolate blended almost indistinguishably into intense black pupils and beckoned males from as far as might be seen. Cheeks, lips and chin were slightly full, almost a commoner's physiognomy were it not for an ever so slightly arched patrician nose. The unsettling combination of common and royal resulted in a remarkably disturbing, provocative effect of total innocence coupled with smoldering sensuality.

If Gwendolyn's face promised sensuality, her body promised the wild delights of utter abandon. Waist-long brown hair hung in a tangled skein upon white, sloping shoulders, parting to either side of an ample bosom which, when displayed under the lightest silk, gave the impression of aching to be touched and fondled. Her waist, a touch thick, flowed into round, low-slung hips and experienced thighs, the secret of a hundred conquests. Perhaps she had another year, two or three at the most, before time extracted its dreadful toll. No wonder the lady sought young lovers: there lay the illusion of youth. Perhaps the reality, Marie thought, for to judge from the list of those invited to her chambers, m'lady had not aged.

Gwendolyn misread the girl's stare. "Come, child. You needn't act as if I'm an ogress. The captain was quite delicious." She paused pensively. "Though I'm afraid he'll be no longer so when my husband finishes with him. How did he look?"

"Fine, ma'am." Marie shook her head positively. "He's a fine-looking man."

Gwendolyn sighed with exasperation, started for the closet. "Not James, silly. My husband."

Marie followed, helped her mistress with a dressing gown before answering. "I'm not one for reading m'lord's thoughts, ma'am."

"Not a very satisfactory answer, Marie. Surely you can do better."

"He was angry, ma'am, though he masks anger well."

"I see," Gwendolyn answered, tapping her left foot, a sure sign of consternation. "And who would think my dear duke would deny me my arrangements and diversions, eh?"

"Well, ma'am, he is your husband," Marie ventured, treading lightly.

"Oh, come, Marie. Don't be such a silly goose. Shall I be judged by servant as well as husband?"

Marie shook her head. "No, ma'am. It's just that . . ."

Gwendolyn suddenly laughed brightly, embraced Marie in a fond hug. "You *are* a silly, naive goose. A dreamer, I think, which is why I love you. Do you know what?"

"No, ma'am."

"You are the only one in the household who has not yet become a cynic. *That* is more refreshing than you think. Now . . ." She turned Marie toward the armoire, seated herself at the ornate French commode and rummaged through jars of makeup. "We must forget about husbands and lovers and decide what I shall wear. Today matters little, but tomorrow? . . . You must help me choose. Something daring, no doubt, for I fear Gregory will join the ranks of the has-beens and I shall be in want."

Marie set to work on her mistress's hair as Gwendolyn prattled on. "Tell me. You've seen most of them. Which, if you had your choice, would you pick? There's young Hanson. A boy of course, but well endowed, 'tis said, even if he is a bit ugly. For that matter, his father might be better. The more years, the more experience. Which should it be?"

"I don't know, ma'am," Marie murmured, answering only for the sake of being heard.

"Hunhh! They say Sir Harold last played with Emily Trepanny." She sniffed. "I should like to give him the comparison there! Emily Trepanny, indeed. 'Tis said

36

you could set a farthingale sideways inside her and she'd not note the difference. I may not be so tight as you young things, but at least I—"

Marie had stopped brushing, stood motionless. Gwendolyn turned slowly and gazed into her servant's eyes. Tactfully, she restrained the laughter that bubbled inside her. "Why, I'll be. You're embarrassed, child." She paused, staring intently, serious now. "It's true, then, isn't it. You've not yet known a man, have you."

Marie stiffened. "No, ma'am. I've not yet found—"

Gwendolyn interrupted with laughter. "Then I must find someone for you. Tomorrow night, with your new gown and all," she winked suggestively, "will be perfect. Would you like that?"

"Mistress, you were always kind, but I beg you not to force anyone on me. I prefer to sleep alone."

"But why, for heaven's sake?"

"Oh, Lady Penscott, I entreat you. Let me follow my own course." She smiled apologetically. "You see, I was taught there should be love."

"Love? Well, so there shall be."

"I do not mean in that way alone," Marie interrupted hastily. "My father said—"

"Father? Fathers are always saying things to which no intelligent person listens. There is no other way, child."

"I must believe there is, mistress."

Lady Gwendolyn shook her head in disbelief. "Still, you are wrong and have much to learn, I fear. And many a cold night ahead. Say what you will, but I prefer a warm lover atop and within to passionless quilts and chilly sleep." She turned back to the dressing table. "But come. I must finish my toilet. We've a busy day ahead."

Marie's fingers flew to work, a talent gained from force of habit. Lost in a thousand intricate details, neither woman spoke for some time, leaving Marie's imagination free to wander among realms far from those of Penscott Hall and Lady Gwendolyn's intrigues.

The stone bench pained his bony posterior and the air was decidedly chilly. Still, Lord Roger Penscott refused to give up the vista of the Thames. His favorite spot was beside the shrub-lined pond in the garden between the two branches of the magnificent country manor. Morning teas in the open would continue until the bitter winter winds drove him indoors.

A figure emerging from the house could be glimpsed between the bare branches of trees and bushes. A moment later he appeared from behind the last hedge and crossed the open lawn. "A brisk morning, m'lord," Captain Gregory remarked in greeting.

The older gentleman took his time answering. This young officer, with small, colorless eyes, a sloping, too-long nose and prognathous chin, irritated him no end. Women found him exciting, but why was a mystery. The hands might have had something to do with it. The lad was blessed with long, tapered, slender fingers, as 'twas said indicated length below. Which had nothing to do with intelligence, of course. Still, the captain would no doubt serve, long or short.

Lord Penscott belched, motioned his guest to sit across the table. "A brisk morning serves to revive one after a night of excess, or so I've found," he grunted acerbically.

Two pewter pots rested amid a craggy landscape of cheeses, smoked fish, oysters and diminutive loaves of steaming hot bread. Penscott pointed to the larger of the two pots. "Coffee. The smaller is tea. I find chocolate an abysmal drink fit for Tories and women. Gwen prefers it, to my undying distress, but I refuse to allow it on my table."

"The tea will be fine, please."

A waiting butler stepped forward to fill Gregory's cup. Wasting little time, the husky young man attacked the platter. The thought of playing a duke for a cuckold, tasting his wife's voluptuous fruits and then those of her husband's well-set table, appealed to the captain's sense of daring. Of course, now that the old man knew, he'd have to be a bit more careful.

Captain Gregory's eyes lifted from the plate to meet an unwavering gaze. Bread and cheese caught in his throat momentarily, but he smiled as if nothing had happened, swallowed and went after the fish. Plate as empty as his host's, Gregory sipped the tea, noticed Lord Penscott had chosen coffee and found himself wishing he had done the same. It wouldn't be the first time a jealous husband had countered an erring wife's contrivances with poison.

A breeze from the north whipped around the corner of the mansion and eddied across the protected lawn to ruffle the surface of the pond. Lord Penscott sniffed wistfully for a scent of sea breeze. It was ages since he had last been aboard a real ship. No more. No more . . . "Have some more fish."

Captain Gregory declined, but his host paid no mind. The breeze promised colder days to come, and soon. Penscott did not shiver but noticed Gregory did, which was well enough.

"My lord," the captain began boldly, "I am grateful for your extended hospitality, but I'm afraid my ship waits. And I must take my leave. You must visit father in London when the snow lies deep."

"Pah! Visit that pestilence-ridden center of disquietude and disease? I prefer the role of country squire. Let your father, my good friend, journey here."

"As respectfully as possible, sir, I might suggest that with our new monarch, London might be the better place. After all, the king's authority—"

"—is fragmented still. The king comes to Penscott on the morrow, but look well at those who ride with him. There are more masters than meet the eye these days."

"But only one England, Lord Penscott."

"Aye." Penscott's eyes narrowed. "I serve her from here—as you will within the next few days."

"I regret not," Gregory answered warily. "There are rumors of strife in Scotland and Ireland, and winter stays neither smuggler nor pirate. A sailor must attend to duties both enjoyable and unpleasant. In truth, one frequently offsets the other."

"And you are a dutiful man, as we have seen."

The captain's facial powder disguised a quick blush. "I hope so, sir." He paused, loath to play verbal games any longer. "I fear this chill ride, but an early start brings a journey's end all the sooner. With your permission, sir? I'll ask your servant to call my coachman."

The nobleman smiled and leaned forward on his cane. "It has been done. He's been sent on his way."

Gregory bolted to his feet. "What? You had no—"

"Sit down."

"I will have a horse, sir!"

"Sit down!" The captain sat awkwardly, subdued by the crackling voice of authority unmasked. "Duty!" Lord Penscott scoffed. "You talk like the quivering bag of guts that fathered you—if he did."

The captain blanched. The blatant insult fired his rapidly vanishing courage and his face froze in anger. "Guard your tongue, sir! As my father's son, I will—"

"Do exactly nothing." The tone was flat and measured. Without pausing, Penscott reached for and broke a piece of cheese, slowly chewed both portions while enjoying the rage and consternation writ on the younger man's face. "Matthew Gregory is more than aware of my opinion, young man. You needn't bristle so."

"But . . . but I thought you were friends," Gregory stammered. "He has spoken of you often and well."

"And wisely so, for he's my man, lock, stock and barrel. As such, he comes in handy from time to time and has been rewarded in kind. An ear at court is always useful. But know this. The name of Penscott survives and prospers not through the affection—though affection is useful from time to time—of servants and lackeys, but through fear."

Again the name of Gregory had been besmirched. "Then I must tell you, sir, I fear no man. Nor will I suffer even a duke to—"

"Suffer? My dear sir, you have no conception of suffering. If you persist in this impertinence, though, I promise you you will."

"M'lord. Perhaps it were best if you knew that I have

fought two duels this past year," Gregory went on rashly. "Both men were so bold as to proclaim themselves my betters. Both are dead."

"I have gout in my leg, James, not in my head. Do not threaten me with duels. I've not achieved success by entertaining the anger of fools. The night is full of dark agents readily hired to seek redress. Choose the course you wish. But beware. Your tongue seeks for you the company of ghosts."

Captain Gregory stiffened. The implication was impossible to avoid. A king didn't travel to visit fools. I should have known better, the officer thought belatedly. Curse the household and seductive invitation that had enticed him to stay too long.

"Now, then," the wily old man continued. "Down to business. Have you enjoyed my wife?" Gregory could only stutter an inaudible reply. "I should think she gave a most marvelous performance. Or performances, if I may make so bold as to judge this morning's lethargy."

"My lord—I—"

"Come, come, young man. You have savored my wife, romped like a playful satyr through bushy park, so to speak. Now you must favor me"—the older man leaned forward and lowered his voice—"and your king."

The captain failed miserably to conceal a growing panic. "What do you mean?" he asked deferentially, the fight gone out of him.

"This!" With a flourish Penscott reached forward and opened a handsomely wrought walnut case. A pair of superbly crafted dueling pistols gleamed in the morning light.

"I do not understand," Gregory said, unable to take his eyes from the guns.

Penscott approved of his interest. At least the man understood weapons. "The king comes to visit tomorrow. With him, an entourage of nobles. Among them will be one who must not leave."

Gregory looked about apprehensively, wet his lips. Like a fool, he'd been trapped. At least the price was cheap enough. To kill a man with such a weapon would be a pleasure. "Who?"

"Jason Brand."

"Brand? Should I know him?"

"He's a Lowlander with an estate near Kelso, north of the border near Tweed. His mother was a Highlander . . . and a Catholic."

Gregory shrugged. "Then he is a Jacobite, I presume."

"Yes and no. He has come to plead moderation."

"A wise policy. Should they choose war, English force of arms will most cruelly prevail," Gregory replied, lost in the confidence of the moment. Then it was his turn to grow shrewd. "You host a king newly crowned. There is more than good courtesy afoot here. A malleable king . . . whose policy you seek to shape?"

The older man chuckled. "Not I alone. There are others."

For a long moment Gregory stared in amazement. The morning was turning into an education. Abruptly, he rose and paced the length of the table. The country lord he had taken for granted as a wealthy eccentric with a voluptuous wife was in truth a member of some inner circle among the Whigs. Perhaps even the Junto, that select, forceful and oftimes secretive assembly of the most powerful men in England. It was they who had long paved the way for the accession of the Hanoverian George to the throne. Gregory glanced at the pistols once again. He had been manipulated most artfully since the invitation to Penscott Hall. Even Gwendolyn—had she known? "What is my function in this charade?" he finally asked.

"Merely to do your duty."

"Which is?"

Penscott smiled. "There are those who dislike our present king. They spend hours wrangling and disputing, conspiring to replace him with another line. Such insidious dissent is unpredictable and, perforce, dangerous. However, if those who oppose us should follow a more overt path, one admittedly anticipated and cut off quickly and at great cost to their cause, the danger is broken. The Crown, victorious and in a position of strength, will be secure beyond all doubt."

"The king is the king. What impedes such a—"

"Again, Jason Brand, who counsels arrest of those leaders who foment open rebellion. And so he hopes to save the peace and gain favor. If there are no arrests, the leaders will rally the Stuart malcontents and an uprising will ensue. The Pretender's support will then be annihilated. To that end, you will issue a challenge to this man. You are reputed a fearless and capable marksman, and have proved so twice. Now you shall do so again. We must not allow this persuasive Scot to sit in council with the king."

"Then sit he shall not." Gregory smiled. "But what then?"

Penscott shrugged. "Your reward may not be immediate, but will be inevitable. Meanwhile, I'm afraid you must be satisfied with Lady Gwendolyn—and, of course, the knowledge you have done your duty."

Gregory stared at the older man, lowered his eyes and took the pistols. "I should like to acquaint myself with their balance."

Penscott waved his hand toward the lawn beyond. "Please feel free."

Gregory smiled tightly. "How long will the king stay here?"

"Three days. Plenty of time to arrange an amusement for Jason Brand."

Captain James Gregory sighed, looked at the pistols, then back at the Lord of Penscott Hall. The old man's eyes glittered like flint in the cold winter sun.

Night crept softly over the land, trailing a bridal veil of moonlight to set the low hills ablaze with silver. The waters of the Thames became a bejeweled playground for the gods. Penscott Hall was waiting for the king. Servants still scurried through the household, finishing required chores. Others wearily trundled off to narrow

43

bedchambers. In the upstairs dining room, Lord and Lady Penscott sat alone at the table, finishing supper. The hour was nine, and early, but the day had been long and tiring. Neither spoke; each sat immersed in his own thoughts.

Penscott gazed at the painting of the *Glorianna,* the ship named after his first wife. Next to it on the wall hung a magnificently detailed map of the Caribbean. His mind's eye beheld the swelling sails. He faced the salt sea spray and welcomed the roll of deck beneath his feet. Lines creaked, sweet music to a seagoing man's ears. A tiny noise from outside distracted him and he tore his eyes from the past to stare out to the dark Thames. Brows furrowed, he considered the dismaying truth. Lord Roger Penscott would never go to sea again.

Gwendolyn dabbled at the sweet. Unlike Roger, she assayed future rather than past. What had happened between James and her husband was a mystery she spent little time trying to solve. James had let her know he wouldn't return to her chambers and that was that. There was always tomorrow, in any case. Edmond Penscott was reputedly the most handsome of the Penscott heirs. From paintings of his brothers, the reputation was deserved. The thought was forbidden but titillating. Her own husband's son! She sneaked a glance across the table and smiled demurely. A stepson might make the affair that much more interesting. How old was he? Twenty? A handsome age . . .

In the bedroom down the hall, Marie finished preparing for the night, double-checked to make sure there were no wrinkles in the sheet and eased out the door. Tired but not sleepy, still excited about the new role she was to play at the party, she made her way down the back stairs and instead of going directly to her room, found a wrap and sneaked out the side door. The stars and moon overhead were the same as on Mysteré. At least there was some contact with home.

The night was cold. It had never gotten this cold on Mysteré. Though this would be her third winter in England, the climate still plagued her with chills and ague.

Nearing the end of the outside wall, she counted the windows to find her room. A light was on. There was nothing to do but wait until Arabella had gone to sleep. Only then could she sneak in and avoid a confrontation. A man's head crossed the window. Marie counted again. The room was certainly hers. . . .

She stood on tiptoes and peeked in, managed to stifle a gasp of surprise and draw to one side that her presence might not be discovered. Slowly, she peered into the room again. Arabella was sprawled on her back on Marie's cot! One of the groundskeepers lay atop the maid, thrusting himself up and down. Two other roisters, younger than the first so lustily employed, stood half naked, their own eager lances throbbing forward in anticipation.

"Hurry it up, Reuben. The little tart will be returnin' soon."

The man atop Arabella grunted. The other youth gripped his staff with a dirty paw. "Let her just. A worthy bit, she is. I've got what she needs right here."

Reuben groaned. Arabella clasped him with her thighs, laughed ecstatically as he rolled off. He scratched his privates and gestured to the last in line. "You'd waste it on the likes of the French bitch. Now here's a lass what knows when and how."

Arabella chuckled proudly, ponderous breasts shaking as she rolled onto her stomach. "A fine wench," Reuben repeated, smacking the maid's ample buttocks.

"Come on, Johnny," Arabella giggled, lewdly spreading her thighs. "Bring me that you've in your hand, and I'll make a cowed repentant of it." The youth next in line hurriedly jumped atop Arabella while his companion cursed aloud, angry he should have to wait.

Gown and party forgotten, Marie stared in horror and disgust as the lean lad named Johnny grabbed Arabella by the hips and hauled her up on her knees before sinking his length between her legs. His lean stomach slapped against the woman's cushioning buttocks.

Animals. No, worse! She had seen animals, whose coupling was untainted. *And they scorn me because I won't indulge in their lewdness? I will never be as they. I will yield to love alone. . . .* The night grew colder, the sky darkening with northern clouds. Marie's cheeks were wet, tear-streaked. Her feet fled along a familiar path across the garden, leading to a friend, a friend to ease a troubled spirit. Few save Lord Penscott knew she visited Behan. When first she arrived at Penscott Hall, a bedraggled, lonely, homesick child, the Englishman had taken her one day to the tutor's cottage, only a few paces inside the garden's sculpted hedges. A former scholar turned buccaneer, Behan had escaped the gallows through a whim of the duke, who granted him a type of freedom if he would teach French, swordsmanship and what he could of ships to the Penscott sons. Valuing his neck above all else—the life of a buccaneer had suddenly become excessively dangerous—Behan had agreed. Besides, a fifty-year-old man had no business at sea anymore, especially as a pirate.

But the sons were gone. One was a major in the Colonies, one dead in France, the third in London. Behan continued to reside at Penscott Hall by the grace of his benefactor, who still appreciated a good game of chess from time to time—even if it did degenerate into fiercely contested discussions on the relative merits of French and English privateers, sloops, brigs, trade winds and tactics. Behan had befriended the orphan of Mysteré on her arrival. Charged with improving her English, he did so, and in the process became the one person in the world she trusted.

Over the next two years, Marie had made a point of using every opportunity to venture to the cottage. Thrush had greatly helped matters by assigning her the task of putting the cottage in order twice a week. Luckily, Behan's conception of order was far different from Thrush's—in fact, he wouldn't allow Marie to disturb any of his "mementoes"—so there was extra time for lessons in reading and writing. As the two became closer, Behan found Marie a willing listener to tales of the old days when the Brothers of the Coast ruled the Caribbean. On her first Christmas at Penscott Hall, he presented her with a short sword. Within a month, she was an ardent pupil.

The door was never locked. It responded to the pressure of her hands and swung open. Comfort waited inside. Junk. Treasure. Memorabilia of countless adventures. An astrolabe near the door. Intricately inked maps helter-skelter on the walls. A grizzled old cat named Fair Weather on the hearth. Cheese and bread on a nearby shelf over a sturdy hammock, relic of nights at sea. Frigates, sloops, Dutch *freibotes* and Turkish carracks wrought from salvaged wood and perfectly rigged from main-truck to martingale. Cutlasses, long swords, claymores and rapiers. Flags and pennants, pistols and philosophic works in Latin and French. A pair of rocking chairs faced each other across a small table and chessboard. Along the wall, shelves held a Bible, small wooden kegs and pitchers. A jack of peasant beer stood upon the table. Nearby lay a pair of eyeglasses, hastily placed beside parchment, quill and ink for memoirs begun too late.

Behan bustled about, happy to have company. He heated some chocolate, knowing the servants received few such treats. Cream and sugar he combined and filled a stout clay cup with the deliciously rich brew, much too hot to drink. Setting the steaming cup on the table, he wiped a kerchief over face and beard, scratched an equally snowy crown of thinning hair. Hardly taller than the girl and almost as agile despite nearly seventy years, Behan was used to both outburst and silence from this young woman he loved as a daughter.

"It's too hot."

"Of course. As are you. Tuck up your skirt."

Marie glared in surprise. "I don't feel like fencing."

"I know. You feel sorry for yourself. The exercise will help. Tuck up your skirt and defend yourself."

"But the hour—"

"—is late and getting later," he replied, sliding the table to one side. Marie pulled the back hem of her dress between her legs and tucked it at her waist, giving the effect of a feminine Pantaloon. Behan pulled down the practice swords from their place on the wall, offered Marie first choice.

The sordid scene occupying her room faded from mind. Attention riveted on Behan's circling blade. "We will see if you've practiced your new riposte, my girl."

Marie grinned, responding to the heft of good steel in her hand. "Well, enough, Uncle, as you'll find. *En guarde!*"

Their blades touched and the brittle music of rasping steel broke the silence. Marie lunged, Behan knocked the wax-tipped blade aside and riposted, his hand a blur as he moved to his right. Marie yelped as the second stripe of the day was laid across her rump. "Ho, then! A score, poor mistress. She'll not sit for a week," he laughed.

Marie, not dismayed by the taunt, sought redress. Behan was again too quick. Teacher's blade deftly turned student's and plucked the maid's cap from Marie's head. Luxuriant ebony tresses spilled about her shoulders. "Why, this is no vagabond, ruffian nor assailant I fight, but a girl! A mere girl, a wisp of a thing . . ." Behan teased.

Marie's lips thinned. She tossed the hair back out of her eyes. "That's the last time for tonight, Uncle," she said in a low voice, at the same time launching an attack. The room rang with the fury of the blades. Steel played in darting whirls, jabs, loops and arcs in the candlelight. Lunge . . . Parry . . . Riposte missed and lunge again. The whir of slashed air. The dance forward and back . . .

"A third. A third, now!" cried Behan jubilantly, controlling a stab as the blade neared her ribs.

Marie grunted with effort, turned her wrist inside. The base of her blade sent his astray and she riposted. The wax-blunted tip caught just below his ribs, bent in an upward arc. "There, poor knave, you're dispatched. By a mere girl!" she panted.

Behan looked down, beamed with pride. "And one

with a tongue sharper than any blade, by my oath," he grumbled, trying to sound angry.

"Luckily for you," Marie good-naturedly retorted, wiping the perspiration from her forehead.

Behand was breathing deeply. "By God, but I'm too old for this nonsense. Give me your blade. I'll put it up. You've learned well, my dear."

Marie straightened her dress, piled the long hair beneath her cap and sat down to the chocolate, cool enough now. Behan pretended to fuss with the rapiers while watching her from the wall. Her fragile beauty had captivated even him, and 'twould be a lie not to admit the existence of feelings other than familial. At that moment he would have sacrificed a dozen years to be young again. Dark tresses, the proud, impudent thrust of still-firm breasts, the delightful contrast of pale flesh, gray eyes and lips the color of rich deep cherries—and as moist . . .

"You know, Uncle? I'm glad I came."

Behan smiled, moved to sit. "So am I. I always am."

"I wish . . . I could stay here with you." She looked around the familiar room, a wistful smile lighting her face. "I'm alive here, at ease and free." Her expression turned thoughtful. "I wonder if I'll ever see it again."

"What, dear?" Behan asked, a little alarmed.

"Home. Mystere."

Behan relaxed. There was no answer for such a question. Home was a futile wish long ago forgotten in the face of a totally harsh world. "Perhaps."

Marie sipped the chocolate, leaned forward to pull a tiny string on one of the models. A mainsail dropped into place. She puffed gently, filling the light canvas. "I think not, Uncle. I think not 'perhaps.' 'Twere better said, I *will*."

Chapter III

Jason Brand rode at the rear of the party. The position boded ill for his mission, but he refused to be discouraged: the plan to salvage peace *would* be presented to the king. An uprising and major bloodshed in Scotland could still be averted, given men of good will on both sides, and Jason was determined to do everything in his power to that end. As for those who opposed him, the self-effacing flatterers who had fought for places closer to the king, to the devil with them.

The black mare strained at the bit, eager to be off and run after three days of rest followed by a long, constrained walk. Jason, with his usual sense of brashness and every bit as bored with the slow pace, decided to let the animal have her way. She needed no more than a nudge to the flanks before bolting to the right and into the woods. One of the dragoons in escort noticed the Scot break from the party. "See here," he cried stuffily. "No one is to—" The cursed Lowlander had disappeared in the woods.

The soldier started to give chase, but a bewigged companion caught his reins. "Let him go, Hubert. Damn good riddance, I say. Anyway, we're near Penscott Hall. I doubt he'll get lost." The first soldier shrugged and regained his place in the line of march.

The mare rejoiced in the exercise. Time and again Jason ducked a low-hanging branch or jerked to one side to avoid being brushed against a trunk. Horse and rider cleared the trees. At a dead run, Jason pulled off hat, wig and coat, rolled the lot into a ball and stuck it in his lap. Now he needn't fear another tree-lined path.

Black mane and red-gold hair streaming in the wind, horse and rider broke onto a path paralleling the bank of the Thames. The king's party, by now far behind, stayed to the left and the high road, separated from the river by trees. To the right was a swatch of diamond-dappled ribbon rolling to the sea. The air was cool and clear, free of the appalling grime and soot and filth of the festering slum, as Jason called London. Better yet, the farther east they traveled, the more like Scotland herself, he thought. Clear as a bell on a winter morn.

With a sharp hand laid to her rump, the mare spurted ahead, at one with the racing wind. A deep creek ahead promised to block the path. Hooves churned the soft loamy bank. Water and flying mud slowed the pace. With a laugh and a wave to a trio of boatmen on the river, the Scot reined left, back toward the trees.

The animal refused the path indicated, fought the bit and won. Swerving between two trees to find a path of her own making, iron-shod hooves ravaged dried gold-enrod, shattered autumn-brown grass and dashed through bewildered shrubs in a flurry of rusted leaves that gave testimony to an early frost. With a great laugh of pure joy, Jason braced, tightened his hold and leaned forward as the mare leaped a fallen tree and took the breadth of a narrow creek in stride. Immediately they bolted across a small meadow to charge a second barrier, a tree split by lightning. One half arced along the ground, the other rose upright, sprouting a decidedly ominous array of low hanging branches. Jason read the mare's mind, realized the curse of refusing to own any animal entirely broken in spirit. The damned fool mare, with a stubborn mind of her own, was going to jump through the arch formed by the two parts of the tree. Hauling on the reins, his lean, muscular body stretched upright in the saddle. The mare defied the cruel pressure of the bit and charged the high curve of the tree. Unable to halt her, Jason surrendered, lay as flat as possible on her neck. If the damned black was determined to jump, there was no point in complicating the issue. "Well then, up and be done with it, Bess," he shouted.

Front legs tucked, rear legs following, Bess erupted gracefully to take the split tree in stride. One dead branch, hooked and hanging down, snagged under the collar of Jason's shirt and plucked him from the saddle. The mare continued without so much as a pause, disappearing from under the rider.

For a second, Jason hung helplessly in the air, arms and legs flailing in a futile search for nonexistent support. Across the small meadow, Bess halted, turned and tossed her head, whinnying proudly. Jason hurled a few choice maledictions against horsedom in general and one sway-backed, bone-brained devil's beast in particular.

The sound of wood cracking brought him up short. He looked down. A good eight feet to the broken half of the tree on the ground. Suddenly he stopped moving, held his breath. "Oh, damn!" he swore in sudden realization. The branch above him cracked again, dropped another half inch. Jason looked to either side. If he could just reach . . .

Laughter? Was someone laughing? Swinging gently, he twisted to the right, caught his breath. A girl in servant's garments stood under an old hawthorn. Her hair was long and black, beautiful to behold. Her laughter was bright and clear, limpid as running water.

The branch gave way with a sharp crack. Jason barely had time to fling out his hands and try to break the fall, still landed with a bone-jarring thud, the branch below driving the wind from him as the branch from above smacked his skull before falling off to the side. Somehow he crawled off the log, lay in the grass, half-dazed and gasping for breath. Running through his mind was the sound of the bright laughter. Had it stopped? He couldn't hear. . . .

Marie ran forward, terrified. She'd laughed at a nobleman, for surely he was a great lord to have such fine if somewhat torn clothes. But he had looked so funny, dangling in the air. Now amusement fled as she hurried across the grassy meadow to try to help.

Jason struggled upright, unwilling to take his eyes from the deep red, sensuous lips which had framed such delightful music. Slowly, he absorbed every feature.

Soft, untouched ivory skin glowed with the flush of youth and embarrassment and confusion. A Spanish nose, without a doubt, hinted of higher blood somewhere in her past as the oval nostrils flared ever so slightly with each breath. High cheeks, sloping in sharp, elegant planes to a determined yet tamed jaw betrayed a lack of the confidence that would come with time and age. Most of all, the eyes. Slate gray, they spoke of curiosity as well as wisdom. Deep and luminous as mist on a quiet, secluded pond, they could not hide the questioning, defensive attitude of one who has learned not to trust too quickly.

Marie took a tentative step backward. Overpowered by the bold appraisal, some sixth sense reassured her that she need not fear. Here was a fair, hearty man, unlike the usual run of visitors to Penscott Hall. Tall, muscular and adorned with red-gold hair streaming down a broad back, his gold-flecked eyes gleamed merrily in spite of a painful knot rising on the high, smooth forehead. When he spoke, his voice was deep, filled with warmth and laughter and the lilt of Scotland. "Well met, lass."

She hesitated, knowing safety lay in flight, instead held her ground when he advanced. Dark hair lay in full rich lengths about her shoulders. A heavy overblouse filled with pinecones and greenery destined to decorate candles lay discarded at her feet. Firm, shapely breasts thrust, not proudly, but innocently against a revealing chemise that made a poor attempt to conceal that which would otherwise be naked.

The forest was quiet now, wrapped in a cocoon of silence. The very air was expectant and tense, heavy with promises unspoken. Marie tried to speak but her throat rebelled, refused to cooperate. A treasure trove of golden-red ringlets on the muscled flesh of his chest revealed where his cravat hung open and the finely woven lawn shirt had ripped. She raised her hands to cover her breasts, suddenly aware and ashamed that the rising nipples should betray her uncontrollable attraction to this total stranger. For some reason, breathing became

53

difficult. Nervously, she dampened parted lips with her tongue.

Jason caught her wrists, slowly pulled her hands aside. Abashed and unable to meet his stare, Marie looked down, only to note the unconcealed arousal where the tight, restraining fabric of his breeches left little to imagination. Alarmed, she raised her head, only to encounter a pair of lips and a searing kiss. As if fused by a great bolt of lightning their bodies pressed together as one. A strong hand slid down her back, cupping rounded buttocks and holding her to him. Hesitating but a moment, her tongue joined in frantic, heated exploration. A silken, sweet moan rose in her throat as the bulging maleness pulsed through the light petticoat and pressed against her.

Marie tried to retreat, but the gesture was hardly more than a deceitful game: his hand would keep her prisoner. He would not let her go. He would hold her . . . hold her. . . . Arms circling his neck, her breasts pressed against the awesome frame and her lips parted, seeking air.

A pealing bell shattered the moment. Jason, in surprise, loosed his hold. The bells of Penscott Hall, closer than he thought—in truth, but a few hundred yards through the woods—were signaling the arrival of the king.

Marie leaped from his embrace. The king had come and she was absent! The dream rent asunder. Brazen Scottish lord and demure maid stared at one another. Marie blushed furiously, gray eyes brimming with tears of embarrassment. Hurriedly, she knelt to grab the overblouse, folded it around the decorations, whirled about and fled into the brush.

"Wait!" Jason called too late. The unknown girl was gone. Jason stared into the woods where she had disappeared. Brilliant, clear tones of a welcoming trumpet echoed through the trees. The mare whinnied curiously. Belief hung suspended in the sunlit air. Never in twenty-six years had he encountered such magnetic desire. Who was she? A creature of the forest? Did Penscott Hall house others like her? Impossible. How could there be another creature of such devastating beauty?

The trumpet stopped and Jason returned to reality. The mare waited, subservient for the nonce. Breeches dusted, shirt smoothed out and cravat retied, the Scot retrieved coat, wig and hat and caught up the mare. "Come, Bess. We've business at hand. For four days we've waited for an audience with this new king who wears a Stuart's crown. At last, we shall see how justly balanced that circlet of power sets on the royal brow."

Foot in the stirrup, hand on pommel, he paused, memorizing the magic glade. A flurry of leaves twisted through the breeze. A jay scolded harshly overhead. Jason, lost in reflection, ignored the brash discord, instead pondered the complexities of the mission that had brought him here, which weighty import was lessened by the fervent memory of a fair lassie's kiss.

Penscott Hall was alive with music. Every room vibrated to the brilliant tones of harpsichord and violin, mellow horns and merry trumpets. In the great hall, couples curtsied and danced, dipping and promenading to the measured, stately strains. Loose clusters of gossipers, held at near arm's length by wide panniers, exercised agile tongues with all the latest bits of news which, given life, grew to outrageously proportioned lies. Great arrays of amber candles twinkled through a mist-white haze, the inevitable consequence of a vast proliferation of heavily powdered wigs and faces.

The very air hung redolent, weighted with a variety of perfumes, few of which blended pleasantly or even much abated the crushing odor of far too many bodies. Civet, musk and ambergris vied with more daring concoctions: orangery, tuberose and the heady neroli, favored by the Duke of Bracciano. From time to time, in an isolated corner, one might catch a hint of the lighter colognes.

In a side room, away from the din, Marie twisted a last curl into place, stepped back to look at Gwendolyn's rebuilt coiffure. *Cruches*, tiny curls along the forehead; *confidantes,* deep coils dangling about the ears, *crevecoeur,* two deliciously provocative ringlets at the nape of the neck: all were in order. Gwendolyn perused herself with the dedicated attention of a field marshal perusing his maps before going into battle. Finally satisfied, she nodded and returned to a broken train of thought. "This Stuveysant, now. No doubt he's the handsomest of the Hanoverians, don't you think? A bit stodgy, of course, but then they all are." She glanced at Marie. "Are you listening?"

"Oh, yes, ma'am."

"Well? Do you or do you not agree?"

"I do, ma'am."

Sorry she'd asked, Gwendolyn scowled and turned back to the mirror. "I thought you would. Powder." Marie fastened the long, tentlike cloak about her mistress, tied it at the neck and handed Gwendolyn the face mask. The long cone fit over the mistress's face in order to keep nose and eyes from filling with powder. Everything set, Marie took a handful of talc, blew it over Gwendolyn's head. The cloud rose, settled. Both coughed. Another handful and a touch here and there and m'lady was ready—almost. "I trust you've seen Edmond, at least," she said, voice muffled by the cone.

"Lord Penscott's had me downstairs 'til shortly, ma'am. He's—"

"—a little rooster with promise, he is. A lad who's had his own way with too many affairs, I think. I've caught his eye, though, and he shall find in me a peculiar conquest, if he dares. Am I ready?"

"Yes, ma'am." Marie set about putting the final touches on an already thickly caked face. On the whole, she could have gone all night without thinking of Edmond. Narrow of build and somewhat effeminate, he affected an innocuous appearance, a charade too late seen through by unsuspecting maids who let him get too close. Always a little too satisfied with himself, hobnobbing with the Court had made the young man even bolder and more obnoxious. This night she'd passed in the hall as he and Captain Gregory talked. Both leered, and Edmond, knowing she was a servant in spite of all her finery, had made bold to pinch her breast. Marie fled their laughter, running to answer the summons from her lady.

Gwendolyn stood, allowed Marie to remove the cape. "I'm afraid we've a surfeit of males," she sighed with a happy, dreamy smile. "Did you see the Scot?"

"Scot, ma'am?" Marie asked as naturally as possible, hoping her blush went unnoticed. "A Scot here?"

"Yes. Lord Jason Brand. To seek an audience with the king, 'tis said, though I fear he has little chance. What he has in mind I know nor care not, but what he hides beneath velvet coat and tight breeches? Now *there's* a secret worth the discovery!" She laughed lightly. "Perhaps I'll find the chance to test our supplicant. I'd hate to think he left Penscott Hall without *some* reward."

Marie's lips formed a tight line of disapproval, which she took care to hide by circling Gwendolyn and brushing the last flecks of powder from her back. The man she'd seen in the forest had been a free, laughing spirit, one who didn't deserve the clutches of Lady Gwendolyn Penscott. If there were any way . . .

"Well? Am I ready?"

The servant girl adjusted a bow, held a mirror while her mistress checked the results. The overall effect was stunning. Lady Gwendolyn, if not the most beautiful woman of her day, was certainly one of the most daring and alluring. Her rich overgown of russet taffeta was stitched with silver thread in an abundance of floral designs that swept to the floor in majestic cascades. The petticoat revealed at the front was of the most intricate Mechlin lace, expensive beyond belief. A diamond-encrusted stomacher sparkled with dazzling brilliance, competing with high-thrust breasts under a simple but elegant corset set off at the top with a brief swatch of off-white silk through which the top half-moons of ruby areolas were revealed. Gwendolyn snapped open an oriental fan, fluttered the gaily painted device in front of her face. A light cloud of fresh powder rose into the air.

"You may return to your other duties, Marie. I shan't need you further."

She was gone. Marie closed the door for a moment of privacy and crossed to Gwendolyn's mirror. How jealous Arabella and the others must be! She twirled in front of the mirror. Three hours has passed since she had dressed, and still she couldn't believe what she saw. Black hair piled in curls, one dangling over her right ear, another partially covering her left eye. Makeup: just a hint of rouge and powder. Plenty enough for a lady-in-waiting, especially one whose complexion needed no assistance in the first place. Lord Penscott's choice of a gown had been perfect. The bone-white silk was cut low to accentuate the natural thrust of her breasts and set off the creamy texture of shoulders and neck. Semiprecious smoky quartz on her stomacher matched the color of her eyes. More yards of silk rustled in the skirt, which was set off with an overlayer of light, light green lace. Though not as sumptuous as Gwendolyn's, the gown's simplicity, in concert with Marie's youth and radiance, contributed to an effect of classical elegance unrivaled by any other woman present.

Half-dreaming, Marie took one last look in the mirror before leaving. Lady Gwendolyn had promised Lord Brand a reward. Of her body, of course. Nightmare visions of the promise fulfilled, of writhing, naked bodies. . . . Marie clenched her fists, whirled from the mirror and ran out the door. *Well, why not?* The door slammed with a great bang that echoed down the hall. *He's probably no different from the rest. Lords and ladies at play. I have no reason, no right, to be jealous.*

Only she was.

Jason Brand cut a commanding figure in the crowded upper hall, now dancing, now skirting the edges of the elegant patterns inscribed on the floor by a sweating throng. Disdainful glances of those he considered mere fops were turned aside with a leering grin, if not ignored totally. The center of attention in the gallery was

58

George Lewis of Brunswick-Luneberg, hereditary lay Bishop of Osnabruck, Elector of Hanover and great-grandson of James I, now better and more simply known as His Majesty, King George I. At fifty-four, he was short, fair-skinned, portly and shy to a fault. Jason found it hard to believe this new king capable of command. That he spoke no English promised to pose but a minor hindrance.

There were factors in Jason's favor. George I, bred a soldier, was reputed to be brave and could be obstinate. He had no particular love of his new subjects and, as had been rumored, was determined not to be led about by a great conniving swarm of English ministers. Unless Sir Roger Penscott and his Whig friends had already convinced the king with their half-truths and filthy innuendos . . . Jason frowned. As had been the case all evening, His Majesty was ringed by associates utterly indifferent to either justice or the fate of Scotland.

"Ah, Brand! A curious horseman, what?" Lord Penscott exclaimed as the Scot approached.

"Curious, sir?"

"My son Edmond, here, spoke of you bolting from the king's party and vanishing into the woods. I trust you found something there to your liking."

Edmond smirked. His dislike for Jason Brand was clearly evident: but one son removed from inheriting the Penscott title and estates, the young man considered his station far above that of any Lowlander. "Yes. For a moment I feared his rash dash"—Edmond chuckled, inordinately pleased— "was a signal loosing a great Jacobite rabble concealed in the woods."

The king's interpreter, M. Bothmer, chortled in amusement. His Majesty looked away, bored with banter he didn't understand.

"Now, sir. That surely must not have been the case, else we would have seen the rump of your well-trained gelding. Word tis, he becomes skittish at the smell of danger, real or imagined."

Edmond blushed, the Scottish lord's unsubtle slur cutting to the quick. That those listening laughed at his expense was even more galling. "Sir! I protest this—"

Jason turned away and bowed low to the king. "My liege," he said slowly, waiting for Bothmer to interpret. "I have waited long for the moment I might beseech an audience. The consummation of this desire has been elusive, for Your Majesty is hemmed about by zealously overprotective souls who make bold to determine what you should and should not hear. But at last I stand before you, and beg you dear pardon for assuming my king himself decides who shall speak and who shall stand silent."

The King listened to the interpreter, stared at Jason with lazy, clear blue eyes. For a long moment he gave no answer, instead sipped from a goblet of pounded gold. Count Stuveysant, George's Hanoverian confidant, knew his lord's mind. The sturdy, middle-aged Germanic leaned toward their host. "What time do we hunt on the morrow, m'lord?"

Penscott, angered by Jason's impertinent indictment, started at the seeming non sequitur. "Will ten suit His Highness?"

Advisor and monarch whispered briefly before King George strode off without another glance at the tense circle. All faces turned to the count. "His Majesty suggests eleven. Afterward, he will retire to his chambers for luncheon. M'lord Brand may join him there briefly." With a quick bow, he too was gone.

Lord Penscott cast a look of alarm toward James Gregory. The captain had joined the circle in the middle of the conversation and stood silently gauging the Scot and devising means to lure him into a situation resolvable through a duel. Some caution had to be exercised in order to assure the king not be angered unduly. Gregory nodded imperceptibly toward Penscott and fell in step at Jason's side. "We meet again, m'lord," he said, irritated at having to walk next to someone as tall as himself. "Do you gamble?"

Jason smiled warily. "I have read *The Compleat Gamester*."

"Then you play at cards."

"Yes. But I do not . . . play."

"And Hazard?"

"I have some small experience with the dice."

"Good. We must game this evening."

"If you wish, Captain."

"I shall look forward to our meeting, then," Gregory replied, a little too jovially. He sauntered away, proud of himself. Lose to the Scot, accuse him of cheating—a little trick would help—and a challenge would have to be issued. The exquisite pair of pistols waited, and this night would seal Brand's fate. As planned.

Great glittering chandeliers overhead smoked and glowed. Candles ringed the walls of the lower hall and added to the glare, keeping busy the one servant whose sole function was to replace those that had burned out.

Marie drifted, as in a trance, from group to group, listening as she'd been told. How exciting it all was! How beautiful she felt! Now and again a woman cast a jealous glance her way, to which Marie responded with secret joy: to be envied by the likes of Arabella was one thing, by ladies of station and the court quite another. Seven times she was asked to dance by earnest young —and one or two not so young—men. Each time she refused, for she didn't know the steps, but each time she felt more at ease in conversation. Twice she glimpsed the handsome Scottish lord, once actually bumped into him. When he winked and contrived to hold her hand, she fled, not having, in his case, the slightest idea of what to say.

Near midnight, her courage bolstered and a speech rehearsed, she found herself searching again, and was dismayed to find him standing beside Gwendolyn. Her heart almost stopped, and the magic drained out of the evening. Oblivious to the surroundings, she fled to the rear of the hall where a servant girl belonged in the first place, and found refuge in a corner of the kitchen. *Why should I care? I have heard the men of Scotland are worse than beasts. Even if he did kiss me, it probably*

61

meant nothing to him. No—and she fought to suppress the tears—*No! I will not care!*

The kitchen air was thick with clashing odors, savory and foul, vying for dominance. Each prevailed in turn as doors opened or closed and fresh air from the outside intruded. A toiling cook's helper, tongs in hand, lifted a golden-crusted marrowbone pie from the fiery hearth. Bubbling currants, dates, potatoes, artichokes and sugar-spiced marrow gave off a rich and palatable aroma which, once the pie was set on a long board to join a battery of cooling companions, melded with the conglomeration of other odors. Quince pies, berry tarts and a delightful array of Florentines, the most marvelous of treats concocted from cinnamon, kidney, currants, cream and eggs stood in long rows, constantly diminished and added to according to demand from the great hall.

The cook's helper wiped a perspiring brow and reached into the flames once again, like an angler fishing for delectable treasures in a fiery sea. Jonathan Ringe, the master chef, strode forth to examine her handiwork. He was a man of immense girth, and Marie could imagine five such as herself fitting comfortably into a single pair of Ringe's breeches. Feared and esteemed, the huge chef ran his kitchen with an iron hand, and woe to the girl or boy, man or woman who gave any lord or lady cause to impugn or criticize so much as a biscuit. At times he was brusque to a fault. Then Marie feared him, for he employed what he was fond of calling his magic knuckle: one great hand would lash out and pop an offender on the skull with the knuckle of his forefinger. At other times he could be curiously soft, even sentimental. Marie—and the others —loved him then, for more than once had he interceded when Thrush overstepped his bounds or when one of their number was ill or in trouble.

The obese chef nodded approval, much to the helper's relief, and moved away to the rear wall, where racks of meats sizzled and spun over grease-spattered coals. Sides of beef, saddles of mutton, collops of pork, all endured the punishment together. Ringe waddled past and grabbed a jack, filling it from a keg at hand and draining the ale without pausing for breath. Massive layers of rippling fat jiggled as he swallowed. Sweat poured in rivulets down his cheeks, only to be lost in the cavernous ridges lining his neck. Overseeing the preparation of fifty-two dishes required total concentration and a vast expenditure of energy. Comments—praise and condemnation—would come the next day, when once again the incredible Ringe would prove that no detail was too small to merit his attention.

Thrush hurried into the kitchen and spotted Marie in her corner. His beakish nose almost touched her face. "What're you doing here, girl? The master wants you in the upper halls again, and enjoins you to mind your French."

Marie nodded in compliance, though there was no joy in the prospect of returning upstairs. Edmond Penscott had more than made his intentions clear earlier in the evening, as had Captain Gregory. The thought of being accosted by either was unpleasant in the extreme, but the notion of discovering Jason Brand and the seductive Lady Penscott was the least pleasant of all.

Roger Penscott paced his private study. The hour was late and he was tired. The festivities continued, and though bed and sleep were devoutly wished, protocol required the host's presence until the king retired. The door flew open and an exasperated Captain Gregory entered. "Well?"

Gregory shrugged. "Two hours I have spent listening to a damned bunch of silly damned nonsense, and lost a tidy sum in the bargain. And still Brand does not show as promised. Where he has got to I know not. However, I am in no position to accuse him of rookery if he refuses to face me at the table."

"And Edmond?"

"Tippling too much of the latest Burgundy."

"Well enough. Make sure he's kept from further altercations with Brand. The lad's tongue outspeeds his good sense, unfortunately."

"Brand rubs me the wrong way. I don't like him," the captain said. "It appears Edmond and I are of like mind."

"But not of like ability, as should be evident. Edmond is rash, headstrong and young. In him are all the attributes of the successful, but he lacks seasoning and experience."

"I have heard he can fire a pistol," Gregory remarked a little too drily.

"Shooting a poacher is no basis for claiming proficiency on the dueling ground."

"A lad must learn. When the spirit is willing, they say."

Penscott thumped his cane on the floor. "Brand is *your* duty. Keep him away from my son."

Gregory, feeling more confident than in days, took the liberty of pouring a glass of port. He smiled most prettily. "M'lord may relax. Edmond has forgotten the episode with Brand. In fact, he has eyes for little more than what he perceives as a vast new harem. Giving credit where credit is due, he's fast, Burgundy or no. One of the easy ones has fallen already, and the lad's working on a second."

"Who?" Penscott straightened, obviously perturbed.

"The black-haired wench who serves your wife. She looks damned good done up in that gown, by the way."

"Damn!"

Gregory chuckled. "Why, m'lord. Certainly you don't harbor plans of a more personal nature for the young thing?"

Roger Penscott stared shrewdly at the captain. "My plans are no concern of yours, Captain, except for that small part you play upon command. The girl is a virgin, upon whom I place a high value. Hers is a treasure not to be squandered lightly, but saved for greater gain at the appropriate time. You will personally warn Edmond away from her, as will I if I see him first. Marie Celeste

Ravenne is my property. Never forget that. Now, get out of here and see to Jason Brand."

Gregory paused but a moment before hurrying out. The old man was on a high horse and best not crossed. When those with power wove sticky webs, James Gregory was wise enough to walk cautiously, lest he become ensnared and found victim with the rest of the unfortunates.

Gwendolyn Penscott sighed, dangled an arm and snared a petit four from the tray on the floor. Two hours' worth of meticulous toilet lay strewn about in disarray. The diamond-encrusted stomacher lay over a chair. Her gown was bunched under her, half draping over the edge of the bed. Only her hairdo had been carefully preserved. A pearl fell from a torn thread and rolled from bed to floor to join three more of its brothers. Clearly the seamstress had never intended the delicately sewn creation to be treated so harshly, and hours of painstaking labor would be required before the garment could be worn again. The heavily iced pastry disappeared. She took another and turned onto her side, making no attempt to cover the still warm reaches of that nest wherein her lover's proud staff had disgorged its fiery contents to the mutual satisfaction of both parties. The wisp of silk that had pretended to cloak her splendid breasts was long since a memory, discarded just inside the bedroom door. "A most delectable repast, Sir Stallion," she cooed, touching the cake to his lips, coyly pulling it away as Jason attempted to bite.

"I trust we . . . dine . . . in solitude, madam."

"This guest room is to remain empty, so to speak," she giggled, once again withdrawing the treat. "There is nothing to fear."

"I did not speak of fear, mistress," Jason answered in a dark tone. "But I should hate to suffer the indignity of defending myself in the altogether." He grabbed a third time, missed. "And at that, for a bawdy wench who denies me . . ." Laughing heartily, he dove across bed and lady, joining the wrestling match with a will.

Gwendolyn switched the petit four to her other hand, warded off the attack. "Sir! Your familiarity is shocking," she laughed, nipping at his wrist.

Jason yelped, rubbed the bright red tooth marks. "Only a moment ago you begged for familiarity, madam." A gleam of mock anger burned in his eyes. "Curse it, woman, will I have the cake or no?"

Gwendolyn, with a look of wild promise, lay back, broke the sweet into three pieces. The first, she balanced atop her left breast. Grinning, Jason rose to his knees, boldly naked and looming over her as he dipped to enjoy the dessert. Gwendolyn sighed with pleasure, placed the second morsel on slightly pursed lips. Her lover took that also, with a long and languid kiss.

"And the last?" he whispered, his voice thick.

Gwendolyn placed the last tidbit on that most intimate center of her passion. "I have saved the last . . . for best, Sir Stallion." Voice husky, her breathing became more rapid, rising in intensity as his flesh slid along hers, as his tongue found the delicacy . . . and more.

Marie smiled and accepted a glass of wine from a Hanoverian aristocrat who had already imbibed to excess. So far she had gleaned little other than the fact the Tories were anathema. Such news was no news, for everyone knew the Jacobite taint excluded them from any serious consideration. Of the Whigs, there was nary a word spoken. The king's advisors, reluctant to choose too quickly between competing, power-hungry Whig factions, had counseled their monarch to bide his time before accepting the earnestly offered friendship of any. In the midst of rumor, gossip and intrigue, the Hanoverians kept tight rein on their tongues, letting slip nothing of use for Marie or any other spy to carry to his host.

On a deeper level, she was engrossed with a more personal problem. Edmond had caught her eye thrice during the night, each time with a lascivious, bone-chilling smile. Now he had located her again. Glimpsing the young lord stalking imperiously across the room in pursuit, she curtsied, ducked behind a knot of revelers and exited quickly through a side door.

At once angry and frightened, Marie attempted to lose herself in the shadowy recesses of a side corridor, a little-used passage that led to the rear entrance of a sculpture gallery. Cobwebs caught at her face and dust choked her throat but she persevered, groping through the pitch-black hall until a narrow door opened with a squeal at the pressure of her outstretched hand.

Fear ebbed. The gallery was being repaired and redecorated, and the main doors had been bolted for the past month. She was safe. Edmond would search for a few minutes and then give up and go back to his Burgundy. A noise in the hidden corridor! The rear and supposedly secret door flew open. Edmond stepped through. A quick smile illuminated by the candelabrum he carried spoke of greed and triumph. "An apt concealment, mistress. For both of us." Marie stared in mute surprise. Edmond shrugged. "You forget I used to live here, and have explored the manor from front to rear."

The light from the candelabrum was enough. Marie bolted across the floor, leaping tools and chunks of wood, darting around scattered sculptures. If she could reach the main door and unlock it, escape . . .

Edmond grabbed her as the bolts flew open. "No. Do not run away, my dear. I've been enamored since the moment I first saw you and learned who you are." Holding her wrist in an iron grip, he retreated from the door, not noting that it had opened slightly. "I've been told you're a virgin. Though I doubt any such good fortune, there is only one way to learn the truth." Placing the candelabrum down on a pedestal, he drew her close. "I hope 'tis true. I've not had . . ."

Marie spun, tried to flee. Edmond lunged, caught a piece of her gown. The bodice tore and Marie slammed into a piece of statuary, sent it crashing to the floor. Edmond whooped and grabbed again as man and girl toppled to the parqueted wood. Pieces of sharp marble gouged Marie's shoulders.

Edmond's fingers dug into her naked breast. Marie's scream of pain and terror was cut off with a drunken kiss. She twisted aside, managed to scream again. Half-insane under the influence of wine and lust, Edmond lost all restraint. An open-handed blow snapped the girl's head sideways. Cruelly sharp knees dug into her arms, pinioning them to the floor. Somewhere a door slammed open. Marie and her attacker were both unaware of the flood of light falling across their struggling forms. Edmond tore the cap from her head, lowered his face. Marie spat in his eyes and he screamed in rage, "Filthy whore!" Again his hand arced through the dust-laden air.

Suddenly Edmond was lifted bodily into the air and, with a startled squawk of terror, hurled to the opposite end of the room, crashing head over heels into a grinning, aroused satyr of stone. Marie was dimly aware of being scooped into the air by powerful arms, felt the heat of a man's muscled chest. Still terrified, she pressed against the golden pelt of curls, seeking safety. "Aye, lass. There's naught that will hurt ye now," a soothing voice said. Musky man-scent and the strong deep texture of a gentle voice allayed her fear. As she lost consciousness, Marie had the distinct sensation she was spiraling upward through darkness to strength.

She awoke some hours later, aware only of aching muscles and strange surroundings. The sordid encounter with Edmond Penscott was a fading nightmare held at bay by the memory of Jason Brand's embrace. She sat up, suddenly shocked into action. Behan's room! The door opened and the old buccaneer entered. A look of grave concern was writ across his face. "At last our girl rises. Good morning."

Marie jerked the blanket over her breasts. "Oh, Behan, my lovely gown is ruined. They'll all be laughing at me, and Lord Penscott must be furious. I'm scared, Uncle."

68

Behan smiled, patted her shoulder. "Don't be. The duke knows it wasn't your fault."

"But why'd he send me here?"

"You don't remember?"

"No. Only that—"

"You asked to come, and I said I'd watch you until morning. Pfagh! Edmond Penscott's not a quarter the man his father is. The insufferable whelp! Brand will take his measure, I wager." He moved to the fireplace, pulled out a pitcher from a warming shelf and poured a cup. "Here. Drink some chocolate. I've been sent word from Thrush you're excused from work today."

"What's happened?" Marie asked.

"Happening," Behan corrected. "Young Edmond did not take kindly to the Scot's manhandling last night. Challenged him, he did, to meet at dawn by the river, there to settle their differences. Why Brand chose rapiers I know not, for the claymore is his weapon and Edmond has a name for using the rapier well. Perhaps he seeks to humble the lad with his own weapon." Behan chuckled. "A cocky fellow, that Scot. By God, he reminds me of me forty years ago. Drink your chocolate, I say, and keep warm. I'm off to watch."

Marie sipped the sweet, heavy liquid, felt new warmth and strength flow through her veins. A half-hour later, with the sun sneaking through the windows as dawn neared, she crept from the bed, wrapped up in a blanket and stole out, resolved to return to the servants' quarters and replace her torn clothing. The morning was cold and invigorating, crisp with the new day as she hurried through the garden.

Brand had come to her rescue, boldly swept her into his arms. But why? She blushed at the memory of their encounter in the woods. Two strangers had been drawn together. But by what? Desire? Love? No. That was only silly, wishful thinking. A serving girl and a great lord? Impossible. She hadn't dared speak so much as a word to him, had only . . .

"My God!" she breathed, the memory of the scene in the sculpture room flooding back. Her beautiful gown torn, skirt halfway up her thighs . . . She'd been half naked! Each nerve ending could remember the touch of soft, masculine hair brushing against her exposed breasts! Never had she felt so . . . so . . .

A duel! Behan had said a duel. "Oh, God, no," she murmured, the thought filling her veins with ice. They must be found and stopped. Where would they be? The servants always sneaked away to watch if they could.

A flash of dull green. A stableboy disappeared around a tree, heading for the river. Of course! On the knoll overlooking the landing on the Thames. A quick glance around showed no one else in sight. No time for new clothes now. Time only to run, to see. If Jason should be hurt . . . *Oh God, please. No. Please do not let him be hurt.*

Beyond the manicured lawns, down through the wild reeds, up the muddy bank of the creek. Small drifting craft filled with curious onlookers hovered on the surface of the Thames. A duel was always worth pausing to watch. Better than a hanging. Breathless, she hurried the last few yards, wriggled through a hedge and rounded the gazebo. Below, men were clustered on the small flat knoll. Their breaths, cloud-white in the river wind, dissipated quickly. The roar in Marie's ears subsided, replaced by the clamorous treble of blades. Brutal, bitter tones. Rasp, strike, slide. A cry, and a shout from the crowd! The blades fell silent and the surging onlookers closed around the contestants. "Too late," she muttered in dismay and fear.

If she could only see! Too many were in the way. On the river, the boats drifted off as the circle opened to allow a chaplain entrance. In that instant, though she could not see the wounded man's face, Marie could see a horrid crimson stain smearing the front of his white blouse. The chaplain kneeled, head bowed and hands clasped. Other, unseen hands swung a coat over the dead man's chest and face seconds before he was lifted to the shoulders of four men and carried from the field.

Dawn and death. A swordsman, white blouse flapping in the breeze, stepped aside from the knot of onlookers. Radiant in the new-risen sun, a shock of red-gold hair told the story. Marie breathed a sigh of relief. *Thank you, God. Thank you, thank you . . .*

The body-bearers, accompanied by the rest of the crowd, passed Marie's hiding place and proceeded toward the house, the fallen man's father leading the sad procession. Jason Brand remained behind, alone. Marie suppressed a wave of panic. What would happen next? What could she do? Call out? What good would come of that, in front of Lord Penscott, to whom she belonged?

Still he stood, motionless and unaware of the anguish spilling from the unseen girl. Challenged, he had fought as any man would. Fighting, he had won the battle but lost the war. What now of the coming audience with King George? As if planned from the start, Dame Fortune had conspired to ruin his plans. It was foolish to think the outcome of the long-sought and all-important meeting would not be affected by the morning's events. The Penscott name was sacrosanct among Whiggery. No good would come of Edmond's death, save to rid the world of a troublesome, useless and tainted adornment of society.

A presaging breeze whipped through his sweat-soaked blouse. Jason shivered, reached to the ground, picked up a heavy cloak and threw it about his shoulders. Slowly, he trudged toward Penscott Hall. Not five hours remained until the impending audience with the king. In the meanwhile, prudence demanded the wise man prepare for a hasty exit, and take care to watch his back.

A stone-faced Thrush rapped on the library door. Lord Penscott, quill and paper in hand, looked up with a resigned sigh. Was there no rest? At but two in the afternoon, the day already felt infinitely long. Edmond lay in the next room, dead. The lad was his youngest, true, yet best loved. He was worth the name of Penscott. So quickly . . . so quickly . . . Grief had not yet caught up with the bereaved. Only anger and the full thrust of hate for the man who had killed his son, even if in a fairly fought duel. One day Jason Brand would die for his crime.

Penscott's turban lay under a heap of papers. He extricated it and coiled the cloth about his scalp. Their plans had been so carefully laid. Granted, the objective of the exercise had been achieved—Brand's suit had been denied out of hand and his compatriots would surely rise in anger—but the cost had been too great, damn it. The cost had been too great!

A discreet tap sounded again. "All right, all right. Come in," he barked, damning all annoyances. Thrush entered. *Damn Thrush, too.* Master servants were the worst of a necessary lot. "Curse it, man. Am I never to be undisturbed? What's happened now? Has he killed someone else?"

"No, sir. Everything has been quiet. He's saddling his horse and will be gone within the half-hour."

"Too bad," came the bitter reply. "I should have liked to see him try to stay until morning and be run through for the delay. What do you want?"

"Captain Gregory has left too, my lord."

"Oh?"

"Yes, sir. He left but minutes ago, and charged me to carry regards and courtesies and bring you this. There's a note too, m'lord," he said, stepping into the cold light from the window and depositing a box and envelope on the desk.

"Thank you. Now get out of here," the master of the house ordered in a voice as cold as the winter sun. Thrush bowed and backed out swiftly, silently closing the wide, paneled double doors.

Alone in the library, alone with his thoughts and memory of a son, the lord of Penscott Hall opened the walnut box and stared mutely at the unused dueling pistols. *The useless bastard! Worst than his father. . . .* Trembling fingers ripped open the seal on the note.

My lord:
    I am called to London posthaste, and thence to

sea. It is with deep sorrow and heavy heart that I return these fine weapons unfired. However, with your kind permission, I shall consider myself your avenger and one day, should God be willing, place your son's murderer in your hands.

I remain, sir, yr. obt. servant etc.

James Gregory, Capt.

Roger Penscott, Duke of Brentlynn, folded the note and sat back. Perhaps Gregory wasn't the fool initial impressions indicated. Perhaps he would serve after all. There was only one problem. "One day" was hardly soon enough.

The tale of the duel and Jason's subsequent audience with the king was all over Penscott Hall. His Majesty had met Brand, listened in stony silence and then dismissed him abruptly, giving him until nightfall to be away from the royal person. Jason's suit was denied and he was chastised through an interpreter for impudence beyond bearing. There was no doubt he would have to ride far and fast, for there were those who would consider the king's declaration adequate license for revenge. White-faced with rage, yet deferential and submissive in the face of absolute power, Jason had backed out of the room. Soon he would ride out the front gate and be gone.

Marie's tears had stopped hours before. Now she stood at the open door to the stable and tried to work up the courage to enter. Thick animal smells mingled with the heavy aroma of leather and the overpowering sweetness of late-mown hay. Trembling, she followed the afternoon sun inside, staying away from the shadows that fell away to either side.

"Oh!" A hand shot out to grip her arm and spin her around, jostling the lace cap from her head. A wealth of midnight hair cascaded around her shoulders. Marie struggled to catch her breath.

Jason stepped from the darkness. "Ah! My little forest nymph." He grinned. "I beg your pardon lass, but considering what the day has brought, it's best I be overly cautious. I've been assured free passage from here, but Lord Penscott wouldn't be the first Englishman to break his word."

"I . . . I wanted to thank you," Marie stammered, handing him a cloth-wrapped bundle. "I tried to avoid him, but he insisted on forcing himself on me."

"A little trick Master Edmond's now free to exercise with the devil," Jason said with a caustic laugh. He started down the aisle, passing lesser mounts until he came to the eager mare he had ridden from London. Marie followed, saw the steed saddled and anxious to be off.

Framed by a shaft of sunlight from an upper window, Jason leaned against the stall and looked through the bundle. Marie stared at him. Golden beams of sun played among the ringlets covering his chest and transformed his shoulder-length mane into a radiant crown. Oh, why was he dressed so? His crisp, white shirt was open to the waist. Tight indigo breeches displayed each knotted muscle of his legs. She wanted desperately to touch him.

"Lass," he said, his voice husky with emotion. "Meat, bread. You didn't have to do this. They'll not be pleased if they learn of it."

"I don't care," she said, her eyes flaring with defiance. "You'll be able to ride farther without stopping. In case someone tries to follow you."

Jason tied the bundle of food to his saddle and stepped close to her. Coppery fingers stroked her cheek and she felt her legs weaken at his touch. A moist, burning insistency flowered deep within her. His hand ran the length of her long, flowing locks. "Eyes as gray as the mists of Mourne, hair as black as the secrets they conceal. Who are you, lass? What matter of woman?" Marie shook her head, tried to speak. "No. Let me glean the answer my own way. Like this," he said, crushing her to him.

Lips hungering, flesh yearning to join his, Marie matched his rising passion. Her breasts ached for his cupping, teasing caresses. Her tongue, on fire with fierce longing, darted against his. His hard strength made a wanton of her. She could not let him leave. Not now. Not ever.

A bell tolled.

Once.

Twice.

Thrice.

Breath rasping in his throat, he released her. "Damn Edmond Penscott," he swore, slamming one hand against the wooden planks.

"No!" Marie pleaded, trying to block out the sound of the tolling bell.

Jason backed the mare out of the stall and swung into the saddle. "I must be off, lass."

"Take me with you."

Jason stared down at her, toying with the idea. "It's impossible, lass. though by heaven I wish it weren't. But this I do swear. If it's in my power, I'll come back someday." He reached down and lifted her until their lips met one last time, held her thus as the mare walked to the doors.

Marie felt as if her very soul were pouring into him. The blood sang in her veins and her head was light and spinning. Then the dirt floor was beneath her feet again and he was riding away. He did not pause or look back but rode like a wild gale across the emerald sward, leaped the enclosing stone fence and disappeared. Marie fought back the tears. He was gone, leaving behind nothing but the indelible memory of a kiss and the promise to come back.

"Oh, yes," she whispered, touching her cheek where his fingers had rested. "Oh, yes, my darling. I'll be here, waiting for you."

It wasn't until she was alone in her bed that night, her mind reeling willy-nilly with breathless dreams, that she remembered she had forgotten to tell him her name. But that didn't matter. Because Jason Brand would come back someday. He had said so.

For her.

Chapter IV

"The galleon outguns you three to one," Behan said, moving a chunk of wood along the map.

"Full sail immediately," Marie cried, eyes wide with excitement. She loosed assorted lines and rigging. Six bits of sail-shaped muslin unfurled and dropped into place on the replica at hand.

"Hard to starboard," she ordered, "I'll cut close to the point and run between the two islands." With a tug on more threads, the square-rigged sails slanted back, the spanker swung to the right to catch an imaginary following wind.

"Remember . . ."

"I know. Beware the reef. We're really too close to St. Kitts to try, but 'tis high tide and the brig draws but little."

"Good lass." He traced her course with a second wood chip. "The galleon cannot follow and must fall off and abandon the chase. You made it." He picked up the chips, returned them to their original position. "Now pay attention."

Marie reefed the tiny sails on the model. Behan did go on and on sometimes. "Another?"

The old buccaneer looked up sharply. "And how are you to learn?"

"But what good—"

"Good? You ask what good? Because you'll to sea in the morning. What else? To learn, of course. Now pay attention."

The old man hunched over the map and Marie bent to listen. Lessons in the art of sailing given in an old man's cottage far inland were next to useless, but what else was one to do? Scrub floors? Besides, the hours spent with Behan were anything but boring. Given the choice, she'd rather be with him and listening to yore collected from a lifetime of daring escapades than anywhere else.

". . . and so you're stuck. It's early morning and the wind is offshore. You're past the reef and have no room or wind to come about and head back to harbor. Another three minutes and he'll cross your bows and ravage you. What do you do?"

Marie studied the chart, chewed her lip. "Send the men aloft . . . and steer northeast by east," she said, moving her marker.

Behan's eyebrow shot up. His chip, the galleon, fell off from the wind a bit, turned slightly to starboard. "You're in trouble now, lass. I'll still . . ."

Abruptly, Marie twisted her chip and called for the rudder put hard to starboard. "And now southeast." She moved the chip slowly past the outfoxed, less agile galleon. "I'll sail close to windward and, making sure to stay close to its lee, duck under most of your guns and lessen the danger of a broadside, for you're heeled to starboard. Then come about sharply, drop tops and foretops and make a parade in your wake. With a pair of two-pounders and my best muskets in the bow, I'll try for the rudder and pepper your stern gunners. With a lucky shot or two and shifting winds—you didn't say what time of morning it was"—she shrugged, imitating her tutor—"the current here is tricky and the reefs deadly."

Behan laughed aloud. In charge of the lumbering galleon, there was little he could do save hold course, put on every inch of sail and run away, smack into the easterly trades. The brig, once glued on astern, would be shaken off with difficulty. "Well done. Well done! Forty-five years ago I first saw that trick, and still it works."

Marie ignored the praise. "I remember father telling stories at night. The same ploy worked for him off the coast of Yucatán. Why is it, Uncle, that being so stupid, they always win?"

Behan rolled up the map. "They?"

"Those in power. They do, you know. Look at you. And me and father." A bitter smile crossed her face. "They always win."

"In the long run, aye, for they're not stupid. They *are* vain, though, and vanity leads to blunders and miscalculations. Don't ever forget that, girl. You may use their vanity and overweening pride to your advantage, but beware. There will come a day when the luck is against you. There will come those who don't underestimate you. On that day your life is in danger . . . or lost."

Lesson over, Behan busied himself with the map case. Marie sighed, rose and carried the brig back to its proper place among the models. The old man smiled secretly. Age hadn't yet dimmed the pleasure of watching the movements of a pretty girl. Far better to contemplate the reality of hips and legs than the philosophy of power and the powerful.

Marie returned, Fair Weather in hand. The old cat stretched its neck and purred with delight. "Do you suppose Jason Brand has sailed past the reefs off St. Kitts?" Marie asked pensively.

"He's had no more than a year at sea, darling," Behan answered. "But no doubt he will, some day. A pirate sails where fortune leads."

"He is no pirate!"

"Buccaneer, corsair, freebooter, privateer, pirate. What's the difference, Marie? Is it so important? Is a pirate such a terrible monster?"

"They call him a reiver, a pillaging freebooter. I believe none of it."

"The same was said of me, once," Behan chuckled, wishing the years could be rolled back.

"Which proves the point."

"What point? I *was* all those things, at least in part. My fortunes were similar to those of your Scottish lord: a lost cause, lost holdings, and a fall from favor and protection set me among robbers. I became as they. A man quickly becomes what the situation demands. That is survival, Marie Celeste. Never forget that and you'll not be so disappointed in this life."

"Disappointed?" Marie laughed bitterly. "Oh, never disappointed, Uncle. On the contrary. I'm eternally grateful. Look at the fine house I live in. The fine clothes I wear. The fine food . . ."

A pair of old and gnarled hands dropped on her shoulders, turned her around. "Stop, Marie. Stop or you'll eat away your heart. There's worse in this world. Believe me, there's far worse."

"All I wanted was—"

"You'll not have him. He's gone. Has been for two years. Forget him."

Marie's gaze met his, slipped aside to the window. Two years? Only two years? It seemed a lifetime. Or a day. She could still feel his lips on hers, the touch of his hands, still see his smile and hear his laughter. Twenty years could pass and she would not forget him. He'd promised to come back. "I can't, Uncle," she whispered. "I've tried, but I can't."

Behan's hands dropped from her shoulders. "Look in the mirror there," he said, gesturing to the wall.

"So?"

"You're young and beautiful, Marie. There will be other men. Believe me, there will be. And now, enough of this. You're entirely too serious. Let's see a smile, eh? A little smile?"

Marie managed the tiniest grin, suddenly giggled in spite of herself. "You're incorrigible, Uncle."

"And alive, you must admit. Now be off before Thrush descends on my door and I antagonize him further with a cudgel."

Marie nodded. She kissed Behan on the cheek and hurried from the room, pausing in the doorway. "Still I may dream, Uncle," she said quickly, before vanishing.

Behan shook his head in dismay, stood in the doorway and tested the north wind. 'Twill be a cold night, he thought with a shiver.

"May dream about what?" a voice asked.

Behan looked up as Lord Penscott appeared from around the corner. "Life, m'lord. The young, too, dream of life. Or had you forgotten?"

79

"I am curious what you teach the girl that holds her so fascinated."

"We are friends, we talk," Behan replied noncommittally, bowing respectfully if a little stiffly before stepping back.

The nobleman entered unasked, dropped cloak and gloves and sank awkwardly into a seat by the chess table. According to custom, Behan took the opposing chair. Penscott was dressed in a warm richly embroidered coat of velvet laced with gold. The scarf about his neck was of exquisite Bruges lace over a more practical muffler of wool. A diamond set about by emeralds set off a fine white lawn shirt. Behan was more simply appareled. The dark peasant's coat was stiffly woven of coarse wool, warm enough but plain and bereft of any decoration. His wig was of flax, stringy and plain in comparison to the great powdered and intricately curled periwig worn by his master.

The persona of Roger Penscott exuded polished elegance. Trimmed and shaped eyebrows and still-long lashes defined clear, hazel eyes. An immaculate layer of white ceruse dusted with fine talc powder was accented by a natural mole high on his left cheek and thin, purposeful lips painted deep red. The lace cravat hid an age-wattled neck, giving a casual observer the impression the nobleman's head, rather than being attached to his body, had been placed there by a matronly collector of wax figurines. The overall effect was one of a doll, sternly brittle, devoid of warmth and perfectly preserved.

Behan appeared more a man of flesh and blood. Full and bushy eyebrows shone silvery white against a background of wrinkles deep enough to be named corrugations. Limpid, inquisitive eyes, strangely baby blue in one so old, viewed a hostile world with the calm paid for with experience beyond recounting. No makeup, no powder lightened the sunken, leathery cheeks. No attempt had been made to disguise the sagging folds of skin lining his neck, nor the wispy curls of white hair poking above the dingy, undyed shirt.

Penscott finally spoke. "What change in her?"

Behan shook his head. "Marie is . . . Marie."

"None then."

"The lass is the same enchanting creature as when first she arrived. Only more beautiful, with age. I had not thought that possible." Behan nudged the board. "White moves first."

"You do not wish to draw lots?"

"I feel gracious, m'lord."

"Which will be your undoing," Penscott snapped, pushing his king's pawn two squares forward. Behan studied the board, a habit that irritated his benefactor, especially so early in the game when the moves should be automatic. This time Penscott sat back and refused the bait, determined to relax and enjoy the game. "Yes, she is very beautiful. The fairest flower. One that blooms yearlong. And pure, by God. I've seen to *that*. A virgin and a valuable asset to be kept until necessary. As in chess, the dramatic, unsuspected maneuver brings victory." He paused, the gall rising in spite of the effort to remain calm. "Are you going to move?"

Behan looked up, smiled. "Chess is a game, m'lord. I prefer to concern myself with life." His pawn mirrored white's opening.

"Both are gaming undertakings for the shrewd, are they not?"

"The girl is precious to me."

The nobleman returned Behan's stare until the tutor lowered his gaze. "No more than to me. She is beautiful, intelligent and therefore potentially valuable. Not for naught did I take her under my roof and see to her learning. Your move again."

The two played in silence through a half-dozen moves. "Suddenly you are interested," Behan finally said. "Why?"

"Ah, that pawn is poison. Do not tempt me, Frenchman. My knight withdraws."

"What are your intentions for Marie?"

Penscott sat back. A forefinger tapped the arm of the chair. "There is a certain prince, who, as princes do,

81

longs for his father's crown and throne," he began slowly. "Among my circle, too close a relationship to such a prince would be considered dangerous. However, if this prince, appreciative of beauty and wit, should take interest in her, he would be in my debt, would he not?"

"M'lord is devious. Potentially valuable indeed. You'll be well paid for your indulgence."

"Come, come, my friend. You need not be so indignant. She won't be lost for some time yet. The moment is not ripe. There are a few months left. Perhaps by then we'll be able to engender a spark of fire in the girl. Her virginity is a rarity with which I shall catch a prince. However, it will take far more to keep him."

Lord Penscott retrieved his cane and rose to leave as Behan's queen's bishop threatened the white queen. "We have not finished the game, m'lord."

"But of course we have. Did you not notice?"

"What, m'lord?"

The end of the silver-tipped ebony cane touched the black king, knocked over the proud and unendangered piece. "I won." Without further comment, the lord of Penscott Hall—and winner of the game—shrugged into the heavy cloak and stumped out the door, leaving Behan alone to reset the board for the next "game."

Outside, a freezing wind whistled out of the north. The vast mound of curled periwig served to keep a gentleman's head, ears and neck warm, but the seeking breeze curled under the cloak and chilled his legs, wrapped though they were. Winter, damned bitter winter, was almost too much for an old man, he thought, heading for his favorite spot overlooking the Thames. Dark images engendered by a gray and featureless cloud-ridden sky abounded. The garden was barren in November. Skeletons of trees and hedges lined the path with bleak, jagged angles. All about, the grass was brown and dessicated, a brittle, cheerless carpet. Pine and holly offered the only color, green patches of hope in a dead landscape.

The pond was frozen. Clear patches of black ice lay

delineated by swirls of light, fluffy snow, blown in whorls and streaks across the hard water. The bench was covered with a pillow of snow, unmelted by a pale, smeared sun barely visible through the overcast and far, far away. Roger Penscott gazed across the land, a sour humor spoiling the elation usually experienced when he stood in the center of the world he and his fathers had built. The wind died down suddenly and that same world fell eerily silent. A premonition? Of what? Trouble? Ruin? Change?

Aye. That was it. *Damn. I'm too old for changes. Now, if I were younger?* He turned toward the choppy Thames. "I'd go to sea again," he said aloud, breaking the silence, "and let come what might." In answer, the wind curled around the west wing and raised the snow on the pond. Gritting his teeth, Penscott grimaced and hurried toward the side door. An old man had no business dreaming of the sea, when what lay in store was a hot toddy and a fire to keep his feet warm while dreams of plots and labyrinthine connivings danced in the flames. Success was all very well and good, but chilblains still hurt.

There was no doubt winter wasn't waiting this year. Marie pulled the heavy shawl closer about her shoulders and poked up the fire. Mysteré had never felt so far away. No matter how many fireplaces were kept blazing, the huge manor remained cold and drafty, cheerless and morbidly gray. It would soon be dark, and if the day had been cold, the night would be worse. Shivering, she moved about the room, lighting candles before pulling the heavy curtains. Below, riders turned into the drive, their horses stiff with cold. Marie paused, frowning. Who was expected? Who, for that matter, would be traveling in such weather?

She shrugged, let the curtain fall and turned back to the fire, thankful to be inside and out of the wind and snow, then she stopped, inexplicably troubled. Something about . . . one horseman . . . Whirling back to the window, she pulled aside the curtain and strained to make out the shadowed faces.

Their leader dismounted and went up the steps, shouting commands to the others, who slowly went on heading north along the west wing to circle the house. The hands of one rider were tied. He was blindfolded. Something about him . . . Prisoner and escort neared the corner. A capricious gust of wind jerked the riding hood from the prisoner's head. Red-gold curls swirled in the wind. Red-gold curls! *It can't be! My God, but it can't be.* . . . The room spun and Marie, barely able to stand, clung to the sill and pressed her face against the freezing glass. *He is back! He is back!* A prisoner, to be sure, but back.

But what if he's been hurt? Shivers of fear raced through her body. Jason Brand was not a man to be taken easily. He might have been wounded, perhaps badly. She had to see, had to know, no matter what the cost. Dropping the curtain again, she checked the room. Candles lit, fire going, bed straightened, clothes laid out. . . . Lady Gwendolyn wouldn't need her for a while. She stole out the door and down the hall, keeping an eye out. Far down the corridor a servant hurried to the master bedroom and knocked. Marie ducked behind a sculpture as the door opened and the lord of the manor, robe flapping and wig askew, hurried out and down the front stairs.

The hall clear again, Marie slipped from hiding and ran to the head of the stairs. The first landing could be seen from the front door, so she hurriedly hid behind a marble satyr. Voices. She peeked around to see a strikingly familiar figure whisk off a heavy riding cloak to reveal a scarlet uniform decorated with gold braid.

"Captain Gregory!" Penscott's voice cut through the dim light. "You've come, then. How was the journey?"

"Cold and slow, but we've an end of it now."

"Aye." The lord gestured and a butler hurried up. "Tea and something to eat in the upstairs library." The butler hurried off. "We'll have you fixed up in no time."

84

Captain Gregory sat and let another servant remove his outer boots, sighed with relief and stamped his feet. "I'll not deny a fire will be welcome."

"Come along then." The two men turned and walked down the hall. "And our prisoner?"

Gregory laughed. "Safe and sound, save for a lump on his pate. Unhappy, of course, but he puts on a good front. I've not yet told him where he is. There are places he'd rather be, I wager."

"I should think so," the older man replied. "I've waited a long time to see that man again."

"I'm glad to see you pleased, m'lord."

"Pleased?" Penscott asked gleefully, stopping at the foot of the stairs. "Pleased? You understate the case, sir. I am delighted. Jason Brand is a most welcome guest."

Jason Brand. It *was* him, then. And unharmed, if Gregory could be believed. Ecstatic, Marie ignored the rest of the conversation. Jason was near: that was all that counted. But they were coming! To be found eavesdropping would be dangerous. Stealthily, silently, she tiptoed up the stairs before Lord Penscott and Captain Gregory reached the landing. Seconds later, out of breath from both haste and fear, she was safely in Gwendolyn's room again, and sank into a chair. Jason, Jason, Jason! Her eyes closed tight and she pictured him. His face, the feel of his arms about her and the touch of his lips. Even his voice. "But this I promise. If it's in my power, I'll come back someday."

He had. At last, he had.

Worse than the Irish Sea in a Nor'wester. Jason's whole body quaked uncontrollably. His teeth chattered unceasingly and his jaw ached. The north wind hit him full in the face, shot down his back and the open front of the cloak. If they didn't get inside soon . . .

What was the English bastard's name? Gregory. James Gregory. An overrated captain who couldn't sail a boy's toy boat on a calm pond. Captured by a fool! *Damn! If I don't get inside, I'll freeze to death. Must be what they want. If I don't get inside, I'll freeze* . . . The words were starting to run around in circles. He couldn't think any more. Just the single word. *Freeze* . . . *Freeze* . . .

The wind eased. They were in the lee of a row of pines. Ahead, a door slammed in the wind and a voice called. Footsteps pounded toward them and someone took the reins and hauled the horse's head about. Rough hands pulled Jason from the saddle, shoved him forward. Barely able to remain standing on benumbed feet, he stumbled, reeled against the jamb and fell into warmth.

"Take off your cloak," a callous voice ordered as more hands pulled him erect. A door closed and the moaning wind was shut out. Words took shape, made sense. Jason raised the manacles to indicate he was helpless. "All right. Who has the bloody key?"

One of the guards who had ridden from London stepped forward, fumbled at his belt and pulled out the key. A second later and the cold iron fell from Jason's wrists. "All right then, mate. Off with it."

He tried. Frozen fingers groped for the tie but couldn't even feel, much less loosen, the knot. "Fer Chris'sakes, mate. Here." With a ringing slap, something touched his hands and they fell aside, too numb and swollen to feel the blow. Warm fingers fumbled at the string and the cloak fell to the floor, followed by the blindfold. Jason stood swaying, blinking, trying to focus.

"Here." Another voice. "Sit down. Drink this."

Gratefully, Jason sank to a bench. A steaming cup of something hot sat on the table. Trembling, he managed to get both hands around it, lifted it and sipped at the liquid. Sweet. Hot! *God, chocolate!* The heat ran down his gullet, spread from stomach to arms. *Hot chocolate!* Nothing had ever tasted so good.

"Come along, then, mate. Up you go." A hand grabbed Jason's upper arm and tugged. Frantically, he gulped the last swallow and allowed them to lead the way. A flight of stairs lay ahead.

A torture chamber. The bloody bastards. So they think they can make me tell them. A door with a small window, heavily barred, stood open at the top of a landing. "Have fun, mate." The same voice preceded a mighty shove which sent Jason sprawling into the room, barely catching himself before crashing into the opposite wall. The door banged shut. He was alone.

At least it was relatively warm. Jason stood, surveyed his surroundings and wondered where this new prison lay. Other than the fact they had left London, there was no indication. A low, guttering and welcome fire burned in a shallow fireplace. A table in the middle of the floor held a single candle. Two chairs, simple but sturdy from their looks, one on either side of the table, were the only other furniture save for a narrow bench on which lay a pile of blankets. A colorless, ragged tapestry, so worn and faded its depiction was indistinguishable in the dim light, hung on one wall. Nothing else could be seen. Nothing else . . . A bucket. A single bucket, thrown into a corner by the window.

The window. Jason hurried over, opened the shutters and peered out through discouraging thick iron bars. Only a hint of light remained, just enough to see the bare outlines of the most important piece of furniture of all: a gallows. Jason stared, unable to tear his eyes from the scene. Hanging by the neck, a body turned slowly in the breeze, turned one way and the next, pirouetting endlessly to the tune of the north wind.

She knocked lightly and the door swung open immediately to reveal her husband waiting at the dinner table. "Ah, Gwendolyn. Come in. Come in," he said, rising. "How long is it? A week? At least, I should think."

Gwendolyn smiled, moved to the other end of the table and let the sallow-faced butler seat her. "I have waited patiently for my lord's call," she replied testily.

"And for that I apologize most humbly, my love. Business . . ." He waved a hand in a vague gesture, cut short abruptly. "But let us not speak of the past. I've ordered a goose killed. You know how much you enjoy young goose. A capon at that. And a kidney pie to further entice your good humor. If you please, Hanley."

The butler set to work carving the goose. Full plates flanked by goblets of white wine soon lay in front of lord and lady, who fell to hungrily. There was little talk for the next half hour. Roger didn't like chatter at table and Gwendolyn, filled with curiosity, felt it imprudent to tempt fate. "You may tell Ringe he's done a marvel, as usual," Penscott finally said, pushing back his plate and reluctantly passing up a final sliver of meat pastry.

"Of course, my lord," Hanley murmured, clearing the table quickly and handing the full trays to a lad in training.

Gwendolyn remained silent, still waiting. "And now replenish our goblets if you will, and then you are free to leave."

Ghostlike, Hanley poured glasses of port for both, then brought separate pitchers to lord and lady, poured for each a steaming cup of liquid and left the room, bowing deferentially before closing the doors. Gwendolyn arched an eyebrow. "Chocolate, my lord?"

Penscott coughed discreetly, chuckled. "A surprise, my dear. Old age makes me mellow. Is it sweet enough?"

Gwendolyn sipped, smiled. "Ringe knows how I like it."

"Ah, yes. No doubt." He smiled, disguising the next turn. "Which brings us to the purpose for this little tête-à-tête, I'm afraid."

Lady Gwendolyn tensed slightly, sipped again at the chocolate. The drink had soured. "I somehow doubt my lord has mellowed sufficiently. A single capon seems hardly payment enough for—"

"I've little time for banter, Gwendolyn."

Eyes snapping with unconcealed hostility, Gwendolyn Penscott leaned forward to retort, reconsidered and sat back with a languid wave of the hand. "My lord has something on his mind."

"You are perceptive, my dear. I will be blunt. You have been told, of course, of our visitors."

"But our table is empty," his wife noted, looking around in mock innocence.

"There are aspects of my life I am reluctant to discuss in public."

"Ah, then our tête-à-tête promises to be intensely personal. How delightful."

"The sarcasm is appreciated. Thank you. May we continue?" Gwendolyn nodded graciously. "Good. So to business. I know you are peeved by our isolation here. For that I am duly apologetic, but plead necessity. I know you have been bored: we haven't had visitors for some time and I admit a certain, shall we say, lack of initiative on my part."

"My lord—"

"Hold your tongue, wife. I won't be flattered or coddled. I'm not overly interested in the rigors of sex anymore and that is that. Especially with one so well used. There are other aspects of this world that more fully hold my attention. Fifty years of dropping anchor between the nearest pair of legs is enough for any man. That's not the point. The point, my dear, is your harbor and those who call there."

"I think my affairs are my own business, my lord. If time has made you exempt, there are those it has not. I shan't be denied one of the few pleasures left in this dungeon."

"Rightly so, and I could care less except . . . when those affairs become a political embarrassment and jeopardize my position in valued circles. Now, I have never dictated yea or nay, but must do so now. Captain Gregory is permissible, Jason Brand is not."

"Jason Brand? Surely my lord doesn't think—"

"Your lord knows that with you once is never enough. The Scot is an embarrassment I shall find impossible to tolerate or forgive."

"But I never—"

"Don't lie to me, Gwendolyn. You may pout, expostulate, weep, decry, argue and generally carry on as women will, but don't lie. I know you once spent part of an evening with Jason Brand. I know to what end he was so gainfully employed before interrupting Edmond's ill-conceived venture. Do you think me a blind fool?"

Gwendolyn sat back, played idly with a knife. "I think my lord tries to dictate that which lies beyond his control. Very well—may I finish at least one sentence without interruption?—Jason Brand and I played the game. He was magnificent, as some are not. I have no intention of . . ."

"Though Hanover be leagues away, I promise you, lady, that should I receive word you've been making the beast with Jason Brand, magnificent or no, you will find yourself packed off to a winter of true isolation."

Lady Gwendolyn laughed nervously in reaction to the threat. "Really, my lord. Exiled for a dalliance? Would you leave Penscott Hall without a hostess? How gauche. What would your vaunted colleagues say should they find the mighty Lord Penscott forced to such silly extremes? 'Power?' " she mimicked in broad tones. " 'Why, the man can't even control his own wife!' "

"There are others, madam, capable of taking your place. Don't forget. Even our king has a wife most easily kept out of the way."

Lady Gwendolyn's chair tumbled over as she sprang to her feet. "You dare threaten, sir?" she hissed, cheeks flushed beneath the heavy layers of ceruse and powder. "I will not listen to—"

"Sit down and hold your temper. You *will* listen. I have sensitive ears. A fortnight after word reaches me that you've sneaked off to the chateau, you'll find yourself on my estate in the Cotswold Hills, with no more than untaught stableboys, gamekeepers and idle gardeners to fill the aching void between your legs."

A deadly silence filled the room. For a long moment a stunned Gwendolyn stared at her husband. Short, rasping breaths rattled in her throat. "Who . . . would . . . replace me?" she asked haltingly, fires of jealousy held in check by fear.

He shrugged eloquently, not deigning to answer. "Does it matter?"

"You would really do this?"

Slowly, Roger Penscott stood to face his wife across the table. "I would, madam," he answered softly. "You may count on it."

Neither said more for a long moment. Finally, Gwendolyn shuddered violently. "Then I concede," she whispered, gaining control with great effort. "To my husband and lord goes the victory."

Penscott smiled, sat down with a sigh. "Good." Lady Gwendolyn still stood, motionless. "That will be all, then. You may return to your rooms if you wish," he said, ringing a small bell.

The doors opened to reveal Hanley. Gwendolyn Penscott, back and shoulders stiff, turned and strode from the table. Well-trained as he was, Hanley pointedly avoided noticing the tense grimace of hate and loathing that distorted his lady's face.

The clock struck ten. Lady Gwendolyn Penscott sat in front of the mirror in her dressing room. Ten o'clock? No civilized person was getting ready for bed at such a ridiculous hour. In London the evening would have barely started, with roaring fires, bright lights and gay chatter, the tinkle of glass and lilting music. Here the fires were damped for the night and the lights dimmed, leaving bleak and gray walls leached of heat and destitute of life and pleasant companionship. Here the only music was that of the north wind moaning through the eaves and rattling the shutters. What could be worse? Gwendolyn shivered. Exile would be far worse.

A candle sputtered and she moved it and another closer, the better to inspect her face. Years of excess had wreaked slow but cruel changes and ravaged once seductive charms. The morning's toilet had become a time-consuming process during which vanity strove to recapture the faded bloom of youth. The truth was evident, now that all vestiges of makeup had been washed away. Lines crept out from each eye. Not great lines yet, but heavy enough to cause concern and require filling. Some sagging here and there—she raised her chin, patted the soft flesh and sniffed a brief disclaimer. Her eyes traveled down. Full breasts, veined and heavy, sagged moderately under the peignoir. It wouldn't do to look at her stomach. Jason Brand would still recognize her, she imagined, but might not as readily fondle those folds of flesh. Two years made a difference, indeed.

Gwendolyn pouted. She had served Roger well, even in bed when he so desired. Granted that had not been often, but the blame lay with the husband, not the wife, who was wrongfully faulted for seeking pleasure where pleasure was to be found. After all, sixty-five wasn't yet totally ancient. The question wasn't one of incapability, but of reluctance.

"There are others, madam, capable of taking your place." His exact words. Others? But who? Damn the heartless passing of time. It wasn't fair. She stared into the mirror, watched as Marie entered with gown and sleeping cap. Two years had seen the serving girl blossom into a ravishing woman whose innocent sensuality had caused many a comment from guests enjoying the Penscotts' hospitality. Gwendolyn could only smile, graciously except such accolades and imagine them directed toward herself. But they weren't, of course, and she knew it. If only she possessed Marie's youth, her pretty perfection. What wiles could she then work on a diffident husband. Why, he'd . . .

Marie!

Marrow made cold as the outer stones of the manor. Blood frozen in the heart with bitter realization. Marie the beauty. Marie the virgin. So that was why the island bitch was under his personal protection. That was why a servant girl enjoyed the tutorial services of old Behan. The transition from servant to mistress would be a simple matter. Roger would be envied and praised, while his true wife passed the rest of her life in obscurity.

The woman in the mirror frowned. The bitch had been betraying her all along, simpering around like a spaniel and waiting for the day when . . . How dare she! "That will be all, girl," she intoned flatly, trying to hold back the anger.

Marie started. "My lady?"

"Do you question? I said that will be all. Leave my gown and cap on the bed and get out. I shan't need anything further from you."

"I . . . I don't understand, mistress."

"Did you hear me?" Control shattered, Gwendolyn screeched, turned on Marie and gestured violently. Veins in her neck protruded and her eyes blazed. "Get out! Get out!"

Marie dropped the nightclothes on the bed, backed away toward the door. Something had suddenly and inexplicably gone terribly wrong. Lady Gwendolyn's face was that of an animal, twisted with hate and rage. "If I have done anything, Lady—"

"Schemer! Brat! Insolent bitch! I see you with a clear eye and will no more of you."

"But mistress—"

"Get out! Get out! Get out of my sight!"

Marie fled, astonished and frightened by the uncalled-for outburst. The door slammed with a resounding crash that reverberated down the spacious corridor. Near tears, she considered anew the dangerous and fickle unpredictability of the aristocracy. For unfathomable reasons, cause or no, Lady Penscott had been offended. Marie Celeste Ravenne, being handy, had received the brunt of the blame. Gwendolyn in a rage. Captain Gregory in residence. Jason Brand imprisoned. Penscott Hall was suddenly a very dangerous place.

Cloud-gray eyes in the dark. Someone has been weeping. Someone has lain abed and heard the tolling of midnight. The booming echo of usually unheard bells is magnified by fear and concern and confusion. A wintry breath mocks the heart. He is there. He is in the chateau. How confused the heart. To laugh, or weep? Forgotten the misery, the cold, the recent rejection and all it portended. One fact fills the night. He is nearby. He has returned.

The room her own, Arabella having been married the past year, Marie was free to sleep or wake, come or go. On this night, sleep futile, she finally gave up trying, rose and pulled on slippers and shawl. The east wing was silent. Servants slept in undisturbed and weary quietude. Thrush's room, the last door on the right, was the only dangerous place, for the master servant, ever watchful and suspicious, slept with the door and one eye open.

She tiptoed safely past, keeping to the wall. Now, with nothing but the rustling sleeping gown to betray her to the midnight cobwebs, Marie glided down the hall. What destination? None really but to move, because heartache was too awesome to bear in stillness. The chateau could be seen—not in summer, for trees blocked the view—from the north end of the west wing. There she headed, making her way down the long hall to the foot of the great stairs and turning right.

Dressed none too warmly, Marie regretted the lack of a coat or heavy cloak. The nightgown and shawl would have to do. Should someone discover her? *They would think me a ghost, no doubt, and take to heels.* The house felt empty, for already the night was long. Cold drained the strength from the strongest and all were asleep, tucked under heavy wool or light down. The home of one of the most powerful men in England felt empty. Yet someone always watched. *I shall be caught and punished. So be it.* Resigned to punishment—a glimpse of the chateau where he lay imprisoned was worth the worst—she continued.

"Forget him, child," Behan had said, "else you court a world of grief. One day he will be killed. Forget him. There'll be another man. What is he to you, after all?"

What is he to me? As well ask what sails are to a ship or wings to a bird. He is my love, my would-be lover, the only man I care for. I am incomplete without him, Uncle.

A streak of candlelight spilled from under the door at

the end of the hall. Marie paused, frightened and frozen in place. Behind her, a door closed and steps approached. She ducked quickly into a sitting room and left the door ajar, ducking back in fear as a dim lantern lit the hall and a bulky figure approached. When the footsteps passed she dared look again, in time to watch Captain Gregory disappear into the study. The door had been left open and she crept near, taking pains to remain out of sight.

"Well, my lord, at long last I have brought you a most recalcitrant guest. By God, but it's cold out there."

"You have been with him?"

"And conversed. For the fifth time since his capture. He's cold, weak with hunger, tired and confused. I daresay he aches as well, yet he guards his tongue craftily. We discussed the whereabouts of his cohorts—in truth, I still believe them to be in England, and nearby—and he answered by questioning the identity of my informant. He wanted to ask where he was, but wouldn't give me the pleasure. In any case, I've saved that surprise for later."

A book slapped shut and she heard a growl of displeasure. "So you've learned nothing. Jason Brand sits within a hundred yards of my rear door, and you have 'conversed' and 'discussed.' 'Sblood, man, but you're a fool. I'll not have my son's murderer go untaught. Tomorrow we shall do more than tell him where he is. He'll be flayed as he hangs by the neck. The rest of the brigands will have scattered by now, so it matters little."

Marie crept closer until she could see into the room. Captain Gregory turned back to the fire and lifted his coat. "With all deference, I must suggest my lord is overwrought. I understand his anger, but beg he not become overly hasty."

" 'Twas not your son who fell!"

"True. Edmond was not my son. He was my friend. Will you listen to reason?"

The men stared at each other across the table. The elder gave in first, shrugged agreement. "Very well, James. I will listen."

"Good. I am more certain than ever that Brand is no ordinary pirate out to reap personal reward. No. He is a dangerous idealist whose ill-gained wealth goes to support the Jacobite cause and rebuild their fortunes so they may try again to usurp the crown. Contraband is smuggled into Scotland and escapes lawful taxation. English shipping is sent to the bottom or captured. The plunder disappears into secret stores or reappears in diverse places on the continent, exchanged for arms or other accoutrements of war.

"Now, 'tis true Brand's cohorts will have scattered since his arrest. We may not expect to find them. But"—Gregory paused for effect—"there is a raft of others, a whole structure not lightly dismantled. Of these we will learn a great deal, if we exercise patience."

"I'm too old for patience, James."

"As I am too young. But we could break every bone in Jason Brand's body, flay him 'til the skin hangs in shreds, torture him to the end . . . and he would remain silent. All that he can endure. But to crush his spirit? Ah, there lies the key. You know it works, I know it works. You've done so too many times in past years, always with the same results. The same blank walls, the tasteless food, the lack of pain to feed resolve? I assure you, sir, by the fourth time our friend drops through the trap and finds himself still alive, even Jason Brand will begin to fear death. At that moment, all he knows will be ours. Then, sir, your revenge will be complete."

Penscott sank into the deep chair. "You continue to surprise me, James. I see a man stronger, firmer than his father. I regret having underestimated you."

The captain leaned forward, knuckles pressed against the tabletop. "I am not the pup you once frightened, my lord. I respect you, yes. You are powerful. You have achieved a great deal. I aspire to no less. Perhaps in your mold do I foresee the successful shaping of my own fortunes."

Amused, flattered and even impressed by Gregory's ambition and candor, the older man smiled in approbation. "You are more like me than my sons, James." The smile disappeared. "My living son," he added with a frown.

"You flatter me, sir."

"Nonsense. I flatter no man unnecessarily." He paused, deep in thought. "So you think you can break Brand, eh?"

"I know I can."

"Very well, then. You shall have ample time to prove it. No man shall stay your hand."

"Sir?"

"Walpole has followed the king to Hanover and causes trouble with Sunderland. Stanhope must abide with Parliament and keep a cautious eye on Townshend's subterfuges. In the midst of this nest of intrigue, I must travel to Hanover. A dreadful fate for an old man in winter, I hasten to add."

"And I, sir?" Captain Gregory asked needlessly, grinning in anticipation.

"As you have guessed, sir. Brand is yours. If he has not talked by the time I return, we will hang him and have done with it. Just make sure you wait 'til then."

"I have waited two years, my lord. Another month or two, with him in my hands, will be a pleasure."

"There is one thing else," Penscott interrupted flatly. Gregroy tensed. "My wife is at times unwisely enamored. I will not, under any circumstances, allow her with our prisoner. Keep her away from the chateau. As for yourself, I do not wish to return home to scandal. Keep your dalliances as uncontroversial as possible."

Gregory dared laugh. "I entertain only the most harmless of fancies, I assure you. A girl for warmth against the chill will serve admirably." He paused, remembering. "The dark-haired wench. Is she still here?"

"Marie Ravenne remains under my patronage. I will not have her touched."

Captain Gregory raised an eyebrow. "A serving girl?"

"Her position is none of your concern, Captain. It is enough to know I have designs for her future. You interfere or dispute my wishes at your peril. Do you understand?"

The threat was unmistakably explicit. "Perfectly, my lord." The girl was a tasty strumpet, but not worth the price. Not in the slightest.

They discussed her as one would a horse. Seething with anger and frustration, Marie watched from the sitting room as the men departed for their respective beds. Lord Penscott's cane could be heard long after he had disappeared down the dimly lit hall. Finally she emerged from hiding and entered the library to stand shivering before the fire. The last hours had been filled with perplexing issues beyond comprehension. Jason's arrival and Lady Gwendolyn's outburst had been bad enough. The disquieting news that her master had "designs for her future" was even a worse threat. What did the strange trio of events portend?

"Aaiii!" Marie cowered behind a chair, weeping with relief when she realized the startling sound was but a nearby branch scraping against the window.

Bolstering what courage she could muster, Marie crossed to the glass, pulled back the curtain, cracked open the shutter and peered into the night. Outside, a ghostly beam of moonlight formed a frigid column of radiance through which motes of silvery snow swirled like stars spiraling in time to the wind's moaning dirge. The chateau lay beyond a fringe of ornamental cedars. There, where a lamp glimmered through a crack, Jason Brand lay captive.

Jason . . .

A leering jest of providence, to be so close to her love. *To my love? I have never spoken to him. How can I love one who . . . ?* A thousand fleeting images danced in the snow. She stood before him in the woods. His ripped shirt and muscled chest. A kiss, long and deep, and her breasts crushed to the golden curls . . . in the sculpture gallery a looming figure interceded to save her from Edmond, later fought a duel and was banished . . .

Was ever a Lady so well served? I must see him again. I must! There would be guards. And Captain Gregory. Jason Brand was special. Those who were consigned to the chateau were watched carefully, and woe to the man or woman who dared interfere.

Do I dare? Behan will scold. If the master finds out . . . The glass was cold. Weak with apprehension, she pressed her forehead to the icy surface. The shock restoring her, she stood, closed shutter and curtains, resolved at last. There was only one possible answer, one possible path. "Forgive me, dear Uncle, but I must find a way. I must!"

Chapter V

Six scratches marked the wall over the fireplace. Six days had passed since Jason had been brought to the unusual prison. All in all, he couldn't complain. As London had proved, there were worse places a man might be thrown, each of which could have meant death within six days.

Wrapped against the cold, the prisoner lay abed and mentally appraised the past week. Where he was, he had yet to learn. The country, to be sure, for surely a city would be noisier. But where in the country? Having ridden blindfolded, their direction from London was unknown. The two permitted to talk to him gave no clue. The first, named Burton, the gravelly voiced one who called him 'mate,' probably came from the south end of London, but that didn't prove anything. The other, Captain Gregory, took great pleasure in dropping meaningless hints.

Gregory was the key. Jason and the captain's relationship was now two years old, having started the day of the duel in which Edmond Penscott died. It hadn't taken Jason long to figure out someone was following when he left Penscott Hall that day. A week later he discovered his pursuer was Captain Gregory. Pursuit ended at the Scottish border, resumed when Jason took to a life of piracy after the horrors of the Fifteen, the tragic rebellion of the Jacobites that brought bloodshed and disaster to Scotland. The chase ended with Jason's capture, betrayed by one he considered an ally.

Since arriving, the captain had visited two or three times each day. His demeanor varied. Once he was friendly and vaguely informative, caring to play at cards or chat about the court or the weather or other minutiae. Next he was abusive or threatening, peppering his prisoner with insult and questions. That they were out to break him, Jason had no doubt, but the methods employed left him confused. Had the choice been his, he would have questioned once and, receiving no answer, set the prisoner adrift or killed him out of hand. Time might have made him ruthless, but he drew the line at unnecessary cruelty or long, drawn-out inquisitions.

Alternately cold and warm, alternately hungry and fed, beaten to near insensibility in London and now coddled, he finally realized what was happening and found himself playing a guessing game with his captors. By the sixth day he had talked himself into not caring, into trying not to anticipate. The chore was difficult, but no alternative existed. Determined to come through the ordeal in one piece, Jason started a regimen of daily physical and mental exercise.

On the seventh morning, he woke fresh and rested. The day before hadn't been bad. Breakfast under the watchful eyes of Sergeant Burton; a game of Hazard in which he won five buttons; then solitude until dinner. The usual bowl of porridge and slice of dark bread, if not kingly fare, was enough to keep body and soul together. Rising and wrapping the blanket about his shoulders, he dug the seventh scratch over the fireplace before throwing the last of the wood on the fire and drinking the last of yesterday's allotment of stale water. He went to the window and opened the shutters. The morning was cold but bright and clear. Sun glimmered off . . .

The corpse on the gallows was gone! Only an empty noose hung over the closed trap. The sound of a mallet on wood broke the stillness. The trap dropped and a soldier appeared, adjusted something, pulled up the trap and disappeared again. A dark feeling swept over Jason. This was going to be it, then. He'd won. Gregory would learn nothing of the pirate network and would take Jason's life for spite. This day was the last. For unknown minutes he stood without moving, staring at the gallows. A thousand preferable endings flashed

101

through his mind. A duel or fight at sea, surrounded by bloody turmoil. A glorious demise, going out in a grand manner, contending against man or nature. But a noose around his neck?

Death lay below, waiting, personified in a hank of rope. *Did I not know it would come to this?* Death lay below, rough-cut boards dull in the brittle sunlight. *Bone and blood is the pirate's lot.* Death lay below, the frozen bare ground beneath a closed trap ready to spring open, drop from beneath his feet. *Should I quail or flinch, then, before fate?* Death lay below. . . . *I shall rob them of their satisfaction.*

The feeling of panic passed abruptly, replaced by a great acceptance, by calm compliance. The time had come to join the others. His father, dead these eighteen years. . . . Two sisters and three brothers, all dead. . . . A wife and dear, darling son, murdered in their beds by the marauding English butchers during the Fifteen. His mother, too, cut down in defiance, flame-red hair clotted dark with gore as she lay before the gate. These last four, no matter how hard he tried, would not quit his dreams. In all, he had seen enough—too much of life's cruelty to quaver before a noose.

There were regrets, of course. He would die without learning who had betrayed him and caused his capture, much less the names of those responsible for the deaths of his wife, son and mother. He could never extend a similar courtesy to his executioners. And how much else? Too many maids, blonde, brunette or redhead, walked the earth untasted: he'd never know them, never ride to feverish glory on and in them. Too many jugs of ale or pots of rum. Too many horserides, sunrises, sunsets, joints of beef, storms, calms, escapades high and low in which life and . . . life's end . . . were confronted. A fleeting twinge of uncertainty was reasonable.

But too late even for regrets. Whatever waited beyond death would have waited in any case. A few years could make little difference. A more elegant departure could be desired, certainly, but the matter was in other hands and he refused to worry longer. Outside the door, the bar was raised. "Stand back, mate." Burton, that would be. Come already? No. The door opened and a tray slid in on the floor. "Eat hearty, mate."

Mutton pie, hot and steaming. A great mug of tea. Bread, covered thickly with butter. A man might as well die on full stomach as empty. It was said men of slight build took longer to die. Dangled and choked. Not enough weight to snap the neck. *Dammit man, quit those thoughts.*

No sooner was the meal finished than footsteps sounded on the stairs. Jason straightened his clothes, stood relaxed before the fire. The wait was over. By the time the door opened he was ready and, if not exactly willing, prepared to face them with equanimity. Gregory entered, a grin dirtying his face. The two men stared, neither giving way to the other. "Well," the captain finally said. "There's no point in waiting." He stepped to one side, gestured. "After you, Brand."

Jason started out, stopped at the table and downed the last swallow of tea. *The last swallow of anything, damn their smirking souls.* The door stood open. The stairs were empty. Soldiers undoubtedly waited below. *Perhaps I could escape. No. He's a fool, but not enough to try to hang me by himself.* The point of a sword prodded his back. At the same moment Burton, waiting to one side in the dark, stepped in front of him and clapped a pair of manacles on his wrists. *So be it.*

Brave he may be, but the last walk of a man condemned to die is never easy. The noose is never an illustrious end. Jason emerged into the sunlight, blinked and followed one squad of soldiers as a half-dozen more fell in behind. A group waited at the gallows, their backs to him. Jason's lips set in a thin line. He forced them to relax and smile. *I'm damned if I'll give 'em the satisfaction of anything less. Jason Brand goes with a smile on his face and a curse for the bloody bastards on his lips.*

A half-dozen steps. Not deigning to turn, he mounted

103

the steps and with a withering expression of scorn, turned to face the waiting audience.

"Well, Brand, are you ready to die?"

Lord Penscott! Duke of whatever it was. The father of Edmond Penscott. So that was where they were. And why. Penscott Hall. "At your hands? Not especially, but then it appears I have little choice."

"I think not. If you'd talked perhaps we could have . . ."

"I'm not an idiot, Penscott. Talk or no, the result would be the same, for there is no talking to men like you. Your kind doesn't care to listen, nor have they ever." He turned and walked to the noose, stood with the loop touching his ear. "I'm used to a man doing his own killing, Lord Penscott. Cut, stab or shoot, the lives I've taken, I've taken honorably. Have your man do his duty, sir, since you cannot."

Penscott smiled. "I'm too old to be hurt by a fool's words, Brand." He nodded and one of the soldiers stepped smartly to Jason's side, slipped the noose over his head, tightened it snugly around his neck and stepped away. "I've waited for your life, lad, so you'll have neither hood nor blindfold. No different than had you been no more than brigand and pirate. Only in this case, I'll watch your face. Seeing you die won't replace my son, but it will help. You may proceed, Captain."

Captain Gregory moved to one side. "Executioner!"

Jason forced himself to keep the smile. The wind cut through the light lawn shirt but he didn't feel it any longer. The years flew past. Home, youth, wife, son, the sea, women, son, horses, home, wife, his father, sunset, sunrise, the sea, life . . .

Gregory's hand dropped and a soldier jerked on the oaken level and released the trap. Time slowed to a crawl. Jason could feel the door dropping, falling out from under him as slow as pitch running down the side of a ship when the sun is hot. An eternity later and it was gone and he was falling, slowly, too, like a feather. The sun glinted off a bayonet and he blinked. There was time, yet. Home . . . wife . . . son . . . father . . . mother . . . How much slack? That too he could hear, the whisper of rope straightening until taut. *Smile! Home! Father! Mother! Son!* The knot bent his head sideways. The muscles in his neck stretched, pulled tight. Still falling. . .

A popping sound. *What?* Still he fell and time speeded to a blur. Not prepared, his feet hit the ground and his legs crumpled. Jason fell to the left, hip and shoulder slamming into the ground. *What? What?* A half-dozen fathoms or rope snaked down from the gaping trap, landed on his right thigh. *The bastards. The stinking bastards!*

A hand grabbed his hair. Manacled and gagging, Jason could do little but try to help as they pulled him erect and marched him from under the gallows. The duke waited, stood rocking back and forth on his heels. A hand jerked on the rope still attached to Jason's neck. "Take it off."

The noose was gone. His neck was sore but he could breathe. His tormenter seemed pleased. "An interesting exercise, eh Brand?" he asked. Jason tried to answer, couldn't. "No. No answer is necessary." The cane reached up, touched Jason on the cheek just below one eye. "I can read it in your eyes. Take him back."

Somehow he made it back to the chateau and stumbled up the stairs under his own power. The fake execution had had the desired effect and Jason was drained of all emotion. To challenge death and come through alive was not an unknown experience, but at all other times there had been a sense of jubilation, of conquest and triumph. To face and accept death by hanging and then learn he'd been played with as a cat plays with a mouse was an entirely different matter. His neck ached terribly and burned as well where the rope had sawed through the skin. Feet and legs, hips and shoulder hurt where they'd struck the frozen mud. No doubt there were lacerations as well.

A cup of hot tea waited, but he could hardly pick it up, rather chafed his wrists where the manacles had bitten into the skin. Gregory lounged against the wall by the door, laughing silently while Jason slumped on the bed, spent and wanting only to be alone.

"So our game continues, Brand. How did you like it?"

"I shall have to learn the rules, I suppose," Jason croaked in return, the words rasping in his throat.

"Not really. There are no rules. I simply do as I wish, when the urge strikes. Our objective—colored, of course, with a certain admitted degree of revenge—is to learn what you know. Your objective is to remain a man, not become a blithering idiot. Until you decide to talk, you'll never know from one minute to the next what will happen." Chuckling, he started to leave, hesitated in the open door. "Who knows? Perhaps the rope will be secured, the next time."

He was gone. Jason stumbled toward the table, managed to grab and hold the tin cup of tea. Grimly, he approached the window, looked out. The rope had been replaced and the waiting noose swung in the noon breeze. Captivity had taken on a new aspect. *A game?* How many times could he take that walk, ascend those stairs, feel the noose slip over his neck and the floor drop?

Life at sea had been perilous. Existence anywhere, for that matter, was perilous. This was different. This led to madness. Jason stood before the fire, let the heat work on aching muscles. Grimly, he determined to hang on. *An unfortunate expression. Persevere is better.* They'd not break Jason Brand. *Not the Jason Brand I am today,* he amended. *But what of tomorrow?*

Fair Weather, frisky after coming in from the cold, batted the fringe of Marie's shawl. Behan chuckled, the first sound between the two for a quarter-hour. "Ten years old and he thinks he's still a kit."

Marie reached down, tickled the cat's stomach. Fair Weather rolled onto his back, caught her wrist and nipped playfully at a finger. "Fair Weather! Stop that!" Marie scolded, pulling hand and shawl out of harm's way. "You're just like all the rest of them."

"Now, darling," Behan started with a sigh of exasperation. "You know . . ."

"I know nothing, save that men are all alike. Jason Brand sits in prison and no one but me cares."

"Be reasonable, Marie. What good will caring do? I'm over seventy. What do you expect? Am I to take up a sword and vanquish a detachment of soldiers just so you can see a man who probably doesn't remember you?"

"He'll remember."

Behan snorted. "You make as much sense as Fair Weather. Use your head, girl. He might as well be in London. You can grouse and complain 'til the tides stop, but there's naught you can do save wait. If they let him go, they'll let him go. If they don't, they won't. It's as simple as that."

Marie jumped to her feet. Fair Weather scurried out of the way. "They took him out and pretended to hang him day before yesterday. God only knows what horrible things they've done since. I can't let them keep on, Uncle. I can't. Now, are you going to help me or not?"

"I don't know what—"

"Are you going to help or not?" Behan pushed from the chair, wearily shuffled over to the ledge and took down a bottle of rum. Marie waited while he pulled the cork and poured a glass. "Well?"

The old man recorked the bottle and tossed off the shot, exhaling mightily as the fiery liquid burned his throat. "No, sweet daughter. I can't, and won't."

So there it was. When all was said and done, Behan would not help. Caught between anger and sorrow, Marie turned and headed out the door, not daring to speak lest tongue say what heart might later rue.

The weather had held. Still bright and clear, the sun mocked her dark mood. Jason Brand, so near, yet so far away. But a scant hundred yards separated Behan's cottage and the chateau. A minute's walk would have found her at the front door. And yet. And yet . . .

Four times since the first night, she had actually begun, heading out resolutely toward the prison. Four times she had come no nearer than the line of ornamental cedars, there to stand and stare at the gray, windowless walls. Once she had circled around to the east side of the chateau and hid in the woods. The shutters to his window were open, but though she waited a half-hour, there was no sight of him. Finally, upset to the point of tears by the gallows which stood between her and Jason, she crept back south to Behan's cottage, there to weep miserably in the old man's arms.

Patience. Resignation. She kicked a loose chunk of ice, sent it skittering along the path. There was no time for patience. They had already "hung" him once. Lord Penscott had left for Hanover, but everyone knew the cruel torture would continue until Gregory tired. Then it would be too late to intercede, for the macabre game would end for good, and Jason would be dead.

The kitchen was quiet. At five in the afternoon, most of the servants were finished with their daily tasks and had stolen off to their rooms. Dinner would be simple with the master gone and none but Lady Gwendolyn and Captain Gregory to be fed. A chewed joint of mutton lay on the table in front of the gargantuan Ringe, who sat nodding in late-afternoon torpor. A young boy with a crutch propped on his hip lay next to the hearth, sound asleep and snoring. Marie gently closed the outside door, stole across to the table and grabbed a half-dozen biscuits which she dropped, along with a pot of jam and a chunk of cold beef in the voluminous skirt pockets hidden beneath her apron. Once in her room she'd be able to eat in peace and quiet and not have to return to the kitchen and chance a chore or sit with the rest of the servants.

Ringe and the boy slept on. Moving as quietly as possible, Marie headed for the corridor to the servants' rooms, stopped in alarm as familiar footsteps approached. Thrush was coming. *Oh, damn! He'll want something and I'm the only one available.* If she could get out the back door before he got to the kitchen . . .

The hem of her skirt caught a bucket bail, sent the metal clanging across the stone floor. Ringe sat up abruptly, looked around. "Eh? What's happening?" Marie stopped in her tracks. "Oh. It's you? Well, what do you want?"

"Nothing, Master Ringe. I was just going out the back way. I'm sorry I woke you up."

"Huh! So'm I." The chef rubbed his eyes, perking up when Thrush swooped into the kitchen.

The master servant stopped, looked around contemptuously so all present should know the kitchen was beneath his station. "I need someone."

Ringe yawned. "There's none here save the girl, as you can see. If she won't do, you'll have to find someone else or do it yourself."

Thrush bristled indignantly. Of all the servants in the house, the fat cook was the one he hated the most, for he had no hold over him. "I'll thank you to watch your tongue, Master Chef Ringe."

"I'll thank you to watch your tongue, Master Chef Ringe," the chef mimicked broadly. "Say what you want and get your skinny arse and rotten carcass out of my kitchen, Master Thrush. You make the food turn sour. I'll have none of ye."

The master servant fairly danced with anger. "How dare you? How dare you . . . speak . . . to . . ." The cook had gotten up and was advancing. "Now, now. Don't you touch me."

"Say what you will and get out, Thrush, before I pitch you in the soup. Or puff and blow you away like chaff."

"You . . ." Thrush extended his hands in conciliation as Ringe stepped forward. "All right. All right. But you'll hear more of this later. Captain Gregory wants someone to fetch supper to the chateau. Whoever takes it needs to carry along hot water, salve and bandages. Brand's neck is infected from the rope burn and must be cleaned. They want him to last a little longer."

Ringe looked around. "There's no one here for that. You'll have to—"

"The girl will do," Thrush interrupted. "She's doing nothing."

109

Marie stood frozen on the spot. "Of course I'll go," she wanted to say. If Ringe would only shut up and let Thrush have his way.

"It's a man's job," Ringe growled. "I'll have no woman carrying for a murdering pirate."

Thrush's lips pursed in a triumphant smile. Here was his chance. "The kitchen may be yours, Master Chef, but the help is mine to command as I see fit. Now, *if* you please?" Whirling, he stalked out of the room, coattails flying.

Ringe stood motionless, fists curled into balls. "'Tis no fit task for a girl," he finally muttered. "No fit task." Still, Thrush had been right. There could be no argument. Angrily, the chef busied himself preparing the evening supper for the guards and prisoner. A slab of beef, a hot loaf of bread and a pot of steaming soup for the guards filled one corner of a large tray. A bowl of porridge and a half-loaf of dried bread for Jason seemed a meager repast in comparison.

Marie waited, hardly daring to believe she was finally going to see Jason. And with Thrush's sanction, at that. Trembling with excitement, she followed Ringe's direction, filled a pitcher with hot water, grabbed a pair of clean rags and a jar of grease for the wounded neck. Ten minutes after Thrush left, all was ready. "Guard yourself, girl," Ringe growled. "Take care around that murderin' scum. For that matter, the guards aren't much better than their prisoner. If anyone tries anything fancy, you tell them Ringe will pay 'im a visit. You understand?"

Marie stared in surprise. Other than Behan, no man had shown such concern for her well-being until this moment. "I'll be all right, Master Ringe."

The cook tossed a towel over the heavy tray. "See that you are. I'll feel badly should anything happen to you, lass." Not waiting for further word, he grumbled an oath and shambled off.

Marie didn't hesitate a second. Before Ringe had found his chair again, she was out the door and headed up the path to the chateau. He'd think her beautiful, of course, and sit in stunned silence while she nursed him. Then he'd take her in his arms and hold her. Together, they would flee somehow. Escape and sail away to the Caribbean. Dreaming, fantasizing, hardly feeling the weight of the combined dinners, she hurried along the path.

The entrance to the chateau was barred from the inside. Marie kicked the door and called. No answer. Kicking again, she stamped her feet with the cold and called louder. Finally a tiny window opened to reveal a bleary-eyed, red-nosed face. "What d'ya want?"

"Open up. I've your supper."

The small window slammed shut and the door opened. "Hurry in, girl, afore ye let all the heat out." Marie slipped through the door, set her burden on the table. Another guard lay fast asleep by the fire. The draft stopped as the door closed. The guard came to the table, pulled the cover off the food. "What's all this?"

"I was told to clean up his neck. There's your food and his. This is water and rags."

"Humph!" The guard suddenly sneezed, wiped streaming nose on dirty sleeve and peered intently into Marie's face. He didn't understand why a prisoner should be so well cared for. A pretty girl sent to clean a tiny burn? 'Sblood, but a damned pirate had it better than a guard in this country madhouse where they hung men ten times over. "A regular little Fulham's Nun, ain't you?" he sneered. "There's beggars enough in London town need service, too. You'd be better off there. That pretty face wouldn't last—"

"I do as I'm told."

"No doubt. Well, he's up there. Watch your step. When you're finished with 'im, perchance me an' me partner'll find a little something else for your warming pan. What do you say to that?"

"No doubt it will be very little indeed, by the looks of you, sir," Marie snapped. The soldier grabbed her arm, started to pull her to him when another spasm caught him and he sneezed again, more violently than the last time. "We'll see what Captain Gregory says when he

111

learns the men who guard his prisoner sleep on duty."

"Now look here, Miss." The guard sneezed again, rubbed fever-burned eyes. "Awww, go on up."

Marie left the soldier in the middle of another sneeze. Heart pounding, she retrieved the lightened tray and mounted the stairs. *I should just leave the food and turn back. It's been two years. He'll have forgotten. Behan was right. He's a killer and a thief. He won't know me.*

The door was at hand. Marie set down the tray and reached hesitantly for the bar when a noise on the stairs startled her. It was the soldier from below. He leered, then brushed past to remove the wooden beam. "I'll replace it after you enter. Call out when you want to leave. If there's trouble," he added with a yawn, "I'll be downstairs."

The door swung open and the soldier, musket cocked and wary at last, slid the tray through the doorway with a booted toe. There was no turning back. Marie took a deep breath as if she were about to dive into a river and entered the room. The heavy door swung shut behind her and the bolt slid home with startling finality.

The room was larger than Behan's, but sparsely furnished with a few pieces of light furniture. The meanest servant's room in the manor was more interesting, more homelike. The single window in the east wall was shuttered against the cold, leaving the room dim and forbidding. Only a guttering fire on the hearth served to alleviate the winter chill and infuse the bleak quarters with a modicum of warmth. The whole effect was one of unrelieved boredom, even squalor.

There was no sign of the prisoner, but as Marie's eyes grew accustomed to the dark, she noticed the bench against the wall. A bundle of blankets raised a long hump on the makeshift bed. As she watched, the bundle stirred and a swatch of color appeared. The fire popped and a flame curled up to enlighten a tangled mane of red-gold hair. Marie tried to swallow, found her throat dry and constricted. Jason Brand!

He did not move again, only moaned in his sleep. The wool cape was suddenly too warm. Without

112

thought, Marie untied the neck string, let the heavy garment slip to the floor, reached down and picked up food, water, rags and salve and tiptoed across the room to the table. Closer at last, she could discern the strong features of the sleeping face. Two weeks' growth of light-colored beard stubbled his face and caught the firelight, casting it off again with radiant glints as his jaw knotted and relaxed, knotted and relaxed in dream-shaken sleep.

What a change there is! That this was the same man who caught her in a demanding embrace, made winter's meadow summery warm with the nectar of his kiss, who saved her from Edmond and was subsequently banished, there could be no question. But two weeks of captivity had made a considerable difference. His cheeks seemed sunken, a little too hollow. A bruise on his right temple was only half-hidden by hair. Marie shuddered. There in the dark room, the presaging shadow of death hung over the bed. She stood next to the narrow bench, gazed down at the wolf-lean face. *He is still beautiful. No matter what they've done, they can't change that.*

So close she could touch him now. If only . . . His eyes opened and locked on hers. Instantly, a hand shot from under the covers and caught her wrist. "Aha! See what I have snared. A new trick?" Marie tried to pull away, couldn't. Jason's left hand flung off the covers. He swung his feet over the side of the makeshift bed and pulled her to the fire. "Let's take a look, then." He stared, recognition slowly dawning. "It's familiar you are lass. I know you. Let me think." The iron grip relaxed and a surprisingly gentle hand plucked the maid's cap from her head, releasing the hair. "Ah! That wondrous cape of night is your betrayer. The nymph of the woods. The poor lass in the sculpture gallery and the stable." A look of puzzlement crossed his face. "What in the name of all the saints are you doing up here?"

Marie retreated to the table. "They sent me with food. And told me to fix your neck," she added, regaining a semblance of confidence.

Jason's hand went to a rag wrapped around his throat, touched the discolored bandage lightly. "Aye. And care it needs." He bowed slightly. "Then 'tis welcome you are, lass, if you'll but tell me your name."

Marie uncovered the tray and looked up at Jason, standing so close. Shirtless, his winter-white torso reflected the flickering firelight, caught and held the hint of flames in the gold carpet covering his chest. Breeches of faded tan did little to conceal the corded muscles of his thighs and calves, set off a trim waist which expanded and decreased with each breath. Not gaunt, he was leaner than she had imagined. Veins like lengths of rope unraveled down bulging biceps and forearms. His eyes grazed frankly and openly, returning her stare of assessment. In all, he resembled one of the statues in the main house, a Greek god, a relaxed but poised Adonis ready to explode into action. Marie wet her lips, lowered her eyes. "Marie, sir. Marie Celeste Ravenne is my name."

"'Tis a French name," he said with a scowl.

Marie tossed her head, suddenly angry that he should so quickly judge on a name alone. "Which in truth proves nothing, save you jump to conclusions."

Jason pulled one of the two chairs around, straddled it. A new light of respect was in his eyes. "You're right, of course. I was hasty." He glanced at the covered tray. "I'm hungry. Where's that food?"

Marie pulled the towel off the tray and Jason moaned aloud. "Porridge again. They mean to starve me. I think I would give my right arm for a chunk of red meat."

"Would you now?" Marie asked, laughing for the first time. "Is that a promise?"

"Aye. And a leg to go along for good measure."

Marie reached under her apron and pulled beef, biscuits and jam from her pocket, nonchalantly tossed them on the tray. "You are in my debt, sir."

"My God! Is't true?" Without waiting for a reply, he grabbed the meat and tore off a huge bite. For the next few minutes he ate without comment, totally occupied.

"Where'd'jou ge' it?" he finally asked, mouth stuffed and a look of bliss softening the chiseled planes of his face.

"From the kitchen, of course." Marie pointed to the bandage. "You'd better let me work on that. Move closer to the fire so I can see."

All argument gone, Jason moved as told. Marie untied the knot from the soiled bandage and started to pull it off. "Yeoow! Easy, lass, else you'll rob me of my hide."

He was right. Marie poured some of the warm water on the bandage, tugged gently and repeated the process until the rag was finally loose. The wound underneath had festered, was angry red, oozing and smelled horrible. "You could have taken better care of it," she commented sharply, already cleaning the long welt.

"With what? The filthy excuse for water I'm given to drink?"

"Hold still." Pouring fresh water on the rag, she bore down and parted the open lips of the wound, scrubbing until it bled with bright new blood.

"You're gentle as a press-gang leader, miss. Do ye think ye might—Ow!"

"And you're as tender as a babe. There. At least it's clean." She threw the dirtied rags away and picked up the salve. "Just a little more and I'll be done." Without preamble, she scooped a glob of the greasy substance from the jar and plastered the open wound, then quickly bound a clean bandage around his neck. "There. How does it feel?"

Again the hand went to his neck, pressed the new bandage. Jason grinned, swallowed the last of the beef. "Good. Very good." He sniffed the air appreciatively. "Smells better, too. Who'd have thought a French serving maid would be a first-class surgeon? Any more tricks up your sleeve?"

Pleased with the praise, Marie smiled shyly. "I'm not much of one for tricks, sir."

Jason stood, suddenly sober. "I'll wager you're not,"

he said softly, placing a finger under her chin and lifting her head.

The very air in the confined room seemed to change subtly. Misty gray eyes swam with confusion. The pressure of his finger on her chin sent chills through her body, immobilizing muscles and weakening knees. "I remember your kisses, Marie Ravenne." The voice had thickened, came from somewhere deep in his chest. "Warm kisses. Soft kisses . . ." A warm kiss. A soft kiss . . ."

Marie was floating through the air, incapable of resisting. Once again enfolding arms crushed her against his chest. His lips covered hers, strangely sucked the very life from her even as she was infused with new life, new awareness. His tongue forced its way between her lips. Half-fainting, Marie wrapped her arms about his torso, dug searching fingers into his back. Two years she had waited. Two long years . . .

Suddenly she was pushing away, fists pummeling his chest as lips tore free. "No. I can't. I'm afraid. You must let me go."

Surprised, Jason released her. "I don't understand, lass," he said, a puzzled look creasing his forehead.

"The guards . . . well, they might . . . I mean, they might . . ." Her mouth was too dry to finish the sentence. Unconsciously, trembling hands rose to cover aching breasts.

"The guards are dolts and idiots. They're probably asleep." Without waiting for an answer, Jason grasped her wrists, pulled her arms apart. "You're beautiful, you know." Caught in a spell, Marie watched as he let go her hands and caught her shoulders. "You're beautiful and I'm lonely and we're alone. And I shall have you, mistress." Somehow he was pulling the shift from her shoulders. She couldn't stop him. Only the light chemise stood between her breasts and his hands. She opened her mouth but no words came out. No words . . .

Now the chemise fell, too, and hung about her waist. Naked breasts were framed in an obsidian mantle of flowing hair. Jason's gaze rose to meet flaring gray eyes, soft as storm clouds lit by lightning. Her mouth was slightly open, revealing a double row of pearl-white teeth. She was breathing unevenly, short, shallow breaths. "May I kiss you again, Marie Celeste Ravenne?"

No answer was necessary. A half-step was all Jason needed, for Marie swayed forward, shuddering slightly as the tips of her breasts met the soft curls of golden hair. Marie's mouth opened and she inhaled a long, deep breath, heavy with man-scent as Jason's lips met hers. Her breasts were crushed against his chest now and she moved from side to side, unable to stop. Against her will, and yet with a will engendered of a starving body's need and soul's deepest desire, Marie welcomed the rising heat of passion. No man had ever held her like this; no man had ever been allowed so near.

Trembling himself, Jason's hands played along her naked back. Long denied the pleasures of a woman's body, held in prison for two excruciating weeks, the touch of breasts, open lips and fevered tongue kindled a raging blaze. Forgotten were the nightmare days of the Fifteen when he stared in disbelief at the massacred bodies of loved ones. Forgotten were the months running, at sea, fighting and running again. Forgotten the interminable days since the door to the Cock and Pilot flew open and the English soldiers captured him, the days of impotent rage, of imprisonment and near death. The only reality now was the woman in his arms and the throbbing ache of imprisoned gender, a second pulse against her bare stomach.

The flames from the hearth felt weak and insipid compared to the furnace of his desire. Marie had dreamed how his arms would feel around her. Now they were, and a wild exultation rose in her breast.

Lips parted and eyes met in the timeless question that needed no answer. Marie looked into Jason's eyes, close enough to see her reflection. One hand stroked her spine, the other entwined in her hair as he kissed her for the third time. Marie closed her eyes and matched the insistent demand of his lips. *Why am I so drawn to*

*him? They call him robber and murderer. All bronze
and fire he is. Brand. Fire. Am I but a moth to perish
in the flames? The girl of Mysteré is gone, must die
forever if she is to know love. So be it. Love me. How
do I say the words? Love me, Jason Brand, love me as I
love you!*

She melted against him in a dreaming dance. The
wind. The silence. A crackling symphony of embers.
Hands upon her naked hips. Naked. . . . How? The
clothes fell in a tousled pile about her ankles, joined by
his breeches and kicked aside. How long and tapered
his legs. Bronze curls gathered in greater profusion,
deeper in hue about his thighs, densest of all at the
junction of powerful limbs, from which sprang the
splendid length, proud scepter erupting from the forest
of gold. Eager. Full. Regal. The root of passion longing
to plant fierce seed in the thirsty field of desire . . .

No man had ever seen her so. Yielding, revealing
love's last and final secret. Her breasts ached under the
teasing lash of tongue. A momentary enticement, only,
for now the urgent need was to be joined, a union begun two years ago though not expected or seen or understood . . .

Jason lifted her and laid her on the tousled covers.
Marie let his hands guide hers, one to cradle the slowly
roiling twinned sac, the other to grasp the sweet length
of tumescent flesh. She stared at his length, grew frightened and forgot her fright as he spread her legs and
stroked the dark hair and soft, parted flesh. What exquisite tremors ran through her body as his fingers
touched the protuberant bud, engorged and impatiently
awaiting that longer, sweeter touch.

Mouth open, eyes misty, seeing far into past and future. The man-form reared over her and she guided the
swollen staff to the feverish gateway . . . and fitted
about . . . and pressed . . . Marie gasped, trembled
with unspeakable passion. She could no longer watch,
no longer bear the thought of him outside her, no longer
stand the emptiness . . .

Feel him stir. Feel the need. *Frightened!* Urgent, insistent pressure held back by membranous gate. She reached out, eyes imploring, fingers digging into muscular flanks. A small frown of incredulity darkened Jason's face as he realized this was her first time. A gentle smile of reassurance lifted the corners of his lips.

"Marie Celeste . . ."

He thrust forward. Marie's mouth opened in a silent scream and her body arched in a taut bow as he sheathed his full length, piercing to the very womb. Over and over he whispered her name in her ear.

Pain receded, replaced by a burning sensation. A hundred kisses scalded her throat and shoulders, consumed the tears of pain and joy. Pain. Joy. Release. Eyes shut, seeing past the room, past England and the oceans. A storm over Mysteré. The sky shattered into thunderous fragments. Broken waves piled one after the other, burst on boulders, curled onto the white virgin sand. A dim awareness of time, of motion, of rising and falling, climbing to the heights and plunging down again.

Waves rolling in, rolling in. From the distance, the mightiest swell of all, a vast wall of curling foam burgeoning from the ocean depths to obliterate the horizon. From what distant sea? Whence come? Why here or now? No matter . . .

Feel it rise, the most magnificent of tides. A roaring tempest to encompass and engulf a boiling, furious sea. Erupting, exploding, crushing all barriers, shutting out the world.

The very fabric of her being riven, Marie tightened around his hardness. Unable to bear the exquisite pain, she cried out once, sharply, before the voice caught in her throat. Jason moaned in reply, buried his face against hers as the spasm rushed over them again and again. The single vast torrent at its height caught the lovers and held them in the paralysis of ecstasy.

Chapter VI

Captain James Gregory slapped down the last card and scooped a small stack of coins from the center of the table to the pile directly in front of him. "Well, Sir Pirate," he gloated, "admit it. I have bested you in every way."

"Bested? An easy term for one with long sleeves and nimble fingers."

"This sullen behavior proves what I have long suspected," Gregory continued, ignoring the implication. "A gentleman would admit defeat and respond more graciously." He leaned forward to emphasize the next statement. "You . . . are no gentleman."

"No," Jason replied with heavy sarcasm. "A Scot, rather."

"A boor and barbarian, then."

"Which is an improvement over a cheater at cards."

The captain tensed, ready to spring over the table at Jason's throat. "I don't relish listening to impudent remarks from lick-tit tongues of Papist dolly-mops, Brand. Your position is a little too precarious for—"

"Nor I of a fawning, pretentious fetch-and-carry fop with stolen gold enough to buy a commission," Jason interrupted coldly. "Your position, Captain, is no less pre—"

"One more word, Brand, and I shall summon the guards."

Jason leaned over the table, unperturbed. "Do you really believe they frighten me, man?" he asked quietly, danger glinting in his eyes. "Don't you know I could kill you twice before they so much as reached the door."

Gregory thought back on the moment of Jason's capture. Two detachments had surprised the pirate and a companion in the Cock and Pilot Tavern in London.

Outnumbered ten to one, the freebooter had slain three good men before being subdued. Gregory had taken part in any number of battles, but the unconstrained fury of the Lowlander had been a sobering, frightening experience which led him to hate the pirate with a far deeper intensity than he bore any other man. Men always hate the objects of their fear.

A disdainful smile concealed the unadmitted apprehension. Brand was, after all, a prisoner and quite helpless. Smugly, the captain relaxed, scooped the coins into his purse. "I will enjoy seeing you die, you know. To watch the noose grow taut. Your tongue forced from your mouth. Legs kick. Watch you soil yourself."

"Save your arrogant vulgarities for the ragged and poor, Gregory. They're ignorant enough to fear you and your kind. I have watched men hang and know the exercise for a cowardly act whose victims are always the innocent or destitute. But know. I have taken toll in kind, glutted my cutlass with the blood of such as you, haughty, foul-mouthed press-gang captains with not enough skill to win honestly at cards or keep a scow afloat in a cesspool."

Gregory slammed his fist down on the table. The chair fell over as he shot to his feet. "The insolence!" he sputtered, in a rage. "I will have my pleasure now! Guards! Guards!" Not waiting for a response, he stalked from the room.

Jason waited, a nervous smile disguising the sinking feeling that he'd gone too far. Five minutes later footsteps pounded on the stairs and Gregory burst into the room again, followed by a whole squad of soldiers.

"Come now, Captain. January is too cold a month for these executions. You'll catch your death."

"You do not believe me?" Gregory ranted, beside himself. "That is a mistake, sir. A mistake, do you hear!"

Jason remained seated, seemingly undisturbed though at great cost. Seven times he'd made the trip to the gallows and had no wish to tempt fate with an eighth. Who knew? Perhaps the rope would catch on a peg or loop around the crossbar. Death by accident, after the past weeks of survival, would be a ludicrous demise.

The baiting had been an idiotic, ill-considered enterprise, but the slur against Jason's Highland mother had destroyed prudence and provoked derision and mockery. Gregory was trembling with anger, his pouchy cheeks red and white, twisted with rage. Pushed to the edge of reason, he was dangerously close to madness.

For the first time real fear struck the Lowlander. There was every possibility Gregory meant what he said, would exceed the dictum of Lord Penscott and continue with the hanging. Jason rose, careful not to give any soldier cause to fire. "Lord Penscott, Captain, left—"

"Lord Penscott be damned!" Gregory shouted. "I'm in charge here. You're *my* prisoner! Mine! You'll hang, do you hear? Hang!"

The soldiers crossed the room at their officer's gesture, ringed the prisoner with muskets. Jason felt the perspiration trickle down his sides. He had to remain calm. The wrong move would be disastrous. To be hanged was one thing: to be hanged by mistake, as it were, was another.

"March him out!"

Sergeant Burton hesitated, indecision writ across his broad features. Explicit instructions had been left by Lord Penscott: no actual harm was to come to the prisoner. If Brand was hanged, no matter that Captain Gregory had given the orders, Sergeant Burton would share the blame, and one lesson learned in twelve successful years in the army was never to share the blame. If the captain could be persuaded . . .

"March him out, I said, Sergeant. Are you deaf?"

"No, Captain. I . . . I . . ."

"The sergeant is concerned for the captain's welfare," Jason interrupted smoothly. "I believe Lord Penscott's orders were that I remain alive until his return. If that is the case, no doubt—"

"I've not asked your opinion, Brand, nor am I accustomed to listening to a prisoner's interpretation of my orders. March him out."

The corner of Burton's mouth twitched but he nodded in compliance. A bayonet pricked Jason's back, but the Scot stood steady. "May I remind the captain?" he said coldly. " 'Twas I who killed Lord Penscott's son, and 'tis on me he wishes to wreak revenge. He'll not take deprivation of that honor lightly." Jason refrained from smiling in reaction to a soft sigh of relief from Burton. The sergeant was in his debt.

Gregory scowled. Vengeance taken independently would most certainly incur Lord Penscott's wrath, for the bereaved father was set on personal retribution, set on watching Brand's face as he strangled. The pleasure denied would surely jeopardize the captain's chances for advancement. Pirate and soldiers, stiff and blankly staring, waited for a decision. Ever so slowly, the captain forced a smile of contempt. "Release him. Return to your quarters."

The soldiers dutifully filed out. Captain Gregory waited until the last had left. "Do not think," he began quietly, the words as deadly as the malignant look of lingering hatred, "that you have escaped, Brand. I promise you, in return for your life, a most unpleasant time from this day forth. And on the day, the very minute of Lord Penscott's return, it will be my great pleasure to see you hang, slowly, by the neck until dead." No more needed be said. Captain Gregory strode from the room and disappeared down the stairs. A second later the door slammed and was barred by the soldier on guard outside.

Relief, accompanied by overpowering weariness, flooded through Jason, dropped him weak-kneed and trembling into a chair. Lord Penscott's words on the occasion of the first mock execution returned, hauntingly familiar. The prediction had been uncannily true. After a half-dozen more near-escapes, the studied facade of insouciance was crumbling. The diabolical comings and goings, the never knowing, constituted a strain beyond the normal. To be jerked back and forth like a puppet manipulated by a madman lay beyond the bounds of bravery or common courage. Endurance and fortitude were meaningless platitudes.

Jason sipped at the stale water, rinsed the brassy taste of death from his mouth. The multiple brushes with oblivion and the constant stress unrelieved by action or adventure were taking an unforeseen toll. His will was weakening, and for the first time he realized desperation. Shaken, he went to the bench, lay down and knotted his fingers behind an aching, throbbing head. The tension was intolerable. Somehow, he would have to escape. Somehow . . . somehow . . . exhausted, Jason slipped into sleep. Mercifully, he did not dream.

Night came early in the middle of January. Marie dug chin into cape and hurried up the walk. The porridge was already cold but it didn't matter: there was meat and warm bread, food that kept Jason in health and spirits, under her apron. No one knew the servant girl carried this secret sustenance. Had they learned the prisoner in the chateau was eating more than the planned diet of porridge and bread, Marie would have been severely punished.

Wood scraped on iron and the door to the chateau opened. One of the guards uncovered Jason's tray for the usual inspection, stirred the porridge and broke open the loaf of bread to make sure no weapons had been hidden inside. At his grunt of approval, Marie started up the stairs. "A minute, miss," a gruff voice called from the dark corner by the fireplace.

Marie stopped, turned. A very serious-faced Sergeant Burton emerged from the shadows and gestured for her to return to the table. Haltingly, afraid something had gone awry, Marie obeyed the silent order, smiled faintly as the burly sergeant sat across from her.

"You've not heard, lass, but I've some bitter news," he began. Marie held her breath, waited. "It's about Mister Brand." He paused, not wanting to hurt the girl but knowing there was no alternative. "Captain Gregory has learned his prisoner knows of Lord Penscott's orders. He was upset, you might say, and insists on some changes."

"What do you mean, changes?" Marie asked, foreseeing the worst.

"From this day on, he's to see no one save the captain himself, and the soldier who carries the food upstairs. There'll be no exceptions, miss. Not even you."

"Captain Gregory knows that I—" Marie reddened.

"He knows only that you deliver meals from the kitchen, but doesn't suspect—" Burton coughed, embarrassed himself. "A man's a man, damn it. I've seen many die in my time, and felt pity for few. But hanging a man over and over again? Well, the lads and me draw the line there. They'll not let your secret out."

"What am I to do, then?" Marie asked in a conspiratorial whisper. "I can't just let him—"

"Orders is orders, Miss. You'll not be able to go upstairs again. I've no wish to be hung myself, and the captain's just angry enough to do so. You'd best run along, then, and put the man out of your mind."

They can't do this. They can't. Panic-stricken, Marie forced herself to think. *There must be a way.* She reached across the table, grasped the sergeant's wrist. "You must let me see him." Burton shook his head. "You must! I've things to give him."

"Things?" Burton asked, frowning.

"Food. Nothing else. I swear it! A bit of meat . . . some cheese." Unbidden tears welled in her eyes. "Just once more, Sergeant? Just once?"

Sergeant Burton pulled on his chin, considered. He'd no love of the captain, to be sure, less for the idea of blatantly going against orders. Still, Brand had done him a favor, had stopped the hanging and so saved the guard from reprisal at Lord Penscott's hands. Perhaps one last time wouldn't hurt, if no one found out. After all, what could the girl do?

"I won't ask again. Truly I won't."

One of the guards by the fire shifted his feet nervously. Burton glared at the disturbance, looked thoughtfully at Marie. What was a man to do in the light of those eyes? "Well, I may be a sentimental fool, but I suppose once more won't hurt." Marie jumped to her feet. "But mind you. Just this once!"

"I promise," she agreed, already edging toward the stairs. "Thank you, Sergeant."

Grinning, Burton followed Marie up the stairs to open the door for her. Alone on the landing, an idea struck him and he paused. "I had a daughter once. She was a fine girl, hearty and strong. Eyes the color of yours. She fell in love with a lad who was pressed aboard a ship much like the captain's. When the boy died, my girl's heart like to broke, it did."

"I'm sorry, Sergeant," Marie said, anxious to see Jason but at the same time sympathizing with the friendly soldier who had done her a favor. "What happened to—"

"I don't know. Disappeared, she did. Into London. Ruined her, the bloody bastards." He paused, looked around to make sure no one was listening. "If a girl was to go around to the back, and if our man here"—he nodded toward the closed door—"was to expect her and let down a piece of string . . . At least she could see he had some solid food now and again. Of course, a person could only do that if no one was watching." He winked conspiratorially. "Me, now, I never go around to that side of the building."

Even the darkest cloud soon gave way to light. At least they wouldn't be completely separated. Impulsively, Marie freed one hand from the tray and hugged Sergeant Burton. "Thank you," she whispered gratefully. "Thank you. I wish there were some way I could repay you."

"Get on in there, woman, before I change my mind. Go on now." The sergeant lifted the bar and Marie slipped through the open door.

The shutters were closed and the room was dark save for a glow of embers in the fireplace. "Jason?" No answer. Rare. He was usually waiting, anxious to see her after a long day alone. What had happened that morning? Was he ill? Wounded? Why hadn't Sergeant Burton told her? Quickly, she moved to the table, set down the tray and went to the bed. "Jason?" Expecting the worst, she touched the bed. "Are you there?"

Movement. "Of course not. I'm in bleeding Edinburgh."

"Is something the matter? Are you all right?" The terse, sarcastic rejoinder wasn't anything at all like Jason. They had spent an hour or two together almost every afternoon since the middle of December, and rarely was he anything other than cheerful and gay.

"Is there any fire left?" he asked.

"Coals."

"Fix it up."

"Of course, Jason." Truly worried now, Marie felt her way to the fireplace, knelt and fished around for wood chips. In a few minutes a tiny blaze sprang up. More chips of wood were followed by chunks and finally larger pieces. Heat crept into the room, slowly spreading past the crouched and shivering girl to the table and bed. By the light of the flames, Marie went about the chores that had become second nature during the past two months. *Almost like a married woman, like man and wife.* She lit a candle, placed it on the table. Two more on the mantel brightened the scene. Meat and cheese were laid out. A still-warm loaf of hard bread, opened and covered with butter.

Still, she didn't know what to say. Jason hadn't spoken more than a dozen words. No kiss, no gentle, teasing banter. Nothing. He lay motionless, eyes reflecting the fire, following her every move. "Everything is ready, Jason. Aren't you hungry?"

The covers heaved upward and Jason swung out of bed. Fully dressed, he headed for the fire. "They're succeeding. After two months, they're finally succeeding," he said, talking more to the fireplace than to Marie.

"Oh?" she asked in a tiny voice.

"This morning . . . Gregory is mad. He almost hanged me. Ready to march me out when I found the words to stop him. When he left and I was alone again . . ." He paused, then continued in subdued tones,

127

the tones of failure. "For the first time in my life I knew real fear. When that door closed, strength fled and I could only sit and stare. I'm as strong as any man, I believe, yet dropping through a gallows trap week after week . . . For a moment, I gave up, and that more than anything else frightens me." The pain-filled voice stopped, leaving a hushed and expectant silence, punctuated by the sound of the fire. "Do you understand that?" he asked angrily, turning and staring hard at her.

What words would have expressed that which needed to be said? Did they exist? Mere sounds were weak in the face of such great need.

Marie walked to him and leaned against his chest. Slowly, Jason's arms encircled and held her closely. The new and despised regulation would have to wait. Instinctively, she knew her man needed support and strength, not more bad news to further depress his spirits. Instead of words, Marie offered her body.

Jason hungrily accepted her kiss. In passion lay relief. Lust was solace, desire a remedy, a shield against troubled reality. Captain Gregory, Lord Penscott, the gallows . . . All could be forced out of awareness, left behind in the fevered carnal rush. Marie felt his body waken, stir, felt the aching pressure of his manhood. *He needs me.*

Hands assumed a life of their own. Marie's clothes fell to the floor, piece by piece, followed by Jason's. Naked, they held each other, sought warmth and comfort from singing loins. Four steps and they were on the narrow bench that served as a bed. Jason entered her immediately. His face was set, serious, almost pained. Rock-hard, he slammed into her over and over, as if the explosive culmination would change the world in which he lived, as if the spending of seed were an affirmation of renewal.

Marie met each thrust, automatically moved from side to side. Uncertain of her role, confused by the violent, mindless rhythm, she felt little save the incessant, driving force of flesh. *It doesn't matter, darling. I love you. I love you.* Suddenly he shuddered violently and stiffened. Marie cried out, imitating unfelt ecstasy, moving violently from side to side to prolong his pleasure, gladly accepting his weight as the spasms lessened and he collapsed against her.

In the aftermath of tension released, the chateau was alive with a thousand tiny sounds. The hiss of candles, the snap of popping wood. The soft breath of exhaustion whispered in her ear. A board creaked, swelling with heat. As Jason's manhood softened she held him tightly inside, satisfied with and unwilling to lose the inevitably receding warmth. For two months they had been together almost daily, sometimes sitting and talking, at other times passionately entwined on the makeshift bed. Their lovemaking had brought intense pleasure, carried Marie outside the physical body in which she was entrapped, far from the English estate so distant from even the memory of Mysteré. This day had brought a new experience, troubling but strangely welcome, upon reflection. A new dimension had been discovered, one of sharing beyond sharing, of giving without needing to take. When only love would do, the unselfish lover gave without thought for reciprocation.

Here was a strange power, too, one Marie had never realized existed, the power to alleviate pain and anguish, at least in some measure, to some degree. A shooting pang of resentment quickly disappeared. Everyone had moments of weakness. Every man or woman on the face of the earth, at some time or other in his or her life, surrendered to despair. Who would resent the momentary weakness of a lover? Better to rejoice that within oneself was the power to help lift the bleak veil, to contend against melancholy and effect a rejuvenation of spirit.

Jason sighed, rolled off her. Marie propped herself on one elbow, ran the fingers of her right hand through the light gold hair on his chest. For long moments, neither spoke. Jason stared at the ceiling, finally turning to look into her eyes. Ebony hair spilled across her breasts. He blew gently until the locks parted and one nipple peeped through, to be rewarded with a light kiss.

A slow smile of satisfaction softened his features and one hand crept between her legs to caress the soft, moist flesh. "I don't know what I'd do without you."

"Shhhh."

"It's true. I stand behind no man in courage or valor. Prison I could take. To be confined, to suffer: that is simple. To die isn't much harder. But to be subjected to death over and over again without the chance to fight back? No man can take that for very long."

Marie's brow furrowed. The task became more onerous with every second. Thank God for Burton. Jason read her mood, tensed in reaction. "What's wrong?"

"Nothing."

"That's not so. What's wrong?" he asked insistently.

She wanted to hide the truth, but they had been together too long, knew too well the little signs and tokens of lovers in distress. The room was suddenly cold. Marie swung from the bed, retrieved chemise and skirt and stood before the fire. "I won't be able to return."

"You what?" Jason asked, sitting up.

"Sergeant Burton was waiting when I got here. Captain Gregory has given new orders. No one is to see or talk with you save himself and the soldier who passes the tray through the door."

"But they can't do that," Jason said weakly.

Marie turned. "Not all is lost. Sergeant Burton said I could—"

"They can't do it. Can't." Jason sprang from the bed and paced the floor, oblivious to the cold. "What will I do? That damned porridge! Day in and day out."

Eyes flashing and hair bobbing, he appeared half-mad himself. His skin leached of color by too long confinement, glowed in the candle light. He appeared a grotesque and naked ghost, stalking restlessly back and forth, back and forth. Marie had never seen him quite like this before. Always he had been full of confidence and self-assurance, ready to face reversal with a laugh, gay and cocky in the teeth of adversity. Quickly, she pulled on the rest of her clothes, picked up his. "You'd better dress, darling. It's cold and—"

130

"Dress? Is that all you can think of? Dress? I've got to get out of here, damn it. Got to get out. Don't you see?"

Marie flushed with sudden anger. "Will you listen or not?"

Jason stopped in front of the fire, sullenly took the clothes and began to dress. "Of course I'll listen, if that's what you want, mistress," he said in a voice dripping with bitter sarcasm. "Speak. Tell me how lovely the world is, how bravely I'll march out there the next half-dozen times."

"Sergeant Burton told me I could come to the window. He said—"

"Nice of him. You do that."

"Will you listen, Jason?" Marie demanded, stamping the floor in frustration. "Will you please listen for just a moment? It's better than nothing. I'll make sure you have a piece of string to lower, and every evening I'll come and bring food. We'll be able to talk and plan. It *is* better than nothing."

Jason stood silently, shoulders hunched. Without a word, he crouched down, extended hands to the fire and rubbed his palms together.

Marie stood behind him, her hands on his shoulders. Something. She had to do something, or lose him forever. But what? As long as he was in the chateau, there was nothing to do. Only if he escaped . . .

Escape? The word was frightening. He had no chance alone, no other prisoners with whom to plot, no friends. She was the only one to help, which meant defying Lord Penscott and Gregory. Could she? What means were given a servant? No matter. A way would be found. Desperate, she kneeled next to him, took his hands. "Escape. You have to escape."

"What?"

"I don't know how or when, but you have to escape. Don't you see? I'll get help somehow and we'll escape. We'll go somewhere far away where they won't find us!"

"Impossible. You'd have to—"

131

"Miss!" A call and knock at the door, the sound of a bar raised.

Marie rose and kissed Jason on the cheek. Not even a vestige of a plan suggested itself, but she was determined. "I'll find a way, Jason. Somehow I will, my darling. You'll see. Good-bye. Listen for me tomorrow night, outside the window."

January, February, March. All gone. April had come, and with it the first signs of spring. The snow was gone, replaced by vast seas of mud and patches of hopeful green. The days had been getting longer. Now a blood-red ball hung on the horizon, swiftly dropped out of sight. The last few months had been bleak and depressing. Since being dismissed as Lady Gwendolyn's personal servant, Marie had been assigned to the meanest tasks. Now polishing wood, now scrubbing granite floors, she had been shifted from chore to chore. The only consolation had been an unusual amount of free time, during which she could make her way through the woods to the rear of the chateau. The arrangement, if not the most felicitous, proved to be better than nothing. Burton had been true to his word and kept the guards away from the rear wall, leaving Jason and Marie in quiet solitude. Food could be passed through the bars, and while the window was too high to permit actual physical contact, the lovers were free to pass the chilly night hours in whispered confidences.

Jason's outburst on their last night together had not been repeated. Gregory's passion had likewise diminished, and although the captain remained adamant and refused to revoke his final orders, there had been no more simulated hangings. But now the equilibrium established over ten weeks was disintegrating. A message had been received from Penscott, whose return was expected within the fortnight. Jason had not yet been told and Marie was under heavy pressure to devise a method of freeing him before the duke arrived. To date, no plan had seemed reasonable. Captain Gregory was a suspicious sort, one who meticulously checked all possible avenues of escape and plugged them before advantage could be taken. Sergeant Burton was kindly, but only to a degree: Marie's visits defined the absolute limits of permissiveness. Worse, no other member of the household save Behan could be trusted, and no matter what frantic schemes Marie proposed, the old Frenchman refused to cooperate and continued to counsel patience.

But there *had* to be a way. A frontal attack? Hardly possible. A hue and cry would sound throughout the estate before the first soldier fell. The walls or window? Impossible. The heavy iron bars were deeply imbedded in thick stone and would not budge. A weapon smuggled to Jason? Burton was too wily, nightly searched the single drab room after Marie's furtive visits to the window, each time with a man at his back and the door barred from the outside. If possible, Marie would have tried to summon Jason's men and bring them to Penscott Hall, there to win his freedom in open battle. But were they still in England? Not even Jason knew.

A sour, sluggish knot of panic lay like a heavy stone in Marie's stomach. A fortnight. Two weeks. Hardly any time at all. Each hour hastened the nobleman's return. Each hour heightened the nagging certainty that Jason's death was imminent. Marie crept the remaining yards along the path, stopped behind the holly bush where she usually waited to make sure the open ground between her and the prison wall was empty. As always, the silhouette of the waiting gallows gave her a start. *How many times now? Seven? Eight? Perhaps the next will be the last.* She couldn't permit such thoughts. Simply couldn't . . .

Behind her, a footfall, the squish of a boot in mud. Marie crouched, pulled the cape about her to blend with the shadows. Discovered at last? Were they to be denied these last few days? Jason's spirits had been holding up well, but what would he think were she never to return? *Go away. Go away!*

"Merde!" Whispering curses in French, a shadowy figure emerged from the woods and materialized before her. Behan!

"Uncle! Over here!" she whispered hoarsely before he should step into the open and attract attention.

The old man paused, peered intently. "Where's that? This damned dark—" Marie opened the cape so her white blouse would show. Behan finally saw her, limped over a fallen log and hobbled to her side. "I waited at the cottage. You didn't come."

"I'm sorry, Uncle," Marie apologized. "Everything has been so . . . so . . . Oh, I don't know. I just forgot, what with—"

"Hush, child." Boldly, the Frenchman stepped into the open, looked the chateau up and down. "Humph. See what you mean. Depressing sight."

"What are you doing here?" Marie hissed.

"Depressing, all right. Never did like a gallows."

"Oh, you're so exasperating, uncle. Please go back before we get caught."

"Caught? Caught? It's been years since I've been caught, young lady. I've learned a bit since then."

"I'm not supposed to be here and you know it," Marie pleaded, almost in tears. "Two of us increase the danger. Please go back. Please?"

Behan ducked into the deepening shadows, took Marie by the shoulders and pulled her close enough to see in the fading light. "So you want to get him out, eh? It means that much to you?"

"You know it does."

"Of course. Well, I've been giving the matter some thought. Interested?"

Earlier, Marie would have grasped at any straw. Now, seeing the old, hunched and lame pensioner, who could barely climb over a fallen log, the glimmer of hope died out. *A woman and an old man. . . . The addition's hardly an improvement.* "Uncle, I don't see—"

Behan laughed softly. "All these years at my side, and you don't trust your old uncle. Just one question. Listen carefully." He paused, waited for Marie's nod. "Do you really love this man, Marie?"

"I can't tell you how much." Tears filled her eyes

and she fought to keep from sobbing openly. "In this whole world, he's the only thing I want, Uncle. The only thing. Nothing else, nobody else matters. Don't you understand?"

For a long moment he stared into her eyes. Finally, with a weary sigh, he let her go, reached into a hidden pocket and pulled out a vial. "Yes, I do," he said gently, and I shan't keep you from him. Here. Half of this in a bottle of ale and the guards will sleep the night through."

Marie gaped in astonishment. Incapable of speech, she grasped the tiny bottle to her breast. Here at last was hope, was the path to freedom and escape. She'd told him of the Caribbean and they'd talked of the island they would find. There, they'd live in freedom, joyous with one another. Suddenly, panic. *The door! How will I get the door opened?* She struggled for speech. Spirits so quickly aroused plummeted to the depths. "It won't work, Uncle. The door is barred from the inside. The guards will sleep, but I'll be locked out. When they learn an attempt has been made, there's no telling what Captain Gregory will do."

Behan laughed aloud, quickly clamped his mouth shut and grew serious. "That's the easiest part. A bar, you say?" Both hands flew up. "Poof! Gone in a thrice. And our young man as well."

The sun was shining again! "How? Will you teach me?"

"Aye, my lovely daughter. As I have for these past four and a half years, I'll teach you."

Had Marie been able to see, she would have noted tears brightening the old man's eyes. As it was, the wistful quality of impending loss touched her through the darkness. *He knows I'll go. Still, he . . .* A burning lump rose in Marie's throat and she threw herself into his arms. "Oh, Uncle. You've given me everything and I'm repaying you so terribly. I'll never see you again, and I love you so much."

"Hush, child. Not a fledgling but leaves the nest. You love him. 'Tis enough for me to see you happy."

"Uncle, I—"

"No. Go to him now. Tell him. Make plans. Rejoice. Come to me tomorrow, and I'll teach you the way of doors." Marie would have said more, but the kindly old man, friend and surrogate father, lay a finger across her lips. Marie smiled through the tears, kissed the sere and age-worn finger. Checking to make sure no unfriendly eye watched, she broke from Behan's embrace and ran across the open field to the window where her love waited.

Behan watched from the shadows. Not until the girl disappeared in the darkness against the wall did he turn and slowly pick his way south to the empty cottage.

The soft chunk of wood meeting wood signaled a point beyond which there was no return. Heart pounding, Marie stood in the shadows by the door, listening to the night and nervously fingered a knife stolen from the kitchen. So far, so good, she thought as calm returned. A crescent moon shone serenely. Peaceful. Gray, shining slate walk, hedges coming to life after winter's sleep. Stirring of sap, the scurrying of small animals through the night.

No turning back. A task to be done. To be gone from here, with Jason. As naturally as if going for a stroll on a sunny afternoon, Marie started up the walk. Strange, how composed she felt, as if action once begun were an antidote to fear. Reasoned confidence took command. Icy calm, now, prepared for all eventualities . . . almost.

The chateau loomed ahead, shadow-deep in the dim light of a subdued moon. Four days had passed since Behan and Marie's meeting behind Jason's prison. New messages of the duke's imminent arrival had come the day before. Now he was expected on the twelfth, leaving the conspirators but one day to spare. Marie slowed, ducked behind the row of cedars and crept along them, coming out near the corner of the building. Dressed all in black, she peered out; no sign of movement broke the peaceful scene.

The night had been chosen with great care. Sunday

was the one day of the week when the guard was split into two shifts instead of three, which meant the same men were on duty from before suppertime until dawn without the usual change at ten o'clock. No new guards would be, or should be, arriving. That is, if the plan was to work. For the last hour she had watched the path and there had been no movement. All indications were that no unforeseen changes had taken place.

Once again she checked her pockets, pulled out the two special strings Behan had given her. Taking a deep breath, she walked out from the cedars and across the open ground, stopping at the door. No sound could be heard from inside. Carefully, glancing around once more to make certain no one was coming, she swung open the small window and was greeted by the sound of heavy snoring. Working quickly, she lowered the first string, to which was tied a flat, hooked piece of iron, along the inside face of the door until it hung inside and below the heavy oak bar. The next step was the hardest. Tying the first string to the latch, she reached inside with the second, to which a ring had been attached.

Nothing happened at first. The small window wasn't large enough for her whole arm and Marie was forced to swing the ring around until she heard the clink of metal against metal. Slowly, holding her breath, she lowered the ring, jerked up quickly. Not until the third try did the ring catch on the hook and form a continuous loop which would raise the bar.

At last. Slowly, she pulled on the second line, sighing with relief as the improvised loop became taut. The bar squeaked against the iron hooks in which it rested, finally broke loose and rose. When it had cleared, she tied off the second string and pulled open the door, reached through the crack and held the bar up while hook and ring were loosened. The first and most dangerous stage, that of entry to the chateau, was a success.

The guards were sprawled on the table where they had fallen next to the drugged bottles of ale. One of the guards stirred, mumbled in his sleep. Clutching the knife, Marie tiptoed past. Behan had promised the po-

137

tion would keep them unconscious for most of the night if they drank enough of the ale. How much they *had* drunk was purely conjectural, though, and she wasn't about to stop and check the bottle. A stair creaked, but the dangerous part had passed. If they woke, they woke. She ran up the final steps, threw the bar from the door.

Jason was ready and waiting. His beard had grown bushier, fuller. "You made it. Good."

"The guards are asleep," Marie whispered, quickly embracing him. "We have to hurry. I don't know how long . . ."

"Let's go, then." Without waiting, Jason led the way down the stairs. Marie followed, more at ease now with him at her side. Jason stopped, took a heavy cloak from a peg on the wall. Marie hovered by the door, silently urging him to hurry. Jason moved calmly, as if he escaped from prison every day of his life. A long sword stood in a corner: he strapped it to his waist. A brace of pistols, complete with powder flask and shot, lay in a box on a low cabinet; passing up a musket, he stuffed them into the waist of his trousers. A quick, close check of the sleeping guards and he was ready.

Closing the door behind them was difficult, but necessary, for the plan included leaving everything as found, in hopes of confusing those who would surely follow, surely search for the traitor who had helped the prisoner escape. Behan must not be suspected. The bar slid into the iron braces. A bit of frantic jiggling and the ring disengaged from the hook and both were pulled from the small window. They were ready.

No sound threatened. Jason and Marie ran to the line of cedars, picked up the package of supplies Marie had hidden there the night before and disappeared from view, heading for the river. Before long the bespeckled waters of the Thames glimmered in the icy moonlight. Slowing, they approached carefully, working their way around the main landing and striking out downstream to a small cove where the locals kept a small boat or two for fishing. Despite vigorous attempts to maintain his physical condition during the long weeks of imprisonment, Jason was far below the peak of endurance, and in truth was forced to rest while Marie ranged along the shore until she found one of the boats. Quickly, she led Jason through the undergrowth to a rickety wooden quay, hauled the rowboat close and dumped in the package of food and clothes.

Jason nodded in satisfaction, then swept Marie into his arms. "You've been a good lass, and it's pretty work you've done this night. In three days, I'll be back. See that you wait upon the knoll where you watched the duel."

"Wait? But I'm going—"

"No. There's none to suspect you, and where I go it were best I travel alone. One can be invisible. Two will be seen and commented on."

Confidence vanished. Verging on panic, Marie protested vigorously. "But we decided. You can't leave me. You're too weak."

"It's strength I'll gain with oars in my hands, I warrant. Believe me, it's for the best. Wait for me. I've friends, but will have to find them. We'll bring a sloop and signal with a lantern. Two blinks and pause and two more. Watch closely. We'll put ashore between here and the main landing. You can take the path. Three days. Four at the most. Captain Gregory will never expect so bold a ploy. Now hurry to your room before you're missed and all is lost."

"Jason!" Frantic now. He was leaving. Her love . . .

"Wait for me, my love," he whispered, kissing her quickly before untying the painter. "Wait." The boat rocked as he stepped in.

"Yes. Yes. I'll be there. Jason? I love you, Jason!"

"Good lass," came the reply. Boat and brigand disappeared into the night, a dark shadow blending with the shore. He was gone.

Three days. Four. A woman waited at the water's edge and remembered stolen moments and sweet caresses and months of fragmented hours. Eternal hours now, vivid in recollection. Lord Penscott had returned, sputtered and fumed in impotent rage. Captain Gregory was gone in pursuit, the mumbled explanations of the guards burning in his ears. If the ale was bad, why did they drink it? Why couldn't they tell? For the price of their thirst, a rogue had escaped. A traitor to England and the Crown had slipped his bonds. Jason Brand was free.

Three days. Four. A woman at the water's edge. Waiting in the night. Waiting in vain.

Waiting . . .

Chapter VII

Roger Penscott irritably paced the gloomy library. What the devil was taking the old pirate so long? An order was, after all, an order. Perhaps five months was too long to be away. Perhaps the servants had forgotten who their lord was, to whom they owed immediate and unquestioning obedience. Obviously, a firm reminder was in order.

The door to the hall opened and closed. The flames in the fireplace shifted in response. Careful not to display impatience, the nobleman waited a moment before turning. Behan stood near the wall, just off the edge of the rug. Lord Penscott gestured to a chair across the desk before stumping to his own. Stiff and hesitant in the formal surroundings, Behan crossed the room and sat as ordered. Lord Penscott placed a manicured hand on a large wooden globe, set the sphere spinning on its axis. Earth groaned in revolution, the only sound in the book-lined room.

Two old men, both nearing the end of full, adventurous lives, faced each other across an expanse of walnut desk that symbolized the vaster distance of place and station separating them. Still, the similarities between the two were remarkable. Both limped: Behan from the old sword wound in his left thigh, which ached more and more each year; Roger from the increasing depredations of gout, aggravated by a harsh winter at the king's palace in Hanover. Both were balding, short white fringes of clipped hair the only evidence of once longer, more flowing locks. Both felt a little short of breath these days, though in truth Behan, living more simply, could have outwalked the other man on any day of the week, notwithstanding five years' seniority. Both had seen action in far-flung places. Both were brave

141

men who could look back with pride on a life of honor. Neither felt the necessity of avoiding the other's gaze, for they were equals as men of arms and action are.

Most revealing was each man's posture. Born and raised an aristocrat, Penscott sat easily erect, at home in lush surroundings, a nobleman at heart and accustomed to the perquisites of high birth. Behan was less at ease, didn't know quite what to do with his hands, which knotted together in a confusion of gnarled knuckles in his lap, the safest place under the circumstances.

The globe creaked to a halt. "It has been some time since we've downed a tankard or two, eh, Behan?"

"Aye, m'lord. Too long. I trust your trip went well. Place hardly seemed the same without you around for chess."

Lord Penscott nodded. "But a most disturbing homecoming. Captain Gregory has been placed in the mortifying position of having to tell me Brand has made good his escape. As far as can be told, from all of England." He reached into a drawer and placed two tankards and a bottle of ale on the desk top.

Behan sucked his teeth. So the subject was to be Brand's escape. He preferred less dangerous conversations and the usual custom of meeting later in the day in the humbler surroundings of the cottage. This drastic change in habits could be regarded with nothing less than suspicion. Still, there was nought to do but wake up, put on a good face, play the game to the end and hope for the best. Behan reached for the bottle, realized immediately it was empty. So that was it. Penscott knew. Pawn to king four, an empty bottle. A defense of casual innocence was the only conceivable strategy. Behan raised an inquisitive eyebrow.

Penscott smiled devilishly. "Be thankful it is empty, tutor, else Thrush would find us in a most disreputable state. Not to speak of the aching heads we'd sport for the rest of the day."

Behan sat down the bottle. Games with Roger Penscott had a habit of turning out badly, of course, for he frequently invented his own rules. Little choice now but to make the next move. A sense of excitement surged through jaded veins. For once they were playing for real. More years than he cared to count had passed since the stakes were more than a petulant curse or mild displeasure. Behan smiled wolfishly, curiously eager for the engagement. "I do not understand, m'lord."

"Then you shall be enlightened, if you repay my effort in kind. The soldiers charged with the responsibility of watching that despicable Scottish ruffian quenched their thirst on ale from this bottle. A sour brew, my kitchen master claims, and cuffed the blackguard responsible for failing to notice. Thus is explained the stupor that beset Captain Gregory's appointed guard and allowed Jason Brand, my son's murderer, to escape."

The old pirate snorted, leaned back and relaxed. "Give a soldier a bottle and he loses all sense of distinction. As long as it makes him belch, he'll down it without thought. Still, 'tis well and good the cause is discovered, I should say. A most inopportune sequence of mishaps."

The nobleman nodded in accord. "Of course we, you and I, know the truth behind these mishaps, do we not?"

A babe's face could not have displayed greater innocence or perplexity. "We, m'lord? I know nothing of—"

"Protestations and denials are a waste of time, Louis. I have sailed the Caribbean the same as you, set foot on many an isle and learned to recognize the taste and smell of potions exotic and deadly. I see Louis Behan's hand in this plot, old friend. And it vexes me."

"A plot?"

In truth. And how else would Brand have made good his escape?" He held up a hand, admonishing silence. "No. Please don't try too hard. The exercise palls. Even with the watch unconscious, the Scot could not have effected his own release. Someone had to lift the bars and open the doors. Someone wily enough to replace both bars, by the way. In that, I smell the touch of an older, wiser fox, a man devious enough to leave behind a

143

touch of mystery. You were too clever, Louis. How did you manage to put back the inside bar?"

"So the bar was replaced, eh?" Behan chuckled. "Very clever. Distressing, I'm sure, but clever." He sat for a moment, seemingly deep in thought. "Who brought the evening meal to the chateau?" he asked, trying to help solve the mystery in the uncertain hope the gambit would be accepted.

"One of the lads from the kitchen. He's blameless, as any fool who asks him a question can see." The nobleman leaned forward on the desk, unable to trap the old pirate, at the same time not fooled for a moment. "No. The fault was not with the lad, nor in whimsical providence. Brand didn't fly out the window. The blame rests on he who drugged the brew and unbolted the door. I know of only one man adept enough at skullduggery of this sort. He sits before me, affecting innocence."

Behan frowned indignantly. "Not I, m'lord."

"You had a hand in it then. With whom did you conspire?"

"You flatter an old man, m'lord. I sit in my cottage and play with models of the ships we sailed in the old days, remember the cry of men, the sound and smell of the ocean, the sight of green islands washed by sun and wind. I've done with adventure and wild escapades," he vowed, barely skirting the truth. After all, he'd taken no real part in the actual escape.

Penscott sighed in exasperation. Whatever the motive, why Behan even should have considered letting Brand free, he was in it thicker than thieves. The prospect of having to punish the old renegade was displeasing. He searched for an alternative, found none readily available. "Return to your cottage, old friend. But mark my word. I will summon you within a day or two, and your tongue had best be limber and put to better use. Think on it. I will hear the truth. I think that's all for now."

Behan rose and bowed slightly. He'd been found out, but would be damned before he incriminated Marie. At

144

least he'd gained time for thought. The doors swung open at a touch. "Louis?"

Behan turned. "M'lord?"

"Please see you don't forget. It was I who spared you from the hangman's noose. Don't let the intervening years lull you. Don't misinterpret my friendship. 'Tis a kindness that can be undone."

The mellow tide of spring, long held at bay by winter, inundated the sluggish, frigid ocean of northern air and replaced it with warm swells of regenerative breezes from the south. The forest was aglow with floral bouquets, congested with creeping vines climbing to the new blue sky and willowy ferns unfolding carpetlike over the drying detritus of deep woodlands. Rolling fields blazed with carnival colors, a buffoonery of orange and yellow daisies, cowslips and buttonknobs. Closer to the forest's edge, demure white spikes of lady's tresses sported with crocuses under lordly oaks. The brief return of cooler temperatures was not inconceivable. Nevertheless, spring had certainly come with a will, determined to impregnate the air with a thousand burgeoning scents and sounds, and give hope to the heart that life was indeed renewed.

A macabre jest, Marie thought bitterly as she sat on a fallen bough and gazed over the greening meadow where she'd met Jason. Who cared about beauty? Beauty could disappear in no more time than it took a faithless lover to say good-bye. A dull anger festered inside her. Thrush would be furious over her absence but she was beyond caring, resolved to endure whatever punishment the master servant devised. Certainly he would assign the most onerous tasks imaginable in retribution for the morning's unfortunate occurrence.

The servants breakfasted about a massive oaken table filling most of an alcove in the kitchen. Marie had arrived early and was joined by Arabella. For a moment, the two sat in isolated silence at either end of the table. Marie registered surprise when the buxom servant moved closer. The two had been at odds for years and there was no reason for a display of friendship.

Arabella scowled at the bowl of porridge before her. "I should like bread and beer. Not watery gruel," she complained. When Marie failed to reply, the woman continued. "I suppose you welcome what there is and are glad for it. But then you've had the more of what's best."

Marie glanced up, eyes questioning. "Don't think I'm as blind as the rest," Arabella whispered harshly. "I've shared your room, know you better than most. I've seen the changes in the way you walk, seen past your moods. You was bringin' more to that roister than food. I'll warrant you spread your legs and offered him a basket more to a man's likin'."

"Enough," Marie hissed, choked with anger at the mention of Jason.

"Not by your life. There's more I've to say. It's up to you whether I do or not."

"Your words are like cards. In playing them, you fail to turn them over."

"No card game this, prissy bitch. Very well. Plainly said." Arabella leaned closer. "You're the one who let him go."

Marie caught her breath, tried not to look surprised. "You speak in riddles."

"You cannot deny it. You drugged them guards."

Marie laughed. "Really, Arabella, but you have a fine imagination. How in the world would I—"

"Don't play coy with me, you island trollop. Actin' like you was a queen or something. I didn't think much about it until the master put up that reward. A whole piece of gold! Law, but what trinkets I could buy! So I got wonderin'." The older maid looked around to make sure no one else listened. "You want to know how I figgered it out?"

"I have no desire to—"

"Shut up!" Arabella's eyes narrowed. Accumulated rancor from years of hating the younger and prettier girl spewed forth. "I seen you come in the kitchen just before the boy left with the food for the guards. Didn't mean anything until the gold was mentioned, but then I got to askin' myself what you was doin' where you shouldn't be. Got askin' around to others, too, sort of sly like so no one would get on to me. Gully says you was at the tray, looking innocent as a lamb when he come to take it to the chateau. Says he seen you tuck something in between them two pretty little jugs, like you had something to hide.

"'Course, that wasn't enough, so I kept on askin'. Florence seen you the night before, slipping out the back way with a bundle. She thought you was goin' to the old Frenchman's place, but I know better. And then on the night he got away, poor little Freddie that sleeps by the woodpile woke up and seen you comin' in the same back way, sniffin' like you'd lost your best friend."

"That's a lie," Marie retorted heatedly, desperately trying to manufacture another and more plausible story to cover her actions.

"Lie? Well, well, now. Then how come you been going out each night and sitting on that knoll over the river? Waitin' for him to come back and get you?"

"I'm doing no such thing!" Of course she wasn't, she thought bitterly. Because he wasn't coming back.

"'Twas Reuben himself seen you first. Comin' back from chasin' that old crinkly-horned cow what got out and was wanderin' in the garden. He asked me what I thought you was doin' traipsin' around by the gazebo after dark. The next night I went out myself, and there you was, just as pretty as can be."

"I go there often to sit and think of home. Just because—"

"Then how come you just now started going there often? You let 'im go, for sure, missy."

"Stories. You can't prove anything."

"I don't have to prove nothing," Arabella said with a smug grin. "All I have to do is tell Master Thrush what I know and he'll take me to the master himself, who'll draw his own conclusions. That piece of gold is my own, dearie, if I want it."

Not knowing what to do, Marie stared across the table. Arabella was right about one thing: Lord Penscott was one to draw his own conclusions. And yet, why hadn't the girl already told her story, collected the reward and had done with the whole business? There must have been a good reason. "Why are you telling me all this?"

Arabella laughed aloud, displaying a line of decaying front teeth. Suddenly she stopped, leaned over the table again. "You're a smart one, dearie. You're a smart one." The look of mirth was replaced with a flat, evil stare. "For years you been too good for the rest of us. Paradin' around like you was some saint or such. Well all that is going to change. Me an' Reuben got to thinkin', talked it over real good. A piece of gold ain't so much, after all. What are we gonna buy that we don't already have? Lady Gwendolyn gives me ribbons. We got food, a roof over our heads. That piece of gold is going to be gone before we can spit, you can be sure. An then we'd have nothing but an afternoon to show for all our pains."

Marie sat back, hands clenched in her lap. "So?"

"So why not buy something that will last? Something we can have for a long time?"

"A piece of gold would buy—"

"—a servant of our own. Just think. We keep our mouths shut and you do what we say, just the same as if Thrush said it. That way you don't have to face bein' thrown in jail—or worse—because we wouldn't say a word, not wanting to lose a servant and all."

Marie blanched, imagining what tricks Arabella had in mind. She was prepared to accept whatever punishment Lord Penscott devised, but being subjected to degradation by Arabella and Reuben was beyond consideration. "I will not."

Arabella's face twisted. "Then I'll tell everything I know. I'll tell the master that it was his sweet Marie

148

Ravenne who betrayed the house of Penscott for the favors of a brigand and the price of a goodly spiking."

Pent up rage and frustration caused by Jason's betrayal exploded in violence. Marie lunged across the table. Arabella tipped over backward and slammed her skull against the stone floor. Screeching and howling, the women went for each other's throats. Arabella outweighed Marie by a good twenty pounds, but the advantage was nowhere near decisive: the orphan of Mysteré had inherited her mother's fiery temperament and been taught to handle herself by a dozen conscientious ex-pirates and Behan as well.

Servants rushed in and gathered around. Asleep but moments ago, the fight brought them on the run, ready to take sides, cheer and wager on the outcome. The men rushed to the fore, eager to glimpse the firm flesh revealed beneath torn garments.

Marie winced as the heavier girl slammed a bony elbow into her side. Arabella wheezed as a fist tore into her stomach. Trying to escape, she rolled under the table, in the process ripping the sleeve from Marie's blouse.

Marie scrambled for position, tearing the buxom servant's bodice from throat to navel. Great mounds of breasts gleamed in the smoky candlelight. Heavy areolas, puckered and taut, elicited a concerted moan of delight from a half-dozen male throats as the combatants rolled into the open.

Arabella tried to claw her attacker's face, instead felt herself hauled erect by the hair. Marie stuck out a foot and at the same time shoved hard. Arabella tumbled over a bench, slammed her head against a table leg and landed on the floor again, a bundle of tattered skirts and naked thighs. Insult was heaped on injury when a bowl of porridge rolled over the table edge and dumped the slimy, still-hot sticky contents on her face, breasts and torso. Marie scooted between three howling onlookers too convulsed with laughter to stop her flight. Stalking from the kitchen, she escaped through the back door.

At least two hours had passed, during which Marie had wandered mindlessly, neither seeing nor hearing. A respite in the meadow of memories hadn't helped much, only renewed the pain of the past few days. The image of Jason—treacherous, faithless Jason—drove her at last from the meadow. Again she walked whichever way the meandering path dictated, trying not to decide how and when to return to the manor.

But what if they came looking for her? Wildly, seizing upon the frailest argument, she tried to find a defense against Arabella's accusations. *My word is as good as hers, isn't it? No one saw me with Jason. They'll blame Gully if anyone. No one saw me near the chateau.*

As if the mere thought had called the place into being, Marie stepped from the trees and found herself standing before the building that had housed both wondrous bliss and the depths of despair. Empty, the stone walls drew her even now. The door stood open, the English soldiery a departed memory of broken tankards, the odor of tobacco, molten stumps of candles and a discarded or forgotten powderflask.

Without realizing, Marie ascended the stairs. The bar was lying on the floor and the door swung outward. She stepped into the room. The window shutters had been left opened. A fresh spring breeze made a valiant attempt to brighten the gloom. The rumpled bench where Marie and Jason had made love, talked and slept together stood as left, the covers disarrayed from when the waking soldiers had thrown them about in the fruitless search for their escaped prisoner.

The floor needed sweeping. Cobwebs spanned the legs of both chairs. Marie crossed to the windows, beyond which a stretch of the Thames, partitioned by the iron grating, glimmered in the distance. A wood wren alighted on the stone sill. Oblivious to the sober surroundings, the tiny bundle of life began to warble happily. The cheerful music was more depressing than a dirge. Angrily, Marie brushed her hand against the bars. The startled bird took to flight.

Regretting chasing away the wren, Marie closed the shutters and slumped in one of the empty chairs. Why had she come to the chateau? Did she expect to find Jason there? Expect, by some miracle, to find time had gone backward in its tracks? Did she seek to affirm the goodness that had transpired between them by returning to the room in which love had defeated the uncaring forces of a hostile world? *The walls are chilly and damp. The iron, cold. The tapestry but tattered cloth, ill-used by time.* A hollow room. No trace of Jason Brand was left behind. *I'll pretend he never existed. I never saw him, never met him, never . . .*

"Girl!"

She spun, frightened by the voice. Reuben the gardener loomed in the doorway. "You should of paid attention to Arry. Too late now. Old Thrush been lookin' for ye. I seen him from across the way. They're waitin' at the big house. Best you hurry, if you know what's good."

He knew already. Everyone would know. Delicious, exhilarating gossip, the story of the fight would have run through the house like lightning. Arabella would be bragging. The rest would be laughing and making jokes at her expense. Marie wanted to say something spiteful, but no words would come. Mind reeling with dread images, she rose from the chair.

Reuben grinned, gripped either side of the door. Near choking with disgust—*Cochon! Animal! Pig!*— Marie stopped a few paces in front of the leering gardener and stared without speaking, her misty, slate-colored eyes overpowering whatever intentions he might have. Reuben stepped aside with a nervous laugh and let her pass.

The sun was nearly noon-high, bathing the spring-green garden with gold light shining through the new growth. Heedless, Marie walked down the path like a sleepwalker. Beauty didn't amount to so much as a pint of ale now. What mattered was the coming confrontation with Arabella and Lord Penscott. As on the night of Jason's escape, necessity demanded rational behavior. Coldly she assessed the chances of success. A cool, calm exterior, a sharp tongue were needed. The day might yet be saved. Penscott, after all, did like her, had seen to her education and made sure her burdens were never too heavy. How many other servants could converse in French with him? How many others could listen to supposedly secret conversations? The benefit of doubt lay on her side. Tossing her head, she determined to put on a good face and act with boldness and confidence.

Thrush was uncharacteristically calm when Marie reported. Thin-lipped and quiet, he led the way to the library. His attitude was puzzling: seldom was the master servant at a loss for a demeaning word. No doubt Arabella had already spoken to the lord of Penscott.

The doors swung open and Marie was ushered into the library. Outside, the sun shone brightly. Inside, gloom prevailed, ruled over by the terrifying form of Penscott's lord, a prim, periwigged judge on whose stern authority Marie's future hinged. She tucked a length of hair beneath her cap, at the same time noted but refused to acknowledge the presence of Captain Gregory. When had he come back? Why was he here? Was her cause lost without a chance to plead? She smiled innocently. "You summoned me, m'lord?"

Penscott nodded. Gregory smiled. A door leading into a side gallery opened and Arabella entered, a look of smug satisfaction evident in spite of a swollen eye, cut forehead and a dark, blue-black bruise on one cheek. Strangely, Marie was not afraid.

"This girl," Penscott began, " . . . ah . . . "

"Arabella, m'lord," the informer said, curtseying daintily.

"Arabella," he continued, irked at the interruption, "brings the most distressing news, namely that it was by your hand that the guards were incapacited on the night Jason Brand escaped." He paused, deep in thought. No one saw fit to interrupt again. "I have, of course, only her word of accusation, and am loath to suspect you. The brew was most deceptive to fool the practiced tastes of Sergeant whatever his name was, and I am more inclined to suspect old Behan's touch. However, the accusation cannot be overlooked. Did you free Jason Brand?"

Marie held his gaze, considered quickly. Here was an unforeseen trap. No matter what else happened, Behan had to be protected. He was too old to sustain punishment, and in this matter there was no doubt punishment would be swift and severe. Clearly, the end of self-deception was at hand. Jason was gone and Marie Ravenne was left behind to pay the price for the hours of bliss and loyalty to one who had forsaken her. Without him, procrastination served no useful purpose. "Knowing where the vials were kept, I stole the potion from Behan. I drugged the guards. Jason Brand escaped by my hand alone, m'lord."

Penscott, not believing his ears, nor that anyone would so unabashedly admit such a deed, seemed genuinely shocked. "Do you know what you say, Marie?"

Marie's cockiness faded and she hung her head. "Aye, m'lord. I do."

Sadly, the nobleman opened a drawer, pulled a coin from within and threw it toward the smirking Arabella. The maid scrambled to catch the money, missed and was forced to get down on all fours and retrieve it from under a chair. The gold piece firmly clasped in her hand, she looked back up and withered under Penscott's contemptuous gaze.

"You have your gold," the unsmiling nobleman intoned flatly. "Now get out of my sight." Arabella rose, trembling, and backed from the room.

Marie waited in the silence that followed. Penscott seemed reluctant to take the next step. Struggling erect with the aid of his cane, he wandered to the window and gazed out a moment. When he turned back to the desk, his face was hard and unforgiving. "Confession to the crime of betrayal implies guilt in a second, more heinous—that you bedded the Scottish brigand. Is this, too, true?"

"The words are yours, m'lord," Marie stated in tacit

153

admission. "I was under no edict not to do so." Penscott jerked back as if struck. Marie recalled the plans for her he had expounded to Gregory. The concept that the wizened man across the desk from her should determine with whom she slept drove her to sudden fury. Suddenly, she was glad she had defied him and knew she would do so again, given the chance. She straightened. "I loved him, m'lord," she said in a low, intense voice designed to cut deeply, "and would not stand idly by and watch you hang him."

Penscott's face grew mottled beneath the covering layer of powder. For years he had waited for Marie to show some spirit, but to do so now and with such defiance was beyond belief. All his hopes and dreams for her soured. Her great beauty, with which he'd planned to snare a prince, was useless now. How much had he invested in her? he wondered painfully. The question was moot, no longer of importance. The orphan to whom he had given so much could not be trusted, and that was that. There was no forgiveness for betrayal, none for traitors, none for those who defied his will. "I am done with you," he declared shortly, lips a tight slash across the drawn face and voice straining for control. Hands clenched about ebony cane, he stood by the grand chair behind the wide desk. "I know not what to do with you. I care less."

"Give her to me," Gregory suggested, speaking for the first time.

"No!" Marie whispered hoarsely, stepping toward the desk. "Please no, m'lord," she pleaded, wincing as Thrush dug his bony fingers in her arm and jerked her back to a respectable distance.

Penscott stared at her, the woman who had let his son's murderer escape. "Agreed," he rasped, the single word knifing into Marie's heart. No better punishment could be devised. Gregory was a brute. She'd learn a lesson at his hand, no doubt. One she'd not soon forget. "She is yours to do with as you wish. Have her away from here immediately."

"Within a fortnight," Gregory answered, a malignant grin spreading across his face.

"I don't want to see her again. Keep her away from me and my house. Take her to the chateau. Now get out of here. All of you. Get out!"

The room emptied quickly. Gregory gripped Marie's arm and led her out. Marie stumbled, almost fell. She wanted to resist but her legs had lost their strength and she could barely walk, much less run. A triumphant expression on his face, Gregory dragged her down the great stairs and past those with whom she had worked. A few wore expressions of sympathy, the rest were obviously pleased. Out across the lawn, through the wooded glade to the line of cedars guarding the chateau. The door was still open, gaping in mute and ironic welcome. *Jason. Why did you leave me, Jason?* Across the guards' room, the dead fire mirrored Marie's innermost thoughts, emptied by dread and the beginnings of despair. The stairs ascended to darkness. *Not up there! No! I can't let them lock me in! Don't let them, Jason! Why did you leave me?*

Gregory jerked open the door. The suction pulled one of the shutters open, slammed it against the wall. The room seemed even darker now, dingier, a waiting presence demanding a victim from whom might be sucked warmth, and life. Marie walked in, arms wrapped round herself. "And now, my dear . . ."

"No!" she screamed, trying to bolt from the room. An iron grip caught her arm, spun her into a waiting embrace. Bruising lips cut off a terror-stricken cry. Marie fought, bit down and tasted blood. Gregory howled, hauled the tigress aross the room, tearing her gown down the front as he threw her onto the narrow bed. Marie tried to get up, found herself slammed into the wall. The room spun in dizzying circles. Helpless, she clung to the bed as the last of the tattered garments were torn away.

The captain's eyes gleamed with anticipation at the sight of perfect breasts, firm thighs and flat stomach. The dark forest concealing her womanhood filled his

155

mind with whirling suggestions of carnal delight. Struggling, he kicked aside boots and breeches. Marie's vision cleared. She watched him advance, his brutal bough enlarged with lust.

"No!"

Gregory laughed, dove onto the bed. Marie squirmed to one side and fell to the floor. If she could get to the door, lock him in . . . Crawling on all fours, panting, trying desperately to scream but somehow forgetting how to make her throat work . . .

Something hit her in the back and she sprawled flat on her stomach. Again the laughter. She caught at a table leg, missed and tried to dig her fingers into the floor as a hand caught her ankle and dragged her back toward the bed. Pain in her side! A piece of pottery, a shard of a shattered clay tankard dug a groove along her right side. Somehow she managed to catch hold of the sharp piece, clutch it firmly out of sight.

Gregory wasn't willing to wait any longer. Letting himself fall from the bed, he rolled her over and dropped on top of her. "Fight, little bitch. Fight!" he crowed, enjoying the struggle which only made eventual victory so much sweeter.

Marie suddenly relaxed, throwing Gregory off balance. Before he could recover she slashed out with the piece of sharp clay. Flesh ripped and Gregory gasped, cried out and struck, one rock-hard fist almost breaking her wrist and sending the improvised weapon skittering out of reach. Cursing, he slapped her across the face, rose and painfully pinned her arms with his knees. "Bitch!" he panted. "Bloody bitch of a tart!" The cheek beneath his left eye hung in tatters, a crimson furrow stretched from cheekbone to jawline. Bits of flesh clung to the makeshift knife, lying safely out of range.

" 'S blood!" he grunted, shocked as his fingers explored the wound.

"Not His. Yours, *cochon*," Marie spat, trying to get a hand loose in order to claw his face.

Very calmly, Gregory slapped her twice more, great buffeting blows that left Marie nearly senseless. Groggy

156

and unable to resist, she felt the pressure ease from her elbows and his weight shift. A knee forced passage between her thighs, spread them wide. The ravaged, bleeding cheek descended, spattering and dripping blood in her eyes. Through a blinding, crimson haze, like the workings of an inescapable nightmare, Marie watched him slide between her legs. Half-fainting, she tried to squirm away, but no use. Elbow on the floor, her attacker dropped an imprisoning wrist across her throat. An iron hand reached under the small of her back and lifted her hips. Paralyzed and choking for breath, she gasped as the unspeakable organ penetrated and drove to the depths, leaving pain, degradation and welcome unconsciousness in its wake.

Alone. Pain. Moonlight, a brilliant silver stream. Pain again. Nausea. Cold. A dim memory of animal grunts and muffled curses, of weight relieved as the satanic incubus rose and dressed in real clothes, bound the seeping wound on its face with strips torn from her blouse. He had spoken before leaving. What? She struggled to remember: the words seemed important.

Sleep, stirring dreams. Pain and despair beyond tears. "You have fixed your fate in hell, bitch." Marie woke, the curse ringing in her ears and filling the night with terror. Groggily, she struggled from the floor, wrapped up in one of the blankets. The moon barely lit the room. She searched. No food. No water. Nothing. The door was barred and Gregory was gone, leaving his victim alone. How long ago? If there were only some water.

Pain again. Blood. Marie fell on the bed, huddled in the thin warmth. Heavy sobs wracked her body. She placed one hand over the violated womanhood. Too late to protect, too late to defend.

When the tears finally stopped, she lay for a long time without moving, feeling hollow, empty and used. *Is that all I'm good for? To be used and cast aside, taken advantage of and discarded?* Vision blurred by pain and exhaustion, she stared out the window to the moon, arcing slowly out of sight. It would have been easy enough to get up and go to the window. *But I don't want to get up. Not now. Not just now. Later, maybe* . . .

Helplessly lonely, she wept again. No tears, just a hoarse, rasping sob that eventually subsided with the realization that crying was a waste of energy. *I shall never again cry. Never again.* With that vow came rational thought, the first since the ordeal of pain had begun. With thought came relief at last. Icy calm, Marie lay flat on her back and stared at the ceiling. Weakness disappeared in the fiery crucible of reasoned introspection, emerged transformed, forged into a bright, hard blade of vengeance.

Pain? Fear? Degradation?

"I deny none of them," she spoke to the night in a soft, clear voice. "I take them to me as clothes, to be worn night and day. Fixed my fate in hell? We shall see. They have hurt me, Papa. They have murdered you. Live, you said. Live. But I am alone. How then live?"

The passionate and unmeasurable treasure of Marie Celeste Ravenne's love, betrayed by one, plundered by another, made the answer tortuously obvious.

. . . Alone . . .

PART II

Chapter VIII

Betrayed. How terrible the word. For one who put trust in love, to find the dearest emotion lacking . . . But then I had much to learn of love . . . and loss.

Three days became four, four days a week. My heartless captor had yet to return, but his parting threat haunted those tedious days. Fearful I might prove as elusive a prisoner as Jason Brand, the cause of my current state, Captain Gregory marched off to London, leaving specific orders to keep any and all visitors from my door. A suspicious Sergeant Burton, once burned and no longer my friend, likewise ordered the rear window closely watched. Thus did he protect a threatened future, and thus was foiled my one hope for effective communication with the outside world.

A change of warm clothes replaced those ripped from my body. Of food, I was allowed a modicum, enough to starve a healthy child. I should have lost all hope had it not been for the intercession of none other than Kitchen Master Ringe, whose bluster and immense proportions—and a judicious bit of bribery, no doubt—impressed the English soldiery enough to let him pass. Six days running this dearly remembered man brought sustenance. I have never ceased to marvel how, in the eight years spent at Penscott Hall, I had failed to recognize the depth of Ringe's goodness. I recall one visit in particular. Ringe smuggled a tiny plum cake past the stone-faced guards, for I had earlier recounted that my birthday fell sometime near the end of April. Though a grown woman, I acted with all the aplomb of one half my age and gulped down the sweet in three short bites. Ringe watched, his eyes shining with tears and pity, a look I recall with great tenderness, but at the time could not bear. But for Ringe, I would have passed those cap-

tive hours in total solitude. Sad to relate, fate never al-
lowed me to repay all the kindnesses done me by this
man whose frightful countenance and immense propor-
tions hid a generous heart.

At last, on the afternoon of the last day of April in
1716, one of the guards beat on the door and warned
me to make ready to leave. Fearful of what my fate was
to be, I hurriedly gathered my meager belongings and
sat down to wait. Within moments, a different set of
steps sounded on the stairs and a young gentleman,
splendidly bedecked in scarlet coat and rose-colored
breeches, entered, sniffed disdainfully, elevated his nose
and gave the empty air above my head leave to address
him by the name of Lieutenant Pulham. No older than
I, and not unhandsome, he impressed me as being a
mere youth plunged into circumstances beyond his abil-
ity to comprehend, if indeed he had ever tried. He
maintained an attitude of speculative contempt, found
my features obviously pleasing though tainted with a
forbidden aspect, the nature of which I was soon to
learn . . .

A sailor. A sailor meant ships and ships meant voyages. But to where? Where would anyone send an out-
of-favor servant? Giddy with speculation, Marie lost her
footing, almost fell down the stairs. The very idea was
exciting. To go to sea! For how many years had she
yearned to escape England? That which her captors
considered punishment might very well turn out to be
exactly what she most desired.

One possibility shone above all others. America!
That had to be it. Captain Gregory was sending her to
America, where she would be sold as an indentured servant. Tales had been told. The crossing could be brutal.
The man who bought her might be a monster, throw her
into the fields to work with black men and women.
Forced prostitution was a definite possibility. The
thought made her nearly faint with fear. Marie Celeste
Ravenne a slave and prostitute? Of such stuff were
poorly scribed tales and unreal nightmares made. She
clutched the tiny bundle of extra clothes to her bosom

and nodded good-bye to Sergeant Burton, who, pleased to be relieved of a dangerous responsibility, waved sympathetically and turned away. Did he know to what shores she was destined?

Four marines fell in step to either side as they left the chateau. Marie almost smiled. Was she truly such a desperate brigand to require armed guards? She glanced over her shoulder, wondering if Lord Penscott was watching the departure. They marched in silence, southeast to the landing. On the crest of the last knoll, the ship became visible at last, at anchor in the middle of the Thames. Marie was startled to think she had not seen it from her window. Surely such a large ship would have been visible.

"Hold there!" Pulham exclaimed. Marie recognized a figure approaching along the shore. Behan!

The old man ignored the officer's command, continued until he was abreast of the little party. The seamed face was sunken and hollow, the clear blue eyes moist with emotion.

"See here, old man. No one is to—"

Behan cut short the young officer with a wave of his hand. "This is my niece. I will bid her good-bye." Before the lieutenant could react, Behan evaded Pulham and enveloped the girl in a close embrace. Marie began to cry for the first time, unable to restrain the tears any longer.

"Take courage, my dear," Behan whispered. "Remember what you've learned. Those long lessons may stand you in good stead one day." While he talked, his left hand slid between their closely pressed forms. Marie stifled a gasp as the cold steel blade of a dagger slid inside her blouse.

Barely in time. A burly marine grabbed Behan's arm and roughly jerked him away. "You heard the lieutenant. Be off, old man, or taste the butt of my musket."

Thrown off balance, Behan staggered and fell to the soggy mud by the path. "Uncle!" Marie cried, rushing quickly to his aid but pulled up short as the same marine grabbed her wrist. "Let me go. Don't you see he's hurt? Let me go!"

"Leave him be, missy. You'll have uncles enough to care for where you're going." His grip tightened, cutting off the blood to her hand. Marie was powerless.

Behan struggled to all fours, managed to stand. Dripping with mud, he faced lieutenant and guards with a degree of dignity no mud could soil or tarnish. For a moment it looked as if he would attack, but age and wisdom counseled better. Eyes red-rimmed, countenance aged and weary, he shook his head. A tiny remnant of a smile crossed his face. "Good-bye Marie Celeste," he said silently, his lips framing the words. Acknowledging superior strength but not admitting defeat, Behan squared his shoulders, turned and limped down the path, quickly rounded a corner and disappeared.

"Uncle!" Marie caught the word, choked back the tears. *No. I will not cry for their amusement. Turn. Turn away. There. It is done. Now walk toward the river. Do not look back. There is nothing to see. Nothing you do not already hold in the depths of your heart.*

A waiting jolly boat rocked gently at the wharf. Prisoner and guards aboard, the sailors bent shoulders to oars and soon had the slim craft bobbing beside the mammoth hull of the *Sword of Cornwall,* the name writ in gilded letters on stern and bow. Quickly, she counted. Twenty guns visible. Another twenty would be mounted on the starboard side. A sixth-rater, according to Behan's lessons. Twenty six-pounders on the main deck, as many twelve-pounders below on the gun deck. Sails furled or luffed and flapping in the breeze, the ship was one of the finest Marie had ever seen. A brightly painted figurine of carved oak under the bowsprit proved to be a dragon's head, bloody fangs and slavering jaws the symbols of ruthless savagery. A forest of masts jutted high overhead like the spires of some warlike temple set afloat and come to raze heaven, not to praise it.

Marie could not help but be impressed. Time and again she had watched ships pass up and down the

Thames, but never since her abduction had she been so close to one. Were circumstances altered, she might have ventured forth enthusiastically.

She glanced over her shoulder. The shore dipped and bobbed in the distance. The manor was visible through the trees, as was a tiny patch of Behan's cottage. Four years. Like the passing of a shadow upon the land, time had flicked by, barely noticed in retrospect.

The master. Lady Gwendolyn. Thrush. Arabella. Ringe. Behan. Figures in the gallery of the heart, to be exhumed during lonely, distant hours. Behan. Marie imagined him at the south window, framed by the memorabilia of the roistering years that had passed for him. Fair Weather contentedly purring on the windowsill. *I do not think I shall see you again, dear uncle. Farewell. Farewell.*

A Jacob's ladder of hemp and wooden steps dropped over the side, swayed like a pendulum above their heads before descending the last few feet and thumping the gunwale. The sailors steadied the jolly boat with their oars and a pair of marines held the ladder. Pulham ordered Marie up first. At the first touch of hand to line, old memories flooded back. The ingrained feel of a ship returned, for those who once set to sea never forget. Quickly, easily, Marie clambered up the ladder, unhampered by the coarsely woven full skirt that flapped about her ankles. For a moment all fear was left behind. The rise and fall of a ship, of the swaying, dipping ladder, was too exhilarating.

Rough, calloused hands gripped her shoulders and upper arms, lifted her over the railings and unceremoniously dropped her to the deck. Smell of line and damp canvas, tar and sweating men . . . Gleaming brass and lustrous teak and mahogany . . . Creak and whispered protest of bound wood, of line running through blocks . . . The soft pop of flapping canvas, waiting to be pulled taut to catch the breeze . . . Seagulls taunting overhead . . . A brisk breeze plucked Marie's hair, blouse and skirt. The wind spoke of the sea and great empty distances, of voyages to unknown destinations.

165

For this punishment, she would have transgressed years earlier. Now, if only Behan were at her side . . .

"My gawd!"

"B'm'oath, but I nary seen such a wench!"

Crewmen surrounded her and stared slack-jawed at the new arrival, plainly dressed and disheveled as she was. Unabashed, for she had grown up around men like these, Marie returned their scrutiny.

Lieutenant Pulham scrambled over the rail and the crowd scurried back to their respective duties, all the while sneaking glances in Marie's direction. At the bosun's cry, the men assigned to the winches began to haul up the jolly boat. An air of expectancy hung over the ship. Men stood to their posts on deck, and others in the yards waited for orders that would set them under way.

Marie looked around, filled with wonder. The tide was running in, holding the *Sword of Cornwall* upcurrent of her single anchorage. The wind was from the southwest, a quartering wind off her starboard beam. Aft, the jolly boat had been swung out of the water and was being manhandled aboard. At the same time came the sound of the bosun's pipe. A hue and cry erupted from above as orders were passed from mates to common seamen, as men called and crawled across the yards, coordinating the tricky business of raising anchor and getting under way.

"Helm hard to starboard, Mr. Riff." Riff, the master's mate, passed the order to the helmsman. The tide started to swing the stern to larboard, or to the left, toward the north shore.

"Brace back the main and mizzen topsails, if you please, Mr. Riff." The foresails still shivered in the crosswind as the main and mizzen topsails were pulled forward on the starboard, or right side of the ship. Slowly, the *Sword of Cornwall* swung across the current to point toward the south bank of the river.

The man at the helm spun the heavy spokes clockwise and the ship started to move ahead, imperceptibly at first, then picking up speed. The order to start hauling in the anchor line was almost unneeded, and Marie could hear the solid chunking of the capstan as it wound in the heavy hemp line. By the time the *Sword of Cornwall* was abreast her anchorage, the iron shank broke through the water. Minutes later it had been stowed and the ship was on a steady course downstream, running on the fresh quarter wind. They were on their way.

Images remembered from childhood, never forgotten, only tucked away to be gazed upon like precious jewels. Sailing vessels of every description anchored on the crystal clear waters of Mysteré's tiny harbor. The ineffably sweet smell of sea breeze, the quickening of the heart at the suggestion of distance, of adventure and romance. Enthralled, Marie watched as the sails filled and the great ship picked up headway as effortlessly as a boy's toy boat on a pond. In the pandemonium, she had forgotten why she was there, found herself totally engrossed in the excitement generated by running, shouting men at work.

Her reverie ended abruptly when Pulham reappeared at her side. "Take this doxie to the captain," he ordered shortly, patting out the wrinkles in his uniform. Two nearby marines saluted in response.

"My name is Marie Ravenne," she retorted sharply. The feel of a ship under Marie's feet had given her courage, and being called a doxie by an errand boy didn't set well.

"The likes of you have many names, no doubt," Pulham sniffed.

"Only one, which I have told you." As a child she had learned the faint of heart seldom survive at sea.

One of the marines stifled a chuckle. Pulham glared at her but could not conceal the blush stealing across his face. He scolded himself. The girl was nothing but a tart and beneath the consideration of speech.

The likes of her. A prisoner. No doubt guilty of a heinous crime. Yet she was not riffraff. Of that he was sure. Her hair was too rich and lovely, fell about her shoulders and bosom like a mantle of expensive velvet. Her eyes were too gray, too limpid, too soft. Whatever

167

she was, she was an appealing creature, one he'd gladly pursue, given half the chance.

Damn it! Was that amusement in her eyes? He straightened his shoulders and cleared his throat. "That will be quite enough, I think," he said, nodding to the marines.

"Let's go, missy," one of the scarlet-coated marines grumbled, hauling her away abaft, toward the stern of the ship. They crossed behind the mainmast, mounted a set of narrow stairs to the quarterdeck, that part of the ship reserved for official functions and from which most seamen were excluded unless brought before the captain. Abaft of the quarterdeck, an oak door flanked by two red-coated marines opened into a passageway leading to the "great" or captain's cabin.

Marie noticed Pulham hurrying up a similar stairway across the deck to her left. The lieutenant continued past the quarter deck to the poop deck, the highest and rearmost deck where the wheel was situated and the ship was steered. One of the escorts nudged Marie through the doorway. She blinked, trying to adjust her eyes to the dim interior. A hammock to one side attested to the fact the captain's aide resided here. A narrower door immediately presented itself, swung inward on leather hinges.

Not even the great cabin on the *Glorianna,* the merchant ship which had brought her to England, had been appointed so lavishly. Glass casement windows cut into the stern admitted copious sunlight that flowed in almost tangible brilliance across burnished brass fittings and highly oiled and shining exotic woods.

"Stand steady, missy. The captain will be along in a minute. Don't touch anything," the marine commanded, stationing himself just inside the door.

Marie waited, wondering why an indentured servant should be brought to the captain's cabin. Through the transom windows she could see the English countryside slipping past on either side of the broad, flowing Thames. The interior was fascinating. Opulence was nothing new to a girl who had lived for eight years in the mansion of one of England's most powerful families, but this was opulence on a different level, compact and therefore more impressive. All the comfort normally provided for a whole suite was packed into one medium-sized, low-ceilinged room. An intricately carved desk, luster of walnut richly defined in the sunlight, sat in front of the windows. A larger dining table, three ponderous chairs to a side and a great armed one at either end, dominated the center of the room. A cushioned settee, royal purple in color and base panels hinged to permit access to storage compartments, lined one wall.

To her right, which was the ship's left, or larboard side, a four-poster bed covered with rich fabrics seemed out of place. Silver and gold filigreed decanters of brandy and French wines crowded a table close at hand. On the opposite wall, between double-tiered shelves of books and charts, was a small stand on which rested a finely worked leather case, open to reveal a set of exquisite dueling pistols. Above them, on a special rack, hung the most beautiful rapier Marie had ever seen. The scabbard was of fine steel, untarnished and glimmering in the sun. The basket hilt appeared to be of silver, wrought in intricate serpentine coils.

"Leave us!"

Marie froze at the sound of the voice. It couldn't be . . . Not daring to look, she listened as the marine answered with a crisp "Aye aye, Sir," and marched out. The door closed. Marie waited silently, the pressure of the dagger secure inside her blouse giving some comfort.

"Welcome to the *Sword of Cornwall*, my dear." A figure passed to her left, continued all the way to the desk in front of the window, turned and sat. The bright sun behind left his face in deep shadow, impossible to make out for certain. "Cat's got your tongue, no doubt. Come here."

She couldn't have hesitated for more than half a second. "I said, come here!" he snapped angrily. "You'll learn to jump when given an order, starting this instant."

Marie reluctantly drew close, stood before the desk and tried to calm the sinking feeling of dread as she gazed at Captain James Gregory. Heavy makeup could not mask completely the puckered scab that ran in a jagged line down his cheek. It was obvious, even in healing, his flesh would be streaked with scar tissue for as long as he lived.

"A pleasant surprise, eh? An interesting development. Just who did you expect to see?" With a soft laugh he rose and crossed around the desk. Long, tapered fingers entwined in one of the jet curls spilling almost to Marie's waist. "Skin white as snow, breasts soft as down, parts below . . . all firm and sound . . ."

Marie stiffened, determined to give no indication of fear or uneasiness. The captain smelled of brandy. "A ballad," Gregory continued, "from whence and whom I know not, nor care. The tune escapes me. Perhaps you know it, eh?"

He jerked her head back and looked down at her face. A cruel smile twisted his lips. "You shiver? Don't worry. Be set at rest. I will not soil myself again within your 'parts below,' though in truth you shall beg on bended knee and plead for my interest before this voyage ends," he crooned softly, letting go her hair.

"I do not think so," Marie replied, desperately forcing a note of calm into her voice.

"We shall see," Gregory said, smiling still. *Damn her insolence, her cursed pride*. He would shatter that spirit if it was the last thing he ever did. "Sergeant Hogarth!" The marine escort reentered the cabin. "Show this wench to the orlop. See she stays there as long as the others."

"Aye aye, sir. Come along, doxie."

The orlop? *My God, no!* The words struck her with the force of a heavy maul. Behan had told her of the orlop. There the impressed seamen ate, slept, fought and took their pleasure, such as it was, with the two or three women carried aboard for that very purpose. The orlop! Tongue cloven to the roof of her mouth, she stared at Gregory's wolfish grin.

The captain slowly spun on his heels to face the

170

broad expanse of windows. Wrists crossed at the base of his spine, he presented a figure of unrelenting discipline and harsh retribution, bound to see Marie paid in full for the grotesque scar which would mark his countenance for life.

Shocked beyond the ability to resist, Marie allowed herself to be led out. Mind reeling under the onslaught of macabre images, she stumbled from the cabin. The orlop . . . She could have found it on her own. Behan had taught her well. Below Gregory's cabin, the lieutenants had their wardroom and dining table. Below them, on the gun deck, the mates and marine noncoms swung their hammocks. Amidships was reserved for the midshipmen and the galley, where the food was prepared—separate victuals of course for captain, officers and the rest of the crew. Forward, among the guns, spare spars and canvas, line and a thousand other pieces of gear, the common seamen lived. Beneath this beehive of a floating city was the last true deck, the orlop, the most unfavorable living space on board. Here the impressed seamen were quartered, living & sleeping in crowded and embittered discomfort. Here, too, the surgeon could be found, forward near the bow. Few sought out the "sawbones," the most gentle of the names given him, for his ministrations were much avoided save in cases of dire emergency.

Marie paused on deck before descending to these nether regions, looked to the north and the shore slipping past. The hope of being sent to America as an indentured servant faded, dissolved in the twisting passages of a fiendish nightmare. Gone were all signs of Penscott Hall or the grounds with which she'd become so familiar. For better or worse, the manor had been home, its inhabitants a family of sorts. How much better if she'd never met Jason Brand, or had at least refused the pleasures of his treacherous arms. His fault. He was free and she was a prisoner on his account. *Damn him! Damn his eyes and lips and arms!*

"This way," Sergeant Hogarth said, obviously mistaking her brief reverie for confusion or reluctance.

171

The dark maw into which she was supposed to descend yawned ahead, engendering a sudden desire to flee. *I can't do it. I can't go down there! They'll . . . they'll . . .* "Where are we bound?" Marie asked in a tiny voice, trying to avoid the inevitable, even if for only a moment more.

Hogarth stared at this girl so unlike the others he'd seen aboard ships. There was an innocence to her, despite the disheveled blouse and skirt. "Why, the orlop. Did you not hear—"

"No. I mean the ship. Where do we sail?"

A grin lightened Hogarth's features. Wharf tramp she may have been, but he liked her just the same. "To the sea, girl. Now come along."

The ship's interior was as expected. Each corner, each shadow held unnamed terrors which only gradually took the shape of familiar objects. A glimpse of cannons, set in a row like so many squatting, black iron beasts. Coils of line. Buckets. Ramrods, barrels, timbers . . . low ceilings, under which even Marie had to stoop. Again the memory of childhood visits aboard the craft visiting Voûte Paix flooded over her. The eternal odor of men in close quarters, of forever damp canvas and mildew. The muted sounds of the world shut out, as if nothing outside the dim circles of lamplight existed any longer. Strange echoes of footsteps, of creaks and groans of wood, the slosh of water and disembodied cries from the deck.

"I'll not serve!!" someone shouted as they gained the orlop. "I've a family in London. A wife, three strong boys—"

"Be glad the bastards didn't take them, too. They'll keep her well until you return," a gruff voice broke in. "As for me, a pox on the king. One of his prison's the same as another."

Hogarth raised a bar and opened the door which made a prison of the whole forward half of the orlop. "Words to bring a man trouble. Treasonous words, I hear," the sergeant said. "Could be a man does not want to serve his king. Such a man ought to answer to the cat."

Two sailors, little more than a pair of frightened faces, disappeared into the shadows and scurried off. "Bleedin' pressers," Hogarth grunted. "What they get for hangin' around where the gang'll find 'em. Ought to know better. Get on in with ye, missy. You'll be let out when the captain says so."

"They're right, you know," a woman's voice sounded from the darkness.

The marine spun about, caught off guard. "Curse ye, Hope. You'll stop my heart one day."

"It stopped long ago, Samuel. Else you'd have a word of sympathy for them two lads you've driven off."

"No heart? If that was the case, I'd have 'em whipped around the fleet. I'll suffer no discourse with the like of you. Here. I've brought a new girl. See she gets broke in right."

The woman stepped into the light. "A hen then to mother a chick?"

The only answer was the door slamming and the heavy chunk of timber as the bar dropped. Sergeant Hogarth was gone.

Marie backed away from the stranger until the door stopped her. Hope, as Hogarth had named her, was a far from wholesome-looking individual. Clothed much the same as Marie, she appeared larger, grosser, with rounded hips and an immense bosom that hung loosely, jouncing in perpetual reaction to her every movement. Plain features that brightened with each wicked smile were heavily coated with cheap ceruse and bright rouge. Her hair was a mousy brown, thinning a little as a result of a poor diet and aged haphazardly with silver streaks. Hazel eyes were peculiarly lifeless in repose, brightening with energy only from time to time, much like a flickering candle flame soon to be extinguished in a wisp of smoke.

"I'm Hope," she said, looking Marie over, appraising her as if the girl were a piece of fruit the older woman considered stealing from a stand. "Actually, Hope Deferred Maketh the Heart Sick. It's from the Bible. Me folks was Roundheads, curse the lot. You can call me Hope."

With the deck rocking underfoot, Hope Deferred acquainted Marie with her new home. The orlop was an unsettling place dominated by shadows and the ponderous bulk of the mainmast, which was stepped at the keel and extended through the ship, joining floor and ceiling.

Beyond the mainmast, the orlop opened up into a large compartment filled with the impressed landlubbers who would be kept under lock and key until there was no chance any of them could jump overboard and escape the king's service. The two women stopped deep in the shadows, out of sight. "Poor bastard souls," Hope whispered. "Not a one of them been to sea, that I know of. Not a one of them but what belongs on land. They're a surly lot. We'd best keep clear of 'em for a while." Taking Marie's wrist, the frowzy ship's woman guided her new charge around the sides of the open chamber, through a tortuous maze of stacked barrels and crates and trunks toward the bow of the ship.

A few minutes later they slipped through an opening in a wall and headed for a curtain of threadbare blankets behind which a smattering of privacy might be had. Behind this partition, Hope arranged some heavy sacks into suitable places of rest. "There. We'll have comfort for a time, until Mister Nohl has need of this grain in the galley."

Marie positioned herself on one of the sacks and arranged the lumpy contents to suit her posterior. Hope added a candle to those already burning beneath a small metal pot, sprinkled some tea leaves into the bubbling water and looked up with a self-satisfied grin. "Courtesy of our own flesh-tailor, Master Gianna."

"Did someone mention my name?" a voice inquired. The blankets to Marie's left were pulled aside and a diminutive caricature of an Italian street vendor stepped into the cubicle. "I was on my way to make the acquaintance of— Aha, but who is this?" he asked with a larcenous expression.

"Speak of the devil," Hope sighed. "This is our saw-bones, and a worse one you'll not find on land or sea. Tries to make out he's an Italian, but I've known him on the streets of London and, to be truthful, was a mite put out on learnin' he was aboard this very ship. His name is Gianna, but we call him Giuseppe. This is . . . What's your name, Tulip?"

"Marie." Her voice sounded weak and hollow. "Marie Ravenne."

"Marie Ravenne," Hope repeated needlessly. "She's new and don't know the ropes."

The surgeon doffed a small pot-shaped hat to reveal a balding head with hair brushed forward to resemble Julius Caesar's. In truth, Marie thought, he might have passed for the conqueror of old were it not for the veined cheeks and jaundiced eyes of a confirmed drunk-ard. A small, rotund Italian with scratchy orator's voice and bleary eyes was the best he could do.

Marie nodded in return. "And are we to be your assistants?" she asked hopefully.

Both old-timers stared, speechless. Hope began to cackle. "Aye, but only if he makes it worth your while, love."

"Hush, woman. Do you not see she asks in honesty?"

Hope sidled forward, squinted at Marie and reexamined her from head to toe. "'Sblood, if you ain't pinned it to the wall, Giuseppe. She ain't from the streets. Who are you, girlie?"

"Marie Ravenne," Marie answered again, "a servant in the house of Lord Roger Penscott until I earned his displeasure."

"A great displeasure, surely," the surgeon grunted, "to be brought to such an unwholesome task."

"I don't complain," Hope sniffed indignantly. "There's worse could happen to a person."

"You were born to draw a fellow's fireworks, and many a ceiling you've seen over a man's shoulder," the surgeon scoffed. "You're like the rest. Give an old whore a home and she thinks she's in heaven, but it's plain as day this lass is cut from different cloth."

175

"No matter. She'll learn to give her greens and find what pleasure she can in the process. You tip us over and we're all of us alike, which the boys well know. Don't matter what kind a' cloth we're cut from."

Marie sat in shocked silence. Gregory's revenge became more and more clear with each word spoken. She had been brought aboard to appease the carnal appetites of the marines and sailors. Behan's offhand portrayal of life in the orlop and the deck-moll's role aboard a military vessel took on new meaning. Two or three extra unfortunates, usually broken-down prostitutes off the streets for whom only starvation or worse waited, were always available to serve the impressed seamen who, given to the lash or cat, cooped up every time their ship came to port and fed on the rottenest, vilest, vermin-infested food and stagnant water, soon became near ravaging animals. The filthy, pox-ridden women were the only outlet permitted for the frustration and rampant belligerence among these captive sailors. Lower than the most common seaman, lower than the impressed seamen, lower even than the ship's surgeon, the orlop hags were looked down on by all the ship's lawful company.

Hope Deferred was obviously one of this status. And so am I. So am I, Marie thought to her own unabiding horror.

Hope bent over to pat Marie's leg. The harlot's bosom sagged against the cheap material of her chemise. "There, there, Tulip. You've nought to concern yourself with for a time. They'll let us be until their anger at being taken wears off and they get their sea legs. Then they'll think the better of us and come to share their grief. You'll see."

The motion of the ship changed. At first slipping along easily through the water, now the *Sword of Cornwall* heaved and bucked without rhyme or rhythm. Marie stirred, waked. Exhausted by the fear and tension, she had fallen asleep. For a long moment she lay quietly, listening to the sounds coming from abaft. Her reverie was disturbed by a sudden rise of voices. Hope was gone, had disappeared. Only one candle still burned, filling the tiny comparment with writhing shadows. Suddenly panic-stricken, Marie jumped up, pushed aside the blankets and stumbled toward the voices, above which Hope's rose in argument.

It was but a few paces to the crowded compartment. Not yet seen by the men, Marie paused in the doorway. They still looked frightening. Large and small, all were dressed poorly, mostly in canvas rags thrown them by the mate. Their faces looked pale and unhealthy in the sickly lantern light. Anger and fear were the common denominators of each visage. Hands on hips, Hope faced a veritable giant of a man, a burly fellow with an enormous belly that looked appropriate in the context of his massive frame. "Say what you will, it's grief you'll be bringin' upon all our heads with your bickerin' ways, Tom Gunn!" the woman brayed, her head thrust forward to stare with malevolent energy at the figure towering over her and everyone else.

"You've a poison tongue, woman. Them slops wouldn't be called food by a starved dog and you know it."

"Dog be damned," Hope shot back. "You'll have a visit from a cat, if you don't watch your mouth. A cat with nine tails and a thousand lives. You'd best learn—"

"Get away from me. Go back to your blanket," the giant shouted. "We'll have none of you. Honest men we are, stolen from home and hearth and our families left to ruination. 'Tis a sad day when we be slaves of our own countrymen. You're the captain's handiwork and we're wise to you." He glanced up and saw Marie, was beside her in three great strides and hauled her forth. "By the mark. Another wench. Two then, to keep us from our yearning?"

It hadn't been difficult for most of the men, newly torn from their families, to agree with Gunn when it came to Hope. They'd all heard the tales of the orlop harlots, knew well their function. But this new one was different, was far too desirable and beautiful! There must have

177

been a mistake. A great silence fell across the orlop as over fifty pairs of eyes stared in astonishment at Marie. No one spoke for a long moment. The ship groaned. A rope creaked. From above, a voice called for a change in sails. Marie lowered her eyes, unable to face the stares. Her mind reeled at the future in store for her. How many men? Visions of being passed from one to the other, used, brutally taken again and again . . .

No! This is a nightmare!

She would not let it happen. Not give Captain James Gregory the satisfaction of enjoying her degradation. One recourse remained. With grim amusement, Marie wondered if Behan suspected she might use the dagger on herself.

"Ain't real," an unseen figure wheezed. "She ain't bloody real."

"A fresh piece of meat, by God!" The voice came from her right and Marie looked up involuntarily. A hawk-faced, thin wisp of a man grinned back from where he leaned against a great beam. "Welcome, dearie," the man continued with a harsh laugh. "On ship or on land, I've a weakness for dark-haired wenches. Why don't you come give us a kiss, or more?"

"She'll not bring her wanton ways among us," Tom Gunn swore. Marie fought against the nerve-deadening grip on her arm, felt herself lifted and hurled toward another man, a beggarish-looking fellow with great open sores on his face who caught her and sent her sprawling into the arms of the hawk-faced one.

The sailor caught her easily, laughed at the prospect of so ripe a dalliance. One hand pawing her breasts, he pulled her to him and tried to kiss her. Marie doubled a fist and drove it into his eye. Howling in agony, he let go and struck back with a sharp blow that sent her spinning to the floor. "I'll show you, trollop. I'll give you a reaming you'll not forget," he cursed, one hand cupping part of his face.

Marie clawed desperately for the concealed dagger as her attacker advanced. The other seamen looked on in various attitudes of disgust and excitement. Removed

178

from the contest, Hope's face was devoid of emotion.

"None of that, Ned Sly," growled the giant.

"You keep to your own, Gunn," Sly snarled, starting to undo his belt. "You ain't no captain, 'spite of your swelled head. I aim to bugger this wench and teach her proper manners. You said it yourself. She's the captain's handiwork."

Gunn stepped between them. "I'll break you, man."

The hawk face paled, reading the earnest meaning of the leviathan's threat. Another sailor stepped forth, recognizable only by his voice, which Marie had heard from the shadows when first she'd been brought to the orlop. "He's right, Ned. The lass is poison. See? One day out and we're already at one another's throats. Go to sleep. The girl's a tasty bit of flesh, but not worth a thrashing."

Sly glared at the man. "Mind your own affair, Joshua," he said. Though already subdued, he refused to back down from Gunn.

The larger man reached down and caught Marie by the arm, hauled her to her feet. "He'll leave you alone. Now get to your blankets and come not among us. Both of you."

Hope chuckled aloud and waddled off with what had at one time been a provocative wagging of her behind. Marie ran to join her behind the blankets. "I'd swear that Tom Gunn reminds me of my father," the older woman laughed caustically. "The self-righteous mongrel of a man." She handed Marie a blanket confiscated from one of the upper decks.

"Give them time, dearie, and they'll come sniffin' to us for comfort in spite of Gunn. It always happens. They talk well and good now, but when their wives are but will-o'-the-wisp memories lost in the months at sea, and when they've leaned down some and grown tired and sore, we'll be hearin' a prettier tune."

Hope glanced at Marie, curious about the girl's continued silence and trying to make her feel better. "I'm tellin' you, there's worse lives to have to live. We're fed here, and bad though it be, it's food. Such as it is, we've

179

a roof over our heads, which is better than a dung-filled alley and freezin' rain down your back. Before long you'll see we have friends, too, who will help us as they can. An extra tumblin' on a bare deck ain't never hurt a soul. And at voyage's end we even get a share of the spoils, same as the others. Cheer up, love." Marie shut her eyes and rolled over on her side, facing away from Hope Deferred. The harlot shrugged. "A body's got to take care of herself, Tulip, the best way there is at the moment. There ain't no fault in that, is there?"

Silence.

"Well, is there?"

Marie couldn't sleep. The rhythm of the ship had changed. Now the *Sword of Cornwall* rose and fell, rose and fell in long, surging leaps as she bit into one wave and then another. Taking the candle, Marie wrapped up in her blanket and stole from the curtained alcove. Working her way back along the ship, she paused at the large room before continuing. The men lay asleep in attitudes of despair. One called out sharply and sat up, looking about wildly. Quietly, Marie turned and headed forward. A dim lantern burned in the surgeon's quarters. Giuseppe sat slumped forward on a stool in a drunken stupor. Marie glided past soundlessly.

Now that they were at sea, the forward ladder to the upper decks had been let down so the men could go to the heads when necessary. Marie doused the candle and made her way up the ladder, past the already nauseating odor from the catwalk under the bow, to the forecastle. Cool, clean night air greeted her as she emeged onto the deck, part of which was fenced off to contain the pigs and sheep brought aboard to supplement the salt meat supply as long as they might last. She peered over the rail, caught her breath. The mouth of the Thames was far behind. A dark line of land to starboard that was England moved steadily away as the ship rode a stiff breeze. Low in the east, behind them, a nearly full moon promised a bright sky for their first night at sea.

The only sound now was the gurgling splash as the bow met the seas, parted them and passed through on the way west. Strangely enough, she felt at home, here on the forecastle. The constant rolling pitch, wind, sea spray, smell of salt, of distance . . . The day had been . . . what? Slowly, she raised her hands, undid the loosely pinned jet-black hair and let it unfurl in the streaming wind.

So beautiful. The ruffled surface of the sea. The wind. I could be happy. If only Jason were with me. She frowned and her heart chilled. Why had she even thought such a thing? *He betrayed me. I hate him. He put me here. I hate him.*

There was no escape. She was trapped, totally and irrevocably, with no way out. Sixty-five men waited below. One day soon they would wake and have their way with her. *No way out . . . no way out . . .*

The ocean listened, considered and whispered back with the sound of wavelets. There was a way. A simple, foolproof way. The logic of the ocean was impeccable, undeniable. All she had to do was climb over the rail and jump. No one would see. No one would hear. It would be so easy. *So easy. What else is left? What else? . . .*

Entranced by the dancing waves, pulled by the whispering water, Marie took the final three steps to the rail. *So easy . . . so easy . . .* The years flashed by, reflected in the water. Mysteré . . . Her father, Jean . . . The little grave on the mountain . . . Penscott Hall . . . Arabella . . . Lord Penscott . . . Lady Gwendolyn . . . Behan . . . Jason . . . None moved to belay her. They were smiling gently, almost beckoning, she thought.

So easy. So easy. The ocean won't betray me.

The rail was damp with salt spray. Extrasensitive, she could feel each tiny ridge of the grained wood. One foot up and over, followed by the next.

So easy. She stood poised over the water. Nothing below but moonlight. Nothing inside, either, save the tiny prick of the dagger point as she leaned over. Only

181

the ghost of Jean moved, rose from the water to stand at her side and hold her hand as the tears streamed down her face.

"Only I am dead, darling Marie. Only I. The others smile because they do not know. Do you remember what I told you, that last day in Mysteré?"

Yes, father, I remember. But . . .

"You have the dagger, daughter. You have your wits. You have the will, *if* you will. Shall I repeat myself?"

But Father, they want me to . . .

"What men want you to do, and what you do, are two entirely different things, Marie. You have many to-morrows. Some of them happy, some sad, but all yours. Do not lightly cast them off."

You haven't seen the faces of the men below, Father."

"I have seen the faces of men all over the world. Never did I fear them."

Father . . .

"My dearest, my little one. I abjure you: live!"

He was gone. The faces in the water below dissolved, disappeared. Marie was left alone. Overhead, the sails spread like motionless clouds. Below, the ship creaked with life. The water whispered. No more messages, only the timeless hiss of passage. Marie touched the dagger and smiled. *Very well, Papa. Very well.* And without thinking further, she climbed back over the rail.

Chapter IX

Crack!

High burning sun. The ocean's blistering smooth surface. Water and fire blending in unholy forbidden union of the elements. Becalmed inferno. Becalmed.

Crack!

The line of marines stand motionless in their stifling uniforms. Hogarth checks them with a watchful eye, noticing who wavers, who slights discipline. They'll answer to him later. As he will answer to Captain Gregory.

Crack!

Captain James Gregory. Supreme and unquestioned monarch of an ocean-borne kingdom, whose sacrosanct word is written on the ledger of command. His feet spread wide in imperious stance upon the quarterdeck. Hands are clasped firmly behind him. His back is stiff and unbending. Emotionless eyes are riveted to the scene below. His lieutenants, lesser echoes of the Crown's authority, share his aloofness and imperturbability. Except for Pulham, who looks sick. Punishment is a messy business. And painful.

Crack!

The boatswain, Ethan Trow, pauses to gulp heated lungfuls of the stagnant air. His shoulders ache from exertion. How many more? The Captain has decreed ten lashes. Hell, Ethan thinks, I'm suffering as much as this bloody piece of meat hung in front of me. He glances through a curtain of sweat at crisscrossed welts streaking Joshua's straining shoulders, then up to the bound wrists lashed to a cleat on the mainmast. Joshua's fingers flutter futilely against the shining, smooth wood. Trow drops his arm for the backswing and the cat whispers across the deck, doubles back and whistles through the air as the boatswain swings across and down.

Crack!

Joshua shuddered and groaned pitifully. His knees buckled and he was left hanging by the cordage binding his wrists. He struggled to regain his footing, but soon gave up and slumped unconscious. The pressed and freely signed seamen exchanged sidelong, mute glances. No one liked the sound of the cat: this could be any of them. And might be before the voyage came to an end. The message was most efficiently presented, and impossible to ignore. Joshua had taken an extra ration of fresh water: now he was paying for it.

Prey to a thousand fears, the motley, shabby crew shifted uneasily. Some fixed their eyes on the horizon, unable to watch. Others, for whom brutality had been their only sport throughout a mean and bitter life, watched with idle curiosity. One man, Tom Gunn, observed each blow and twitch to insure Joshua's punishment was seared indelibly into his memory. He wanted it that way. He would not forget.

Crack!

Marie winced as the leather thongs bit into Joshua's torn back. She stood near the wooden railing of the pig and sheep pen, now occupied by only a half-dozen swine and one lonely ewe. Many were the tales she had heard concerning the cat, but never had she actually seen the whirling tails at work. The scene was one from a bad dream. The silence, as the ship lay becalmed, was eerie. Before her eyes stood almost one hundred ninety men, none of them with a sound on their lips. Where lay the necessity of such treatment? she wondered. The sea was a stern taskmaster, but flogging an unconscious man was discipline beyond the meaning of the word and all bounds of reason. Men worked better when treated like men.

"That will suffice, Mister Trow." The Captain's voice sliced over the deck. "The point has been made. I will have order aboard this ship. Am I understood?"

The marines and ship's crew, knowing the procedure

and their captain, answered with a loud "Aye!" The impressed men stood silently. "Answer, by God, or I'll see each and every one of you covered in your own blood!" Gregory roared. The words lashed the men and spread out to disappear in the quiet expanse of sea and sun.

For a half-second, nothing happened. Then, reluctantly, the impressed men answered with a grumbled response. Gregory hesitated as if he would demand more, then thought better of it. "Lieutenant Schell. Break out the boats. We'll pull our way to wind," he ordered curtly, then turned aside and disappeared into the passageway leading to his solitude.

Marie followed Joshua's limp form down to the surgeon's quarters. The pair of marines unceremoniously dropped their burden on the table and left. The Italian rolled up his shirt-sleeves and began searching among his supplies for a bucket of salve. Marie watched and dabbed at her face with a bit of rag. The stifling closeness in the orlop was all but unbearable, especially in the horrendously cramped living space given to Giuseppe. For the last three days she had wondered how the swarthy Italian could stand the closeness and stench, now wondered anew as he set to work as if he were in the great cabin itself. "Is he dead?"

Giuseppe looked around, startled. "You! I should have suspected. Sneak around like a ghost. No wonder the men fear you. That's why they won't lie with you."

"I have done nothing."

"True. You work in the galley and say little. Like a shadow, you are. It unnerves me. I prefer Hope."

"To the devil with your opinion," Marie said, irritated by the heat and the surgeon's attitude. "The man needs help, not talk."

Giuseppe swung a bucket of salve onto the table and wiped his hands. "Well said. There's fire in you, right enough. Woe be the man who finds it." His sharp eyes drilled into hers. "Or has someone already done just that, and left the rest of us to go hungry?"

Marie turned away. "Shall I tear up this cloth?"

185

The surgeon shrugged. "He'll be needin' something of the sort," he grumbled.

Joshua Stemple stifled a moan as Giuseppe wrung out a rag full of water over his back and began to wash the torn flesh. Marie wetted another cloth and dabbed at the wounded man's cheek, at the same time whispering soothing words of comfort to help thwart the burning pain. Joshua sighed, as much from the pleasure of a woman's gentleness as anything else. "You're a good lass," he managed, then fainted again.

The job finished and Joshua resting peacefully, Marie washed the blood and salve from her hands. The task had not repulsed her, for she was not a stranger to the viciousness of men. Ships had put into Mysteré with wounded men aboard. More recently she had nursed another back to health, a golden-haired lover who had repaid her ministrations with caresses—and then betrayal. Her face hardened and she resolved, again, to force him from her mind forever.

"Bring me a bucket of water like a good girl," Giuseppe whispered before Marie had a chance to leave. Marie shot him a look, followed by a meaningful glance at Joshua. He had been nearly killed for the precise offense the surgeon was asking her to commit. Giuseppe avoided her gaze. "There's a barrel aft, on the gun deck. You needn't worry. There'll be no one below. They're all off in the jolly boats or working on deck." Afraid to go himself, he had little compunction about sending someone else.

Marie could read his mind like a book. But there was little choice. Joshua had to have water, and if Giuseppe didn't dare fetch it, she must. Grimly, she grabbed the bucket from the surgeon's outstretched hand and started aft, through the open orlop and up the ladder to the gun deck. Shadowy and silent, squat, brute shapes lent an air of pending violence to the gundeck. Taking care for her head, she moved in darkness alleviated by little more than light blue squares where the gunports had been left open to let in what air there was. Hammocks and makeshift bedding were slung hither and yon, in

186

much the same fashion as in the orlop. The water barrels were kept near the aft where the marines might watch over them. Today, with all hands on deck and surly with heat, thirst and the just-completed flogging, the barrel stood unguarded.

A quick glance around showed she was alone. Marie slipped the heavy oak lid from the barrel, dipped the bucket full, closed the barrel and sneaked back to the orlop and the surgeon's quarters as silently as possible. A half-hour later, in the stifling cubbyhole, the realization of her folly hit full force and she lay trembling, cold sweat beading on her forehead. Surely, she would have died if Gregory had discovered the theft, for she never could have lasted the flogging received by Joshua.

The sun, fat and red, lay only a few degrees above the curved line that told the horizon. The *Sword of Cornwall* drifted like a dead beast upon the water. High in her rigging, a midshipman searched the four directions for any hint of wind ruffling the glassy, low swells. Twenty yards ahead, four boats filled with the larboard watch pulled to a slow beat against the great weight of the becalmed ship. When the glass next emptied, they would be relieved by the starboard watch, now asleep or resting on deck.

Marie picked her way through the jumbled bodies to the quarterdeck ladder. The tray she carried held supper for the officers. The men had been given their biscuits, grog and pease soup earlier—enough to still the grumbling in their stomachs, certainly, but nowhere near enough to sustain the efforts demanded by the calm. Already they looked gaunt and drawn. Two or three cocked a jealous eye at the passing tray of hardier sustenance, then sank back to stare up at the flaccid sails and beyond to the infinite, windless blue.

The door to the officers' quarters stood open and Marie passed through on her way to the great cabin. Captain Gregory and the lieutenants, Schell and Pulham, were relaxing, oblivious to the men who served under them, though, of course, as anxious as any to get under way again. Marie tapped on the sill with her foot. "What is it now?" Gregory inquired.

"Your suppers, sir," Marie answered docilely.

"Well, what are you waiting for? Bring it on in. What is it?"

"Chicken, sir."

Gregory's eyes raised. "Chicken? How's that?"

"One was about to die, sir. From the heat, the cook says."

"Humph. Damned calm."

"Yes, sir. He's done it up in sherry. And there's cheese and bread."

"Well, set it down, for heaven's sake. Let's have a look." Marie set the platter in front of the captain, then stepped back to await his pleasure. Gregory stared at the quartered fowl, then reached out with his knife, speared the breast and dumped it on his plate before shoving the rest toward his lieutenants. Schell paid no attention, merely grabbed a leg and thigh, but Pulham inspected the bird closely. The chicken had been close to death when culled from the diminishing flock and he had no desire to eat tainted meat. He would have preferred the white meat, but dared say nothing, much to his undying chagrin. Having to adjust to getting second best from one he outranked socially was difficult at best.

"A fair weather fowl," Schell laughed, digging into the cheese the second the captain pushed the plate across the table, then pausing as a knock sounded on the door.

"Will I not be allowed to eat in peace?" Gregory demanded through a mouth full of chicken. "Damn it, man, what is it?"

"The glass is run out, sir. Request permission to pull in the larboard watch, sir."

"Granted, of course. No wind, then?"

"None, sir."

"Very well. Continue as you were."

"Sir?" the boatswain asked apologetically.

"What?"

"It's the men, sir. They can't pull much longer without rest and a bit more water."

Gregory rose abruptly, knocking down his chair. "Damn your impudent tongue! They'll get water when I say so. Until then they can make do, d'you hear?"

"Aye aye, sir."

"Now get out of here. And make sure double watch is kept on those casks. I've had one flogged today, and there'll be more to follow if so much as a drop is missing."

"Aye, sir," the boatswain answered hurriedly, backing from the door.

Gregory sat again. Eyes blazing, he glanced around the table. Schell was eating as if nothing had happened, but Pulham was staring at the nibbled leg that lay before him. "Troubles, Mr. Pulham? Something the matter?"

"No, sir," the young lieutenant answered quietly.

"You think me too harsh, no doubt. Never been in calm before, have you?"

"No, sir. But yourself said we were only four days from St. Kitts. I understand water is critical, but if the men row better for it, we'll be that much closer to a new supply."

"The trouble with selling commissions, Mr. Pulham, is that the navy buys inexperienced men." He paused, glanced at Marie. "Where's that wine?" Marie hurried to the table, poured him another goblet. "Mr. Schell. Would you be so kind as to educate Mr. Pulham in the mystery of drinking water."

Schell washed down a bite of wing and grinned. He had worked his way up in the navy and enjoyed sticking it to the son of a nobleman, a delight he shared with the captain. Pulham's face was beet red. Ridicule was bad enough, but in the presence of a serving maid, intolerable. "Begging your pardon, captain, but Lieutenant Schell needn't—"

"Begging *your* pardon, Lieutenant, but I'm the one in command here. Proceed, Mr. Schell."

"Yes, sir. Drinking water. A very important commodity, Mr. Pulham. You see, none of us—not even the men—can drink sea water. A pity of course, but there you are. Now, 'tis true we are but four days from St. Kitts. And 'tis also true we have at least eight days of water to hand. But . . ." He leaned forward to emphasize the point. "We have no wind."

"I understand."

"Now wind, of course, is another important commodity aboard a naval vessel. Without it, as you have seen, we sit here like a bashful boy a'play with a harlot's teat, bobbing up and down but going nowhere. Worse, we don't know where the next wind will come from. It should come from the east or northeast, but that we don't know. Therefore, Mr. Pulham, it could take us *ten* days to get to St. Kitts—or other landfall—in which case we would be in dire trouble."

"As we shall be in any case, sir," Pulham commented, barely able to control his voice, "if there are none left alive to sail the ship."

Schell laughed again. "Oh, but that won't happen. The weak ones will die—like this chicken—and good riddance. But there will be some left. There always are."

A cry from outside broke the uneasy silence that followed. Captain Gregory jumped to his feet. "Wind!"

Schell wiped his mouth, slapped Pulham on the shoulder. "So it's moot, after all. You worry too much," he said, hastening after Gregory.

Pulham slumped in his chair, having forgotten Marie was in the cabin. When she started to clear the table he sat up, chagrined. A frown gave evidence to the war raging in his spirit. How desperately trying it was to despise one so beautiful for being privy to his embarrassment. Marie smiled at him. "It was good of you to think of the men."

Her lips were red and inviting as the most lucious fruit, and engendered wild fantasies fueled by the enforced celibacy aboard a naval vessel. Still, one had to keep up appearances. "This is the king's ship, and as such is required to exemplify his justice and authority."

"Still, it was very brave of you to speak up like that," Marie insisted, reaching across him to remove his plate.

Pulham leaned forward so his shoulder touched her breast. "A pity bravery sometimes goes unrewarded," he said, his lips brushing her hair.

In that moment, Marie knew the young lieutenant was the one man on board ship who might help her. He had the aristocrat's penchant for getting his own way with women, yet was terrified of Gregory and Schell. Would he, then, to prove his mettle, allow himself to be led into a trap? Could she snare him? She had but one weapon, and that she resolved to use. "A brave man sees to his own reward," she said, forgetting the plate and gazing down at him.

Pulham rose from his chair. His eyes raked her body. "It is customary when aboard a naval vessel not to initiate relationships with one's subordinates. But then, one rarely finds suitable subordinates with whom to have relationships, eh?"

"Do you think *any* man may touch me unless I desire him to, Lieutenant Pulham?" Shocked by her own boldness, Marie tilted her head and allowed a cascade of long jet curls to spill to one side.

Pulham glanced to the empty doorway. If Captain Gregory should see him there'd be the devil to pay. But oh, to hold this temptress for a moment, to taste the cherry sweetness of her lips. Unable to resist, he gripped her arms and pulled her to him.

Marie did not resist, rather savored the sensation of newfound power. Adroitly led, this naive and passionate young lieutenant could be the key to her eventual escape.

"Mister Pulham!" The lieutenant almost knocked her over in his haste to shove her away.

Gregory's voice drifted down from the deck and the mate's took up the call. "Mister Pulham!" The lieutenant bolted out the door and up the ladder, leaving Marie disheveled and alone. She straightened her blouse and grinned mischievously. She had a chance now. A chance.

Hope wedged her plump buttocks into the jumbled pile of sacks she used for a bed and place of business. "Best pull the blanket shut, dearie." Marie glanced questioningly at the woman. Except for a few snoring, totally played-out souls aft, the orlop deck was empty. "The men will be coming down soon. They'll be tired and in no mood for bein' put off." Marie didn't move. "What's wrong, Tulip?"

The younger girl sighed, pulled out a greasy rag from under her blouse. "Nothing. Here." She dropped the wrapped-up remains of the chicken on Hope's belly. "Chicken."

Hope's eyes widened and she grabbed for the packet, tore it open and bit into what for her was a rare treat. "My Gawd, but that's good," she mumbled.

Marie pulled the blanket closed and slumped onto her pallet. The conversation in Captain Gregory's cabin had unnerved her. She knew as well as anyone the need for strict rationing of fresh water, for she had seen ships pull into Mysteré with half the crew dead from thirst. Behan, too, had expounded at length on water rationing. But never had she heard the men's lives so callously discussed. Water rationing and rowing to wind were instituted to save men's lives, not to take them, as Schell had implied. She had returned to the galley, passing along the deck filled with men beyond swearing or caring, yet working hard to recover the jolly boats, trim the sails and get the deck in order for whatever fate the weather should bring next. She marveled that though driven to the point of exhaustion, they could still function. Schell had equated them to chickens, but there was no doubt they were men. Deprived, weak, tired and heartsick, but men nonetheless.

Hope belched, rummaged beneath her ample frame and brought forth a dusty bottle of rum. "Nothing like a dollop to wash down a good meal, I always said." Marie glanced around nervously at the sight of the bottle. "I stole it, so keep a tight tongue. If the sawbones sees it, he'll not leave a drop. It anyone else sees it . . . Well, 'tis best to enjoy the crime." Eyes twinkling, she tilted

192

the bottle and took two throat-blistering swallows, then extended the rum to Marie. "You want some?" she wheezed.

Marie shook her head. Hope shrugged, slapped the cork back in and returned the bottle to its hiding place. "You've not much use for me, have you, Tulip?"

Marie, lost in brooding silence, ignored the question. Hope shoved her face in front of Marie's. Heavy-lidded eyes struggled to focus. It was obvious she'd had more than those two swallows this day. "Why don't you speak? Say something. Always sittin' off by yourself. A silent one. You think they'll forget you're here? They know. There's a hunger in their faces. I've seen it before. The heat, the calm, the work . . . Why don't you speak?"

Marie's eyes narrowed. "Leave me alone, Hope," she said, angry and ready to strike out. A scurrying of claws on wood caught both their attention. Dark gray, silken fur, gleaming eyes. A rat perched on a beam overhead. Giving vent to a curse, Hope grabbed a block of wood and hurled it at the rodent, which darted off unperturbed.

"A cup of grog. A man deserves that, if nothing else."

"Who's seen to poor Joshua?"

"The hell with him. Stealin' water—"

"Mind your tongue. We'll have no more of that."

"A pox on your 'no more' I say."

"Aye," a half-dozen thirsty voices grumbled in assent. "He deserved what he got," one continued.

Tom Gunn, hunched over in the confined space, glared about him. "Forget it. Not a one of us but would have taken some if we'd the chance, and you know it."

"So you would have. And gotten more than a boot in the arse for it," laughed another.

Gunn searched for the speaker. Being kicked was something he'd hoped the rest had missed. "That mate plant a boot to me again and I'll toss him to the fish," he grumbled menacingly.

193

"Aye. And put yourself before Hogarth's bayonets. And your neck in a noose," Ned Sly replied.

"They'd have to go some to hoist him," a man named Tremain retorted, grimly amused. "Now the likes of you, Ned Sly, would swing to a fare-thee-well, I warrant."

The smaller, hawk-faced man lunged at his companion. "I've enough of you, Ben," he shouted, his fingers closing about the older man's throat. Though short and slight, Sly possessed surprising strength in his bony arms and, to the raucous jeers of the others, soon overpowered his older opponent.

Tom Gunn intervened, parting the struggling sailors with a sweep of one massive forearm. "That's enough, I say!"

Sly, enraged, rebounded to the attack. "And I've a gutful of you, Tom Gunn! You're forever buttin' in where you're not wanted. Do this. Do that. No fightin'. Keep away from the women. Hell!" he shouted, then doubled over as the larger man drove a fist into his midsection. As if the blow was a signal, pandemonium erupted. Tempers long held in check were released in self-destructive disregard. A sailor leaped for Gunn, missed his back but hit his knees. The giant, head and neck already hunched over to clear the ceiling beams, dropped to his knees. Another man landed on his shoulders, only to be tossed aside like a sack of grain. A third tried his luck, and then a half-dozen more.

Gunn fought like a bull. On his knees, he crawled and slugged his way to an upright beam in order to protect his back. Assailants were sent stumbling across the room or dropped beneath short, clipped punches. Sides changed with each blow. One unfortunate lay entangled in a jumble of hawser and screamed as the fight passed back and forth over him. Finally, Ned Sly grabbed a three-legged stool and hurled it with all his strength. The stool caught Tom a vicious swipe to the head, and the embattled giant pitched forward.

As Gunn slumped unconscious to the floor, Sly roared in triumph. "So much for him. Now the women!" he howled. Before the others could take up the cry, he had darted to Marie and Hope's quarters and torn away the flimsy blankets. Marie rose, backed away toward the bulkhead as the sailor advanced. Hope reached out and caught his leg. "Oh hell, dearie, if it's a tumble you want, have a go," she said, hitching up her skirt to reveal pale, fleshy thighs.

Sly kicked free of her grasp. "I prefer younger petticoats," he said with a leer, lunging for the girl.

Whatever happened, she couldn't let him touch her. Blindly, like a cornered animal, Marie darted past him when he tripped over a sack of corn, only to find herself surrounded by his randy cohorts.

"Aye, Ned. Give her a taste of the stick!"

"Hold her for him," someone else roared.

"Him, hell! Hold her for *me*!" another demanded.

A sea of leering faces, featureless in the dim light. Panic-stricken, she turned to the right and left. There was no escape. Hands groped for her, ripped her blouse and spun her about. One lad managed to seize her from behind. "There you go, Poole. Pin her arms."

"Somebody get her legs!" Poole howled, dancing about as Marie's heels found his shins. He did not see the swirling skirts nor the buxom assailant who stepped from the shadows and, missing his head, brought the treasured bottle of rum down upon his shoulder. Covered with rum and bits of glass, Poole let Marie go and staggered out of reach, writhing in pain and screaming for help.

The brassy taste of fear in her mouth, Marie backed toward Hope. Ned edged forward, heedful of the broken neck of the bottle the older woman still held. "You broke Poole's shoulder for sure," he growled, furious at having his sport interrupted.

Hope Deferred looked sadly at the puddle of rum at her feet. "To hell with that," she wailed, "I've broke my heart!"

Ned turned his attention to Marie. His voice was soothing and calm. "Well, sister. Enough of this. Tom's down and there's no more waitin'. The captain brung you aboard for one thing, and we all know what. It's time you started earnin' your keep. Now, you ready or not?" Poole's scream had brought her back to her senses. She breathed deeply, regaining control while she eyed Ned speculatively. Finally she smiled grimly. "If that's the way it's to be, Ned Sly, I'm ready." Ned's face brightened and as quickly fell as a steel blade appeared in Marie's hand. "Ready to slice you into gobbets if you come one step closer!"

The men sighed collectively, shifted awkwardly. No one had bargained for knives. Ben Tremain, grateful no more violence had come his way, giggled inanely and stepped behind the nearest beam. Ned stopped and scowled, stared at the torn blouse and the barely concealed mounds of flesh so deliciously rising with each breath. He stared at the knife. The girl held it steady, but that was probably no more than show. Chances were he could take it away from her.

The door in the aft end of the orlop flew open and Sergeant Hogarth barged in. "Here now. What's going on?" he roared. Ten well-armed marines, bayonets fixed and gleaming in the lamplight, filed in behind him. Marie quickly hid the dagger in the waist of her skirt as the sailors parted before Hogarth. "Is it trouble you're after, lads? Not worked enough this day to sleep without mischief? Then it's some more you'll get. When I can see the moon reflected on the deck I warrant you'll rest well enough. Topside, now. Get along double time!"

The marines stationed themselves in facing lines leading to the door. Grumbled protests from the pressed seamen faded before Hogarth's stare, and the men started out. Ned Sly, the last to leave, cast a look at Marie, then disappeared with the rest. Only the two women and Gunn were left behind. Hogarth tarried momentarily, gazing from one to the other in turn. "What happened?" he asked shortly, pointing a finger at Hope.

" 'Twas an accident, Sergeant. He bumped his head on that beam, and—"

"Never mind. Who gives a damn?" He turned to

196

Marie. "You tend him. The sawbones is topside." Two steps put him in front of Hope. "And I'll have a word with you, mistress." He reached out and grasped her wrist, pulling the broken bottle to chest level. "In my quarters, if you please."

Hope grimaced at the incriminating evidence in her hand, opened and relaxed her fingers. The bottle neck crashed to the floor. "Why, how did that get down here?" she asked in wide-eyed innocence.

"Aye. All the way from my own stores, too," Hogarth rasped. "Which is what we'll be discussin', among other things." Changing his grasp, he pulled her along behind him, out the door and up the ladder.

Marie sagged with relief and headed for her quarters, only to stop when Tom Gunn groaned and struggled to his knees. "Sit down," Marie ordered. "I'll be back in a minute." Before he could answer, she was off to Giuseppe's quarters, there to retrieve a mug of water, bandages and salve. When she returned, the sailor was leaning against a sack of grain and watching Marie suspiciously. She tucked in her blouse, flicked the long jet locks away from her face and set to work washing the blood from his face before cleaning out the inchlong cut on his forehead.

"I want nothing from you," Gunn grumbled, wincing as the water stung. He tried to avert his sight from the proud thrust of her breasts, so close to him, but his gaze seemed drawn to them. She was beautiful. Too beautiful. And so near.

"Don't you?" Marie scoffed. "Are you so different from the others? You pretend to be, but I doubt it."

"You are Gregory's wench, here to leach our anger between your legs. The others are fools and will gladly be gulled, but I know you for what you are."

"Do you?" Marie asked. The awful, sweat-soaked stillness and the abuse of the hulking seaman combined, and suddenly she didn't care whether she angered him or not. Fingers gentle but a second past turned rough with haste as she slathered some salve in the open wound and bound it with the torn bit of rag. Her eyes flashed with wild spirit and her temper flared in defiance. "And I think you are like all the rest, no matter what you say. A brigand and a lout that calls himself honorable."

Tom Gunn's arm shot out to imprison her before she could move away. Marie clawed for the dagger but Gunn's hand was faster, captured her wrist and twisted. The knife dropped to the floor and Marie found herself beside it on her back with the sailor over her. "I'll show you," Tom said. "Trollop!" Straddling her, he ripped the blouse apart to expose her breasts completely, then leaned back that she might see her own helplessness mirrored in his triumphant face, Marie clawed for his eyes, but once again he caught her wrists and held them in a bone-crushing grip. "Maybe Sly was right," he whispered hoarsely between gritted teeth. "Maybe he was right, after all."

Tears of fear and frustration sprang from Marie's eyes. "I cannot stop you," she said, suddenly relaxing and giving up the fight. "And in truth, it will not be the first time a man has forced me against my will."

"Force? No one need force an alley cat."

"Then what are you doing now? You make me sick. You and all *honorable* men. Honorable, pfah! Since when was rape and cruel abuse honorable? The first such honorable man who took me was Captain Gregory, and you're to be the second. You malign him, but there's not a jot of difference between you."

Anger. Silence. Sweat. Salt air seeping through the very walls. Flickering lamp and sickly amber light. Dark and heavy shadows, deepening to black. Hoarse and rasping breaths in the eerie gloom. Then, to the girl's surprise, Gunn released her wrists. His head fell back and he let out a long sigh then swung off her and sank against a jumbled pile of hawser. "A wife. Two darlin' boys. I was a carpenter. Oh, I'd been to sea before, but a fine family cleans the yearning for a bobbing deck and grand sights from a man's soul. For me, the grandest sight of all was them two lads. Growin', sturdy lads, they was. We were poor, for sure, but who wasn't along Betner Lane? Life was hard, but the folks was honest friends, good men and true." He stopped, staring into the darkness. Marie lay without moving, all energy spent. When he went on, his voice was a crooning lament.

"Friends, family. Two fine lads. I'll not see any of them again in this life. Not a one of them. Not Jeremy. Not Michael. Not my own sweet Jill." He shook his head, trying to dispel the pain, then focused on Marie, noting without caring as she pulled her blouse together and replaced the dagger in its hiding place. "But I am an honorable man. I am."

There was shame in his face. And weariness. Sailor and girl sensed an unstated hint of inner torment shared. Tom Gunn was a simple man and could no longer find words. His broad rustic features softened in the dim light. That was all. Marie knew no words needed be said. She reached out and patted his massive forearm. Her hand left a smudge on her cheek as she wiped away a tear. And then she did a most curious thing. She smiled. And Tom Gunn smiled back.

They were under way, running west by north to St. Christopher Island before a fair wind. Marie curled in a fetal position and pretended to sleep. From without the blanket, the sounds of half a hundred snoring men was a constant cannonade accompanying the creak and groan of the ship. Across the cubicle, Hope stirred and mumbled in a dream. Marie had tried to thank the woman for her help, but Hope had shrugged aside all offerings of gratitude and muttered sourly, "What with the scarcity of spirits, and what I had to do to make amends with the sergeant, I only hope it was worth it."

Finally, Marie slept. Outside the curtain, a giant form stirred and crept away from his self-appointed post into the darkness. He moved softly, hunched over under the low overhead, stepping over sleeping bodies until he reached the one he sought. "Ned Sly," he whispered, poking a hard finger into the smaller man's ribs. "Wake up."

"Ah . . . wha . . . what? You—"

"Quiet. Hear me, man. You're not to touch her again. Ever again, do you hear?"

"What? Who?"

"Marie."

"You're daft, man. I'll—" His sentence was cut off as a large hand grasped his throat and lifted him to his knees. "Let me be!" he gasped, choking for air.

"You are not to ever touch her again. I'll be watching. Do you understand?" The hand tightened. Just enough.

"Yes. Yes!"

"Very well. Oh, and it was you who threw the stool, I'm told."

". . . Yes."

"It hurt." Amid deafening snores and grumbling dreams and the eternal creaking of the ship, the loud smack of a fist against flesh went unnoticed. As did a startled grunt of pain, and a slow, unconscious exhalation as Ned slumped to the floor, asleep again.

Chapter X

St. Christopher. Small, palm-set island dominated by the towering Mount Misery. Given a northeast wind, her harbor offered safety and haven from the brutality of the open sea. Totally in British hands since 1714 and the Treaty of Utrecht, artillery batteries on Brimstone Hill commanded the calm waters where the *Sword of Cornwall* rested, rising and falling almost imperceptibly on the gently flowing currents captured from the sea. The sixth-rate was not alone. A magnificent third-rate ship of the line anchored on the far side of the harbor was having a new set of masts stepped. A pair of island traders, battered and looking the worse for wear, rested close in to shore.

St. Kitts, as it was called, Nevis and the smaller outlying islets, had become an important British outpost in a generally hostile Caribbean. The tranquil complex offered a promise of fresh water and provisions, land to stand on and a respite from the monotony of shipboard life. The impression was of quiet and peace, until one looked toward shore. There, the mansion and grounds of the Admiralty officers was the showplace of Basseterre, the thriving port town where ship chandlers, blacksmiths, gunsmiths, sailmakers, coopers and a dozen other shops jammed the steaming, shell-paved, narrow streets. In the streets and along the docks, men cursed and sweated and loaded the specially built, wide-beamed victuallers with barrels, bales and crates to be rowed out to the sea-going vessels. Food, too, passed from shore to ship: live animals, salt pork, flour, beer, peas and, most importantly, cask upon cask of fresh water.

By night the scene changed. A new and more rapacious set of merchants appeared to hold the stage until dawn. Men who have been at sea for months on end develop ravenous appetites. The Admiralty, in its infinite wisdom, took great care to see these appetites assuaged. The policy was both lucrative and sensible. Pounds and pence were quickly spent on the host of carnal fare to the unending profit of those who were lucky enough to hold the correct purses, and the sailors, penniless but appeased, were ready for another hitch at sea.

This night was perfect. Low clouds cut off all light from the sky and muffled the harbor in inky blackness. Gregory had accompanied the governor to Nevis for a hunt and would not be back until late in the morning. The whole crew had been confined to ship for fighting aboard. Marie lay hidden behind a bale of goods along the starboard bow. The nearest guard was twenty feet away, and dozing. She stifled a gasp, then scolded herself silently for being frightened by a creaking line. It wouldn't do to attract attention—not when she was supposed to be below and in the orlop, locked away with the others. But a pox on the guard. This night was worth any risk. The soft thud of wood against wood allayed her fears. She peered over the side and glimpsed the deeper shadow of the jolly boat, quickly slipped over the side and lowered herself on a thick hemp rope and into the boat.

"Damn if we're discovered," Lieutenant Pulham whispered nervously. "It's a wonder I made it. Never did learn how to steer these things."

"Hush!" Marie rasped, shoving away from the side. "Give me the oars, then, and keep an eye out." The little boat slipped swiftly and silently through the water. It was the first time Marie had rowed since her abduction from Mysteré, and she thrilled to the feel of the oars in her hands.

The boat crunched into the shelving sand. Pulham groped for her arm as she started to leap out. "Remember. On your honor," he said. "If Gregory finds out, I'm done for."

Marie leaped onto the sand, whirled about for the

202

sheer joy of standing on dry ground. "He won't be back until late tomorrow. You said so yourself. Don't worry so much."

"Nevertheless, he has many ears. So mind yourself." Taking her arm, he led her along the beach to the outskirts of Basseterre and a tiny hut at the mouth of an alley. "In here. I've arranged clothes for you."

Moments later, Marie emerged from the one-roomed house. "Do you like it?" she asked, whirling about. A white cotton blouse decorated with lace had replaced the shipboard shirt, and her sailor's breeches were gone. In their place hung a billowing skirt patterned with blue and white flowers.

Drums sounded in the distance. Pulham's eyes gleamed in the weak light. "Very much. You're more beautiful than I thought." He jerked his head toward the sound of the drums. "A wedding. The entire island will be there. I don't know who's married, but this is what the women and girls are wearing. Hurry. We need to get back before dawn."

Marie followed in a daze. The sounds, smells and sights of the Caribbean bombarded her senses. Shell streets, crunchy underfoot. Thatched roofs. Palm trees: how stately and grand they were! The perfume of exotic flowers and the sweet succulent odor of fresh pork fat dripping into open fires. Wild bird calls intermingled with the sound of pulsing drums, the treble and bass of the tropic isles. How intensely she had missed it all. Her heart swelled to near bursting with exhilaration. Thank God for Pulham! She glanced over at him. His fresh handsomeness had taken on a boyish quality and a wide grin softened his usually prim features. He looked as excited as she, and in a flash Marie decided she could learn to like him very much. In truth she must, for only through a friend would she ever escape.

They followed the main avenue now. Torches lit the night. The streets were crowded with colorfully garbed islanders mingling with English colonials. Revelers with mugs of heady rum in hand passed by on all sides. Somehow Pulham obtained two of the mugs, and he and Marie, eyes bright with adventure, drank a silent toast.

The center of activity was a large square directly ahead. The crowd closed in the closer they got. Laughter and shouts of greeting filled the air. Mixed in with the merriment were impassioned embraces and occasional fights. The crowd parted for one pair of brawlers. Fists swinging, faces ugly with alcohol-induced rage, they nearly knocked down Marie before they passed on and disappeared. "Maybe this was a bad idea," Pulham said, looking about nervously.

Marie cut him off with a kiss, one arm about his neck, her body pressed against his. Pulham's eyes widened but a second. Fight forgotten, he almost dropped his rum as he returned the kiss. When they parted, both were smiling and Pulham had decided that spiriting Marie from the ship had been a good idea no matter what the consequences.

The crowd around them cheered. Pulham blushed. Marie gave her long raven locks an imperious toss and took her escort's arm. Pulham had surprised her, as she had surprised herself. He was actually appealing. And malleable, she hoped. What frightened her a little was the way his kiss had awakened her own long dormant desire.

A huge pit had been dug in the center of the square and flames jetted upward from it into the air. The potent contents of their tankards drained, Marie and Pulham wound their way to the fire. A platform had been set up to one side. Fully a dozen drummers with large and small battered hollow logs held court with an ages old rhythmic exchange that stirred the soul.

The pounding drums! And on the other side of the fire, dancers. Women in flowery dresses, a veritable bouquet of patterns, spun and undulated in time to the drums. Octoroons and mulattos, Carib and fair of face. Men dressed in abbreviated breeches, now bending, now leaping, always in time with the drums, wove in and out among the women.

Drums. Faces. Chants in disparate tongues. Bodies

pressed close. Rum. Hands clapping. Always the drums. Marie stared, in a trance. The sound of the islands. Unconsciously, she began to sway in time to the drums. The aphrodisiac of sound and smell and motion. The rum, fire and heat of bodies warmed her. Perspiration formed on her forehead. Pulham stood behind her, his body pressed to hers, his hands on her stomach, moving as she swayed back and forth to the drums.

She didn't know how it happened, but suddenly she was moving into the stream of dancers. The sound of the drums and the thudding feet reverberated through her whole body, set up vibrations that awakened primitive, animal instincts hidden deep inside her. Nothing existed but drums and movement. Savage rhythms flowed into her, there to marry with the gypsy blood from her mother, blood that yearned to be one with the tribe.

Moving. The drums were her lovers. Spinning. The black cape of her hair whipped out. Whirling. The skirt billowed higher as the drumbeats increased to muscle-wracking intensity.

The dancers fell away one by one. Not Marie. She had only begun and the drums and chanting voices were not satisfied, demanded more and more. The skirt rose higher until her thighs were bare; and as she danced, driven by the insistent rhythm, the skirt billowed higher yet as her body arched back, breasts taut and straining . . .

The drums! Hips and womanhood revealed. Spinning. Spinning. The primal woman, caught in the chant and the throbbing drums . . .

A scream, long and drawn out. Marie slumped to the earth and the drums . . . ceased.

The crowd roared and surged forward, maddened. Women, caught in the arms of their lovers, were carried into the shadows. Marie felt herself lifted. Through slitted eyes, she glimpsed the scarlet of Pulham's coat, and then darkness.

She woke in candlelight. A room. Outside, the myriad voices of festival, but inside, with Pulham, only silence. She lifted her hips as he drew the skirt from around her waist. The blouse followed with equal ease and she was naked, lying before him, pleading with her eyes. Pulham breathed shallowly, slowly unbuttoned his coat and let it drop to the floor. His shirt followed, more rapidly. Quickly, then, he kicked away his boots and undid his belt. Marie's eyes narrowed as he stripped away the tight breeches and stood before her, hard and eager.

She could not deny the terrible need, the fire that raged in her loins. He stepped toward the bed and she reached for him, grasping his manhood, then opening her legs and guiding him into her. Warmth sinking into warmth. The sweet pain of fulfillment caught them both by surprise.

Sighing as he filled her. Thrusting, rising high and plunging again into the desperate heat. Thrusting. Her fingers dug into his buttocks, challenging him while she rocked from side to side. Now caught in the timeless rhythm, she could not stop. The dance. The drums. She could hear them still, building, faster and faster, to excruciating climax.

And finally his flooding seed. Taut, arched high against him, holding him deep within, Marie cried out. As did he.

Later, lying in the warm aftermath. A single candle guttered, filling the room with orange light surrounded by deep shadows. Pulham lay propped on one elbow, gazing down at Marie. What had started out as a mere lark, a way to still the rising need for release, had become a mystery he couldn't solve. This was no simple serving maid, to be used and thrown away. This was a woman, complete and proud and passionate, one that only the most fortunate of men would ever hold. "Who are you?" he asked in a hushed whisper. "What manner of woman are you?"

Marie lay still for a long moment. The question cut through to her heart and laid bare her innermost soul. Jason had asked the same questions. Jason, whom she

206

could not drive from her mind, whom her body could not forget. Another man's woman, she wanted to answer, but could not: that other man was gone. Though she wanted to, she would not weep. Swiftly, she rolled from the bed. "It's late," she said. "We'd better get back."

Pulham seemed oddly distant on the walk down the beach to the boat. Somehow, it didn't surprise her. Would the fear return now that he had defied Gregory and Schell? She hoped not, for if he were to help her, he must be strong. He had to be strong. Had she not given him her body?

The clouds were breaking apart and ghostly starlight cast a sheen on beach and water. The jolly boat lay another hundred yards down the beach. Suddenly, a figure rose from the boat and Pulham stopped dead in his tracks. Gregory? No. Impossible. It had to be Schell. "Come along, Lieutenant Pulham," he said with a sneer. "It's too late now to do else. We'd best be back to the ship before anyone else notices your absence."

Pulham faltered, then grabbed Marie and dragged her to the boat. "She tried to escape," he explained nervously.

"Come, come, Lieutenant." He held up a hand. "Please do not insult my intelligence. I'm not an utter fool, you know. I saw her leave and thought I'd let you have your sport. You needn't fear that the captain will discover your little indiscretion, though. My silence will be kept as a favor to my friend." He chuckled. "Of course, favors must be repaid from time to time, no?"

Pulham felt sick. "I'll think of something."

Schell laughed aloud. "No, Lieutenant. *I'll* think of something. And when I do, I'll be sure to let you know. And now, if madam pleases?"

Marie was forced to take his hand to be helped into the boat. She sat alone, near the bow. The night had ended in disaster. Pulham was terrified. His fear of Schell would override whatever delights she could offer, and she knew he would never dare so much as talk to her from that moment on. All had been for nought.

207

A tense atmosphere permeated the *Sword of Cornwall* this day, for the proximity to land had fueled the dissatisfaction of those relegated to the orlop and fired the imagination of the others on deck. So close to freedom! The distance of a musket shot, perhaps doubled. As a result, sweating marines in heavy scarlet coats had been stationed every few feet along the rails. Quietly debating who would be allowed ashore first, they waited for the first sight of the gig which would signal the captain's return from his hunting trip and subsequent visit to the Admiralty.

Shortly after nine, a brigantine limped into port. Lieutenant Schell watched the battered ship as he paced the quarterdeck and growled at Sergeant Hogarth. Marie, inconspicuous at the bow, did not try to guess the cause of his discontent. It was enough to know he was angry. The prudent person would keep a wide berth of him. Of Pulham, she saw nothing. On the main deck and in the yards, the crew worked hard to put the finishing touches on the ship. The task was easy for the voluntary seamen for they would have their chance in town if Gregory was pleased. The pressed men, though, had nothing to look forward to but being locked up for the night, and had to content themselves with heavy-hearted glances toward shore.

Marie saw from the beginning the tragedy that followed. One of the pressed men suddenly set down his tools and wandered from his task, heading in dazed fashion toward the rail. Marie was the first to recognize him, for she had tended his injuries. Even now, five days later, the multiple lacerations from the flogging had barely started to heal. His back was crisscrossed with line after line of puckered scabs, dark against the pale flesh.

Joshua Stemple was not a brave man, and it was with matter-of-fact indifference that he headed for the rail. His family—wife, daughter and son—was waiting, and if he hadn't stopped for a spot of ale in the Knoxbury Lane Pub, he'd be with them now, sitting down to a meager supper and recounting the day's misadventures.

But he was late: the fires were lit and it was past time to go home. The first step was to leave this ship, on which he so unaccountably found himself. Strange. He didn't like the sea, even if it stood at his back door. But never mind. He could swim to shore easily enough. A ten minute walk, then . . . He stared at the island and saw another in its place: an English countryside, but ten minutes away.

"Hold there!" one of the marines exclaimed, noting the unfortunate seaman at last.

Joshua didn't answer. He straddled the railing and, as the marine attempted to grab him, leaped into the water. Other marines, and then Schell and Hogarth rushed to the port side. "Come back, you fool," Hogarth called. The sergeant watched the seaman's head bob up through the clear blue water as he started to swim for shore. His hands slapped the water in short, furious strokes, and though the salt water must have stung his back, he made no cry.

"He's fevered from the wounds, sir. I'll lower a boat," Hogarth offered, turning to the men who had rushed to the rail to watch.

"The devil you say," Schell replied, his voice carrying like the crack of a tension-snapped hawser on the warm, still air. He dragged a pistol from his belt and cocked it. Tom Gunn shoved his way through the marines.

"Let me go over, sir. I can bring him back."

"Speak again and I'll have you flogged and clapped in irons," the lieutenant said tersely, not even bothering to turn to look. His arm straightened and the flintlock spewed black smoke and flame. A loud crack followed and a plume of water shot upward a scant foot away from the escaping man. "Dammit, Sergeant, bring him down."

"There's no time to lower a boat, sir. We can—"

"Anyone attempting an unauthorized departure from this vessel will be considered a deserter, and shot. Now, kill him!"

"Aye aye, sir," Hogarth answered. "Horton. Cooper.

Smith." Three marines stepped forward. "Prepare to fire." As one, the men cocked and primed their muskets, sighted on the helpless swimmer who showed signs of tiring while not yet sixty feet from the ship. "Fire!"

"Joshua!" Marie screamed. Her voice was drowned in the roar from the muskets.

Joshua tried to dive. For a moment, no one could tell whether the shots had struck home or not. Then he began to thrash about as the water around him became tinted with a faint crimson. The marines reloaded and primed their muskets. "Again, Sergeant."

"Sir—"

"Again!!"

Hogarth's lips were a tight line as he ordered his men to sight and fire. The muskets gouted flame for the second time, and blood spurted from the floundering form. Joshua thrashed but a moment more before all struggle ceased. His body drifted a few yards, then slowly sank through the bright clear water as the scavenger fish began to explore.

"Let that be a lesson. A traitor's death waits any and all who choose not to serve their king and country." The officer spun on his heels and strode back to the quarterdeck, ignoring the unveiled hatred that followed him. Silently, reluctantly, the men set back to work.

"Faster, man. Faster."

The liveried driver plied his whip and the small brown mare plunged around the corner and into the square. Cursing aloud, men scattered to left and right. One, bearing a bale of goods on his shoulders, tripped and fell. The mare shied and the driver tried to haul her to the left, but the carriage skidded, throwing the passenger against the side.

"Damn your hide! I'll have you flogged." The curse was interrupted by a scream of agony and a jarring thump as the right wheels ran over the unfortunate victim's legs. The driver paled, but kept going.

Captain James Gregory rearranged himself and glanced out the window. If the damned fools had any sense, they'd move their worthless carcasses out of the way. His lips pursed. Here they were, three days in port and not ready to put to sea. Damn the governor's hunting party. Now they'd be hard pressed to gain the next morning's offshore breeze. The carriage slowed at the dock where his gig waited. Gregory jumped out. "That will be all," he ordered curtly, then strode rapidly across the wooden planking.

The men were lounging in the shade, not expecting their captain for another hour or so. Trow, the boatswain, leaned against a handrail and stared across the water. "Dreaming, Mr. Trow?"

The boatswain jumped to attention and his face turned bright red. "Begging the captain's pardon, sir, but I—"

"Never mind, Mr. Trow. Get the men. Immediately." He hardly needed to speak, for the crew of the gig had seen him too, and came running across the deck. Within seconds, they were in the light boat, sitting at attention at their oars. Trow was the last aboard and cast off the painter as soon as Captain Gregory was seated.

The second the gig touched the side of the *Sword of Cornwall,* the captain, his face even grimmer than when they'd started, hurried up the ladder without waiting for help. "Mr. Schell! Mr. Pulham! I want both jolly boats in the water to help the lighters. Lock the pressed men below and keep them there."

"I've done that already, sir. One tried to swim for it after you left this morning."

Gregory's eyebrows rose. "Oh?" he asked darkly.

"Yes, sir. I had him shot in the water."

"Good," he said, unquestioningly accepting the decision. "Mr. Pulham. I want you on shore coordinating. Mr. Schell, you'll stay aboard and make sure everything is stowed properly. I want this ship ready to sail at dawn. Now, if you please . . ."

It was pitch black in the orlop. No candles or lanterns were allowed until further notice. Every pressed man—and Marie and Hope—had been locked inside within five minutes of Joshua's death, there to sit and swelter and wait with only a minimum of food and water. Sometime after four bells on the noon watch, a flurry of activity that was to last until well after midnight started, after which an uneasy calm prevailed. At eight bells, or four in the morning, the *Sword of Cornwall* came to life again. The orlop prisoners waked and wondered as the capstan turned and the anchor hawser came in. Soon, from the pitch of the deck, they knew they were at sea. The stay at St. Kitts had been short indeed.

Captain James Gregory deemed the world, as transformed by ruby Burgundy, a most appealing place. He lowered the glass, sipped once and looked across the table to his subordinates. "A most excellent vintage, gentlemen."

Pulham concurred, raised his glass in salute. Schell followed suit. "That which is captured from Spaniards is sweeter," he noted with a lazy smile.

"But we're at peace with Spain," Pulham replied, his boyish face excited by the prospects of adventure. Schell smiled patronizingly. Pulham suddenly felt a distinct hollowness in the pit of his stomach. He prayed Gregory would never learn of his indiscretion.

Captain Gregory grinned most uncharacteristically. "I'm afraid, Lieutenant Schell, you will have to postpone your colleague's introduction to the dubious delights of the Caribbean."

"Sir?" Pulham paled noticeably.

Gregory rose and strolled to the large map on the wall. With the point of a dagger, he traced the *Sword of Cornwall*'s intended course, running straight through the West Indies, then turning north and heading through the Florida straits.

"But, Captain," Schell said, rising from the table in alarm. "Bonnet and Roberts were reported to be in the Caribbean. Thatch was heard to say he would sail for these waters."

Gregory faced him, eyes blazing with zealous ambi-

212

tion. "There are other pirates on the sea, Mr. Schell. One I most particularly want. Jason Brand."

Pulham looked confused. He'd heard of Brand, but not enough to explain the strange behavior of the captain. Schell knew more of Gregory's vendetta. "I don't understand, sir," he said. "Brand is in England."

"So we all thought," Gregory admitted. "But erroneously. He was a pirate before we caught him the first time, but confined himself to more local haunts. Now it appears he's gone further afield. You saw the damaged brig that limped into port this morning?" Both men nodded. The *Mary Anne.* Brand's work. He holed her and left her to sink, taking for ransom one Hosea Bellspin of Charleston in the Carolinas, for which he is no doubt headed." The tip of the dagger touched the Carolina coast and paused. "He sails a poor excuse for a pirate vessel, named the *Banshee.*"

"A colloquial name," interjected Pulham. "From folklore."

The Captain frowned, displeased with the interruption. "She's old and slow and Lord only knows how or where he found her." Striding back to the table, he unfolded a sketch of an old merchant ship, overhauled slightly, but obviously past her best years. "This is the *Banshee.* No doubt a poor likeness, but the best the *Mary Anne's* mate could do. He can't outrun us, and will probably have to put in to port two or three times before he gets to Charleston."

Schell grinned. "Then we hound the villain through the islands and up the coast, eh?"

"Precisely. As far as necessary. I will have this Brand, gentlemen, if it is the last thing I do. I will see him brought back to England and hanged."

"I shall miss the warm blue waters and the willing maids of Hispaniola," Schell observed, his mind basking in the glow of fond memories. "What say you, Mister Pulham?" He clapped the younger man's shoulder. Pulham's coughing spell was the lieutenant's only reply.

"You will have your fill of blue water and willing

maids, gentlemen, when I have my pirate. That I promise you. Are there any questions?"

"No, sir."

"Good. Then get this ship moving. I want every inch of sail she'll carry. Our course will be west northwest for the next day after we clear Tortola."

"Aye, sir."

"Now get out. Send in the boy to clear this mess, get the louts out of the orlop and to work. You have your orders."

Schell and Pulham hastened out and the cabin boy hurried in, gathered the dishes and cloth and tried to get out before the captain paid him any attention. He almost made it. "Fetch me the girl," Gregory snapped.

"Sir?" the youth asked, pausing in the doorway.

"The black-haired wench from the lower deck. You know the one."

"Yes, sir!" The youth hurried off, glad to be gone.

Gregory turned to the window. They had cleared the shallows, and their wake spun out behind like a maiden's tresses. Many men avowedly loved the sight, but Captain James Gregory was immune to the beauty, could see in that awesome distance only the end of a chase and the satisfaction of revenge. The door closed behind him. Had he not been alert, he would not have heard a sound. Turning, he touched the ridged scar tissue. Some nights, his cheek hurt so . . .

She wasn't broken yet. Her face, still haughtily beautiful, was only a bit weary about the eyes. She was an enchantress, right enough, even if bedraggled. "You sent for me?" she asked quietly.

Though Gregory smiled, his voice lacked any trace of mirth. "Time has robbed you of your timidity, which was one of your better qualities." The girl shrugged and watched him warily. "I hope I didn't summon you unduly from a warm bed," he added sarcastically, approaching her.

Marie recoiled inwardly as his hand reached out to stroke her hair. She felt the pressure of his left hand as it pressed against her stomach and then slid downward.

Her own fingers shot out to claw his face, but he shoved her away violently, slamming her against the bulkhead. "Not again, my pretty," he laughed. "A most unpleasant symmetry, by my oath, to have one cheek match the other."

Marie steadied herself. Gregory dusted one already spotless coatsleeve and followed the girl's line of vision to the pistols in the case on his desk. "They're loaded." Marie looked up guiltily. "But not primed. In any case, I doubt you'd get to them in time." He paused, strode to the desk, closed the walnut case and sat in his chair. "I have some news for you, if you're interested." Marie nodded shortly. "It seems an acquaintance of yours is in these waters, one whom we shall no doubt meet before long. You, of course, know him more intimately than I."

Marie watched him, tried to think. What could he be up to? Where were they going? Had he heard of Mystéré? But who was still there that she might know?

"You do, of course, remember one Jason Brand?"

Jason! Her heart leaped in her throat at the sound of his name. No! reason answered. He was a liar and a traitor. Had he not left her, she wouldn't be facing Gregory. He deserved nothing but hatred. Her predicament was his fault. His.

"Your brawny Scottish cocksman. I envy him. To have been the first to gain admittance . . . Ah, yes. A portal worth knocking on, eh? In truth, I feel a kinship for the rogue. We are bound in mutual bliss, along with so many others. I wonder what he would say to see you now?"

Nothing . . . Nothing.

"But perhaps that is a question soon to be answered. An interesting prospect, you must admit."

Marie lowered her head, let the long dark locks hide her face lest her tormenter see how his words had cut to the quick. Gregory poured a healthy measure of Burgundy and stared at her through the gaudy veil, then downed it with one swallow and poured another. "Get

215

out of here," he snapped, suddenly sick to heart of her. "Get out of my sight."

Quickly, before he should change his mind, Marie obeyed. Behind her, Gregory waited until the door closed, then slumped in the chair, tore off his wig and loosed his coat. He'd slept little and his mouth tasted foul. Damn Brand's soul anyway. The wench had given herself freely to him. Whatever pleasure he, Gregory, had taken by force could never compare to the heady enjoyment of her wanton, willing surrender. Was that why he hated Brand? Because the Scottish rogue had tasted a vintage forever denied Captain James Gregory? The answer was no more comforting than the question, for in reality it was no answer at all. Gregory hated Brand, and that was answer and reason enough.

Forlicar stared into the murky depths of the clay mug. "Chains! I can still smell them." He turned and spat onto the floor. "Pfah! That I, Forlicar, should sail on a slaver!"

Ramahd shrugged in reply. A smaller man, a Turk, he had the patience of the East. All things came to those who waited. All things. Even reason, from a captain whose motives were as inexplicable as the cursed proverbs. "Get used to it, my friend," he counseled. "Better now than at sea."

The Breton downed the remains of one mug and called for another. A stocky, hard-muscled five foot ten inches, his hair and beard were jet black shot through with silver. Newly put in during a drunken carouse the night before, a gold ring dangled from his left ear. If nothing else, the earring drew attention from the great marks the pox had left on his face.

Forlicar might have enjoyed Mobile under different circumstances. They'd left England twelve weeks ago, only two days after Jason had wandered into Portsmouth and found him and Rahmad in the Empress. The three of them rounded up five more, and in a bare dawn light, took over the old merchantman as it set to sea. If they'd been desperate before, there was no hope in England from

216

that moment on. Underhanded, on a tub long past her time to cross the Atlantic, they'd made the West Indies, but at terrible cost. One man was dead, another had a broken arm. All were exhausted.

The last three weeks had been doubly difficult, for low spirits followed high with distressing regularity. They'd found the *Mary Anne,* then lost her when Stillwell, the miserable excuse for a gunner, had holed her beyond repair. The venture wasn't a total loss, for they'd gained the twelve-pounders, plus the owner. Trying to reach north to the Carolina coast, they'd got lost in a heavy squall and found themselves in the bleak morning, committed to the windward passage. High spirits followed when it was discovered Bellspin, despite the fact he was an Englishman, had interests in Mobile, which they had a chance of making—with luck and more hard work. Two weeks later they had arrived, more dead than alive. Now, just as Forlicar had found his land legs and was getting used to the suffocating July heat, Brand, the damned fool, had gone off and bought a slave ship. Bitter gall spewed from the Frenchman. The stench left over from all those rotting bodies could kill a man. "Damn!" he swore aloud. "Why? Why, Goddammit? Why?"

"Because, Monsieur Powderflask," a voice answered, "she is, as every slaver must be, swift as the wind." A figure approached from the tavern's smoky depths and stopped to loom over the table. The boldness of his carriage added to the effect of rolling, trim muscles as Jason Brand lowered himself onto the bench. "The secret, my friends, is speed. Which this one has. We'll name her the *Banshee,* too, and without a cargo of wretches below decks, there'll be ample room for stores. We'll be able to go twice as long without putting into port, and with ten nine-pounders, she'll be able to hold her own in a fray."

Ramahd sat back and stroked his pointed goatee. Brand had done well. Six new nine-pounders. A three-for-one trade for the twelve pounders taken from the *Mary Anne* wasn't bad at all. Still, there were unanswered questions. "You have never told us how we are to pay for such a wondrous ship."

Jason laughed. "Why, John Law is helping us."

"John Law?" Forlicar hissed. "And who in the name of the living devil is John Law?"

"A Scottish gambler, an English outlaw and the head of the French Company here. He is powerful enough to have influenced the governor's appointment," Jason answered smoothly. "Mr. Law is a compatriot of mine and hates England's George as much as we do. As for how he's paid? I gave him the ransom money, plus the old *Banshee*. Mr. Law has advanced our provisions and allowed me one year to raise the second half of the price."

The Turk shrugged. He knew the Gulf and Caribbean well. A year would be very little time. "Which, of course, we won't."

"Which of course we *will*," came the emphatic reply. "And don't look so astonished. We need a friendly port in French America. Besides, Mr. Law introduced me to the governor, who has a sweet bonny lass of a daughter.

Forlicar snorted in disgust and downed a slug of gin and beer. "Chains," he muttered sourly. "The smell of chains sickens me."

"At least they are not your own chains, my friend. They would smell much worse, I promise."

A tambour and bells ended the conversation, and brought the whole tavern, to a hush. Men craned and jostled for a better look at what was to come. These were hard men with but a rare honest face among them. A weak one could not be found. The tavernkeepers of the burgeoning French port of Mobile were noted for their lack of curiosity about their patrons' backgrounds. As for the authorities, they held orders from Law and Governor Bienville to turn a blind eye to everything short of an outright riot, so long as the rogues confined their carousing to the waterfront area.

Jason glanced about. He'd fallen in with a brutal lot, and though he held himself above their station, there was no doubt his honor had already been besmirched

218

beyond hope of redemption. On the whole, he couldn't complain, even if there were moments in the past that he regretted. One above the rest perhaps—his sins were many, but only once had he betrayed a trust, and to one whom he owed much.

A cry of pleasure erupted from the rogues' den, and Jason drove the lingering guilt from his mind, construing it as a weakness he could ill afford. A bevy of mulatto and quadroon girls danced among the tables. Pawing hands reached out to stroke the nearest. One in particular, a lithe, dusky creature, avoided a dozen grasping fingers and leaped onto Jason's table. It was plain to all that the handsome golden-maned pirate had keyed her interest.

A pair of reedy flutes joined the assemblage of sounds that passed for music and the mulatto began to undulate wide, sensual, low-slung hips. Full rounded breasts strained the light fabric of a gypsy blouse, and her peasant skirt, slit to the waist, shifted from side to side as she strutted and posed. Her flesh gleamed coffee-colored beneath a sheen of sweat. Her head, a cap of dark, tightly coiled ringlets, was lightly oiled and glistened as well. The rhythmic din rose to a pitch and the close tavern reeked with musky intensity. The sensuality reached a climax with a crashing of drums, and the girls froze in an improvised tableau. For a second nothing happened. Then, with an electrifying war cry, one of the brigands sprang from a nearby table, caught the girl nearest him about the waist and carried her from the room. Immediately, everyone else tried to follow suit. Arguments and tempers flared as forty men vied for a half-dozen girls. Violence erupted, to the tavernkeeper's dismay, the villainous throng set about crashing tables, and battering one another with benches and chairs.

Jason shouted to his two companions to meet him at the ship, then grabbed the mulatto temptress by the hand, led her through a rear door and into a narrow alley, slammed the door closed and leaned against it. The noise of the riot quieted, but the girl at his side

219

continued to cling to his arm. The heat of her flesh in the comparatively cool alley was a searing reminder of the celibate weeks at sea. Not since . . .

Jason thrust his memory of Marie from his mind and brutally crushed the girl in his arms. She came to him eagerly, willingly, her lips moist and seeking, her breasts soft and yielding through the thin fabric. Suddenly, something or someone crashed into the door. They wouldn't be alone much longer. The girl caught Jason's hands and pressed them to her breasts.

"Earlier in my dreams, I chanted the words and saw us together. I would come with you, Jason Brand," she whispered huskily, "for the future, once seen, must be obeyed."

The world about him grew hazy and dull. As if placed under a spell, Jason faltered, his mind reeling before her beauty. He cared not how she came to know his name. Danger, aching desire and the heady, flattering eagerness of a woman so blatantly offering herself merged to become a powerful aphrodisiac that overrode all sense of caution. "So you shall, then," he promised as another body struck the other side of the door. "So you shall." Laughing, he caught her arm and together they ran for the harbor.

The captain's cabin was small but private. A cot along the transom lay half in, half out of shadows. All tangled in the rumpled bedclothes, Armide, as the girl had at last revealed her name, slept the sleep of the innocent. An illusory innocence, Jason thought, distracted from his maps and charts when the mulatto stirred. No woman that adept at drawing a man's fire could profess to innocence. A week had passed and she had proved to be an insatiable and demanding bedmate. "Just what I needed," he mumbled under his breath.

A soft rapping on the door diverted his attention once again. The door opened at Jason's permission and Ramahd entered. "Fresh meat and the last of the water is aboard, Jason." The Turk stood silently, his eyes focused behind Jason where he could glimpse the chocolate-brown thighs and faintly lighter-hued breasts of the woman on the cot. Armide was awake and, made mischievous by the man's scrutiny, nudged away the last of the covers and stretched languorously. Ramahd's eyes slitted and his breathing slowed as he stared at the dark, full nipples. If the woman belonged to any man other than Jason Brand . . .

"Is that all?" Jason asked, repeating himself.

Ramahd stirred as if awakening. "It is all we need. Wind, tide and current will do the rest, come morning. By the time the day is an hour old, we will be well out in the Gulf."

"Tell the men to be ready then," Jason ordered gruffly in dismissal.

Ramahd's eyes flitted once, briefly, to the woman, then back to meet his captain's. Any other man's, he thought. But not this man's. Slowly, his head dipped a quarter of an inch and he turned and left the room.

Jason angrily spun around and glared at the woman. Her nakedness explained the Turk's behavior. Ducking under the low beams, he crossed the cabin. "You are not to do that again, Armide."

The mulatto pouted playfully, tugged open Jason's dressing robe and sighed with pleasure at the corded musculature of his thighs and the soft, golden curls. One lazy hand reached out to tease that which had so delighted her only hours ago. "Armide does what she pleases," she said in a silken whisper. "And she does please you, no?"

Jason's hips tensed as she brought her lips to his manhood, lingered there until heated interest was assured. Dusky arms reached up to stroke his back and help slide his robe off and to the floor. Jason smiled as he caught her wrists and forced Armide back against the pillow. His mouth covered hers, then seared her neck and breasts, eliciting a throaty laugh. Hungrily, she accepted his pulsing length, sheathed to the hilt between her thighs. The powerful, rhythmic coupling increased in intensity, reaching and demanding climax.

Without warning, Jason withdrew and his weight

sagged against her. Armide fought to free her arms but his grip tightened until she cried out in pain. "No!" she rasped, unable to reach the peak of ecstasy without his efforts. "No." Yet he held back. "Please, no stop . . . *mon amour* . . ."

"You will do as I please. As I tell you, from now own," Jason growled, managing to restrain his own passion. "Say it."

Armide tried to refuse his mastery, yet her own overweening hunger would not be denied. She hovered on the brink of release, yet its refusal brought nothing but more pain. Confused, she tried to think, but thought was deranged until more animal needs should be fulfilled. She had spied this outlaw among the denizens of the Broken Spar, gone to the trouble of learning his name, danced for him and chosen him for her paramour. Now she was trapped in a web of her own devising. Her guile was two-edged, and had made her captive to the fierce rogue's whims.

"As you please," she whispered finally in surrender. "Armide will do as *you* please."

Jason grinned victoriously and abandoned all restraint. Letting go her wrists, he eased his weight from her. Armide moaned in relief as he entered and his sweet length plunged to her very center. Now both were lost to the inner torment of the dance. Man and woman . . . immutable demand and release. A cry now . . . and another. At last the feverish melding subsided into grateful satiation, and their turbulent natures, by passion tamed, drifted into loveless sleep.

Chapter XI

The salt sea song of wind in sails. Rigging humming. The sound rose to a whining pitch as the *Sword of Cornwall* crested watery slopes all gray-green and turbulent. A search for the will-o'-the-wisp, elusive Jason Brand, was under way. West northwest, they sailed, with the wind on their starboard beam. Distant islands were lost in the passing stream as nights slipped into days, inexorably multiplied into weeks. Always they steered to the north, keeping the wind from the Atlantic on their right, trying to outrace the *Banshee* to Charleston. Turk's Island, the Caicos, Mayaguana, Long Island and Deadman's Cay; Great Exuma, Cat Island and finally Nassau itself. No man had seen or heard of the *Banshee*; no word of the pirate Jason Brand preceded them.

Each day that passed saw Gregory's fury grow. Impatient to begin with, he paced the quarterdeck while the crew crowded on all the canvas the masts would hold. Finally, the last of the Bahamas behind them, he retired to the great cabin, emerging only once each morning to check the log. Their next port would be Charleston. No one aboard cared to anticipate the captain's wrath if his quarry wasn't found there, for Brand had become an obsession that filled his days and nights with bloody and frustrating dreams of vengeance.

As predicted, Pulham's fear of Gregory was more potent than his desire for Marie, and he pointedly ignored her. She had chosen the wrong man to help her escape. Time blended into maddening tedium. August had come, and though the sea breeze was cool, the orlop was denied the fresh and sweet air. As the long weeks wore on, accidents and sickness reduced those in the orlop to less than fifty. The living functioned as if in a trance, eating, sleeping and rising to repeat the tasks of the day before, all the while becoming more and more surly and uncommunicative. Hostility was kept in check solely through the threat of punishment—either the cat or a caning followed by a week on bread and water. The mood in the orlop was one of barely suppressed violence, waiting only for the one indignity that would release it with an explosion of uncontrollable rage. Marie labored in the galley and helped Giuseppe when the need arose. The rest of the time, she avoided unnecessary contact with the men and went her own way in peace.

Charleston helped in some measure. With the *Sword of Cornwall* at anchor, the men were finally given a rest, and though not allowed ashore, they were permitted to lounge in the sun and sleep, as well as share in the fresh meat and vegetables and fruits brought aboard. Marie managed to spend most of each day on deck, and her glimpses of the Colonies left her much impressed. The air was alive with the cries of gulls and the land was pregnant with a whispered promise of freedom. If only she could escape here, she thought wistfully. It didn't matter that the Colonies were wild and untamed. Given a ghost of a chance, she would gladly brave the thousand dangers beyond those shores, where, it was said, the forests went on for a thousand or more miles. The unknown was better by far than the grim reality of life aboard an English vessel. As the hours passed, the dream grew, and more and more she found herself resolving to gain her long-denied freedom.

They had been in port but three days when the idyll came to an abrupt end. Captain Gregory suddenly arrived, and with him returned the tension that had been dissipating slowly. By the next bell everyone aboard had learned the unpleasant truth: Brand had never come to Charleston and probably never would. The chase had been for nought. The *Banshee* had eluded capture. How, no one knew. Shaken out of their lethargy, the marines swept the grog shops, taverns and bawdy houses to collect a grumbling, still drunk and tattered crew. By morning the muster was complete. By the next, the fresh-water casks were full and the ship ready for sea. The moment wind and tide allowed, the *Sword of Cornwall* headed south again for the Caribbean, the wind now on her larboard beam.

If the trip north had been difficult, the return was a nightmare. Angry at being deluded, embarrassed by failure, tortured by the thought of laughter behind his back, James Gregory became a raving tyrant impossible to please or appease. Conditions on board worsened until the marines were standing armed guard around the clock lest the angry men take matters into their own hands. Worst off were the pressed seamen, for Gregory had decided that they secretly applauded the escaped pirate and held their captain to constant and irreverent ridicule. As a result, they were forced to work harder and harder at more onerous and dangerous tasks. At night, for their efforts, those off watch were thrown into the orlop and locked in, with reduced rations of little more than a bowl of watery burgoo—minced saltpork and biscuit crumbs—for their supper.

On one such summer night, steeped in misery, the men took to their pallets or hammocks and lay in dispirited silence. Marie sat with her back against an empty barrel, dreamed of escaping and listened to the hypnotic slapping of the waves against the hull. From time to time she glanced toward the curtain of blankets and wished Hope would hurry and finish. Finally, a bawdy laugh followed by a voluble masculine sigh issued from the enclosure. Marie knew she should be appalled at Hope's conduct, but the woman loved a healthy tumble, made no excuses for her actions and saw herself honestly. Beneath the harlot's tawdry exterior there beat a heart, not of gold, but warm, human, caring.

Full of the devil's mischief, Hope's laughter seemed to linger futilely on air heavy with dejection and weariness. The emotions were so palpable Marie struggled for breath and strove to rid her soul of the awful weight. She closed her eyes and let fragments of memory slip into place. Uneven recollections merged into a single, pleasant whole to replace the grim reality in which her daily life was steeped.

Father. She saw his face. A man of authority, of clear conscience that lent a special nobility to his features.

Mother. What had mother been like? "How do you describe a sunrise?" her father had asked. "You cannot do it justice. Your mother . . . was a sunrise. Do you understand?"

The dream daughter nodded. She didn't understand. Not really. But she didn't want to hurt her father's feelings.

Images dimmed, faded. Now a sound stole into the background, swelled to displace the shipboard noises. *What is that, father? What do you sing?*

"A song, daughter. One your mother sang, long ago." *Teach it to me.*

A gentle, lilting, melancholy tune filled her then, brought the peace of memory, of contact with a mother she had never known. There were no words to be sung, only a melody played upon the heartstrings, a thousand different meanings to a thousand listening souls. Unaware, the sound became real and the sweetly intimate notes spilled from her throat. Disgruntled conversation died. Visions of other times, better times, filled the dank and fetid depths of their prison. Now remembered by each man were the days when their lives were tinged with innocence and purity, and they had been worthy of love glimpsed and touched and lost. Now recalled were sweet hours when walls were not so close, nor lives so desperate. Echoes of untold dreams permeated the stagnant air. And when that voice ceased, silence remained, communion reigned, evident in the rugged faces, softened and at rest, puzzled by their new-born tenderness for the girl who had sung.

Ned Sly was the first to reject the transformation from hostility to camaraderie. A scowl rapidly replaced the look of peacefulness even his face had held. The others were more reluctant to forsake the tender moment that had offset the brutal passage of their days. Ben Tremain, the oldest of the lot, crawled sheepishly

226

from Hope's blanketed enclosure. It had been he who had sighed in pleasure only moments ago. "And what tune will you sing us, old man?" one of the crewmen asked with a laugh.

"A dismal ditty, no doubt," Gunn answered, amused himself, "for a gallows bird knows no other."

Ben attempted a look of indifference, but a blush seeped across his face and much of his bald head. "It's no different than the one I'd hear from the likes of a lug like yourself," he huffed as laughter and good-natured derision followed him to his pallet.

Tom Gunn ducked across the room and squatted before Marie. "Then it's up to you, mistress, for we've nary a minstrel among us."

Marie hesitated. "I . . . don't know," she stammered. The dream had been so real.

"Come, girl. We'd hear a tune from ye," said Ned's cohort Poole in a surprisingly mellow tone. A dozen soft ayes from the shadows agreed.

The blankets were shoved aside and Hope Deferred made a grand entrance with a clay jug of rum in each hand. "It took two months to find where Hogarth hid these. We're far from taverns and merrymaking, but there's enough for all if each takes short swallows and makes careful not to call Gregory's officers down on us with brawling." She paused to search the dimly lit room, singled out Poole with a fixed stare. "And I trust there's none among you will cause me to waste another pot of good English rum."

Poole shifted in discomfort. His right hand stole up to massage his left shoulder. The pain had vanished long ago, but the memory lingered.

Hope's gifts were greeted with a chorus of muffled but enthusiastic cheers. Men crowded around to receive their portion of spirits, watched over by the beady-eyed harlot who made sure no one took more than his allotted share. As the bottles emptied, the harlot began to sing a bawdy, mischievous tune, and when the last drop disappeared—down her own gullet—she set the jug in the middle of the floor and started dancing around it.

227

Most everyone followed suit, and though the men were forced to bend over to avoid the low-slung beams, they were warmed by the rum and made a mellow crew.

A slight lad, no more than seventeen, shyly approached Marie. His freckled face reddened beneath a shock of once sandy-colored hair bleached white by the sun. "Would you take to the floor with me, miss?"

Marie looked at him a long moment. The lad had been one to keep to the background, do his work and stay out of the way of others. So much so, she couldn't remember his name. When she didn't answer, he lowered his head and coughed nervously. "My name is Shelby. I wouldn't want to bother you none, but if you would—"

"I would be proud to dance with you, Shelby," Marie interrupted with a warm smile. And so she did. It didn't matter she didn't know the steps, for neither did he. Nor any man, for that manner, and so they proceeded with clumsy, improvised but jaunty steps set to country tunes they could all remember from such childhood as had been theirs. After Shelby, she danced with Tom Gunn, who crouched awkwardly and kicked his legs in grand if undescribable patterns. And then with others, most of whom she knew little, for they were a closemouthed lot not caring to reveal too much of themselves to any man or woman. Yet it hardly mattered. This new-found effusion of warmth was acquaintanceship enough, for it defied their common hardship and cemented them in comradeship.

The clay jugs had run dry long before, but the sailors' enthusiasm continued and they danced like boys inebriated by their own togetherness. It was a festival for the mad and the doomed, without ale or musical instruments or freedom. Here was the timeless release of the unvanquished spirit, that in the end left them limp, exhausted and laughing in the morning's wee hours.

Hawks of the night, wings billowing silver against the starlight. Jason paced the narrow quarterdeck, eyes

228

checking the line of the sails, ears keen to the whisper of the rigging. Ahead, a Spanish trader plunged obstinately forward, determined that the *Banshee* should work for her capture, though barring a sudden storm the outcome seemed inevitable. Come morning, the pirate ship would reach the Spaniard with cannon and grappling hook.

"Steady as you go," Jason called to the helmsman. "We're close enough to keep them awake. You men on the starboard watch get some rest."

Figures flopped down on the deck where they stood. Morning would come soon enough. Jason returned to his thoughts. Gloomy thoughts they were, too. Here he strode a fine quick ship. A sweet wench waited for him below. He was as free as the wind and the stars.

Free. Aye. Because of another. There was the rub, for he couldn't abide the thought of being in that kind of debt. Money was one thing, but a man's life? And owed to a woman? But why think of her now?

The sea slapped the hull in reply. The black sea. Black as her hair. Curse it all! Why couldn't he drive her from his mind? The world and everything in it existed to be used. That was the nature of life, as the tyrants had so aptly taught him. What was in a man's heart had nothing to do with anything.

And yet, if he believed that, why the soul-wearying feelings of responsibility and guilt? Buccaneer, heartless cutthroat and rogue. That's what he had to be if he wanted to survive. Conscience and love must be driven away. The past was past and there was no going back. Not now, not ever.

But, oh, the bitter blackness of the waves. And how he burned with the image they evoked. Thinking and pacing, he walked the night through. Only when dawn brightened the eastern sky did he find relief, and that in action.

A half-mile. The *Banshee* literally sailed circles around the wallowing galleon, peppering away at the rigging and any man who so much as showed his face.

However foolish the *Escobar*'s captain, he did not lack for bravery. Throughout the duel he refused to strike his colors, knowing the pirates would not sink her, for they would then lose the booty they sought. He, too, waited for morning and the moment of boarding, when the galleon's more numerous crew would have the advantage. It didn't work out quite that way. Before dawn, the *Banshee* slipped in close enough to let loose broadside after broadside, raking the decks, putting the *Escobar*'s few cannons out of commission and dealing death and carnage to the terror-stricken Spaniards.

The moment of truth came as the sun rose. The *Banshee* closed in from the east, the sun behind her, and a host of howling brigands swarmed over the side. It was pistol, pike and cutlass, fist, dagger and even feet. The Spanish, not nearly so overwhelming in numbers now and demoralized as well, fell back against the onslaught. A pair of Spanish marines cornered Jason near the poop deck ladder. The pirate lost his pistol parrying a vicious sword swipe, ducked under another and simultaneously ran his cutlass through the man on his right. The marine to the left, shaken by his comrade's death, lunged awkwardly and Jason dispatched him as well, then looked around to see where he was most needed.

Forlicar and the men under his command had forced the surrender of most of the Spaniards around the foremast. The last pocket of resistance centered about the quarterdeck, where the Spanish captain discharged a brace of pistols into the melee and drew his rapier. Jason bounded up the short ladder to meet his counterpart, but there was no need. A glittering flash of metal arced suddenly down from the shrouds, and a Sicilian dagger buried itself to the hilt just above the medals that dangled so vainly from the silken coat. As the captain collapsed by the wheel, the remainder of his crew threw down their weapons. Ramahd leaped to the deck and retrieved his dagger. At the same moment Jason leaped onto the wheel housing and held aloft the *Escobar*'s colors. A triumphant cry rose from the pirates: the galleon was theirs.

Alone with wind and sea, Jason stood gazing down at the wake of the *Banshee*. As he watched, the faint glow in the east expanded and the dim, twinkling phosphorescent path aft dimmed. The sun would rise soon. There would be work to do, decisions to be made.

The raid on the *Escobar* had not been an unmitigated success. True, they had come away with enough Spanish gold to pay Law that which was owed, plus enough to give each man a share. True, they had totally replenished their stores: for the first time they had powder and shot to spare. True, they had loaded a small cask of jewels from the commander's cabin, plus other sundries. True, true, true. But they didn't have the ship itself, the most valuable prize of all.

No one could really be faulted. By the time they'd reduced the crew above decks, the fire started by the ball that had found its way to the galley stove—which any damned fool in his right mind would have extinguished, knowing battle was imminent—was out of hand. There'd been little enough time to get off the silver and gold, not to speak of themselves. Jason sighed. Two men lost. Another dozen with wounds which would take time to heal. Still, they'd been lucky. The mostly green crew he'd picked up in Mobile had done remarkably well. He pounded the rail futilely. All the rationalization in the world wouldn't take away the sting of having lost the ship. But enough. There was no sense reliving the anguish of watching the flaming galleon, her sailors frantically diving into the water and swimming for the few boats they'd managed to lower, slowly settle in the watery depths.

A banging on the deck under his feet drew him from the dreams that would plague him for as long as he remembered the *Escobar*. The dull knock was repeated, and Jason remembered with a start: he and Forlicar and Ramahd were supposed to meet at sunrise. Shaking off despondency and fatigue, he turned and dropped down to the quarterdeck and entered his own quarters.

Ramahd had the charts out, and Forlicar stood to one side, pulling at the ring in his ear, turning it slowly

231

in the still-inflamed hole. He trusted Jason's judgment on most matters and, once used to the slaver, had openly agreed the sloop's build and speed were an invaluable asset. Of course, if they'd taken the galleon . . . He stopped as the door opened and Jason entered. Like everyone, the taller man was stooped and haggard from lack of sleep, and no doubt still damning the *Escobar*'s demise.

Ramahd started the conversation, pointing to the charts. They'd sailed southwest by south as the *Escobar* sank. A divider touched a spot a hundred leagues from the northernmost coast of Colombia. "We are here," he said softly. "More or less. If anyone finds them, they'll look south and west of here." A sly grin narrowed his lips. "Which will make Señor Murcia very curious. Why, he will wonder, did we sail directly toward him?"

Forlicar looked on. Their destination mattered little to him as long as it was somewhere he could wench and carouse at leisure. Every so often he cast a slitted eye to the curtain behind which Armide slept. She was a choice bit of dusky flesh, right enough. Only two days ago she'd stuck out her tongue at him and meaningfully wiggled her full, dark breasts in his direction. He, Forlicar, had been honorable and not even thought about fighting Jason for the woman, but if they didn't reach a port soon . . . Reluctantly, he turned back to the chart.

Jason, new to the Caribbean, relied on Ramahd's knowledge in all matters of navigation. They had talked the night before and decided they needed a haven, a refuge from Murcia's vengeance, for there was no doubt the Spaniard would be infuriated by the loss of one of his ships to an English pirate. Ramahd's long, tapered fingers tapped lightly on the chart to indicate Barranquilla, where the malevolent don, a tyrant virtually unopposed in this corner of the world, held court. "So now it is time to turn back north, my friends. We have come too close for comfort as it is. Here, I think, Jason, is the place we should go."

"There is nothing on the chart," Jason said.

"No matter. There are islands there, I know. One in particular, with a harbor. I do not think they will look for us there."

Jason exchanged glances with Forlicar. Neither wanted to accuse Ramahd, but the lack of a mark on the chart was disquieting. "It is a long way to go for an unmarked island, Ramahd," Jason observed tactfully. "Are you sure?"

"I was pressed aboard one of Murcia's ships six years ago. We raided there. Burned a stronghold."

"Murcia?" Forlicar asked. "You were with Murcia?"

"I have been many things to many people, my friend. It was serve with the butcher or be flayed alive and thrown to the sharks. We took many prisoners, but were wrecked on the return to Barranquilla. I was one of the lucky ones rescued by an English merchantman. Thus I came to your country."

"Not my country," Jason scowled. He turned back to the chart. "This island, then. You can bring us to it?"

"Yes. There will be food and water. And who knows. Five years is a long time. Maybe even women, for Forlicar." He laughed, a shrill, unfamiliar sound, unusual from one so implacably dour.

Forlicar grinned uncertainly. Anywhere with women was fine with him. Anywhere at all.

They had been to sea, by any meaningful reckoning, for over four months. There had been stops, of course, but none to give the men any real rest. Not since St. Kitts, some ten weeks past, had they taken on provisions other than fresh foods, which had disappeared rapidly. Of water they had plenty, for they had replenished the casks in both Nassau and in Charleston. Still, the ship rode higher than when she left England, and though the men had been honed to razor sharpness by weeks of drill, their efficiency was hindered to a greater degree by overwork and abuse. Thus impaired, they met the morning of the second Thursday in September.

Lieutenant Schell, with his weather eye and a hint from the mate, was the first to foretell the storm. The

233

glass had been inching down since he'd checked at the beginning of the middle watch, at midnight the night before. Now the sky took on a sickly greenish-gray hue and the water appeared oily. The wind veered to come out of the south with a rush and they were in the middle of a squall, the first of the hurricane's progeny, slung out along with others to the east and west. Torrential rains followed for a half-hour, leaving men and lines soaked. The men didn't matter so much, but the lines would be more difficult to handle.

By four bells on the noon watch, or two o'clock, the hurricane held them in its grip and an unnatural twilight—it lacked a good seven hours until sunset—fell over the raging sea. The *Sword of Cornwall* reared and bucked in the terrible chop created by long swells from the Atlantic mixing with the northward flow of water pushed by the hurricane. The wind howled through the masts and rigging. Without warning, the foresail let go in a great rending explosion that pulled all eyes upward in spite of the bulletlike salt spray. Hurricane or no, four men had to be sent up the wildly swaying masts to cut away the wreckage before the flailing halyards caused more damage.

The waves rose higher and higher, and the ship was hard put to keep her bows to them until a sea anchor was put out. Then she rode, rising up the terrible windswept walls of the waves and crashing down into the ever-deepening troughs. Green and white water pounded the hull, broke over the bow and railings and swept across the deck, threatening to tear men from their tenuous holds on the lines and carry them into the unforgiving maelstrom and watery graves.

Into the teeth of death, into the very heart of the tempest—there was no outrunning the hurricane now—they sailed. If it could be called sailing. By now the jib had been torn away and the storm-tossed ship—no more powerful or impressive than the tiny blocks Marie had moved around on Behan's map—was left to fend, with only her rigging and the sea anchor to keeping her from falling broadside to the mountainous waves and floundering. Night and day no longer existed. Only the slashing green darkness, the continuously groaning and screaming wind, the stiff, mechanical movements of men battered by the elements and their own deepening despair.

Below decks was a hellhole. Helpless should they capsize, those not fortunate enough to be occupied with the pumps held on to beams and stanchions, trying their best not to be defeated by the fear that clutched at their guts and sent silent screams surging to their throats. Giuseppe had moved aft and set up on the gun deck, there to ply his gruesome trade. With the women's help, he had sawed off a man's shattered arm. The procedure went for nothing, for the crewman died, his screams lost in the thunder of waves and loose gear rolling about and crashing into bulkheads. Marie was glad the poor soul's suffering had come to an end. But he had died, as would they all, for what? The white faces in the gloom had decided already: for Gregory's chase of Brand.

Rinsing the horrid crimson from her hands, Marie fell and slid across the deck as the ship lurched violently. Wide-eyed, she stared at the gun carriage she'd fallen against. If it broke loose, all two tons would roll over and crush her, then go on to tear apart the ship from the inside out. She could see the lines, tight as a bowstring, tight to the point of snapping. Why they didn't part was a miracle that could hardly be believed. The *Sword of Cornwall* hesitated on the top of a wave, started the long slide into the valley below. Marie slid across the deck, now on her belly, now rolling onto her back to fetch up against the mainmast housing. Desperately she tried to rise, but strength, breath and hope failed and she could only wedge herself between two beams so she would not be thrown about. The unbearable dejection of the men—beaten men—and her own gloomy prospects filled her with desperation.

How much longer? I'll never be free. But I must. Help me! Is there no one? Jason? No! Father, help! I am alone.

Suddenly all was quiet, or relatively so. The waves

235

still tried to tear apart the frail wooden vessel, but the wind was quiet, no longer howling through the rigging. An unnatural hush fell on the ship, followed by a cry from the main deck. "The eye. We're in the eye!" Gregory's voice sounded then, wild as the waves. "Clear this mess away! We've but a moment!"

Footsteps pounded above her head. Marie, more in a dream than waking, listened without comprehension as the more level-headed rushed about and frantically did what little could be done against the coming onslaught. And then it was upon them again and the *Sword of Cornwall* reeled with the mighty blow of wind. Reeled and shuddered and found her head. Once again the hurricane played its deadly tune in the rigging, set wood and line shrieking and groaning in concert with the devil himself.

Hear the mad laughter! How the wind shrieks! Yes, like the Sirens, calling them all to doom. We have you now. We have you and will keep you! Marie closed her eyes and tried to pray, but no words would come. Instead, a malevolent, sylphlike figure loomed above her. The apparition's hair streamed out like sodden whips flailing the sulphurous air. Ever closer it leaned, with tapered fingers like serpentine waves undulating before her eyes, threatening to pull her into its horrible grasp. The Siren's song was a wailing shriek of glee and triumph. "I have you now," the apparition said. "You are mine!"

Darkness. Awake, finally. A cool cloth was pressed to her face.

"Hope?"

"Yes, Tulip. Giuseppe and me carried you to your pallet. Everything's all right."

The ship no longer bucked about like a mad thing, rather rose and fell easily, as though under sail. "The storm?"

"Passed. You frightened me more than the wind. Here. Drink some water."

Her lips were parched and she spilled the first drops, then swallowed gratefully. "Hope . . ."

236

"Yes."

"I'm going to escape. We all are."

"Yes, dear."

"You don't believe me, but we are. I swear it." She leaned back against the sack of flour. "We are."

Chapter XII

Anguilla, set at the northeast corner of the Leeward Islands, was their first landfall. The low island, sixteen miles long and two across, lay like a green haven in the crystal blue waters. The *Sword of Cornwall* limped in from the Atlantic, borne on the crutches of the mercifully subdued trade winds.

Harbor. A place of rest for the worn and frazzled crew. A place to patch the storm-battered hull, calk the seams and attend to the myriad tasks of repair. Just to be on deck was a blessing beyond Marie's fondest hopes. Gradually, she lost the pallor of the orlop. Color came back to her cheeks, put there by sun and the sea breeze scented with the perfume of exotic blossoms. As on St. Kitts months earlier, thought strayed to home and Mysteré, the very thought of which gave her courage. As the days went by, courage grew and, fed by the hours of quiet and contemplation, a plan of escape slowly evolved, unsummoned at first, then as an exercise, until it was full-blown and waited only for the proper moment.

With the plan came a necessary time of introspection. Was she capable? Would the men go along with her? Sheltered for the first seventeen years of her life, Marie had spent the past five years a servant or prisoner. What experience had she that led her to believe she could lead men? Would the well-remembered words of Behan be enough? It didn't really matter, when all was said and done. The choice was simple: either remain Gregory's slave, or not. If she failed, it didn't matter anymore, for at least she would be free.

Wistfully, she looked back. How simple her life had been, in retrospect. All that would have to change. Grim-faced, she sought for and reconstructed the times in her life when she was forced to summon unusual strength, intelligence and courage. True, there had been no terrible trials as a child. But daring and impetuous ways had been hers. She had lived through the ordeal of Murcia's vengeance. She had learned the art of subterfuge from Lord Penscott and survived even Gregory's cruel abuse. She'd effected the release of Jason. She had held her own against the rapacious crew of the orlop. The truth was, she could do everything necessary—if the need was great enough and she was determined.

As September eased into October, the time came. Lieutenant Pulham and half of the marines had gone ashore to bring back the newly filled casks of fresh water and the starboard watch, on their last foray before sailing from Anguilla. Lieutenant Schell had the deck watch and was making the rounds of the ship to see to the completion of any last minute tasks before the *Sword of Cornwall* sailed on the morrow. Captain Gregory had retired to his cabin to dine as he always did at noon. Fully half the impressed seamen were on deck, the others at rest below.

Marie was helping in the galley, where Nohl, as usual, was in a hurry to finish and get to his hammock. When Marie volunteered to retrieve the captain's tray from his cabin, the cook accepted without hesitation. Heart pounding, she strolled from the galley to the main deck and crossed to the great cabin. Inside, she paused, took a deep breath. *This is it. If I falter, or fail . . .*

No. She would not think of failure. Desperation would lead the way. All she needed was five seconds at his pistols. Just five seconds to cock and prime them. A tiny five seconds. She touched her hair, fluffed it slightly. *Don't overdo it. He'll be suspicious.* Quickly, she tore a hole in her blouse with the dagger, then replaced the blade in the back of her shirt where it could be gotten in a hurry. The tear shouldn't be too large, she thought, tugging at the light material. Just enough for him to catch a glimpse and take the bait. A toss of her head, and she was ready, strode forward, knocked and entered.

"Get it out and leave me—" Gregory looked up in surprise. Clad in breeches and shirt, he had taken off his wig and was lying on the cot. The wide desk where the empty dishes lay was cluttered with charts. The pistol case lay next to a bottle of wine in the corner closest to the bed and furthest from the tray. Marie tried not to look at them. Gregory sat up on the edge of the cot. "What the hell are you—" He paused, noting the girl's slumped shoulders, her downcast face, the long hair spilling forward to hide her breasts. His scowl freshened into a satisfied smile: perhaps he'd won at last, by God, succeeded in humbling her proud and obstinate spirit. For the space of a few seconds he found himself gloating, but the sensation passed rapidly. Now that he had won, he had no further use for her. "Take the tray and get out."

Marie tossed her head, sending the midnight tresses flying to reveal the torn blouse and glimpses of her breast. "Let me stay." A mask of despair distorted her features into a thousand anguished pleas.

"Why?" Gregory toyed, momentarily interested by this unexpected turn of events.

"I don't want to go back. Not down there." Overcome with emotion, she lowered her head. "Please keep me here."

"But you detest me," Gregory protested, feigning hurt.

"No," came the hurried reply. "I do not . . . detest you."

Gregory laughed cruelly. "Look at you!" he snapped. "What should I expect from a whore to fifty men? Diseased, full of the pox and God knows what. Do you really think I'd stoop to . . ."

He paused, slowly came to his feet at the sight of the dagger gleaming in Marie's hand. "What the hell! How'd you—"

"They have not touched me," came the quiet reply. "You were the last one . . . for me." Without waiting for reply, she tossed the dagger onto the desk. "Let me stay with you. I will do anything."

240

Gregory scowled, chewed his lip. Here was a totally unexpected turn. But could he believe her? Was it possible that she had escaped contact with the filthy whoresons? Once again her eyes rose and he delved into them. A man might fall into those eyes, would she but let him. And if not? There was uncommon strength in this woman. Enough to match her beauty. If he could tame her, she might be worth the scar he bore. Marie Ravenne taken against her will had been an enraged tigress. What would she be like if she came to him willingly? He had wondered before, but without hope of ever being granted that favor. Now it appeared as if she was willing. His breath quickened and he became aware of a dull ache in his loins. "Prove it," he commanded huskily.

Marie's fingers slowly slid to the fastening of her skirt, unbuttoned it and let the material drop about her ankles. Gregory's eyebrows rose in appreciation of the long, tapered legs flowing up to the tight V of her thighs. His gaze ranged down her flat stomach, lingered on the soft nest of provocation. *Five steps around the table. If he'll only stay there.* Stepping lightly, she walked out of the bunched skirt.

Gregory's eyes were narrow with appraisal. He stepped away from the bed, reached her before she got to the end of the table. The girl stopped, and he could not tell if she was being bashful or cringing from him. One hand reached up to move her hair to one side and touch her breast. She shivered slightly as his fingers went to the tie on her blouse.

Panic-stricken, Marie felt the tug on the string holding her blouse shut. She had to get him to the bed, get him to lower his breeches and give her a chance to get to the pistols. They were plainly visible from the corner of her eye. He kept them loaded, she knew, and the powder flask stood next to them. Priming would be a matter of two seconds. Suddenly she realized her breasts were free. His hands cupped her, gently kneaded the soft flesh. Revolted, she fought to remain calm, to smile shyly, and reach for his shirt . . .

A perfect solution, Gregory thought fuzzily. If her

tale was true—and he would check it out for a surety—perhaps this would be a better solution. After all, a man at sea did need a woman from time to time. The hell with Brand. He'd be caught sooner or later in any case. There was something about the way it felt when a beautiful woman pulled out a man's shirt. The fabric tugged just so, arousing him to greater heights. Of one thing he was sure. She was ready for him, by God, wanted him.

At last he was backing toward the bed. *A little closer* . . . Marie tugged insistently, she hoped, at his belt, made her hand touch the bulging shaft so badly concealed beneath the constraint of breeches. His hands were busy removing his shirt. The time would be perfect. Boldly she tugged at his breeches, trying to pull them down and so trap him.

Gregory dropped the shirt, felt himself falling backwards onto the cot. Flailing, his right arm caught her wrist and pulled her with him. For a brief second he thought she hesitated, but the moment passed and she fell on him, her breasts nearly smothering him. One arm locked around her waist, the other helped rid him of the damned breeches, and he groaned as the quivering organ met her thigh, laid along the warm flesh . . .

No! What had happened? *No!* She'd been so close to success, and was now being mauled and grappled. Obscene kisses covered her breasts and his hand caught the flesh between her legs. *This is not real—not happening. It can't be.* And yet she could not stop now, could not give up before the whole horrible game had been played out, before she had, perhaps, another chance.

A game then. *Yes, call it that.* A ruse. A child's pretense. There. The laugh, bright and lusty. *I have learned to dissimulate well, have I not, Lord Penscott?*

Her body, once a treasured loveskeep, had become a weapon as effective as any blade or courtly contrivance designed to befog the opposition. Moaning now, she moved against him, feigning ecstasy and accepting his length. A simple plan whose price, so easily considered, paled before degrading reality! Would she be free then? He shuddered, nearing climax. *Yes!* Steeling herself to

242

continue the sham, she moved beneath him, trying to match his hurried mating. A cry of pleasure. His fingers dug into the creamy texture of her shoulders. Then a long, quivering sigh as his fluids unleashed.

Marie turned aside, grateful he could not see her face. Repulsed by success, she blinked back tears for a certain innocence forever lost. The world seemed horribly predatory in that moment, an awful place in which to dwell. And yet, there could be no stopping so short of the goal.

She forced her expression into a mask of further hunger and began to coax him further. A slow, lazy smile drifted over Gregory's face as he sank back, relaxed and spent. For a second his eyes closed, but they snapped open again. "Why? Why only now, not before?"

Marie glanced down shyly, stroked the softened flesh. "The last time . . ." she said haltingly, almost whispering, "you frightened me. Hurt me." She looked into his eyes. "Do you understand?" she asked.

Gregory chuckled, pleased with himself. "Hurt you, eh?" The memory of the gash on his cheek returned and the look in his eye hardened. "As I remember, you deserved to be hurt the last time. But see here. I'm not an ogre, you know." The soft flesh moved beneath her fingers and he laughed. "As you will see in a few minutes." His hand moved to touch the tip of her breast. "When I am rested a little."

Marie caught his hand, brought it to her mouth and nibbled on his knuckles. "Perhaps you would recover faster with a little wine."

The same laugh, denoting overweening pride. "Can't wait, eh? Very well. And bring a glass for yourself as well."

Heart pounding, Marie kissed the outstretched fingers once again and climbed slowly out of bed. This was the moment for which she had waited. But he must see no haste, must not suspect. The wine bottle sat next to the dueling pistols, gleaming in the box. She glanced back, blew a kiss. Gregory wasn't even looking, was lying flat on his back, hands behind his head and staring at the ceiling overhead. The impulse was to grab the pistol, but caution kept her movements soft and fluid. Left hand clinked glass to glass and right hand nudged the stopper from the powder flask, propped up one of the pistols against the edge of the box while she poured a glass of wine with her left hand. Only now, with everything ready, could she take the final step. One deep breath.

"What's taking so long?" The voice from behind almost paralyzed her.

"Nothing."

Marie turned and sent a full tumbler of wine flying into Gregory's face. For a startled second he couldn't understand what had happened, covered his eyes and jerked back in the bed. Somehow her fingers did the right things. Thumb snapped back the flint. Shaking hands sprinkled a dab of powder into the pan. Turning, she stood with leveled pistol.

"What the hell . . ." His voice trailed away. The shy lover of but a moment past had been transformed. Gregory hesitated, wiped away the last traces of wine and perched on the edge of his cot. The warm flesh, only a half-minute past entwined with his, looked cold and forbidding. The pistol was aimed directly at him and the girl acted like she knew how to use it. He cupped a futile hand over his groin. "Bitch. Whore. I should have—"

"Shut up!" Marie spat.

"You're mad."

"Do not make me repeat myself, *cochon*."

Gregory scowled. She might accidentally shoot him. What to do, then? Humor her? What else? She wasn't going anywhere, naked like that. "This little game—"

"Lie down. On your stomach."

"Eh?"

"You heard me. Lie down on your stomach and face the wall. I am quite good with a pistol, so don't underestimate my ability to kill you. Now move."

Gregory hesitated. The weapon did not waver, nor

did the determination so evident in her eyes. Finally he shrugged. What could she do, really? Slowly, carefully, he lay down and rolled onto his stomach, head facing the wall. A rustle of clothes behind him indicated she was dressing. Very well. She would leave. Where? The ship? He chuckled silently. Anguilla was no place to escape. They'd have her back within a day, see her . . .

"Get up."

Gregory rolled over and sat up. She was dressed and held the second pistol, cocked and aimed at him. "I suppose you think you're escaping?"

"You are going on deck with me," Marie declared, ignoring his question. "If you attempt to run, or think to attack me, or call for assistance, I will kill you. Now move."

Humor her. Damn! Gregory reached for his breeches.

"Leave them."

"What!?"

"You heard me."

"The hell—"

The pistol in her right hand lowered until it was aimed at his flaccid manhood. "All right, curse you," he exclaimed, hurrying to the door. *Once on the deck, distract her . . .* "You will never escape, you know. We'll hunt you down." The death-cold muzzle against his naked shoulder blade prodded him through the brief passageway and onto the quarterdeck. Speechless with rage, Gregory marched to the railing.

Riff gaped in amazement, unable to believe his eyes. "Tell him to pipe all hands on deck," Marie ordered.

Gregory glared at the master's mate. "You heard her."

Riff turned to the boatswain. "Pipe all hands on deck, Trow," he said, slowly and clearly. Hesitating only momentarily, Trow put the silver whistle to his mouth. The shrill sound of the bosun's pipe brought the attention of every man on deck. The hatch opened and more men spilled out from below to stare in mute astonishment at the sight of their captain standing naked on the quarterdeck. Lieutenant Schell fought his way aft through the crowd and started up the ladder.

"Hold, sir," Marie said shortly, leveling the pistol in her left hand at the man. At the first glimpse of the pistol, Schell stopped abruptly, uncertain of his next step.

Tom Gunn charged up from below decks, forced passageway between two marines too taken aback by the unusual circumstances to resist. "Good God, lass. What are you doing?"

The entire ship's complement held their breath waiting for her response. No matter what she did, she had already committed mutiny and would have to be punished for it. The thought of Marie in chains and taken back to England to be hung was one they'd never contemplated.

Marie faced them. Outwardly calm, inwardly she was a seething mass of doubt. All would be lost if she faltered for even a moment. Violence had never been her way, yet the men of Gregory's world had treated her violently and she was left with no recourse. The impressed seamen were the key. Alone, she was helpless and on a fool's errand. With Tom and the others at her side, she might prevail. In any case, the die was cast and she must put aside all qualms. Her course set, she became as cold-bloodedly calm as on the night she freed Jason. Her voice was incisive and controlled. "I am taking this ship."

A wave of shock surged through the company and the men rocked back visibly, as if struck. Gregory forgot his embarrassment. A surge of fury engulfed his very being and his face turned white with rage.

"Tell your men to throw down their weapons," came the deadly voice from behind. Gregory stiffened, fighting to recapture the impetus of command despite his shameful state. He nodded toward Lieutenant Schell.

"If this barracks-hack does not put down her arms, kill her. I will count to three."

Schell nodded, drew a flintlock pistol from his waistband.

"One . . ."

No one moved. Not a sound could be heard other than the soft lap of waves against the hull. While the brief drama played, no man so much as breathed.

"Two . . ."

Schell cocked his pistol, advanced up the stairway. The men waited.

Smoke spumed from the breach, flame from the muzzle. The heavy weapon bucked in Marie's slim grip. Schell staggered backward, his own pistol falling from nerveless hands. He gaped in horror at the wound and tried to speak. "No . . ." he whispered weakly, then tumbled backward to crash in a crumpled heap on the main deck, a crimson stain, slightly darker than his uniform, spreading outward from his lifeless body.

Gregory was at last confronted with the enormity of his predicament. Schell's abject demise was a harbinger of his own mortality. "Murderess," he whispered in a trembling voice. "Murder and mutiny . . ."

"I say your men will throw down their weapons. Now give what order you deem best, only know this: if you refuse, I shall see you dead before any man can lay a hand on me."

Gregory stared at Schell's corpse and felt courage ebb. The field of honor was one thing, but to stand naked and be shot in the back? His gaze rested on Sergeant Hogarth. "Do as she bids, Sergeant," he said wearily.

Muskets clattered to the deck, followed by as many cutlasses. The disarming complete, the men stood without moving. Marie knew the moment might soon be lost. "Well?" she shouted.

The impressed crewmen lowered their eyes. "What? Are you truly beaten? Tom? Ben? Are you men no longer? Your freedom is here for the taking. Have you lost the strength to grasp hold?"

Her voice rose, shrill, almost desperate, then tinged with disgust. "So be it. Four months now I've heard you bewail your fortune. Four months you've cursed the fate that brought you to the press gang. And for what?

247

You're not worth your freedom. The cattle pens are forward. Get to them. That's where the likes of you belong, for that's what you've become: meat for the butcher's block, mewling, bleating animals fit for spiritless labor with backs bowed to the cat and the whim of a tyrannical captain. I'll sail alone if I must. Better than that a crew of supple-spined—"

"Enough!" Tom Gunn bellowed. Grabbing a musket from the deck, he leaped Schell's body and lunged up the stairs. "Who'll join us in hell, lads?" he asked, turning to his companions.

A moment more of stillness as each man numbly contemplated his past and future fate. Mutiny was a terrible crime, even if a man had been pressed. The decision was not easy. Not easy at all . . . "I will!" a voice suddenly shouted in agreement. Two score and ten heads turned as one to see Shelby, the youngest among them, leap to the shrouds.

As if awakened by the lad's voice, the throng came to life. "And I!" yelled another. "And I," answered a dozen more.

"Wait!" Marie ordered, her voice ringing out above the chorus. "We don't have much time, for they'll see us from shore." She glanced around. "They've not much, but they can send longboats and marines, so we must work fast. Those who would go with us, to the starboard rail and take the weapons with you. Those who would stay, to the port, and no lagging. Someone get below and let out the rest. I need two men here to shield us from shore, if they haven't seen already. Tom, watch them closely. Shoot the first man to signal for help."

Hogarth and his men hurried to port, as did virtually every one of the men who had signed aboard of his own free will. Sly secured the keys to the orlop and disappeared below. Soon the remainder of the impressed seamen were on deck and given their choice. Most cast their lot with the mutineers, but some joined the loyal seamen and marines on the port rail, for they feared the

248

long arm and heavy hand of English justice more than the scorn of their companions in slavery.

At last all was ready. Tom had assigned duties to the thirty-nine men who had decided to go. As unobtrusively as possible, they heaved the anchor short and prepared to get under way. At the last moment, as the men were going aloft to free the sails, the sullen, cowed crowd at the port rail was given the order to jump. One after another, they leaped into the water and struck out for shore. The last to leave, Hogarth had watched the takeover of the ship with indifference. He doffed his scarlet coat and handed it to Hope. "'Tis a foolhardy deed, Hope Deferred," he said.

The harlot shrugged. She had cast her lot with the mutineers. "No less than the rest of my life. There's little that awaited me in England. Less, now."

The soldier shook his head despairingly. "I cannot swim."

Hope laughed. "Don't worry. A bag of guts like yourself will hardly sink. Just lie on your back and someone will tow you to shore. And if a shark comes to nibble, well, there'll likely be enough left over to walk home with anyway."

"And I suppose you'll be enjoyin' my rum," Hogarth glared.

Hope posed coyly. "Of course, you could stay and help me drink it," she said, leering as she advanced.

"I'd sooner face the sharks than that ravenous appetite of yours," the sergeant said, getting in the last word. And with grace and speed belying his age and girth, Hogarth vaulted over the side.

She had permitted him to dress. Captain James Gregory of His Majesty's Royal Navy watched from the quarterdeck as his ship spread sails, swung from anchor and eased from the harbor without benefit of official sanction. The wind was little more than a light breeze, yet enough to give them headway until they cleared land and caught the stronger winds offshore. He could see a flurry of activity on shore. "Fools. They're too late!" he muttered, casting a malevolent sideways glance at the seaman holding him at gunpoint until Marie's return. Ben Tremain nodded, returned the captain's stare. He wouldn't admit it, but he secretly questioned the rationality of his own actions. The thought of a London gallows and his head on a spike was not a cheerful prospect, but he tried to behave as if the whole venture were nothing at all out of the ordinary.

Below decks, Marie rummaged through Lieutenant Pulham's sea chest. He had been weak and ineffectual, to be sure, but she harbored a warm spot in her heart for him. Luckily he was ashore and could in no way share the blame for the mutiny. A blousy cotton shirt with sleeves gathered at the wrists with a bit of cordage was an ideal find. To her surprise, a number of island-crafted items and a journal gave evidence of his intent to one day compile his memoirs. She wondered if the young lieutenant would write of St. Kitts and their moment of sudden passion and shared bliss. Smiling, she continued the search. Underneath the shirts she found a pair of black breeches which she donned quickly. A pair of leather boots completed the ensemble. Completed? she thought. Not quite. She turned to the contraband confiscated from the captain's quarters and unwrapped a cloth bundle in which she kept her prize. The rapier, scabbard and crossbelt, the silver basket hilt gleaming in the lantern's glow, brought a smile of satisfaction to her face. This, then, is how she would appear.

A burst of frenzied activity and cries of alarm from above jolted her from daydreaming. Quickly, she slipped the belt over her right shoulder and balanced the hilt on her left side, then hurried out and onto deck. The air rang with the cry of frightened men. Tom Gunn shouted from the quarterdeck for all to hold their peace, but it was Marie's sudden arrival and dramatically transformed appearance that calmed them.

Gregory beamed victoriously and pointed toward the bow. "I'll not have too long a wait to see you gallows bait," he chortled, then grew mottled with rage to see his prized possession scabbarded at Marie's hip.

"We're done for," one of the crew bleated. A chorus of protests accompanied the man's remark. Ned Sly stepped forward. "The man in the tops reports a ship of the line around the headland. The *Breston,* he thinks. If it is, we haven't a chance, for we're outgunned and out-manned."

Problems already! No time to be afraid. The rest of her life hinged upon the success of this adventure. Marie tried to remember all Behan had ever told her, all the men of Mysteré had said during the tale-telling. There was another mile before they hit the channel opening into the Caribbean. "How long before he's in full view?" she called to the man in the tops.

"Five minutes maybe," came the answer.

Five minutes. Running with the trades, he'd have to continue past the last bit of headland. His next move would be to come about before he ran aground on the southern bank, only a hundred or so yards inside the estuary. "How fast are we going?" she asked Tom.

"No more than three knots," he said. "We'll be abreast of her shortly after she comes about, then be past in a moment."

"A moment's all she needs to blow us out of the water," Gregory sneered contemptuously. "You might as well—"

"Why should she?" Marie interrupted. "For all they know we're legitimate. Our captain's on deck! They'll not harm us. We've but to—"

"The signal flags!" a voice shouted. "Young Shelby raced to the quarterdeck. "They'll expect the flags."

Marie almost panicked, forced herself to remain calm. "Who knows what signals? . . ."

"I do," the lad broke in without waiting.

"Get them up, then," Marie answered, even as the bowsprit of the coming ship appeared around the head-land. "We'll be safe for a while, at any rate."

Gregory was amused. "A while?" he asked mock-ingly. "How long? The minute they reach port they'll learn the truth. I congratulate you on your long-lived mutiny, madam. Tomorrow you'll be dead."

The speech had the desired effect on the men. Once again they faltered, terrified of what the next hours would bring. "Then it's seek terms and bargain for our lives," muttered one of the crew. A head shook in agreement, then another.

Marie looked at their desperate faces. What would Behan have done? What could they do under the circumstances? There was but one solution. With the ship of line crippled, they would have all the time they needed. "Quiet on deck!" she shouted suddenly, stilling the growing murmur. "If you're men enough, we'll see she doesn't follow us."

"How?" scoffed Ned Sly.

"By striking the first blow," Marie cried. "You know how. Quickly, man the port twelve-pounders with chain shot and aim high for the rigging. The sixes will want grape, to rake the decks. If there's time for more, use balls and aim for the waterline. Get everything ready, but don't open the ports or run out the guns until I give the word."

"My God," Ben Tremain paled, "Fire on the king's ship?"

"You'll set us on a course from which there's no return," Poole shouted, utterly frightened yet holding to his place at the helm.

"We're on that course already. Freedom or death is our only choice now. There is no going back. No other choices to be made." Her long curls were an ebony banner flying in the breeze.

"Mayhaps it's easy for you to talk of death, Marie Ravenne," grumbled Hope from the gathering.

"Aye, 'Raven' indeed. An apt calling," Ned Sly added.

All beheld her then, their imagination fired by the allusion. She stood before them, a creature of darkness and mystery, above them on the deck. For a long second, she did not move, and the men waited with held breath. When she spoke, her voice carried clearly and seemed to be addressed to each man. "The ship you fear so much," she said, "the *Breston*, is starting to enter the harbor. Fifteen minutes from now, we will pass each other. If she passes unhampered, we die. If we fire and disable her, we live. It is as simple as that, my friends. Inaction and death, or action and life. I . . ," she paused meaningfully ". . . prefer life."

As before, Tom Gunn was the first to break the mood of defeat, and his example stirred the others into action. "Life, then, lads! Step to it!" he roared. Without waiting for an answer, he began to hand out assignments, naming those who would follow him below to the guns.

For a moment all was confusion. Once the inertia was broken, men scurried to their stations while Marie looked on and gave low-voiced orders, transmitted by Tremain and Shelby, who reported that the ruse with the signals had worked as far as he could tell. Everything appeared normal, save for the low number of men on the deck of the *Sword of Cornwall*. In another ten minutes the fight would be over with and they would be on their way.

"You are mad," Gregory said, frightened for the first time by the woman. Here was no deck trollop, no serving maid from an English manor. No. A distinctly more powerful, assured personality stood before him now, disturbingly confident in manner and style.

Marie didn't bother to answer. What Gregory thought didn't matter anymore as long as he stayed in full view. She checked quickly: it was vital that the pistol flush against his spine shouldn't be seen by the *Breston*. Equally important, she must not unduly attract the unsuspecting captain's attention. But the time for worry had passed. Anxious eyes were turned toward her for the signal as the *Breston* came about and started across channel toward the *Sword of Cornwall*. "Ready to put your helm to port," she called to Poole. The maneuver would put the two ships beam to beam. Another lesson taught to a foolish, frightened girl. *Dear Behan, thank you.* "Get below and tell Tom to be ready, Shelby.

When he feels us start to turn, he's to drop open the ports, run out the guns and fire at will. There'll be time for only one or two broadsides, at the most." Shelby nodded and ran off.

Less than two minutes now. Marie could see the rival captain talking with his officers. It was plain they knew something was wrong, but couldn't figure out what. They'd soon find out, she thought acidly. "Hail him!" she whispered harshly to Gregory.

"No."

"Hail him or die with him, damn your aristocratic soul."

"I refuse—"

Too late. "Helm!" she cried, "Now, Tom! Now!"

Poole spun the wheel, warming to his task. The *Sword of Cornwall* answered, swung to the port and presented her side to the *Breston*. At the same time Marie heard the chunk of gun ports opening and the rumble of cannon being run out. Consternation was evident on the *Breston*. Never had they anticipated an attack by a sister ship. The captain turned white and his officers began calling commands. Men rushed to the masts, more disappeared below. But no matter how well trained they might be, total surprise lay with the attackers.

Marie stepped into the open and fired her pistol. Immediately, from below, the cannons erupted with a ragged, uncoordinated series of thunderous explosions. Tom Gunn may not have been a master gunner, but at the distance involved, he could not have missed. The elevated muzzles sent a withering hail of chained ball into the *Breston*'s rigging. The six-pounders filled with grape raked the unsuspecting warship's decks and sent the bleeding, stunned crew diving for cover.

The *Breston* was in a shambles. Grape had mowed down half her officers. Her rigging was cut and her sails in shreds. The foretopmast was gone and the mizzenmast cracked: new ones would have to be stepped.

The main battle was won with one broadside. Marie checked quickly. They could hold their present course but a moment longer. If Tom and his men could reload and fire once more . . .

Another ragged cannonade belched from the *Sword of Cornwall*. A dozen balls tore into the *Breston*'s side. With luck, one or two would damage her badly enough to put her out of commission for even longer. But now there was no more time. The *Breston* would be firing back shortly. They had to swing downwind again and get to open water and the brisk trades before they, too, were mauled. "Hard to port," she called to Poole. "Now we run for it."

At the same moment the *Sword of Cornwall* started to swing back onto course, Gregory lunged. His hand connected with the side of Marie's head and she stumbled and fell to the deck. Her emptied pistol clattered across the deck. By the time Ben Tremain realized what had happened and turned to fire, Gregory leaped for the rail and dove overboard. Ben's shot went into the air. He started to reload but Marie, climbing to her feet, stopped him. "Let him go," she said, angry at herself for letting him surprise her. "We've more important matters to contend with."

And so they had. Every inch of available sail had to be crowded on, and rapidly. The *Breston* was wounded, but could still fight. All depended on how rapidly her stunned officers and crew recovered and put the cannons into play, and if her captain could hold her broadside to the *Sword of Cornwall*'s stern. Tom Gunn and the crew had emerged from below and were racing into the rigging to set the rest of the sails. Pushed by wind and tide, they picked up speed.

As the final brace was pulled tight and the men started down to the deck again, one of the gunports on the *Breston* dropped open and an iron snout emerged. Seconds later, a billow of smoke followed by a clap of thunder signaled it was the mutineers turn to face deadly fire. The ball missed, but each man knew the next would be closer. In another minute, balls of iron, each weighing twenty-four pounds, would come crashing down on them, rending wood and flesh with equal ease.

"Helm two points starboard," Marie called. The new course gave more of their sails to the wind, and would take them into the unimpeded trades a few minutes sooner. Hopefully, too, the maneuver would delay the *Breston*'s gunners from finding the range.

Suddenly the *Breston* shuddered and her stern, pushed by the outgoing tide, started to swing toward the *Sword of Cornwall*. Given the grace of another minute, not another one of the vengeful guns could be trained on the escaping attacker. And yet for that minute, there was nothing anyone could do save count the seconds and hope. As for any further shots . . .

Two clouds of smoke erupted simultaneously. Two thunderous explosions. Muscles tensed, then relaxed as one ball sailed harmlessly overhead and another skipped across the water and sank twenty yards to starboard. A quick succession of three shots followed. One ball sang through the main topsail and plunged into the sea. Another was never seen. The third whistled over the poop deck and landed amidships, tearing out a chunk of the gunwale, killing and carrying overboard one of the men. Everyone stared at the empty spot. One of them had already paid the frightful price.

Her face set, Marie turned from the scene. "Three points to port, Mr. Poole, she ordered quietly, becoming more authoritarian with each passing moment. "The rest of you! Man the braces as quick as you can," she called, giving everyone something to do to take their minds off the danger. The heavy spokes turned and the *Sword of Cornwall* answered slowly. Another ball flew through the rigging, parting a line. "Get that line spliced!" Yet another splashed but a half-dozen yards before their bow. Back a bit and it would have shattered the bowsprit and wrecked the rigging. Still another smashed through the stern, luckily missing the rudder.

Then, as suddenly as it had all begun, the attack was over. As fast as the *Breston* gunners had been, they could no longer bring their guns to bear. It took Marie a moment to realize the *Sword of Cornwall* was no longer in danger. When the realization dawned, the men erupted into cheers. They had fought and survived. Escaped! Behind them, the unhappy *Breston* lay hard aground, her deck cluttered with gear and covered with huge flaps of canvas. Ahead lay the Caribbean and safety. They were free! Free of Gregory and officers and the navy that had made virtual slaves of them all.

Marie was so overjoyed she wanted to dance. She had remembered well. Once the need was established, she could lead, could command a ship. Behan's lessons had not gone for nought. The self-congratulatory fog lifted. They were shouting at her. "Three cheers for Captain Raven!" Poole cried out, the metamorphosis from former antagonist to enthusiastic convert complete. His cry was followed by a roar of approbation.

Tom Gunn stepped to her side. A wide grin split his face. "'Twas your doin', lass. The men want you for their captain, and I agree. Will you serve?"

The deck grew silent. Every eye was turned to her. Thoughts rushed pell-mell through her mind. Would they really accept her? How long could a woman command a ship without trouble? A half-hour was one thing, but did she know enough for the day-to-day decisions that would have to be made? And yet, who else of them knew more about sailing a ship? Who knew anything of navigation, of the hundred tricks Behan had taught her? Who of them had ever been in the Caribbean, knew anything of the waters and the islands? Who else possessed the strength and determination necessary? In all honesty, she had to admit none other aboard could do as well as she. Raven, as they had called her, *would* be their captain. She was strong and capable of leading them. Taking a deep breath, she drew herself up proudly. "I accept," she said calmly.

"But I don't." The negative statement cut through the beginning of a cheer. Ned Sly, a confiscated cutlass in hand, stepped forward. "I'll not be captained by a woman!"

257

"Why, you—" Tom Gunn growled, moving to answer the challenge.

Marie put out a hand to hold the giant back. "No, Tom," she said quietly. "They must all see I am capable." Marie leaped to the main deck, her heart racing with exhilaration. She hoped the long hours of practice with Behan would bear fruit. It had been many a day since she had touched a sword. "Come then, Ned, for I've had my fill of you," she challenged, drawing the blade taken from Gregory. "But you'd best hurry. We've a ship to sail and the wild sea before us."

The hawk-faced crewman hesitated before the cold gray fury of her eyes. "I've never fought a woman," he said, noting the hard glances from the rest of the men.

"No man here is to hold grudge against Ned Sly for fighting me, do you hear?" Marie shouted. "No man."

Arrogance overrode caution and Sly lunged. Marie dodged to the right and tripped him as he rushed past, sending him to his stomach with a grunt of surprise. "You've lost your footing, Ned. Best get up and try again."

With a cry of anger, the man scrambled to his feet. His blade sliced the air where Marie had been but a second ago. A silver hilt seemed to float out of nowhere to slap him across the throat. Ned staggered back, gasping for breath. "And now your voice," Marie taunted.

Sly attacked, this time more carefully. Blades glinted in the early afternoon sun. Marie parried and twisted, careful not to let the heavier cutlass break the long, thin rapier. Sly bore down on her, pressing her back against the bulkhead below the quarterdeck. Suddenly, she moved inside, swept upward to send her opponent's cutlass spinning from his hand, then caught it in the air.

"You've lost both footing and voice, and now your weapon as well. Would you lose your life, Ned?"

She had toyed with him, could have killed him at any moment. There was the galling truth. Ned lowered his head. "No."

The spectators did not laugh, rather were as impressed as Sly by the performance. "Then I would have you as my friend, Ned Sly," Marie said, extending the hilt of his cutlass to him. "Can that be?"

Ned Sly looked at Marie. She wasn't merely a tool to be used to still the carnal lust that plagued a lonely man. The truth hit him, and he bowed to it. It had been she who had masterminded the mutiny, she who had reduced the *Breston*. And she who had bested him, by God. The ship was beginning to buck in the heavier waves outside the harbor. He had to decide. Suddenly the hilarity of it all struck him. A woman captain, by God! And why not? There'd been others, and good ones too. If this one could beat him in a fair fight, she'd do. His hawkish features softened and he took the cutlass, thrust it through the rope around his waist. "We've an ocean before us and a ship to be sailed," he said, the grin spreading over his face. "It'll be friends to the end, Captain."

Marie turned slowly, facing each member of the crew. Not a man demurred. The solemn moment lasted but the space of a sigh, and then she turned and leaped onto the quarterdeck. "There's work to do, lads. Until we've time to talk, Tom Gunn's the lieutenant, Ned Sly the mate. The wind's fair and the more leagues we cover the better off we'll be. I want every inch of sail we can spare. Poole . . ."

Sunset. Marie Ravenne, now Captain Raven, stood at the bow and watched the pastel sky darken at the end of her first day of freedom. The ship had finally quieted down, and other than the watch, most everyone was asleep—though not a man could be found in the orlop. As the *Sword of Cornwall* plowed through the deep blue water, there was time to think. Thirty-eight men—thirty-nine, actually, for they'd found Giuseppe asleep in his quarters—and two women. There would be a great deal to learn. Freedom was a heady draught and the men had spent the day doing as little as possible. Some were even drunk, having discovered the ship's rum cache. The discipline that came from necessity rather than physical punishment must be taught before any-

259

thing else or they would not survive beyond the first week. In addition to order, it was imperative they learn how to handle the ship. They all knew a little, but would have to teach themselves a great deal more before the next storm caught them. Luckily, the ship was newly provisioned. Forty-one people enjoyed access to supplies for over four times their number. If they were not profligate, they had enough to last at least five to six months.

But then what? The question she had refused to ask could no longer be avoided. What were they to do? Sail aimlessly about the Caribbean? Of course not. What about Mysteré? Could she find it? Did she even want to find it? Scenes of fire and pillage, of blood seeping into the sand, overrode the brightening stars. Marie shivered. Not Mysteré. Never again, Mysteré. There was too much pain there, too much anguish. But where else? Where?

Too many questions. Too many. She had to sleep. At least they had some time. It would be a week before word of the mutiny reached St. Kitts. From that moment, whatever decisions she made would be influenced by one overriding, inescapable fact: the *Sword of Cornwall* and its crew would be the hated quarry of every English ship in the Caribbean. Survival against those odds would be difficult indeed.

Chapter XIII

"The fresh water! Great Jesus, the fresh water!"

The cry wakened Marie. Confused and for a moment at a loss to remember where she was, she lay without moving, staring at the unusual conformation of beams overhead. Suddenly she realized it was light. Light? In the orlop? The day before flooded back instantly. The sunlight pouring in through the transom windows of Gregory's cabin signaled the beginning of her first full day of freedom. Captain of a forty-gun English sixth-rate ship, she mused wryly. What did fate hold in store next?

Springing from the cot, Marie pulled on Pulham's breeches and shirt, considered whether or not she should wear boots and discarded the idea: the backs of her heels were sore from wearing the unaccustomed footwear the day before. She'd have to get used to them gradually. But sore heels were a small matter compared to the joy that welled from deep within her. They were free! Free to live as they pleased, sail where they would!

The sudden realization of the words that had cut through her sleep froze her in midthought. What had been said? Fresh water? She sagged to the chair behind the desk. "Fool!" she muttered. How could she have forgotten such an important detail? Of course the fresh water hadn't been brought aboard. It never was until the last moment. Each hour's delay in filling the new casks could make a huge difference when, a month or two later, they were opened at last to slake the terrible thirsts of hardworking men restricted to a diet of salt beef and pork. Water adulterated with green slime could hardly be called a palatable beverage.

The victory of the day before dissolved into dust. The

ship would be doomed before they'd been at sea a week. A week? Possibly only a day. She had to find out how badly off they were, how much water remained. Frightened, she ran from the cabin to find the whole crew milling about the entrance to below decks and waiting for Gunn and Sly, who had gone to inventory the remaining supply. Marie's spirits sagged anew. If there wasn't enough water, she and she alone would be blamed for the omission. Another mutiny was a distinct possibility. It wouldn't be the first time an angry, mutinous crew, cocky with success and newly won power, had turned on its leader.

The deck fell silent as the hatch opened. Tom Gunn emerged first, followed by a white-faced Sly. Seeing Marie, they joined her on the quarterdeck and turned to face their mates. "We've a little over five hundred gallons left," Gunn announced flatly. "Enough for eleven days at full rations. It's water we loaded at Charleston. Might not be the best, but it's drinkable."

A half-hearted buzz of relief swept through the crew. Marie stepped forward and stood between Tom and Ned. "You men. Listen to me!" she called. Conversation ended and the men stared discomfortingly at her. She would have to make each word count, get them to work and then confer with Gunn and Sly, the two men she depended on more than all the others. "You've heard what Tom has said. Eleven days isn't much, but it's enough if we remain calm and maintain discipline. Until yesterday, marines protected the water supply. As of today, we must assume that responsibility ourselves. If any man takes more than his allotted gallon per day, all his mates will suffer." She paused to let the words sink in. The men glanced about at each other and Marie hurried on: to make them suspicious of their fellows was as dangerous as letting them drink as much as they wanted.

"Our best solution is to put someone in charge and let him dole out the rations." She inspected the noncommittal faces. Tremain was the oldest, perhaps they would respect him a little more. "Ben? Would you see to the water until we replenish our stores?"

Tremain looked embarrassed, pleased at being offered the responsibility but worried about the reaction of the other sailors. "If you say so, miss," he finally mumbled.

"Good. Then let's have breakfast. Tom, Ned and I will try to figure out our best plan, and then tell you. Will you give us the morning?"

Thirty-eight heads nodded agreement and Marie sighed with relief. The first crisis, while not yet solved, was at least in hand. Now they would have to find a solution. "Good. Let's keep on due west for now."

"Starboard watch, eat first," Tom broke in. "Trim all sails and get the deck in shape. Port watch, eat second, then see to cleaning up below decks before it becomes a pigsty down there. Free we may be, but we've got to keep healthy and alive."

The crew divided into smaller groups and set to their assignments. Too slowly, Marie thought, but that was natural enough. It would take time for them to get used to working without the threat of the boatswain's cane playing on their backs.

Marie preceded Tom and Ned into the captain's cabin and led them to the large chart of the Caribbean. The three stood for a long moment, staring at the blank expanse of water to the west and south. "Eleven days," Ned groaned. "Where the hell we going to go in eleven days? How the damned hell did we manage to leave without water?"

"There's no sense in lingering on the past," Tom growled, trying to cover the one mistake Marie had made. "We are free men and alive. That is enough."

"Not quite enough, Tom," Marie broke in. "When I was a girl I saw ships short of water come into port. Half the men were dead of thirst on one. We have to find water."

"And keep our heads," the giant said soothingly. A stubby finger jabbed at the chain of leeward islands behind them, stretching to the south. "We daren't come about and reach for a single one of these. Not a sailor but will question where we got such a fine ship, even if we could beat our way back against the trades in the time allotted to us. We've got to go somewhere else."

"Here?" Ned asked. Unable to read, he pointed at a large island to the north.

"That's Puerto Rico," Marie answered. "It's Spanish. We might . . ."

"Spanish or English doesn't matter," Tom broke in. "They'll know we stole this ship the second they see us."

"So what? Where else are we to go?" the smaller man asked, his voice rising. He indicated the long sweep of the Caribbean to the west. "That there's open water, and probably a half-dozen hurricanes by the time we get across it. We've got to——"

"Tom. Ned." Marie's voice was firm. She had to put a stop to the bickering before it started. "If we argue among ourselves, we're lost. There is an alternative." A delicate finger touched the map and moved. "South. Less than two hundred leagues. To the islands off the northern coast of South America."

The two men studied the map. It was possible. Five hundred miles, the trades abaft on their quarter. "Four, five knots an hour," Tom figured. "Five days, more or less, if we don't run into a storm. It could be dangerous."

Dangerous was an understatement. Any storm they met would drive them north, away from land and water. They could sail for three or four days, lose all they'd gained and soon die of thirst. "Any more dangerous than sailing into an English port?" Marie asked in a low voice. The answer was obvious. Their only course was south.

Their luck held for three days. Driven by the trades, Marie kept the ship on line with the compass, but pointed away from the tiny arrowhead indicator. The three days were invaluable. Necessity, adversity and constant reminders from Tom, Ned and Marie started to mold the men into a single, hardworking crew which

264

took pains to keep the log and attend to the thousand and one other details which, if ignored, would soon sink a ship. Better yet, the crew had grown to realize how little they knew, and each day saw them spend two or three hours practicing the same exercises to which Captain Gregory had subjected them. There were three differences. First, the ship was theirs and they were their own masters. Second, with Marie in command, Hope cooking and Giuseppe too frightened of being caught to help, there were but thirty-nine men left to do the work of a hundred and ninety. Third, quite simply, they didn't want to die, which is what would happen if they didn't find water or if, unprepared, the *Sword of Cornwall* encountered an English ship or a vicious storm.

A dream woke Marie before sunrise on the fourth morning. The wisp of memory, fleetingly recalled in sleep, faded with the return to consciousness. Knowing only that the dream had referred to where they were going, she lit the lantern and paced back and forth in front of the large chart on the bulkhead until the name penned beneath a small island less than a hundred miles off the coast of South America caught her eye. "Orchilla," she said aloud, puzzled, repeating the word twice more. Orchilla meant something, but what? Where had she heard that name?

Perhaps the charts and books held the answer. Hurriedly, she tore through Gregory's book locker and pulled out the one for the Caribbean, leafed through it until she found the right page. Generally, the island was low and featureless save for an old and worn-down volcano sloping off to east and west. Nothing there prompted her imagination.

There would be water on Orchilla, at any rate. For that matter, any one of the half-dozen outlying islands they might sight would do for water. She smiled, wide awake now. The world was a good place to be in, no matter what the past had thrown in her path. A fine ship, a crew willing to work, the same Caribbean Behan had sailed so many years ago . . .

265

"Behan. That's who." He'd told her about Orchilla. Someone he'd known had gone there. Of course! Behan's old *matelot*, the French word the buccaneers had used to denote a brother and companion-in-arms. Louveteau was the man's name. Tiring of a pirate's harsh existence, he had chosen solitary exile on Isla Orchilla, where he vowed to live out the remainder of his days. If he were still alive, perhaps they could find him.

Beside herself with excitement, Marie rushed from the cabin. Ned and Poole were aft and she hurried toward them, stopping suddenly when she realized the wind had shifted. Ned left his place beside Poole and the wheel as she mounted the stairs. "Wind's coming to the south. Fresh, too. I've called Tom."

Before she could answer, a voice from the dark hailed them. Tom Gunn, shaking sleep from his head, joined them on the quarterdeck. "What the hell's happening to the wind?" he asked, sniffing the air suspiciously. The wind shift was ominous, for the storm it signaled would delay their landfall. There were only seven days of water left.

By now the ship was close-hauled and barely making headway. If the wind turned another point to the south they would have to change course. The three fugitives shouted against the rising wind. Without the resources of a navigator or older hand who knew the Caribbean, all were in trouble.

"Damn!" Ned swore. "Another two days and we'd have sighted one of them islands."

"You can belay that talk, Ned," Gunn said immediately. "There's no sense in complaining."

The wind gusted and Marie heard the ominous sound of the foresail popping. Every minute saw the wind closer to the south. They would have to fall off with it. Worse, it was rising steadily and whipping the waves around them until she had to grip the rail to keep her balance. "We've three choices," she shouted. "East, west or north. What do you think?" Neither man answered. "To the east are the Leeward Islands and the

English. Perhaps the storms, too," she went on, giving them the alternatives. "To the west we might not make land until Central America, which is too far away."

"What about north?" asked Ned. "This wind will give us at least six or seven knots. We could chance Puerto Rico."

"What happens if it blows out two days from now? We'd have to turn around again."

"What the hell do you want to do, then?" Ned retorted angrily. "We've only got seven days left."

"Keep on the way we're going as long as we can," the giant answered doggedly, in spite of the obvious impossibility of sailing into the wind. "I'll not sail into English hands again."

Marie had to calm the rising tempers. "Can the men ride it out if we have to, do you think, Tom?" The crisis had driven Isla Orchilla and Louveteau completely from her mind.

Gunn hesitated, considered the crew. "I think so," he finally answered, "so long as it doesn't get as bad as that last one."

"Then that's what we'll do. Get off all sail save for the jib and heave to until it blows out. When we've a fair wind again, we keep on south. What do you say?"

The ship bucked and heaved under the steadily growing waves. Forward, the foresail popped again. The decision couldn't wait much longer. "Agreed," Tom finally said.

"Ned?"

"We'll have to cut the rations."

"Three quarts a day, then, for two more days, then only two if the storm hasn't ended."

The smaller man acquiesced. "I'll see to it. We'll need all hands."

The decision made, all hands were called on deck to bring in the sails and tie down everything loose. As a dim, bleak dawn brought gray light, the *Sword of Cornwall* settled down to the unwelcome task of riding out the storm.

Five days later the storm had finally done its worst and passed them by. On the morning of the sixth, the wind came back around to the northeast and they could once again steer for the South American coast. The situation was desperate. An attempt to gather rainwater during the storm had ended in failure when the wind drove salt spray into the clean water as fast as it pooled in the spread sailcloths. One keg of fresh water had been found to be adulterated with salt water and unusable. Little more than a hundred and twenty-five gallons was left—only six days' supply at half rations.

The next morning brought no relief. With luck, they were but two days from land, but no one could be sure. The men were listless and dreamed of clear, fresh water. None tried to steal more than his allotted share, though, a miracle for which Marie gave silent but heartfelt thanks. "Sail ho!" Every eye went to the man on the mast. "Four points on the starboard bow. She's still hull down, captain."

Glass in hand, Marie was the first up the shrouds. "It's an island trader, the *Niño Muñez* Spanish," she called down a moment later. "They're no doubt heading for Hispaniola and will have water."

"But not likely any they'll want to give us," Gunn said sourly.

"The hell with what they want!" Ned broke in. "We've got the guns and position."

The point was inarguable. Thirst was a stern dictator and, like it or not, the smaller trader would be forced to share with the larger ship. Marie took charge. English flags were run up quickly, for it was imperative their prey not suspect anything out of the ordinary. Once again the twelve-pounders on the lower deck were loaded and left behind closed ports, ready for the crew to dash below and run them out and fire at a moment's notice if necessary. By the time the two vessels could see each other's decks, the six-pounders on deck had been loaded and a man lay hidden behind each of them.

Short-handed as they were, luck held and the ruse worked. The two ships came closer and closer, and by the time the trader figured out the English ship might mean harm, his wind was hauled and he was under the *Sword of Cornwall*'s guns. Before long, two boats carrying a total of twenty men were rowing across the hundred and fifty yards separating the two ships.

Tom Gunn balanced in the bow, waved across to Ned in the second boat and admonished his own men to greater speed. Marie crouched directly behind him. "I don't like you being here," the giant muttered. "There's still a chance of trouble. Not a fit place for—"

"A woman?" Marie grinned. "But a captain, Tom. What about a captain?" Her eye narrowed as she scanned the trader and noticed a figure slide down from the rigging. Hurrying to make a report? No doubt, for from the crow's nest one could see into the *Cornwall*, whose empty decks would surely invite curiosity and suspicion.

Her mind working rapidly, Marie tried to put herself in the Spanish captain's place. An English warship, but without the hundreds of men usually peopling her deck. Two boats approaching, each with less than a dozen hands aboard. Mutineers? Pirates? He would take precautions. Every available man would be armed and waiting for them. How many? Thirty? Forty? Once the foreigners had boarded his ship he needn't fear the warship's guns. Unmanned, the *Sword of Cornwall* would be, in these lawless waters, a tempting prize. With a sinking heart, she knew they would get no water without a fight—and might even be lucky to escape with their lives. It didn't matter. Death in a fight or death by thirst. They must continue, boldly and fearlessly. "Pull close to Ned," she ordered. Jesse Crandall, the man at the tiller, nodded and complied. He was the only one of the mutineers who spoke fluent Spanish, and Marie was relying on him to make their demands understandable.

Half a hundred yards separated them from the trader. "They plot to take us. I'm sure of it. What's the signal to open fire, Tom?"

"I told Ben to look for a pistol, waved butt first."

"Stop rowing!" The men on the oars rested. "Give the signal."

Tom paled. "But we're too close. If they fire low—"

"Give it!"

Tom acquiesced, yanked a pistol from his belt and held it upward in the agreed upon fashion. Behind them, the men lying hidden beside the six-pounders sprang to their feet and a ripple of cannon fire spouted from the English ship. Those in the small boats ducked instinctively as a column of water erupted in front of them. "Row!" she shouted. "Row!"

A cannonball shrieked overhead, followed by the brittle crunch of wood. A deadly hail of splinters filled the air. The trader shuddered under the combined impact of another half-dozen balls striking home. The smoke hadn't cleared when the *Cornwall*'s jolly boats bumped into the scarred hull. Anguished moans of the wounded on deck could be heard as Marie leaped for a trailing rope and started up, hand overhand. Behind her, the men followed.

A face appeared, a torso leaning over the jagged railing. Tom Gunn, steadying the jolly boat, fired upward. The Spaniard jerked back and dropped his musket into the sea. Marie found purchase for her foot and with a desperate kick of her leg leaped onto the deck to face, alone for that first dreadful moment, a host of heavily armed seamen who had lain in wait for the boarding party.

Indecision. Under any other circumstances the defenders would have rushed forward to repulse the boarders. But the sight of a woman, beautiful at that, left them momentarily confused. Across the deck, a handsomely garbed gentleman, obviously the captain, stared thunderstruck and failed to give the command. His indecision was all the advantage the boarders needed. Hesitant to attack for those first critical seconds, the defenders were soon faced with the *Cornwall*'s men, who were scrambling aboard as rapidly as possible.

Marie hesitated too. The capture of the *Sword of Cornwall* and the disabling of the *Breston* had been life-saving measures. Here aboard the *Niño Muñez* they were facing innocent men whose blood she didn't want to shed. The sword in her hand was no longer a beautiful piece of workmanship meant to impress. Now it was a weapon, designed to kill and maim. A line of faces across the deck. Peaked helmets, brawny arms. Mysteré reduced, left to burn, ravaged by Spanish dogs. Her father . . . her home . . . dead . . .

The blood drained from her face and the world went blank. Time ceased to have meaning. Marie raised her sword and let loose a blood-curdling scream. Instantly, the battle was joined.

Like two maddened beasts, attackers and defenders met amidships. One man howled as a line of crimson welled from a slashed cheek. Another grunted, his cutlass dropping from nerveless fingers as Marie's rapier skewered his shoulder. Marie cursed them at the top of her lungs even as the Spaniards unabashed now at the thought of killing a woman, sought her flesh with their blades. Charging among them like a tigress, she fought with deadly intent, mad with the lust of battle and only half aware of those who fought at her side.

Vengeance! "Try me! Come for me now, dogs. Murdering bastards!" A sailor stumbled away, clutching his throat. Thrust home, spin away to avoid a killing slash. Parry. Slide along his guard as Behan taught, then twist and thrust home again. More men around her now. Tom, Ned, Jeremy. Steel against steel. Cries of savage slaughter.

The Spanish captain stood before her, his eyes wide with hatred and fright. Before she could react, he dropped his sword at her feet. The fight was over. They would survive.

Too much. Too much, the price of water. Blood-washed decks. The wounded crying for help, the dead, silent and torn. Drained now, Marie watched her crew at work. Her limbs felt lifeless and her eyes stung from powdersmoke. The rapier dangled from her dull fist.

What had happened? She remembered climbing over

271

the rail, then little. Patches of memory. Exploding light. Punishing, frenzied sound. Had she seen Murcia? Had she revenged the rape of Mysteré? No. She had taken water. That was all. And now she felt weak. And sick at heart.

Two hours later, with five hundred gallons of fresh water aboard, Marie gave the order and the warship pulled away from the *Niño Muñez* and steered southeast, hoping to trick the Spanish captain into thinking they were heading for the Atlantic. Once out of sight of the trader, the *Sword of Cornwall* resumed its course due south.

The men were ecstatic. Each was allowed an extra quart of water immediately to ease the throat-constricting thirst that had plagued them for the last three days. With enough for another eleven days, they would surely make land before running out.

Another hour had passed when Marie became the last to learn the whole story of what had happened aboard the *Muñez*. The water hadn't been all they'd taken. Ned Sly, prowling around below decks, had checked the cargo and the captain's tiny cabin. There he'd found the only thing other than water—or women—that could have interested him. Gold. A chest of pieces of eight, Brazilian *moidores,* and four small bars of bullion which, with Poole's help, he wrestled into one of the water casks while everyone else was busy above. Six thousand pounds in English money! News of the fortune had swept among the crew, each of whom was now rich beyond imagination.

Marie listened in amazement. The gold was a godsend. With it they could buy a haven, a place in which to hide from English justice. As excited as anyone else, she rushed to the quarters Ned had taken over from the absent first mate. "Is it true?"

Ned, Tom, Poole and three others looked up. Hope, sitting in one corner and staring at a fistful of coins, more than she'd ever held in all her life, was so entranced she didn't even know Marie had walked in. A medium-sized chest stood open on the table around which they were gathered. Fascinated, Marie felt herself drawn to the table and gold. Ned handed her one of the pieces of bullion. "You ever see anything so pretty, Captain?" he asked proudly. "We was going to surprise you with a bag of coins later on."

Marie hefted the bar, turned it over to see a simplified crest and the name Murcia stamped into the heavy metal. Her eyes widened and her face turned white as new sailcloth as joy turned to dismay.

"What is it, Raven?" Tom asked.

"Do you know whose gold this is?" she whispered, hypnotized by the name that had been burned indelibly into her memory.

Sly laughed. "Ours." His companions' grins proved they agreed emphatically.

Marie held out the bar so they could see the crest. "Murcia's. Do you know who he is?" The men shook their heads. "A Spanish don. He controls the *guarda costa* and is the most powerful man in this part of the world. He will want his gold back and will go to any lengths to get it."

Ned shrugged and an evil grin slid over his face. "I don't think that will be easy," he said quietly, "but he is free to try."

Tom, though of a far different temperament than Ned Sly, couldn't help but agree. An even-tempered man, he brooked no challenge. "I've heard how the Spanish mines are worked. Slaves. Maimed and branded. If he's a Spaniard and this rich," he said slowly, indicating the gold, "your Murcia is little more than a pirate. What we steal from him he deserves to lose. A pirate's gold is fair game for—"

He stopped, interrupted by a fit of laughter from Hope. Unable to fathom her outburst, everyone turned to stare at the woman. Even Marie, in the angry gloom brought on by seeing the Butcher of Mysteré's name, stared in unabashed amazement. Gasping, Hope forced back the laughter and tried to speak. "Pi . . . Pi . . . Pirates!" she finally managed. Tom and Ned's faces were blank. "Don't you see? *We're* pirates!"

273

Despite her fears, Marie could not but help realize their ludicrous situation. Pirates! Not a one of them had planned on being a pirate. Not in their wildest dreams had the idea even occurred to them. They'd been plain men when taken by the press gang. Their only hope had been to get back to homes, wives and children. When that hope was dashed, they had given up until the day of the mutiny. But even during and after the capture of the *Sword of Cornwall*, they still thought of themselves only as mistreated men who had taken the law into their own hands and whose one goal was peace and freedom: to find a place where they'd be left alone to live and die according to their own desires.

Sent to find and reduce pirates, now they were pirates. Unwittingly, pirates. The notion swept through the ship like wildfire, leaving each man stunned with the enormity. No one knew what to do. Pirates were desperate men: murderers, pillagers. Mutiny had been hard enough to accept, but piracy was even more difficult. Men looked at each other and quite suddenly broke into laughter. Who could think of young Shelby as a pirate? Or nervous old Ben Tremain?

The night was beautiful and the ship nearly sailed itself. Someone broke out a keg of rum, and soon all were on deck, singing and dancing. Only Giuseppe stood aloof: when the surgeon had waked to find himself an unwilling party to mutiny, he had been frightened. Now fate had dealt a devastating blow and he was aboard a pirate ship, and terrified beyond description.

Marie came on deck sometime around midnight. The booty had been distributed and the party was going strong. The whole crew was pleasantly drunk and the men were laughing and enjoying themselves and their new image. Two or three had taken to wearing cutlasses in their belts. More had bright rags tied about their heads. Martine, the only one to boast a ring through one ear, was a hero and envied by all. Hope, in a mad display of extravagance, had pounded holes through her share of the coins and made them into a crude necklace which clanked as she danced and shimmered gaily in the torchlight.

Standing alone in the shadows, Marie couldn't help remembering Behan's tales of the adventures he had shared so many years ago. *Perhaps I have stepped back in time*. Back in time. The scene misted and she had to blink. How she wished she could step back.

But to where? All the happy times had become sad. Mysteré was haunted, Jason only a memory. In spite of herself, she looked up to the moon. *Does he sail some ocean under your light?* But no. That was foolish. Jason had abandoned her, left her to save his own skin. He was a past she must forget at all costs. She emerged from the shadows and stood at the rail, forced herself to watch the gaiety.

Spanish Jesse, as he was now christened, was the first to see her. He let out a piercing whistle and the laughter and dancing came to an abrupt halt. One of the men ran to Poole and handed him something wrapped in a sailcloth. Poole vaulted to the quarterdeck and faced the crowd. "As first helmsman of this ship—"

"He couldn't steer 'is way acrost a horse trough," someone jeered.

"Shut up, let 'im get on with it," growled another.

"As first helmsman of this fine *pirate* ship," he corrected, "I'm proud to be chosen to give this little token of the men's esteem—"

"Stow the gaff, man! We've drinkin' to do."

Poole bit his lip. He'd composed a fancy speech and resented not being allowed to give it. But what the hell. If that's what they wanted . . . "Captain Raven," he said, turning to Marie, "the men wanted me to give this to you."

Marie took the package. The sailcloth had been dyed black and grommets had been placed along one edge. She undid it carefully, laid down the piece of wood wrapped inside and shook out the cloth. "It's your new flag, miss . . . Captain . . ." someone called from the pack.

"As pirates fly, or so they say."

Marie didn't know how to respond, but the crew was in such a good mood she could hardly condemn them. They were hard men, but fair. No one had asked them to be pirates. Instead, they had been forced to piracy through the inequities of the very system that would now hunt them down. She looked from the flag to the faces staring up at her. There was no doubt they looked the part. In the torchlight they looked an ominous, fearful lot. And it was to her they bestowed the honor of the flag.

"The board!" a voice shouted. "Look at the board."

Startled, Marie handed the flag to Poole, picked up the board and held it to the light. The letters leaped out of the wood. Carved and then painted red, there was no mistaking them. *Ravener* it said. *Ravener*. Bird of prey. One who plunders.

The night closed in and a terrible roaring sound filled her ears. Marie clutched at the nameplate which would take its place on the bow. Suddenly, the roaring passed and a great exhilaration filled her very being. "Live!" Jean Ravenne had said. And so she would—as few others had.

The men waited expectantly. Not a human sound could be heard. The wind sang through the rigging, the water played along the hull. The whole ship hummed and throbbed as if a beast alive. Suddenly, Marie thrust the nameplate high in the air, held it over her head for all to see. A pirate then. She would live the legend. Live free, to love whom she would. Sail every sea! Who was there to stop her? None. Eyes glittering with excitement and heart beating wildly, a cry escaped her lips. *"Ravener!"*

The men stirred as the spirit caught them. *"Ravener!"* a voice echoed in reply, followed by all the rest, cheering, crying aloud until the sound spread over the wide waters and filled the night.

PART III

Chapter XIV

They followed the gulls and found land as the sun rose on the fourth day. Rearing out of the hazy southeast, the badly charted and useless group of naked rock islands called Islas Los Rocques told them where they were. Isla Orchilla lay fifty miles due east, more than a day's sail in the square-rigged ship, for the wind was dead foul, blowing directly from their destination. Late the next morning, after long tacks south and back to the north, a welcomed cry came from aloft. "Land ho!" Reward enough for all their efforts. Isla Orchilla was just over the horizon.

Caution was essential. As the green island rose out of the water, Tom had the guns loaded and run out. They might as well have saved the time, for as they passed along the southern and eastern coasts, not a sign of inhabitation could be noted. Marie herself was on the mainmast tops when she gave the order to wear about and run along the northern shore. Again, nothing.

The only suggestion of a harbor was a deep indentation on the southwestern end of the tiny island, and it was there the *Ravener* finally dropped anchor. Sheltered from the trades, the mock bay would be treacherous if the wind shifted to the south, for any vessel resting there would be driven aground without hope of escape. Only two hours were left in the day. Marie, Tom and Ned spent the first quarter of them high in the rigging, meticulously inspecting the shoreline for signs of danger. When none could be seen, one of the boats was allowed ashore long enough to fill a pair of casks from a gurgling stream that danced down the precipitous slope to the east. Then, full of fresh water and a heavy meal under their belts, the crew mounted watch and waited until morning for a more thorough investigation.

Morning dawned bright with an excited air of expectancy. The jolly boat was let into the water and Marie and fifteen others glided across the glassy bay and scraped onto the sandy beach. Ahead, an even line of trees allowed the black volcanic sand fifty yards of freedom before cutting off further encroachment with a barricade of ribbed trunks topped by emerald fronds.

Marie cast a cautious glance toward the anchored warship and took comfort in the open gunports and ugly snouts of the twelve-pounders. To one side, the men had hauled the jolly boat onto the beach and were waiting patiently. Nothing could be gained by delaying. Dead ahead, a gap in the trees offered entrance to the interior. Marie lifted her pistol and pointed the way.

Silence. For the first time in over four months, complete and absolute silence. No creaking of wood or line. No splash of waves. No keening wind through rigging. Nothing. The small party stood in the center of a small grassy clearing. Sweat poured down their faces and bodies. Marie was soaked to the skin. Not even a bird sang. The silence began to tear at their confidence, and some primal protective sense urged them into a crude circle.

There should have been people on the island. Dearam, called Poacher from his former occupation, had seen footprints along the ill-defined path they had followed for the last quarter-mile. Perhaps they should return, Marie thought bleakly. It was silly to expect to find an old pirate no one had seen for the last twenty years. He was probably long dead. They should turn back, retrace their steps and fill the water casks. They could rest for a few days, load up with fresh fruit and, if they were lucky, meat, and be on their way.

"Hssst." It was Shelby. "Someone comin', Captain," he said in a scared whisper.

Marie—and everyone else—looked where the lad pointed to see a dusky figure emerge from the choking ground cover. He was clad in ragged sailcloth breeches faded almost white. A hat of bamboo cuttings woven into a shallow dish shape shaded the dark features of an Indian who approached without fear, despite the menacing armament of the seamen. "A Carib," someone muttered. The protective circle tightened slightly.

The Indian stopped ten paces away. A flashing smile revealed teeth filed to points, indicating cannibal origins. Marie uttered a silent, fervent prayer that he had abandoned his peculiar and revolting penchant for human flesh. A quick glance to the rear showed no others in sight. Perhaps this one was truly friendly.

"I welcome you," the Indian said in pidgin French, the words and accent harshly guttural in the silent clearing.

Marie stepped forward a pace. Ned Sly sought to restrain her. "I don't like this, Captain."

"It's all right, Ned. All he said was that he welcomed us." She turned to the Carib who was staring frankly at her, obviously surprised to see a woman carrying weapons and clad as a man. "Thank you," she replied, thinking rapidly. Her questions would have to be phrased simply. "I look for a man. A very old man. Captain Louveteau. Does he live here?"

The Indian pondered the question and answered with another. "You English? Spanish? Dutch?"

"We have no flag," Marie answered truthfully, "save a black one. We are of no country."

"It is good," the Carib answered. The smile returned and he gestured for the pirates to follow him. "Come. Come."

"What about Louveteau?" Marie repeated.

The grin disappeared. "No ask more. White-skin no ask more. Come." Without waiting, he turned and left the clearing.

Isla Orchilla was shaped like the blade of a spear, broad and rounded to the east and tapering to a point at the west. The party from the *Ravener* had penetrated halfway across the pointed end, and from there the Indian led them across the blade, over the flank of the old volcano to the southern shore, almost a mile and a half from where the ship lay at anchor. Sweating and cursing the thousands of insects that plagued them, the white men stumbled after the nonchalant Indian, who slipped through the jungle growth and trotted uphill and down with no more effort than had he been taking an afternoon stroll through a park.

It took a moment to realize the trek was at an end, for at first glance the clearing they entered looked much the same as the previous three. A more thorough inspection revealed a small thatched cabin nestled among the trees, concealed from the prying eyes of passing ships yet within a few yards of the pristine beach and whirling gulls. Marie turned to ask the Indian a question, but he had disappeared into the dense foliage. They were alone.

"Worse and worse, Captain," Ned whispered. "How do we know what they got waiting for us?"

Marie didn't know, but wasn't about to let that stop her. "Form a half-circle at the edge of the clearing and stay with the men," she ordered. "I'll find out."

"But Raven—"

"I'll be all right, Ned. Just do as I say."

"I still don't like it," her second-in-command repeated, his eyes narrowing with suspicion.

Shelby, his boyish face lit with excitement, crouched behind a nearby shrub. "Captain Raven can watch out for herself, Ned. You of all people ought to know that," he remarked impishly, eliciting a rumble of muted laughter from the others. Ned grumbled, pulled his hat forward to hide his embarrassment and signaled the rest to take cover.

Marie refrained from smiling until she was safely beyond the hawk-faced pirate's scrutiny. Then the time for smiling was past, for the shack loomed ahead. Pausing, she took a deep breath, rounded the corner and stopped abruptly. Before her, in profile, a wizened shape, back straight and hands on knees, sat on a twisted, multilegged stool carved from a root. He sat so still, and his deeply sunburned flesh so closely matched the color of the bark that for an instant she suspected man and

282

root were one, a grotesque sculpture chiseled by a sun-maddened artist.

Marie thought she had approached silently, but the old man rose and turned to face her. Never had she seen so strange a creature. Clothed in nothing but a ragged loincloth, his age was undeterminable. His skin was dark copper in color, wrinkled with age and, the girl thought wryly, perhaps even tanned. That it was Louveteau was certainly possible, for Behan had described a nose of immense proportions jutting from a profusion of curly black hair. Though the hair had turned white and only the beard was left, the nose fit the description perfectly.

With a distinct shock, Marie noted one more striking characteristic: he was blind. Milk-white orbs stared sightlessly at her. "Welcome, Captain," the man said in a surprisingly clear voice, his French nearly as mutilated as the Indian's. "You must excuse my poor welcome. It has been many years since the Brethren have chanced to pause at Orchilla."

"You . . . are you Captain Louveteau?" Marie finally managed to stammer.

The old man started at the sound of her voice. Recovering quickly, he chuckled with delight. "Brotherhood? Sisterhood I should have said. Jamil, one of the Carib friends you didn't see, told me of your ship without a flag." He paused and took a tentative step toward her. "Damn! At times like these I would pay gold to see again. From the sound of your voice you are a beautiful woman, no? Come. Touch an old man's hand. It has been a long time."

Marie hesitated, then approached and slipped her fingers into his. The bony fingers tightened. He was amazingly strong and Marie winced. "And how might a young lass have heard of Louveteau?" he asked, not letting go.

"I am called Raven. Captain Raven of the *Ravener*. I was told of you and this island by an old comrade of yours and my teacher, Louis Behan."

The bony fingers relaxed suddenly and the wizened

283

figure shook as if palsied. Louveteau began to laugh with a high, piercing, almost mad sound that caused Marie to shiver and brought her crew on the run. Seeing her in no immediate danger, they stared in mute amazement at the strange figure as the wheezing laughter died away. "Behan Blackheart, eh?" He struggled to contain his mirth. "Well then, lass, or Captain, or whoever you are, Orchilla extends her hospitality. Jamil!"

A native stepped from the trees nearby. He was not alone. With him was the Indian who had led them across the island and nearly two dozen companions, all armed with spears and, from the looks of it, ready to use them. Realizing they were in the open and outnumbered, and not having understood Louveteau's French, the pirates backed into a protective circle and drew their pistols. Quickly, lest someone cause an incident which would bring their stay to an abrupt and unhappy end, Marie translated and ordered the men to put up their weapons.

"Jamil," Louveteau said, lapsing into even worse pidgin French. "Provisions for our guests. Fruit. Meat. Fresh water. They are friends. Friends."

The Indian grinned and nodded as if the old man could see. And as quickly and silently as they had come, his menacing companions vanished into the forest.

The moon was a pale globe of liquid amber tipping the incoming waves with a ghostly fire, a path of flickering watery candles leading to the starry horizon. Marie, roused from sleep by nightmares of burning ships and the crash of guns, followed the fringe of black lava sand away from the stretch of beach where the crew slept. Almost two weeks had passed since their arrival at Orchilla. Louveteau had not failed in the slightest courtesy and the *Ravener,* sails mended and ready for sea, rocked impatiently on the Caribbean's timeless berth.

Now, alone at last and floating on the surface of the star-filled bay, she pondered the problems that faced the *Ravener* and its crew. One thing was clear. They would have to leave Orchilla soon, for the island could not support an extra forty souls. But where to go? Where lay safety? Where would the civilized world *not* harry them to death, or worse?

Warm and sensuous, the water laved her body, dulled her mind. Unbidden, the past intruded. The episode with Guy: how she wished she could return to that time of innocence. Vivid recollections of his hands, the shape of his body. And Jason's. How she ached for him. They had talked of sharing nights like this, surrounded by the silent, swimming stars. She could feel him in her, his weight crushing her, feel the rolling spasms as he stiffened against her and called her name. And then left? Yes. The memory of his treachery was like a dash of frigid arctic air. Marie turned over and swam to shore, dressing quickly by the light of the moon.

The sound of bare feet padding on the sand. Marie grasped for the hilt of the rapier that so rarely left her side. A knowing chuckle overrode the sound of the distant surf. "You must learn to listen more closely child. And be much faster."

"I thought I was alone," Marie explained lamely, ashamed at having been caught. She glanced up to check the triple stars of the Hunter's Belt. "It is late."

"I know. Sometimes the fear of darkness wakes me."

"Fear?" Marie asked, surprised. "The Louveteau I have heard of would spit in the face of Satan."

The old man shrugged. "I do not understand either. For ten years now, I have seen nothing. I have grown used to eternal night and even come to enjoy it. Waking, I am at peace. And yet, during sleep . . ." He trailed off absentmindedly.

"Yes?" Marie prompted gently.

"During sleep the dreams come, and so long as I sleep I am a child again. When this happens, I must wake and walk and listen. Tonight I heard you, Captain Raven. I heard your restlessness." He tapped his breastbone with a stubby thumb. "Here. So I come."

"But how did you find me?" she asked, confused.

Louveteau pointed down to the waves lapping at the

285

island's apron of sediment. "I follow that. Do you not hear? No. I forget. I couldn't either until the blackness came. The hearing is a gift more precious than sight. I have walked around this island many times and heard Neptune's hundred voices, each different. They say ancient mariners were driven mad by the song. Mad? Not so, Captain Raven. Not so, unless it was the madness of truth and the knowledge of things as they are."

The aged figure shuffled forward and directed his sightless eyes to the sea. "Now you for instance, lass. Behan's charge. I wonder if he taught you to hear the truth?" The old man turned suddenly and started to leave.

Marie shifted, unsettled by his strange behavior. "What do you mean?"

Louveteau hesitated. Once again the cackling laughter rose over the soft sound of water. "If you've come for answers, Captain Raven, you must listen for them. Listen. And farewell."

Perturbed by his eccentric and unsatisfying answer, Marie started to call after Louveteau's disappearing figure, but then thought better and continued her walk until she reached the western tip of the island. There, alone with the waves, she paused and found a seat on a boulder covered with Medusa-like tresses of purple lichen. As she watched, the moon gathered its veil of pearly light behind a passing cloud and the stars seemed to swell and fill the sky.

She could hear the wind now, bustling around the island and sweeping out to sea. Listening, she hung suspended between earth and sky like a wraith in the corridor of passing hours, surrounded by a sea song without beginning or end.

My heart is a heavy burden. Odd that emptiness should weigh so much. What truth am I meant to hear? Where do I go now? I've refused to ask for three weeks, but now the time for leaving has come and I must now. Where? I am lost, Father. I can follow the stars, but there are no stars within me. Only a restless, searching sorrow.

The sea rolled onward, its rhythmic cadence a soothing lullaby.

Where?

And the sea song without beginning.

Where?

The seasong without end . . . answered.

Hope Deferred woke up as Marie entered the
sprawled camp. "Is that you, Tulip?"

"Yes."

"Are you all right, dear?"

"I . . . Yes. No. I don't know."

Hope nodded. "It's this island. Friendly or no, that
blind, leather-pated coot and his cannibal friends give
me the quinseys."

"You needn't worry about them any longer," Marie
replied.

"You mean we're off at last?"

"On the morrow, as soon as we fill the water casks
and take on the fresh food."

Hope nodded. "Good." She patted the hard-packed
sand. "I'm getting as bad as the worst old salt you ever
knowed. Restless, bein' on land so long at a stretch.
Now, isn't that strange?" Next to her, Marie yawned
and curled up in her blanket. It wasn't until she was
almost asleep that Hope thought to ask, "Aye," she
whispered, a trace of concern in her voice. "But where
are we bound to, darlin'?"

Marie rolled onto her back and stared up at the sky.
When she spoke, her voice echoed the wind and repeated the hypnotic message of the waves. They had
told her where truth began. "Mysteré," she whispered,
spellbound. "Mysteré."

Marie's excitement caught them all, and from the
barest of light the beach had been a beehive of activity.
She stood at the edge of the sand and watched Tom
Gunn and his crew manhandle fruit-laden nets into the
last jolly boat. Everything else was aboard. Louveteau
kept his age-wrinkled face to the wind, as if skin and

ears were endowed with the magical ability to see the *Ravener* bobbing at anchor. "So you're set on Panama no matter what I say?" he asked, a tinge of worry shading the question.

"I am," Marie answered. She wondered if he could hear the lie in her voice. It didn't matter if he did. Let him know she wasn't heading for Panama, just as long as he didn't know her true destination. She wasn't eager to entrust their plans to a man she considered partly mad, no matter how kind he was. "Panama is as good as any."

Louveteau squinted, an old habit. "You'll be tempted to steer due west, but you'd do better to set a course north first, then drop back down. And keep a sharp eye out for Spanish warships all the while," he cautioned. "I'd fly my English flag, too, if I was you."

"Oh?"

The old man cackled. "Healthier. Murcia's agents are on every island from here on west. If the trader you took that gold from was smart enough to go back to Barranquilla, there'll be ships out looking for you. If you're lucky, the flag will help, for he fears angering the English. But, of course, one can never tell with Murcia."

Maria chewed pensively on her lips. Murcia. The Butcher of Mysteré. She had tried to forget him and the cayman-faced Captain Solia, but fate kept throwing them in her path. Tom Gunn was speaking. "What?"

"I said we're ready to cast off, Captain Raven. This is the last of it." The big man frowned, puzzled at the strange and dangerous glimmer of hatred in Marie's mist-gray eyes.

The fire faded and Marie forced herself into the present and concentrated on the thousand details of setting sail. Perhaps when she reached home—how easy it was to think of Mysteré as home again, once the decision had been made—there would be time for thoughts of vengeance. Louveteau stood next to her and she took his hand. "I take my leave of you, Captain Louveteau. My thanks for a safe harbor and your hospitality." The

288

words sounded strangely stilted in French, now that she was leaving.

Louveteau squeezed her hand. It would be a long time before a woman's hand rested in his, and he wanted to remember. Especially this one. The girl had a cagey streak in her that he liked. Behan had taught her well. Perhaps she would survive. Too bad it was impolite to ask where she was really going. But no matter. The voices would tell him. Sooner or later, he learned everything. "Fair wind and full sails, Captain Raven. And if you see Behan Blackheart, tell him Baptiste Louveteau . . . But never mind. I'll see him soon enough in hell, and tell him myself."

Willing hands set the sails and a sea chant reverberated through the ship's timbers as the crew pulled in the anchor. Tightly braced, the *Ravener* slipped from the small bay. Once out of the shallows, they swung west to clear the tip of Isla Orchilla before heading north.

Marie waited until the last second before land cut off her view, then stole a look behind. Hiding the gesture, she brushed a tear from her eye. On the sands of the island whose shores defined the limits of his universe, Louvetcau stood alone, a mad, frail, strangely majestic soul, vanishing into legend. Thus time treats some men.

Chapter XV

The wind sang in the rigging and the whole ship reso-
nated in harmony. The sails, taunt, snowy expanses of
canvas, thrust the *Ravener* into a repetitive procession
of watery blue summits. Gracefully, the bowsprit
pointed to the sky, then slid into the following trough as
the stern rose to let the blue Caribbean pass underneath. Like a mote of dust on a shimmering sapphire,
the queenly craft kept to her course.

Occasionally the tip of the rigging of a distant ship
was sighted on the rim of the ocean. Then, their eyes
alight with the fire of adventure, Ned Sly, Spanish
Jesse, or young Shelby would plead to give chase, only
to have their enthusiasm dampened by their captain's
gentle but adamant refusal. Now that she was bound for
Mysteré, Marie had become one obsessed. No course
but the one they held would do. Once she overheard
Ned grumble to the small gathering of shipmates that
"Captain Raven was immune to the fever brought on by
Spanish galleons crammed with silver and gold." Which,
he added with a sigh, was a malady he hoped never to
be cured of.

Night sounds. The creak of spars as tightly wound
ropes chafed against wood. The whispered hush of a
dreaming sea. A melancholy restlessness drove Marie to
pace the deck and wrestle with troubled thoughts engendered by almost forgotten faces. Murcia, a gentle-
manly countenance hiding his cruel nature. Captain Solia, his horribly mottled face a leering mask as he bent
to inspect his captured prize. The dead of Mysteré, lit-
tering the burning paths and blood-soaked sand. Ashes
swirl and settle. Ashes of the dead, for the end of
dreams.

But I still dream. Of what? Marie drew the cloak

about her, forced aside the relentless flow of questions before they led to the inevitable outcome—a shock of flaming hair, handsome, guileless eyes, nose, mouth, the hardened strength that had been her pleasure . . . and pain. Ardent promises unfulfilled left a bitter residue insoluble in time and loneliness.

Companionship was the remedy prescribed for intro-spection. Escaping the solitary confinement of her cabin, she sought fresh air on deck. Tom Gunn's massive sil-houette loomed behind the wheel. "Evenin', Captain." His deep bass was a balm for troubled spirits.

"Tom. You were drilling the men on the guns all day long. You've no business here, but should be below, asleep."

Tom shrugged. "It's better to be awake this night. Too many memories below. Too many dreams."

Marie nodded, understanding more than he could guess. "Then keep to your post, my friend. But see you rest tomorrow." From her vantage point, she spotted another familar figure strolling toward them. Giuseppe ascended the steps and stopped at the rail. "What? Is the whole crew awake tonight?" Marie asked. "What brings you topside, doctor? Change your mind?"

"Change his mind?" Tom's grip tightened on the wheel. "He's too damned stubborn to change his mind."

"I'm disappointed in you, Giuseppe," Marie said. "You'll miss a fair share of the gold. You're with us, why not accept it?"

"I do not want to hang," came the dogged reply.

"Yet you're here."

"Not of my will. I slept through the mutiny."

"Slept indeed. Drunk, if you want the truth," Tom grunted. "On half the ship's rum!"

"Nevertheless," the doctor whined, indifferent to the big man's anger, "I didn't ask to be part of this."

"You've been free to leave any time you wish," Marie snapped back, angry at last.

"What? On a godforsaken island with a blind pirate and cannibals for company? Or do you recommend I bet set adrift in a jolly boat to be rescued by the Span-

291

iards and spend my remaining years in slavery? No. Better an unwilling participant in piracy than either of those fates, though in any case I am doomed." His eyes rolled to heaven and his hands followed in an exaggerated display of morbid theatrics. "Doomed." With that brief denunciation of fate, the doctor morosely ambled off to wallow in misery.

Left with nothing but gloomy thoughts for company, Marie and Tom stared at his departing figure. For Marie, the dejection from which she had sought relief had deepened, added to by the lurking fear of recapture by the English. A muffled grumble that sounded like a large animal in distress but was really Tom's version of a chuckle came from the darkness. "Doomed!" he said, throwing up his hands in imitation of the dour Italian. "Doomed!"

Hands off the wheel, the ship lurched as the rudder was given its head. Marie caught the spinning wheel, turned it back. "Tom! Pay attention."

"Doomed!" His voice rose. "Oh, woe is me!"

"Tom, quit being so silly, damn it!"

Gunn took the wheel and the ship steadied. "Look at it, Marie." His head jerked up toward the sky. "I'm a simple man, but I know when I'm well off. If I'm to be doomed, I can't think of a better way. You ever see anything so beautiful!" As if in answer, the sails slowly turned a soft gold color. Marie glanced to her right in time to see the moon rise dripping from the eastern sea. Tom was right. Without thinking, she hooked her arm in his and held it tight, grateful for the companionship of this giant of a man who was her friend, who put things in perspective. Dejection and gloom faded, replaced with a quiet joy. Giuseppe could be sad for all of them. She was on her way home.

Neptune's children at play in the deep. One day flying fish burst from the water to arc across the white-flecked waves. On another a mother whale and her baby lazed in the sun as the *Ravener* passed no more than a hundred yards away. A trio of dolphins followed

292

them for a time, offering an assortment of tricks that left the pirates laughing and joking, full of boyish antics and practical jokes. That night the crew lounged on deck, grew pleasantly tipsy on rum from Gregory's private stores and spun yarns of childhood while the sky showered stars to wish upon.

Neptune angered. A series of squalls forced them to furl all but the smallest scraps of sail. Those who could be spared took cover below while the wind whipped capes of water across the main deck. The *Ravener* plunged and shuddered like a madman's conscience, caught in the anger of the elements. Marie did not complain, for each pounding mile brought her closer to Mysteré. After the storm, the clouds broke, leaving azure skies dotted with airy clumps of whipped sugar scudding to the west. All sails spread, the *Ravener* followed and later, after dark, raced their shadows across the night.

"Land ho!" came the cry that brought Marie to the quarterdeck. "Land ho!" the cry again. Poacher, lost among the dizzying heights of the topmast, was pointing to port. Twice before they had made land, only to be disappointed and veer off. The first had been Jamaica, which they had avoided like the plague. From there they had gone too far north to find Grand Cayman where, under the cover of darkness, they'd stolen ashore to fill the water casks. By morning they were off at sea again, heading west southwest.

"Deck, there! Three points on the port bow!"

That had to be it! Marie's heart pounded in her throat as she hurried to the wheel. "Southwest by south," she ordered, trying to sound natural. "Tom! The guns!"

The air crackled with excitement. The deck watch trimmed the sails, then hurried down to ready the six-pounders. Below, the rumble of wheels and hurried footsteps indicated the twelve-pounders were being run out. They dared enter no harbor without taking precautions.

A half-hour later, the island was visible from the

deck. Ben Tremain hurried up to Marie. "Is that it, Captain Raven?"

No longer than five miles, nor broader than three at the widest, an island barely visible through a sea-kissed mist lay like a teardrop falling toward the heart of the Caribbean. Hidden in the shrouding vapors, a mysterious face in the cliffs had been carved in rock by human hands or the elements themselves.

"Mysteré," Marie whispered. "Yes. That is Mysteré."

Like a curtain parting to reveal the island, the mist dissipated as they entered Voûte Paix. Marie clutched the rail in astonishment. Where the charred, pitiful wreckage of La Cachette had been, now lay a bustling new settlement. Further inland, cultivated fields could be seen. As a flower takes root in a wasted land, so Mysteré had renewed itself and become the garden she remembered.

Lest she forget, it could be a garden of menace as well. Four unmarked ships lay at anchor in a pattern that afforded crossfire to any point in the harbor. None were so grand as the *Ravener,* but there was no question their guns outnumbered hers, especially since the crew of the new arrival wasn't large enough to man all forty guns. Even as she watched, the ports on two ships opened and she was treated to the unnerving sight of cannons pointed at her from near point-blank range. Perhaps entering so boldly had been a grievous error, Marie thought belatedly. In any case, they were committed and must make the best of it. As she pondered her next command, more gunports opened and a dreadfull hush fell over the harbor, a hush which could at any second dissolve in a thunderous barrage.

The *Ravener* was barely making way. They would soon have to drop anchor. Still, no one had hailed, not a face could be seen aboard any of the other ships. She couldn't wait any longer. "Anchor!" she called. "Get in the sails."

The next ten minutes passed as if in a dream. She

heard the heavy hemp line rumbling through the hawse-hole, saw the sails disappear one by one. At last the *Ravener* was at rest. The men on deck scurried below to man the starboard twelve-pounders. If there were a fight, the heavier guns would serve better than the six-pounders on deck. The tension grew tighter and tighter, increasing with the wracking, oppressive heat of the blistering tropic sun. If only they *knew*. Throats grew dry. Muscles held too long in one position cramped. No one dared take the first step.

Marie stood on the quarterdeck, trying to figure out what was expected. All the pirate ships that had put into Voûte Paix when she was younger had been known. Only once had a total newcomer entered the harbor. He escaped being sunk by running up a black flag. But in those days everyone who entered Mysteré knew it was a pirate haven. Had that changed? Were the vessels that faced her English ships, just waiting for the chance to retake her? They were a motley lot, to be sure, but that proved nothing. Such a ruse was not un-heard of. She counted again. Sixty-two guns of all sizes. Never could the *Ravener* survive against that kind of firepower.

An hour passed. She reached out to pick up the spy glass and . . . *Damn!* The sun had heated the metal so she could barely touch it. *Damn!* They had no right to treat her this way. *Mysteré is my home. I was born here, lost my mother and father here.* Anger swelled rapidly and her temper heated to vie with the hot black metal. "Pass the word!" she barked to Shelby.

"Captain?"

"Get forward and tell everyone to stand ready on the guns, and then run up the flag."

The youth started, looked about apprehensively. "Aye, Captain. Uh . . . which flag?"

"The black one for heaven's sake," she snapped without looking. "Run it up smartly. We'll find out who they are and be done with it."

The crew seemed to know what was happening without being told, for it had become very quiet after the quick shifting about as the men eased sore muscles and checked the guns. *Twenty twelve-pounders to sixty-two of all sorts. And not enough men to reload all of our twenty. Worse than three to one odds.* Speculation vanished at the creak of a halyard, and she craned to follow the ascent of the bit of black cloth.

At first nothing happened. The crew tightened holds on lanyards in expectation of the crash of heavy balls. Suddenly, they heard the rumble of heavily loaded wheels across the water. Then more wheels. The guns were being run back in! A dull thud sounded, followed by another and another. Gunports were closing on the four surrounding ships. And then faces appeared. Faces and bodies, as men came into sight, climbed over rails and into light boats to return to shore.

Marie and the crew heaved a collective sigh of relief. The danger was over. As preparation got under way to put Marie and half the crew ashore, few could restrain their excitement. One thing was for sure, the welcome given them by the pirates already there lived up to the island's name. Mysteré was precisely that, a mystery.

With the black flag aloft on the newly arrived ship, the inhabitants of Mysteré breathed their own sigh of relief. Goods that might have been concealed lest a squadron of marines came ashore were allowed to remain on their shelves and on display in stalls in the hopes of exchange for whatever booty the newcomers might have. Weapons were placed aside. Bandages put away to await another day. One after another, buildings emptied and men and women and the few children streamed to the shore to greet the new arrivals, who were already skimming across the water in a sleek, shining cutter fit for a king.

Ben Tremain, Poole, and a dozen and a half more had been left behind to guard the *Ravener* until their position on shore was secured and a friendly reception assured. Marie's heart beat faster with each stroke of the oars. The beach loomed closer and closer. A thousand fleeting images. Here lay her mother, Pia. Her father's lifeblood had spilled into this very sand, there but twenty yards up the beach. The house! It still stood, barely visible through the trees. A hot lump rose in her throat and she swallowed hard, forced herself to concentrate on the landing and the confrontation that would follow.

She stepped to the front of the boat so all could see her. The crowd on shore stilled, taken by surprise. Here was no ordinary pirate, rather a wild beauty clothed in black breeches, boots and a dazzling silk blouse. A scarlet scarf tied around her forehead kept the windswept ebony hair from her eyes.

The cutter ground onto the sand and Marie leaped lightly from the bow. Tom Gunn, Ned Sly, Hope and the rest followed in quick order as the crowd gathered around and pelted them with questions. "Who be ye?" one asked in a rasping voice.

"Men of the brotherhood like yourself," blurted Hope as she flounced ashore, her ample bosom jostling with every effort.

The incongruity of her statement sent a ripple of laughter through the crowd. "Men, she says," another voice broke in. "Never did care much for men. Guess I'll have to change my ways." More laughter. "Aye, but the rest of them don't look as fitting. Best we search them and see what they hide."

"You want to start with me?" Tom Gunn asked, straightening to his full height and stepping forward. Though his voice was low, not a man there missed the threat. Behind him, the crew of the *Ravener* inched forward and returned the flint-eyed stares that surrounded them.

"Who's your captain?" the first speaker demanded, his voice as threatening as Tom's.

A disturbance at the rear of the crowd interrupted the confrontation. Three or four of the watchers stepped aside to make room for a man decidedly smaller than his fellows. He had the hooked nose, pencil-thin moustache and jutting beard that marked him for one of the East. Daggers fitted into wrist sheaths on either arm and a brace of pistols in his belt marked him for a dangerous man. "What say you, Ramahd?"

The Turk ignored the questioner. If he was at all surprised to find a woman pirate, much less one of such great beauty, his face didn't show it. "A tale has been told in the taverns of an English ship and mutiny. Of a bold *kadin* who captured one ship and disabled another. They say the *kadin*'s hair is dark as the black rose of *Maçaçkala,* a flower few know of and fewer still have seen. She is named for the spirit bird that haunts all men." His expression continued unchanged, but he looked out to the *Ravener,* then back to the woman. All eyes were on her now.

"I am the woman you speak of," Marie said clearly enough for all to hear. How quickly word spread, she thought, pleased with the advantage her reputation gave her." "I am Captain Raven."

A murmur went through the crowd. Ramahd nodded. "Then you are as welcome here as any. When you have found a place for you and your men, the captains in port will hope to dine with you. Perhaps you bear information important to all of our persuasion. Until then, govern yourself and your men as you will. The only code here is that of the ancient brotherhood, of honest thieves." He laughed then, revealing an uneven row of yellow teeth.

The tension, held so long, dissolved in a flurry of laughter and greetings. As if all were old friends, the throng turned and headed for the streets of La Cachette. Many a man stared hungrily at Marie's lithe form until confronted with the flat glare of Tom Gunn or the evil grin of Ned Sly. Hope Deferred cast an invitational glance toward one leering freebooter, happily suffered the pinch of another.

The afternoon became a party. The crew of the *Ravener* were led into town by their hosts and soon Marie, Tom and Ned were left alone as the rest of the men found their way into the few taverns and grog shops, there to sate themselves with rum and talk. The three found themselves a table at an outdoor tavern set up

298

under a thatched roof. Tom and Ned engaged in light banter with men at nearby tables, but Marie could only sit numbly and sip the cool drink set before her. Smells and sounds from the past assailed her. Fresh bread, crusty and golden in the sun. Children laughing, running among the tables. Heady aroma of fruits free for the taking, piled into wooden bowls. The chatter of women arguing over men, the teasing whispers of women enticing men in contrast to raw, burly male discourse and bawdy jests. The succulent fragrances of sizzling grease dripping into open fires. The cloudy perfume from a smoke-shed where meat was prepared for long journeys at sea. The smells and sounds of life, thought Marie, where but five years ago had been the terrible clangor and stench of death.

Though the laughter and talk continued, Marie sat in a cocoon of silence. *Here, father. I am here again.* Mysteré in spite of all, had raised itself from the ashes of defeat. *And so, perhaps, can I.* Eyes alight with newfound hope, she turned to share in the merriment.

They hadn't wanted to come at first, but now that the bustle of the village had fallen behind, Tom, Ned and the rest of the crew followed more willingly as they crossed the freshly plowed fields and enjoyed the feel of warm, turned earth beneath their toes. Emerald twilight beckoned and Marie began to hurry ahead, ignoring the scarlet, spiny crescents of lobster claw and the violet-red, pendulous blossom of banana trees. Blind to both beauty and the musical accompaniment of countless birds, she paced along what had been the old trail leading to home.

These are steps I have taken in dreams . . . Images of sweet childhood, of disastrous tragedies, rushed pellmell to meet her. The cumbersome branches of the *ycao*, where father sat. *No, don't think of that now.* Running now, out of breath, she left her puzzled companions behind so she might reach the spot and stand alone for a moment.

And there it was! The home of her youth, set on a

299

mound of earth jutting from the long slope and looking out over La Cachette and Voûte Paix. The sinking sun lit a face suffused with anguish and love and shining eyes bright with threatening tears. The house was just the same as she remembered it, the rock walls only slightly besmirched by fire, the roof newly thatched, as was the custom every few years or when someone new moved in.

Newly thatched!

"Hold there, missy," a voice growled from the shadows. A stocky brigand complete with a patch over one eye and a gold ring in his ear, stepped from around the corner. Marie paused at the single step leading to the porch. "And just where do you think you're goin'?"

"This is my home."

"The hell it is," the pirate said, stepping closer for a better look at the strangely attired woman. "A smart tidbit you are, Lady Jane." His eyes paused on her breasts, traveled down to the tight breeches. "I'd be glad to give you a portion of the place. Say one side of my cot." He reached out to grab her arm, but Marie reacted on the instant. A yard of glittering steel sliced the air inches from Forlicar's nose. He gave ground, blinking in surprise. At that moment the *Ravener*'s crew burst into the yard, pistols and cutlasses at the ready.

"By my oath—"

"I am Captain Raven," Marie interrupted brusquely. "These are my men and this is the house where I was born and raised."

Taken aback by this sudden and dramatic turn of events, Forlicar could only stutter a feeble protest. "But you can't. We fixed—"

"I'll pay you for your troubles. With gold."

"We do not want your gold," a woman's voice answered. Marie spun around. A proud, coffee-skinned mulatto stood in the open doorway. At her side, a mestizo servant clad in coarsely woven trousers brandished a musket. There was a disturbing familiarity about the servant with the gun. The mulatto woman stepped confidently from the safety of the house. "Forlicar at bay! The others will laugh to hear it."

Forlicar scowled. A woman had threatened him with a sword, had interrupted him twice. Now another woman mocked him. His blood boiled. "By the devil," he growled, starting toward Marie.

"You'll have to fight us all." Tom Gun stepped to Marie's side.

"Tomás!" The mulatto's strident voice cut through the men's lower-pitched threats. "If these men do not drop their weapons, kill their captain," she said, spitting out the last word contemptuously.

The crew looked from one to the other. None would be able to move fast enough to protect Marie. " 'Sblood! Put 'em down," Hope broke in, slightly tipsy but sobering fast at the sight of the musket pointed at her Tulip. "I'll not see harm come to——"

"No," Marie said sharply. "He will not shoot. Not me."

"Do as you're told," the mulatto ordered, her voice brittle and full of hate.

"Tomás. Do you not remember me? Have I changed so much in five years? I am a long time in returning, true, but surely you have not forgotten your Marie and that this is, in truth, her house?"

The half-breed's eyes bulged as if he'd seen a ghost. "Shoot!" Armide cried. "Kill her, damn your slow-witted soul!"

Tomás's eyes widened with horror, then he tossed the musket to the ground and fled into the trees. "Tomás!" Marie called after the fleeing figure. Armide lunged for the weapon, but Marie planted a booted foot across the path and sent the woman tumbling. The pirate captain swept up the musket as her crew crowded around.

"The house belonged to my father, and I intend to regain my rightful property," Marie announced with finality. "Now be off, and quickly."

Forlicar, recognizing the wisdom of retreat in the face of overpowering odds, casually hooked his thumbs in his belt and started down the path, not deigning to

301

talk. His fists and sword would talk for him. Later. Armide leaped to her feet. "You will pay for this. When he returns from the hunt, Captain Brand will have you flogged."

Marie stiffened to keep from falling. "Brand?" she asked weakly. The world spun and she was forced to cling to Tom for support. "Jason Brand? You know him?"

Armide thrust her full breasts forward to strain the material of her blouse. "I . . . *know* . . . him well," she said.

Marie did not mistake the woman's intonation. "Tell your captain," she said, biting off each word in order to maintain control, "that I shall be pleased to display adequate proof of ownership if he so desires. He will find me here, in my home, if he wishes to call."

The years had added dust. Vandals had stolen what simple treasures Marie and Jean Ravenne had possessed. Oddly enough, she recognized her father's handiwork in one of the heavy, crafted tables. One piece, at least, had escaped the burning. Newer, more crudely constructed tables and chairs were scattered about the house. Like a silent visitor resurrected from the past, she made her rounds while the rest of the crew settled down where they could find room. Hope undertook to sweep the floors and set a large iron stew kettle to boil on the hearth. Marie roamed the house, stopping in the room that had once been her father's and now bore unmistakable signs of Jason. A pair of his boots. A shirt. The bed, tousled, his shadow still indented . . .

"The men would like to return to town, Marie."

Marie jumped guiltily. Tom Gunn had entered unseen. "Very well. What about the guard aboard the *Ravener*?"

"Taken care of," Tom grinned. "Ned swore a blue streak and cursed me from stem to stern, but he's aboard for the night with ten good lads. Tomorrow night it's my turn."

Marie gazed through the window. A gust of warm sea

air wafted a wayward curl on her cheek. "Best post a guard here. Two men will do, I think."

"Aye. Done, Captain."

"Then be off and mind you keep together for the first night. We may have troubles with those who were here earlier."

"None we can't handle. I mounted a swivel gun by the window in the front room. You set her off and we'll come runnin'." Marie nodded. Tom started out, then paused. "Maybe I ought to stay here with you after all."

"No. Go ahead. I can take care of myself."

Gunn looked around, only a little skeptically. She'd handled Ned. And the burly one called Forlicar as well. "I guess you can, Captain. But be careful," he added thoughtfully, and left, disappearing into the gathering dusk.

Alone again, as she would have it, but confused by the ghosts of a long-dead mother and a murdered father, she was plagued by a tide of memories that flowed unabated and collided with the turbulent maelstrom of present unhappiness. Jason was on Mysteré, of all places. *Fate.* Her flesh felt heated. Veins throbbed and heart pulsed with what she strove to call anger. *He betrayed me. He used me.*

"Tulip?"

"Oh!"

"I didn't mean to startle you, darlin'," Hope exclaimed, flouncing into the spacious room. Her cheeks were the fiery pink of a morning's first light and she held a cup in one hand, a bowl of fruit in the other.

"I thought you went with the others."

"I've had enough of men for one day, dearie." The buxom harlot sighed contentedly and eased her plump buttocks into a chair. She gestured toward the haphazard arrangement of precariously piled fruit, two of which had already thumped to the floor. "The fruits of the branch," she declared grandiosely, then sloshed her cup upward in salute. "And of the vine," A purple-red liquid splashed over her hand and dress. "Someone cached a goodly number of stout jugs against the scul-

303

lery wall. A good Christian soul, it must have been, to leave such a generous gift for one so thirsty."

Marie smiled, grateful for the older woman's company and humor. What other pirate captain, after all, was called "Tulip"? It was an odd assortment of humanity she had brought to Mysteré, Marie reflected, not the least of which was herself. "Not of the vine. Palm. A particular type that grows only on the highest slopes. But be careful. Too much can——"

"Raven! Captain Raven!"

Hope looked up in startled amazement. Marie froze in recognition. *His* voice. He was here! What would she say? What would she do?"

"'Sblood," Hope swore, staggering to her feet. Marie moved quickly to a shuttered window. Through the cracks she could see a cluster of torches and shadowed man-shapes. One stepped forward and she glimpsed a shock of red-gold hair.

"I've accepted your generous invitation, Captain Raven, and come to call. To settle accounts, if you will."

As if he read her mind, the man who could only be Jason continued. "Your friends are in town and of no use to you. And those left behind sleep soundly, helped to their dreams with a belaying pin."

Several menacing voices laughed at that and the crowd drew closer. Marie recognized the Turk. And there was the one called Forlicar. The mulatto, Armide, pranced triumphantly forward. And now Jason, stepping again to the fore. Laboring for breath, Marie closed her eyes. God, it was him, his terrible beauty revealed in the savage, sputtering light. Hope lit the coiled, slow-burning match and held it over the breach of the swivel gun.

"No!" Marie ordered curtly.

"But it will warn the others. And handle not a few of them as well, I warrant."

"Put it away." Sighing, Hope Deferred acquiesced to Marie's inflexible tone of voice.

"Captain Raven. A reckoning. I would see this deck

harlot that steals English ships and captain's houses."

Laughter again. Marie trembled with cold fury and lunged for the door. "Tulip!" Hope exclaimed, and made a tardy attempt to stop the girl. Then Marie was through the open doorway and standing in the shadows. Jason squinted, but failed to recognize her.

"A lass indeed. And well for you, else I would have come with pistol and cutlass in hand. But Ramahd tells me you are too lovely to carve. And Forlicar attests to your spirit. Armide here would have you flayed, but I'm of a mood to be generous. Come, I could force you out, but there's no need. You'll find another place for your crew, but this is mine."

"I think not," Marie replied quietly. Unable to see her, Jason searched the shadows. An unsettling look of vague recognition crossed Jason's face, but he rapidly dismissed whatever recollections were called to mind. "This plantation is mine."

"By what right?" Jason blurted, unused to such inflexibility from a woman.

"By birth, if you must know. And even if that were not the case, I don't doubt you would gladly relinquish any claim to this ground and these walls. It is a small enough gift in exchange for that which I have given you."

"Ha! You speak in riddles and I have not the time for wild guesses. What have you given me?"

Marie stepped forward into the revealing torch glare. She undid the scarlet band about her hair and let the luxurious dark locks flow down her shoulders and breasts. "Your life, Jason Brand," she said softly.

Jason's strong, noble features seemed carved from marble, for all they revealed. Only the lengthening silence betrayed his surprise. Ramahd stepped forward. "Captain?"

"Leave us," Jason croaked in a hoarse whisper. "Go back to town. Find a new place."

Armide hissed and lunged forward, dagger in hand, but Ramahd caught and held her. Forlicar and the others, bewildered by their captain's behavior, looked back

305

and forth, trying to make sense of the order. Jason gave
no sign of his motives, even when the murmur of dismay grew behind him. "Leave us!" he repeated, his
voice rising. "I'll join you at Caron's Grog Shop."

"Let me go!" Armide howled, clawing at Ramahd.

"Forgive me, little one, but captain's orders."

"I will kill her myself. Pig! Worm! Great stinking
ape! Let me go!"

"Armide!" Jason roared angrily. "All of you! Go!"

Forlicar and the others quickly disappeared among
the trees, followed by Ramahd and the struggling, cursing Armide. When they were gone, the flame-haired
Scottish rogue drew closer, drawn by the wondrous
beauty of the girl he had loved so many months ago.

Marie noticed that lines of forced laughter and cruelty furrowed his once smooth, aristocratic face. They
did not mar his handsomeness but rather lent a hint of
inner wisdom that made love all the more desirable.
Neither spoke. Holding a mirror to time, they played
again, though in a far corner of the world, that first
instant when they met. Yet something was different.
Then, the breathless certainty of love had drawn them
together. Now, doubt and suspicion engendered by pain
given and received kept them apart. Then, the moment
had climaxed in a kiss. Now, Jason reached out to
stroke Marie's cheek, as if to reassure himself she was
there in truth.

*Deny the gold-flecked treasure of his eyes. Deny the
sun-kissed ringlets of the hair that lies matted against
his muscular chest. Deny his firm appealing build, his
evident desire I have known and longed for. Deny the
pain, the torment suffered? Never!* Mist-gray eyes grew
wintry and cold and Marie's cheeks and jaw tightened.
Jason's hand paused, then slowly withdrew, leaving her
untouched. Marie closed her eyes, shuddered and heard
his footsteps on the path. When she looked again, he
was gone.

She ignored the sound of men hurrying up the path,
ignored the shouts of alarm as Tom Gunn burst into the

clearing, his towering anger abating as he saw she was unharmed. She ignored their questions, ignored Hope's puzzled stare over what the older woman had seen transpire. At last, in the private sanctuary of her father's room and safe from further inquisition, she slumped forward onto the bed, curled into a tight ball and surrendered to the overwhelming sense of loss that sent burning tears streaming down her face to soak into the pillow where the faint perfume of prior lovemaking still lingered.

Chapter XVI

Ramahd watched as the stars shimmered and dimmed before the onslaught of dawn. The faint sounds of footsteps alerted him to danger, but he relaxed and eased his fingers from the hilt of his knife when he recognized Armide. Armide the beautiful, the mysterious, to whom he was drawn as a moth to a candle, yet secretly, so no man should see his weakness. Anyone who could weave a spell to see the future deserved respect. The others laughed at her claims, but Ramahd had ridden the wastelands of home, the far empty places of the East. He had drunk from the Euphrates, had strode the shores of Rhodes and glimpsed the eerie limits of what could be.

"You do not sleep, little one?"

Armide pouted, irritated that he should have discovered her without turning to see who approached. "Nor do you," she said seductively. She stood next to him. "The tavern was too warm." Her voice faded.

"And the bed too empty?"

She turned to go. "You mock me."

"No," he answered. His voice was truthful, so she remained.

"I do not find him anywhere. The tavern he chose stinks with sweat and crawls with lice." Somewhere in the dark water, a fish jumped. "Why did he not kill her? I do not understand, Ramahd. He sends us away and returns alone." She shook her coffee-colored face in bewilderment.

"I do not ask for reasons," the Turk replied. He removed a knit cap, brushed the palm of his hand over his shaven skull and replaced the cap in thoughtful ritual before continuing. "No man knows why Jason Brand does one thing rather than another."

Behind them, from the tavern, sensual laughter, treble and bass, lingered on the soft land breeze. Armide cursed beneath her breath. "Do not begrudge poor Forlicar his amusements," Ramahd said wryly. "His needs are as great as yours."

Armide shrugged, walked a step into the tiny waves breaking on the beach and watched the lazy, faintly phosphorescent water foam about her ankles as she stirred the sand underfoot. "What would Ramahd know of Armide's needs? I thought you took no notice of me," she said, turning to stand in front of him.

Ramahd watched cautiously as she tilted up her chin and thrust melon-round breasts forward, daring him to caress her. "I noticed you, *kadin*," he said, his voice controlled and even, carefully noncommittal. "What man would not?"

"It is not yet morning." A simple fact stated as invitation.

"But it is, Armide." The sun had yet to appear, but a faint glow dimmed the stars.

"How can you tell?" Armide asked, puzzled by the man's behavior and not understanding how anyone could spurn the gift of her body.

Ramahd stepped closer, took a thread from her white cotton blouse, another from his worn, black coat. "In my country, when the difference can be seen between a white thread and a black, it is morning."

"I do not understand you," Armide snapped.

Ramahd dropped the threads onto the sand. "You are many things in the night, as are all women. But in the morning, like the threads, you cannot hide your love for Jason Brand. In the face of this love, all other men must be content with the shell of your body. It is not enough, Armide. Someday, perhaps when you have left behind the tortured vanity that will not let you admit he does not love you, I will come to you. But only then."

He caught her wrist before slashing talons could rake his face. "Offal!" she spat. "Turkish pig!" She tore free of his grip and ran toward the town. As she entered the rutted path that served for a street, a mongrel puppy yapped at her heels before slinking off, thoroughly frightened by a string of violent curses and well-aimed kicks.

Still breathing heavily, Armide burst into Caron's. The main room was littered with the crew of the *Banshee*, some with women at their sides, others alone. She stared at the ceiling. Above was the room where she had waited for Jason. She knew he would not be there. "What is it? What has happened?" A sleeply-eyed brigand, awakened by her entrance, rose from his chair near the door.

"Where is Captain Brand? Has he come in?"

The pirate gestured helplessly. Then a crafty smile broadened his stubbled face. "Perhaps I can be of help, eh?"

The glance Armide gave him was answer enough. He slumped into his chair and snatched up the jug of palm wine left over from the night before. Peering around the bottle, he watched as she climbed the stairs. The sway of her hips heated his blood and the wine scalded his throat. It gave him back his courage. Almost.

"Eggs! Damn me! Damn my eyes! Real eggs!" Ned beamed with pleasure and attacked the platter. The rest of the crew, already having served themselves, crowded around the table and looked from one to the other in amusement. Tom Gunn watched in open amazement as his smaller counterpart ladled a half-dozen eggs onto his plate and began mashing chunks of freshly baked bread into the steaming orange-yellow yolks.

"Are you sure you have enough?" Tom asked, his voice the epitome of politeness, making the whole interchange all the more ludicrous. He held the platter before Ned who, ignorant of the larger man's sarcasm, nodded gratefully and scooped another pair onto his plate.

"Thankee, Gunn," he muttered, and fell to with a relish.

The strapping giant beside him was left exactly two eggs with which to make his breakfast. Shelby was the first to lose control, and soon the rough-and-tumble souls were all laughing while a perplexed Ned Sly looked up to see what was so funny. He grew even more confused at Gunn's icy stare. Hope saved the day, though, with another platter of the delicacy which none had seen for so many months.

As the eggs disappeared, the room heated with the rising sun. Two of the thirteen men crammed about the cedar table left to take their turn aboard the *Ravener*. Hope, tired from cooking, just fitted in the bench space left behind. "What about Giuseppe?" she asked. "He comin' ashore today?" Rum thief though he was, she couldn't help liking the diminutive Italian.

Ben Tremain finished his coffee. Poole scowled into his cup then looked at the older man. Ben took the cue. "We tried to coax him ashore, but he'll not hear of it. Won't set foot on this 'pirates' den,' as he calls it. He's fearful lest Gregory find us and take him for a mutineer."

Hope scoffed. "How's he think staying aboard is going to help? Gregory will send him back to hang along with the rest of us."

Poole laughed harshly. "He's taken precautions. Last night he got into the marines' supplies and found a set of shackles. Keeps 'em by his hammock. If the *Ravener*'s taken, he'll clap himself in irons and make out how we forced him along."

"Aye. Not a day passes but what that sawbones don't feel a hangman's noose about his neck." Talk of hanging and the long arm of English justice filled the room with a heavy silence.

Hope grunted. The time for worrying about English justice was long past, and she was damned if she was going to live under its pall for the rest of her life. "Let Gregory find us," she said bravely. "I'd welcome him with open arms—and trim his length of rope so's he'd rue the day. And I don't mean hemp, neither," she finished wickedly. The threat restored the equilibrium and the crew broke into smiles.

311

"And I doubt you'd need a knife to do it," Ned added with a wink. "Chew it off, she would!"

A lady might have blushed. Hope threw her clay mug. Ned ducked and the cup shattered against the wall. Then the whole table heaved as Hope struggled away from the bench. Weak with laughter, Ned ran, the harlot in hot pursuit. Ribald catcalls from the crew followed them both.

By the time Hope reached the outer yard, Ned had stopped and was staring up toward the slope above Marie's house. As Hope ran up, he waved her into silence and pointed up the hillside. "See her, then."

"Who? Marie?"

"On horseback." He paused, squinted at the retreating figure. "I wonder where she goes, our Captain Raven?" he added in a strangely gentle tone. Hope's brows furrowed in speculation as the mounted figure blended into the trees and her night's-cape hair became one with the shadows.

The stout little mare easily ascended the slope, her hooves finding footing in the generous layer of thick loam. Marie guided the animal toward the towering *genipa,* familiar beacon of old, below which the rusted gate and weathered headstone lay vivid in her mind's eye. She cleared a masking hedge of interwoven cedars and brought the mare to a halt beneath the tall palm tree she had climbed five years earlier to see the burning town below. Everything was the same. No. Not everything. There were two markers within the wrought-iron enclosure. The stone with Pia's name carved in the grainy surface was a trifle more eroded by rain and wind, but generally bore few traces of the years. Next to it a second marker, obviously newer, had been jabbed into the soft earth. No name was carved on this piece of wood, which had already started to decay. Curious, Marie knelt and touched the marker. *Father?* . . .

But who could have found him, carried him that long sad way up from the beach? No matter. Not now. Too many memories overwhelmed this chanced-upon puzzle. Her fingers strayed to the cold stone over Pia. Had she expected warmth? She stared at Pia's marker. "You have him now," she whispered numbly.

Marie sank to the ground.

The grief nurtured since the cruel day five years past now spilled over in blinding, burning tears. Jean Ravenne. Of the quick temper, of the gentle words that healed a child's heart. Even in death his love had sustained her. And what had she to give in return? Emptiness? Grief? Tears? *Good-bye, father. Good-bye* . . .

She had to leave this place of tears. Quickly, she rose from the wreckage of her youth and left the tiny clearing to the ghostly vespers of the wind in the boughs. The mare pawed at the loam, eager to be off. Marie vaulted to her back and the animal sprang away, following the winding trail that led to the emerald summit. Scrambling upward over rocks and roots, Marie felt at one with the steed, bent forward for balance into the flowing mane whipping her throat.

Cresting the top of the summit, she paused. The Caribbean lay flung out below as if some magical dragon had scattered his treasure trove of harbored sapphires, then melted them with his fiery breath. To the north lay Point de las Pleurs, the cape of tears, forbidden playground of youth. Shading her eyes, she peered southeast. A ragged fringe of trees hid the top of a knoll, beyond which was the cliff with the mysterious face that the island's first settlers had seen and Pia Ravenne named. From the top of the cliff, a spring-fed waterfall dropped past the pool whose crystal surface was shaded by surrounding *ycao* trees. Smiling now—once past the visit to the grave she could remember her father fondly, rather than with pain—she heard once again as he cautioned against the wild boars who coveted the delicious fruit. They had not worried her then, and most certainly not now. She cast a final glance down the way she had come. If only Jason . . .

Jason again. Better to have forgotten him. The rogue was a rock hurled into the placid pond of newly achieved self-assurance. His presence had ruined her return. Why couldn't he have just gone back to Scotland? There was plenty of shipping on those storm-tossed coasts. He had no excuse for intruding on Mysteré and her life. Cursing herself for a weak fool, she fought the thought of him and savagely urged the mare into a gallop designed to outrace the sweeping tides of passion, however unadmitted and denied.

She kept to the shallow slopes, the game trail that wound along the spine of hills that ran the length of Mysteré. Overhead, the spiny columns of rosary palms cast jagged, irregular patches of shadow. Then she was past them and in a gully, emerging a few moments later on the brushy crest of a stubby knoll. To the right loomed the dark, almost malevolent caricature of stone, mammoth and misshapen. Portrait of god or devil, the face was carved into an escarpment of hardened lava embellished with cindery fragments of scoriae, chunks of which littered the trail and exploded into powder under the mare's hooves.

Descent was less precipitous on the eastern portion of the cliff, where the strange alchemy of seasons had sculpted the surface into ropy footholds of solidified magma. Marie dismounted and cautiously led her mount along the treacherous path leading to the base of the cliff. The morning sun was intense and heat radiated from the lava. Strands of hair clung to her streaked cheeks. Sweat stung her eyes and blinded her with salty indifference. Now, beyond the face itself, she could see the tiny waterfall plunging into the thick exotica, above which rose the cool, tinkling laughter of water on rocks. The mare snorted impatiently, lunged ahead and almost trampled Marie. Half-slipping and half-running, Marie was dragged the final short yards to the beckoning glade, deep in verdant shade.

No more than fifteen feet in diameter, the pool was surrounded by a belt of level ground encircled by trees. Marie let go the hackamore and allowed the mare to drink, then wander around the pool to crop the sweet grass. Two handfuls of the fresh, clear water were enough for Marie. She tugged free of her boots and

314

sank to the earth to lie and stare through the leaves to the startlingly azure sky. Here at last, in her secluded fairyland retreat, was surcease from painful memories and disquieting longing. Here at last, after the torment of the night before, was sleep, sweet and deep and untrammeled with dreams.

She woke a half-hour later when the mare snorted in alarm. The sun was · high overhead, a bright glare through the cooling canopy of trees. Nothing seemed to be amiss. A dozen feet away, the tinkling waterfall called. The pool was dappled with slatted beams of light, diamonds on jade. The ground all about was littered with amethyst-colored fruit, evidence of the generously laden branches that formed a latticework stretching across the water. Quiet. Stillness, delightfully broken by the high furtive piping of a small, green-plumaged parrot. Marie laughed and the tiny bird, misunderstanding, took alarm and fluttered to a higher branch for safety.

Rested and lazy, suddenly full of joy, Marie rose, stripped off her blouse and weighed it down with the flintlock pistol carried in her belt. Breeches followed quickly and, naked, she turned slowly and luxuriously in the warm air.

It was almost like being a child again. Innocence. Purity. The real world had disappeared, to be replaced with a land where squalor and pain and degradation and doubt didn't exist. Marie crossed to the edge of the pool, chanced a step into the chilly water, gasped and took another. With a shriek, she toppled into the pond. There had been no gradual incline, rather one step and then an abrupt, total and most frigid drop. Remembering she had made the same mistake as a girl, she laughed anew and struck out for the far side.

The cold water was a refreshing change. She dove beneath the surface, plummeting through the pool's jade-colored gloom, her hair streaming back in jet tendrils. Like a water nymph, she was a creature of mythic beauty in ivory nakedness. Abandoning the quest to touch bottom, she shot to the surface, whipped her hair

315

and sent a cascade of droplets dancing in the air. How beautiful it all was after years of absence. How heart-achingly beautiful. Awed, she climbed from the water and flopped down to the warm ground.

Body alert and eager, she smiled at the fractured sky. Here was rest. Here was what she wanted, what had drawn her across the Caribbean. She would gladly sacrifice ship, crew and adventures to end her days in such perfect solitude. At peace finally, she rolled onto her back, flesh tingling, petal-pink nipples extended and taut, rounded breasts provocatively full with the beauty of youth.

And then the sound! Something was in the brush. Man? Beast? Horror stories from childhood had no sooner flashed through her mind than a feral boar, jaundiced-yellow tusks jutting from brutal, foam-specked snout, emerged from the fringe of undergrowth. The animal paused not fifteen feet away, his bristled hide and chunky frame adding to his vicious appearance. Marie held her breath and her fingers edged toward the pistol, woefully inadequate in the face of the beast's obvious menace.

The boar grunted and lowered his head. Marie's hand froze, inches from the pistol grip. Like a macabre painting, mindless beast and frightened woman posed on the brink of action. *If I could get into the water again . . .* Trying not to move her head, she calculated the distance. *Roll to right . . . jump and dive . . .*

Without warning, a jagged chunk of lava shot past her shoulder and struck the boar. The animal grunted and jumped back. For a brief second a comically startled, almost human look passed over his face, then he squealed in fright and vanished among the trees, losing no time in putting as healthy a distance as possible between him and the strange she-creature who could hurl missiles without moving.

As startled as the boar, Marie spun in time to see Jason, an appreciative grin lighting his face, step from behind a tree trunk. Half-angry, still half frightened, she scooped up the pistol and leveled it at him. "What are you doing here?"

"Saving you from wild beasts," Jason said laconically, his eyes wandering approvingly over her supple form. His shirt was open to the waist. She centered the gun on the red-gold ringlets matting his muscular chest and, acutely aware of her own nakedness, tried to keep the gun from wavering.

"Come no closer," she ordered, taking a step backward at the same time he took one forward. "I mean it."

"I rescue a fair maid in distress," he said, slowly circling the bank toward her, "and am threatened in return? But I doubt your intentions, mistress."

Marie thought of Lieutenant Schell. He had doubted too. Something in her eyes made Jason pause a half-dozen paces from her. It was maddening to be so close. He wanted to hold her, crush her in his arms and feast on her kisses.

"You followed me," Marie accused.

"I watched you climb down the slope. I was here before you, by my oath."

"And said nothing?"

Jason stroked his chin. A mischievous expression crossed his face. "There were other matters demanding my attention."

Marie blushed despite herself. She tried to conjure up all the reasons she should hate him, enumerate betrayal, pain, lies . . .

"Marie—"

"No. I am no longer a silly child to be taken on the whim of a great lord. I have known prison and humiliation, blood and death. I have known betrayal of the basest sort, by one who lied in his teeth and ran like a coward." Tears welled in her eyes as she continued. "How quiet you've become. What? No denial? I should think so great a Scottish lord, once so facile of tongue, could find something to say in his defense."

Jason flushed at her allusion to the past that could never be relived, never repaired. "In this world," he

317

finally answered, "only a fool allows his life to be ruined by the mistakes he's made. Only a fool allows himself to repeat those mistakes. I am what I am. I deny nothing. Can you say the same?"

"I have nothing to deny," Marie blurted in astonishment.

"Oh, no?" Jason responded softly. He moved toward her. "Prove it." Marie's hand tightened on the gun but he was drawn on by the slate-gray, misty eyes, by raven tresses, by the supple, exquisite flesh made for heated desire. Drawn to fulfillment or death.

The gun exploded and flames licked from the iron maw. At the last moment, Marie jerked her hand upward. Leaden death creased the flesh across his shoulder and left a line of crimson where it passed. Without breaking stride, Jason brushed aside the smoking weapon and, ignoring the pain of his superficial wound, swept Marie into his arms.

The gun slid from her fingers, thumped to the earth. *No! I will not love him . . . No!*

"Marie," he whispered, his lips tantalizingly close, moving closer.

No! The last vestige of a ruse. The soul's unbounded leap into the swirling, cruel maelstrom of passion. Holding back, and then . . . released . . . by the searing touch of his lips.

Soft, silent crush of grasses. Bronze flesh beneath caresses. Someone has been spinning darkness. The fire of her love is daybreak, her hair is nightfall. Her eyes are the misted mystery that lies between. Eternal woman, infinite.

Marie slid her thigh between his. Her fingers found the puckered ridge of a scar, a pale corrugated crescent from ribs to hip where a recent wound had healed. She bore a similar memento, though invisible, for her wound was of the heart. Had it healed? *No. Do not doubt. Love, instead. Love only. Not as an excuse for the past, but a reason for now.*

There his gold-flecked eyes. Sad Adonis. Why sad? *I*

318

will quench your sorrow with a kiss. Muscles ripple along his back beneath her ministering touch. His hips are supple stone. Now his pulsing strength surges against her breast. Delicious enticement! *I will clasp you close . . .*

Her hair drapes him. She yearns to the core of her being for his proud length. But not yet. Not quite . . . yet. From its mantle of burnished ringlets, upthrust scepter of creation rises to meet eager kisses. Feel the hot strength that longs to fill her own moist emptiness. Fierce fire, incomplete.

Now? Wait. No longer, Jason. No longer, my love . . . She rolls atop him. Their fingers interlock to form a temple to Venus. *Banish this hollow ache.* His heated manhood presses at the feverish gateway. *Vanquish longing . . .* Eyes shut, they stare into the spiraling explosion of ecstasy. His hands grip her rounded hips.

Then sweet impalement.

Oneness. Marie yawned drowsily, stretched her right leg and pointed her toes at the treetops, vague against the dusk. *Good heavens!* She nudged the sleeping form at her side. Jason stirred but did not wake. Marie smiled, rose on her elbows to stare down at him.

How peaceful he looked in sleep. Relaxed, the hard lines of his face had softened and she thought she could catch the telltale signs of innocence long since covered with layers of self-centered cynicism and disillusionment. Doubts threatened the idyllic afternoon but she shrugged them aside. *This moment. Now. Here is happiness enough. Let sorrows lie where they may, for the while.*

Jason grunted and rolled over, revealing the wound on his shoulder. A line of caked blood marked how close the lead ball had come. Marie shuddered. An inch lower would have shattered his collarbone and done serious injury. Six inches lower? She wouldn't think of that. In any case, the wound wasn't inflamed. He was strong and healthy, would heal quickly. An impish smile suffused her features with gypsy daring and she stifled a

319

giggle. Rising to her knees, she leaned forward and tickled his chest with her hair. Moving her head from side to side, she swept down across his stomach and bronzed thighs. A hand suddenly cupped her naked buttock. "Hey . . ." he said, gently.

"The little prince is restless," she teased as the light touch of her tresses elicited the desired response.

"He would be king," Jason replied.

"Alas, he has no court," Marie countered. Knees touching his side, she sat back on her calves.

"But he does have a queen," Jason rasped, aroused now. He heaved forward. Marie, head back and hair spilling capelike down her back to the ground, thrust her breasts forward and shivered as his lips coaxed her nipples into taut life. She sighed as he traced a path down her smooth stomach, then moaned with delightful anticipation as his kisses found the nest of her desire.

A year without him! The muscles in her legs were weak and she sank to the earth. Jason kneeled beside her, his hands playing up and down her breasts, stomach and thighs in time to her cries of endearment. *A whole year!* His fingers moved inside her until she arched high in the air, and clutched at the rampant member lost in the mists over her.

Gently, Jason loosed her hand, reached down and lifted her hips, swung her to him. Still on his knees, he entered, pulling her tight against him. Marie clutched the ground lest she spin into space, then abandoned herself to the sweet convulsions.

Beyond thought, beyond reason. His face was a blur as he lifted her up and down, up and down until she reached the next impossible summit, only to find another more lofty, and yet another still to conquer the last. Each climax was but an interlude blotting out the one before until the world was lost to the harmony of their motion. At last, one exultant, final, sweeping explosion. She tightened about him, weeping as his smoldering seed emptied, joining their souls in a torrent of timeless ecstasy and sweeping them both to a distant starlit sea of satisfaction.

The hands. Horny, calloused, groping hands. Thrust them aside. Cry for help. Cry to whom? Oblivion? Oblivion never answers. There the dagger at her guarded waist. Seize it, then. A horrid wilderness of pawing brutes, eager to defile an unwilling catch. Somewhere, thunder. Draw the dagger forth! See how the lightning plays along the steel.

As the straining, faceless, brute forms pummel her to earth, the girl plunges the biting blade deep into her breast. She laughs horribly, having cheated them of their satisfaction. Her voice rises an octave until it becomes a piercing shriek of pain, ever and ever spiraling higher.

Marie bolted upright, stared into the heart of night, her senses gratefully relieved of the weight of the dream. "What is it?" Jason mumbled, half-awake.

The sun had vanished beyond the earth's rim. "I . . . I must go back," she answered, shivering involuntarily at the last vestiges of the nightmare.

"Not in the dark. Better wait for morning."

"Hope, Tom . . . The others will be worried."

"A pirate's lot is an uncertain one," Jason replied facetiously. "They'll survive." She could feel him shrug. His indifference was galling but she swallowed the retort. "I'll make a fire," he said, finally sensing her discomfort.

Marie drew her knees up beneath her chin, sat there unmoving while Jason gingerly picked a way to his horse, lost in the near total darkness, then rustled about for fuel and tinder. Sparks from a flint glimmered, jettisoned outward like threads of fire, winked and disappeared, vanishing as if they had never existed. Like promises, Marie mused gloomily, lying back again. A flickering flame, another, and soon a friendly campfire cast a cheerful glow to dispel her moodiness. In the soft light, Jason posed, peering into the bush. He seemed molded of burnished bronze. Golden hair hung thick and tousled. His chest, arms, legs were covered with a light down that gave him a quality of unrealness, as if there were no dimensions to him, as if he were a dream concocted of air and night and fire. A figure of treachery and fulfillment . . .

Eyes half closed, she watched as he built up the fire, disappeared into the bushes where his horse was tied. He was so competent, moved with such animal grace, with no lost movement or wasted energy. So natural, she thought, sleepily. As if this were an everyday occurrence, as if he were a creature of the glen, as if there had been nothing special . . . *I am a fool to love him*. Caution contended with sleep and she jerked awake blinking her eyes. *Ha! Love? I doubt he knows the meaning of the word*. Her eyes closed again and she forced them open a crack, pretended she was just resting them. *I know what love is. Love is* . . . A frown. Now that was disturbing. *Love is* . . .

His footsteps as he returned to the fire were a handy excuse for not admitting the sentence had been left unfinished. Somewhere beyond the clearing a horse snorted. A piece of metal clanged. He was kneeling now, putting something by the fire. Sound and sight blended. Her breathing deepened. Comfortable, comforting sounds. "Jason?"

"Hmmm?"

The world was too heavy. She dampened her lips. It was important that she tell him. "Love is . . ." But it was only a mumble.

Jason rose, stood smiling down at her, then reached for his shirt and spread it across her nakedness. For a brief second, his hand touched her hair, then left her lest she wake. For a brief second he remembered England, what she had gone through to free him and how he had repaid her valor. But that was long ago. He'd been an utter cad. But he had survived. Escaped Penscott's den. That he had in the process hurt Marie was unfortunate, of course, but all was well that ended well, even if it had been the devil's own luck.

Smiling at his good fortune, he pulled on his breeches and went back into the trees to bring the horses closer in for the night. From the pommel of his saddle he took a large sack filled with a cooking pot, vegetables, fruit

322

and dried turtle meat. Working swiftly, he dumped a cup of water in the pot and hung it over the fire, sliced the meat, onions and cassava roots and threw them in. The fruit took longer, but by the time the pot was hot enough to set the water boiling, they were peeled and ready to take their place with the steaming turtle. Moments later, apricots, banana and star apple were all bubbling away to form the succulent stew that had been a mainstay of pirates for the last hundred years.

The aroma woke Marie. Foggily unaware of where she was or what was happening, she stirred and rolled over. There was a fire, and behind it a man squatted on his heels, elbows wrapped around knees and chin contemplatively resting on forearm. An aroma long forgotten—sweet, with meat overtones—filled the clearing. She let her eyes slide closed again to continue the dream, then waked with a jerk.

How long had she slept? A glance upward told her nothing, for the trees confused the stars. Embarrassed for displaying weakness, Marie struggled to her feet, pulled on the shirt and advanced to the fire. Jason grinned up at her. "Hungry?"

"You let me sleep too long."

"Not at all. I dozed myself. In any case, the stew had to cook." He peered into the pot, poked the contents with a hastily carved wooden spoon and tasted. A broad smile split his face. "It's ready. Supper's on." Without waiting for yea or nay, he rocked to his feet, caught up the bail and swung the pot to a flat rock set up as a table. "Nothing very fancy," he said, plopping down a clay jug of palm wine and stack of ship's bisquits. "You use it first," he said, handing her the spoon. "Watch out. It's steaming hot."

It was the first time since her abduction from Mysteré that Marie had eaten turtle. She couldn't remember tasting better. Jason dipped bisquits into the broth and bolted them down while Marie wielded the spoon. Then they switched. Both were ravenous and the stew disappeared rapidly. Neither spoke until the bisquits were gone and the pot and jug empty.

Jason settled back on his elbows. Marie stretched out lazily, poked the fire with a stick and sighed with contentment. "For a pirate, you're a pretty good cook, sir."

Jason shrugged modestly. "You did it justice, I'll say that," Marie looked around, smiled and turned back to the fire. Jason watched her without speaking, suddenly filled with wonder. Marie Ravenne . . . Raven . . . Timid serving girl, meek lover to pirate captain. Insatiable, sensual mistress. She was as much a mystery as the island from which she claimed to come. A prize like her wasn't to be had in just any port. He scowled as past caught up with present. He had wronged her then. Should he make excuses? No. Not now. Someday, perhaps, when the time was right.

But who knew what someday would bring? Who could predict what an enigma would do next? Eyes slitted, he marveled at the sleek form of the woman who had been a fever in his blood, whose image had plagued him whether alone or in the arms of other women. *Why this one? Why this one woman, of all I have seen?*

"Asleep again?"

She stirred, moved one foot until it touched his. "No."

"There's much to discover about you, Marie. But we will have time. You and I, together."

Marie suppressed the sudden thrill. Caution had become second nature to one badly treated. "Together? Where?" she asked.

"Here. On Mysteré. The plantation house for our headquarters. We'll enlarge it, of course. Even put in windows. Real glass, by God, if you want."

She turned to look him in the eye. "Lord and lady of the island?" she asked, with a touch of sarcasm.

Jason frowned. Marie caught a glimmer of sorrow, emptiness and pain to match her own. It was a quality she had not expected in the man, one which his brash nature had kept well hidden. "No. Not lord," he said in all seriousness. The more familiar devil-may-care attitude returned. "King and queen," he proclaimed with mock grandiosity.

"And what will . . . Armide is her name? What will Armide say?"

Jason had recovered sufficiently to handle the question without hesitation. "Armide? A pretty problem. My crew will be content in the village, as will most of yours. But Armide? I suppose I shall have to give her up."

Marie cursed herself for blushing. "I think she loves you. Yet you would hurt her?"

"Loves me?" he chuckled. "No. Not Armide. Armide loves Armide only. Which does not mean she won't be hurt, even if for only a day or two. However, it is us who concern me now. You and I. Think of it. A sixth-rater and a slaver. What prizes I can take!"

Marie sat up abruptly. *"We* can take."

"Of course, we. I'll shower you with Spanish gold. English and French, too, with luck. What is it?"

"The *Ravener* is my ship, Jason. Its crew, mine."

"Well, yes . . ."

"What prizes there are, we take together."

"Are you mad, lass? You're no buccaneer."

"I took the *Ravener.*"

"True enough. Fortune was kind I'll warrant. But pirating is altogether another business. Why, you're just a girl!"

Marie shot to her feet, her fists clenched and knuckled against her waist. "You . . . you . . . Oh!" She stamped the ground, then with growing fury began to gather her clothes.

Jason sat up, partly amused, partly concerned. "Here, now. What's this?"

"I'm leaving."

"But you'll get lost."

"Not hardly. I was born here, remember." She bent over to pick up her boots, realized the immodest display of bare flesh and quickly straightened. "Oh, I hate you!"

"No you don't."

"I do! Don't correct me!"

"If you did, you wouldn't have missed." He grinned, reached for and handed her the empty pistol.

She tore it from his grasp. "And I wish I hadn't. Missed, that is." Beside herself with anger, she started toward the tethered mare. Jason caught her arm, spun her around. Marie slapped him with the flat of her hand. He yanked her close, forcibly kissed her. Marie struggled to no avail. She was imprisoned in his powerful grasp and try though she might, her own ardor rose at his demanding virility. And then she was free. Jason stood a pace off, laughing uncontrollably. "What's so damned funny?"

"You. Me. Look at us. Fighting like a pair of children."

"It's you who started it. You and your high-handed ways."

"It doesn't matter who started it, Marie," he said soberly. "It's how we end that's important." He reached out a hand. "I'm conceding. You've spirit enough. More than most men. As far as I'm concerned, it's together we'll roam, lass." He gestured to the campfire. "Come back to the warmth. I'd not be having you break that pretty neck of yours."

Marie held back. "I'll not be a servant to you, Jason Brand. You or any other man. My ship, my crew."

"For as long as you wish it, on my oath. But mind you, girl, you need me. A strong man to—"

"I need no man," Marie retorted.

Jason stretched out near the fire. His handsome, reckless features glowed with amusement. He patted the blanket, caught Marie's hand and pulled her down next to him. "We'll see," he said as she lay back. And repeated softly, "We'll see."

Chapter XVII

Forlicar rubbed the ponderous expanse of his belly, belched royally, wiped a grease-encrusted sleeve across his stubbled jowls and tossed over his shoulder the beef bone he'd gnawed clean of flesh. A scruffy hound of indeterminate lineage, spurred from a doorway vigil by the clatter of bone on the floor, bellied carefully across the tavern, retrieved the prize and returned to his resting place. Forlicar had just grinned at Ramahd and muttered something about doing his good deed for the day when his single eye darted about in its socket. Armide had started down the stairs.

"Ah!" he sighed, loud enough for her to hear. Armide stopped and stared at him as if he were some new and despicable form of animal life. Forlicar struggled to manufacture a witty comment, but nothing came to mind. Resigned to his own illiteracy, he settled for a second, more lascivious and heartrending "Ahhhh!"

Armide disdainfully looked around the room and pointedly ignored the hopeful stares. Everyone there knew she had slept alone, and not a stouthearted man but wished he would be chosen to rectify the situation. The moment was broken by the mongrel pup at the door: growling and snapping, he ran for safety as Tom Gunn, followed by a dozen of the *Ravener*'s crew, burst into the room.

"Found ye then," he bellowed, leveling a pistol at Forlicar. "Where is she?"

Incensed by the intrusion, the men in the tavern set up an angry rumble. It were best you put that pistol aside," Ramahd spoke up coldly. "It is the law. None is to bear arms against another on Mysteré. If an issue cannot be settled with fists, then it must be resolved offshore."

"Curse your rules," Shelby shouted from the safety of Gunn's back. "This goes beyond rules."

"You will turn the whole island against you," warned Ramahd, his voice calm and level, "and find no sanctuary among the Brethren ever again. As for you, cub, either leash your tongue or step into the open and speak like a man."

The ensuing stillness could have been cut with a knife. It ended with the harsh, metallic sound of Gunn's pistol being taken off cock. What should have been an easing of tension ended abruptly when the mountainous pirate strode forward, fists clenched and his homely, usually good-natured face mottled with rage. "Damn you, then. Where is she?"

Forlicar, who had always believed the bigger a man, the more of him there was to hit, was not to be cowed. He struggled to his feet and stepped forward boldly, anticipating the brawl that was sure to follow. "You haven't said who you're looking for, mate. Not that it matters. I, Forlicar, have enough round-heeled wenches to service without adding another to my list."

"Service!" Hope screeched, elbowing through her cohorts to confront the lout who had insulted her Tulip. "Why, you barrel-gutted, carrion-eating son of a crook-assed dungclerk from Bedlam, *service* indeed!" She jabbed a bony finger into Forlicar's belly. "We've come to see what mischief's been done, and woe be to him who's to blame."

"We'll not be threatened by the likes of a run-down, worn-out half-shilling whore and her scurvy mate," shouted Armide, ready for a fight herself and fueling the flames.

"Aye. Why don't you take this slut—" Forlicar began. He never finished.

"Slut?" shrieked the quick-tempered harlot, hoisting her voluminous skirts to midthigh the better to move her legs. "Slut!" Hope Deferred Maketh the Heart Sick brought up her foot in a rousing kick, sickening not his heart, but that most vital and sensitive place all men seek to protect as well as employ.

Forlicar yelped and doubled over, one hand cupping his crotch, the other wrapping around his bosomy assailant and pulling her to the floor. Ramahd shouted, "Wait!" but his call for order and sanity was interrupted as his shipmate Loupe treacherously felled young Shelby from behind with a crudely manufactured but deftly wielded chair. Tom spun about at the sound and swatted Loupe over a nearby table. The battle was joined.

Fists hammered into heads. Teeth latched onto the nearest limb or appendage. Tables were overturned and smashed. Clay jugs of palm wine and bottles of rum became deadly missiles, arcing across the room to crack into unwary heads. Franco Caron, the roly-poly tavern keeper, and his wife Diana, clutching a frayed nightgown about her buxom frame, appeared in the doorway to their room. Their pleas were lost in the din. Eyes appealing to the heavens, they threw up their hands and returned to the safety of the bedroom, barring the door just in time to avoid catching the poor, unnamed soul who crashed into it head first.

The battle raged on, with the only voice rising above the general destruction coming from the rafters where a mottled green parrot Forlicar had won in a game of chance showered obscenities, the cleanest of which was "Let's put it 'tween your legs, mate," at the brawlers. Tom Gunn, momentarily buried under a struggling swarm of humanity, rose like Leviathan and sent bruised and battered men to the ground with his ham-sized fists. Loupe and Ned Sly engaged in an awkward duel with benches at four paces. The wall of the tavern facing the sea had been laboriously constructed of bamboo shoots, woven to be raised or lowered as needed. Now it disappeared in a shower of yellow splinters and a quartet of contorted bodies tumbled out, followed by Poole. The helmsman howled in pain and tried to pull a biting, scratching, kicking mulatto girl from astride his shoulders.

Amidst a host of trampling, booted feet, Forlicar and Hope grunted and cursed, the pirate trying to dodge her

329

clawing fingers and free himself to carry on the fight with his brothers. There was one problem. The more they struggled, the more pleasurable this contest became, for Hope was a great deal of woman and her undulations served to press full thighs and ample breasts against Forlicar's body, already heated with the lust of battle.

Hope, her skirt bunched up around her waist and one breast pulled free from a ripped blouse, suddenly realized Forlicar's breeches had come undone and that the pulsing pressure thus freed was indelicately demanding entrance. Worse, the great oaf was grinning. He had totally forgotten the fight. "You big ox!" the harlot spat.

Forlicar nodded in agreement. "'Tis true. I'll show you, yes?"

The hilarity of it all impressed even Hope and overrode her anger. Guffawing outright, she opened her legs and pulled him to her, giving herself up to that more delightful contest between man and woman.

A shot sounded. Men froze in attitudes of warlike statuary. All looked to see who had broken the code. Those inside the tavern rushed outside. Jason and Marie, their horses pawing the moist sand, stared at the group. Jason held a smoking pistol. Tom released a bedraggled pirate named Cantu who slumped to the ground, muttered, "Thank goodness," and rolled over unconscious.

"Raven!" Tom beamed. His face darkened immediately. "If that lug has harmed you, I'll—"

"For shame, Tom," Marie interrupted. "These are your mates."

"Aye, men," Jason echoed. "Will you war with your own?" The combatants stared at one another in amazement, and then at their captains. "These energies were best put to use building shelters, for there aren't enough taverns to host you all. And one fewer it would seem," Jason added, indicating the shambles.

Diana Caron trundled out through the missing front of the tavern. "Captain Brand," she moaned. "Look what they've done. A shambles, and after all the work my Franco did."

Jason couldn't help laughing. "Don't worry, lass. Yours'll be the first to be repaired."

"What's this about my mates?" Ned Sly asked, scowling as he staggered toward the horses.

"It's true, Ned. Jason. . . Captain Brand and I have decided to join forces and work together from now on. So will the crews of our ships."

Sly faced Jason. "Just so it's understood," he said clearly, so all could hear. "Raven's my captain, and none other." A chorus of assent sounded from the crew of the *Ravener*.

"No one is asking otherwise," Jason assured them. "Separate crews, but allies, strengthened by our compact. Are the terms agreeable?"

Marie and Jason sat on their horses while the men conferred. At length, Ramahd stepped forward for the *Banshee*. "We're in accord," he said flatly, "and accept the compact."

Tom Gunn spoke for the *Ravener*. "If this is what you want, Raven, we're with you."

"Good. Then let's to it," Jason shouted. "There's ships to be worked on and beds to be built, unless you'd rather sleep on the sand."

"Sand's good enough for me if it's good enough for you, Captain." Loupe offered. Fighting, drinking and wenching filled enough of his time without having to stoop to more mundane affairs.

"He has another place," Marie announced quietly, almost shyly.

Behind them, Armide soundlessly vanished down the beach. Realization was slower to strike the men, but when it did, knowing grins spread across swollen faces. As if in approval of the match thus announced, a deep groan of unadulterated male satisfaction accompanied by a mellow female counterpart echoing his bliss came from the shadowy recesses of the tavern. Jason looked questioningly in the direction of the sound, but Marie

331

turned aside to keep from laughing outright. She would have recognized Hope's voice anywhere.

John Law hated waiting unnecessarily, even for tea. His swarthy bulldog frame tense, he pondered the frivolity of the French. Here they were in the Americas, in a town but recently hacked from the swamps and forests, and the library looked as if it sat in the heart of Paris. Rich wooden panels of mahogany reflected candlelight and fire. Thin, exquisited carved furniture with brocade seats and backs had been designed for drawing rooms in town houses. The paintings had been transported across the ocean at great expense to reflect the tastes of a civilization far removed from reality. There was even glass in the windows, an undreamed-of extravagance. A beautiful room, to be sure, as was the whole house. But still out of place.

His pacing continued until Angelique, the governor's daughter, entered and directed an accompanying servant to place a tray of tea and honey cakes on a table between her father and his visitor. Law bowed and gallantly kissed her hand.

Angelique, a beauty of seventeen summers, curtsied demurely. "Monsieur," she said softly, the word ripe with teasing overtones as his lips brushed the back of her hand. Her honey-blonde hair fell in heavy curls and confidantes to bare shoulders. Hazel eyes twinkled from under heavy lashes, darkened to contrast deliciously with whitened cheeks. "If you will pardon me?" With a brief, coquettish smile, she swept from the room, her richly brocaded gown rustling on the hardwood floor.

"A most exquisite creature," Law declared heartily. "She illuminates the whole settlement."

Bienville nodded absentmindedly, well aware of his daughter's beauty. "However, this does nothing toward settling our dispute. The English captain is on his way. His men have already searched the taverns along the waterfront."

Law scowled. "We could open fire on his ship. A good dose of heated shot would cure his insolence."

"With Colonel Guilbert off among the Alabamos? No, John. Hatred for the English has warped your good sense. Mobile cannot afford open hostility between ourselves and the English. Nor would Louis ever approve. Such a course would be disastrous. The Royal Navy is far too strong, and we are much too dependent on—"

A knock on the door halted the conversation momentarily. A servant entered. "Monsieur, Captain Gregory of His Most Royal Majesty's Navy.

"Give us a moment, then send him in. And Raoul. Another log for the fireplace."

"Oui, monsieur."

Bienville gestured toward an anteroom to the side. Law hesitated, not in the least liking the conditions for the interview with Gregory that he himself had stipulated. Wielding unseen power was all well and good, but did leave something to be desired from time to time: facing the Englishman himself would be far more satisfying. "Remember who appointed you," cautioned Law, "whose financial resources are responsible for Mobile's continued existence."

"I will do what is best for the colony," the governor replied, closing the side door, then turning as the main one opened and a tall, angular Englishman stepped into the room. *"Bienvenue,"* Monsieur Bienville said, striding across the room to greet his visitor.

Wrapped in an imposing greatcoat, Gregory ignored the greeting. His fierce eyes inspected the room and the governor with a single glance. "I speak no French, but was told you speak English," he stated flatly and without the slightest pretense of civility.

"Yes, yes. By all means." Bienville gestured to a chair.

Gregory remained standing. "What I have to say will not take long."

The Frenchman nodded politely, pretending not to notice the furrowed scar tissue marring the captain's cheek. Straightening, he found himself staring into Gregory's eyes and shuddered inwardly at the depth of hatred displayed there. It was better Law had retired to

333

the outer room, he thought, turning his back on the Englishman and heading for the fire. Such hatred would have found an equal, and there would have been bloody hell to pay. "Very well, monsieur."

"Your colony is indiscriminate in its choice of friends."

"I do not understand."

"I will explain," Gregory sneered. "Pirates, sir. Mobile is a haven for pirates who make prey of English shipping. My officers have gleaned that from the taverns they have searched."

"Monsieur, I protest—"

"Nothing. You will protest nothing. Governor, there is an agreement between our two nations to discourage these sea dogs whenever and wherever they are encountered."

Bienville stiffened. "In that case, my dear sir," he countered, "I must inform you that your high-handed, arbitrary and felonious expedition in our city has violated a similar agreement, violated the sovereignty of our colony and insulted His Most Christian Majesty, King Louis the Fifteenth. Your monarch will hear of this."

"As will yours that you offer sanctuary to pirates."

"How are we to know the purpose of those who choose our harbor and come to trade?"

"Come, come. I am no fool, Governor. Neither are you. If you persevere and I discover you continue to succor these swine, I promise that not so much as a longboat shall arrive in these waters with supplies of any sort. Mobile, such as it is, will not survive long under those conditions."

Bienville paled. "You wouldn't dare."

"I would. And I have the ship to do it. More, if I need them. However, there is an alternative."

The Frenchman sat, shaken at the prospects. Mobile was an insecure colony, barely holding onto life. Any interference such as Gregory threatened, legal or not, would inflict a mortal wound. Reprisals would come too late. "What is this choice?"

"Two ships. Two crews. I have received information that Jason Brand has visited here and will no doubt return. When he does, you will take him prisoner and hold him for my return."

"But he has done nothing, has interfered with none of our trade. So far as I know, he is a legitimate merchant, operating independently and within the law. I find your insinuation that he is a pirate deeply disturbing."

"I insinuate nothing. The intelligence garnered in your taverns is most explicit. Brand bought a ship here, a slaver, which he has armed with ten six-pounders. Need I go on, Governor?"

Bienville cursed silently, damning the loose tongues of the waterfront riffraff. Still, he was damned if he'd let the Englishman run completely roughshod over him. "Of course, if you have proof—"

Gregory stiffened. "My proof, sir, is my word."

The governor inclined his head respectfully. "Of course," he murmured graciously. "And the other?"

"An English ship."

Bienville's eyebrows arched quizzically.

"The *Sword of Cornwall,* a sixth-rater with forty guns and a crew of mutineers, captained by a girl, one Marie Ravenne."

"Mmm." Bienville could not help but be intrigued. And amused, though he considered it politic not to display amusement. "A most unusual occurrence," he said drolly. "I did not think the English allowed girls to steal their ships."

The question faded before the English officer's withering stare. "Do not forget what I have said. Comply with my requests and I will be lenient and overlook your indiscretions from time to time."

Governor Jean Baptiste le Moyne, sieur de Bienville, rose. The offer of leniency was really too much. "I will consider what you have said. And now, if you please, there are other matters to which I must tend. You have proved a most unwelcome guest, Captain."

335

Gregory paused at the door. "On the contrary, Governor. I have been no guest at all. Good day, sir."

John Law reentered the room the moment the outer door closed. A vivid sheen of anger darkened his face. "The next time we will be ready," he said in a strained voice. "I will take great pleasure in sinking his ship—ships, if he has them—and listening to the pretty tune this popinjay of a captain sings then."

"Surely you jest?"

"We are a long way from England, Jean Baptiste." Law paced the room a moment, then stopped. "Brand owes me a good deal of gold. We obtain supplies necessary to our well-being from the Brethren. What else would you do?"

Bienville shrugged. He needed time to analyze all the complexities involved. There was no need for haste. Not yet. "Have dinner," he shrugged, accompanying Law to the door. "Remember, my friend. We are a long way from France, too. I'm sure the English will be most ingenious in their attempts to recover from the embarrassment of losing a ship to a mere woman. And as for Brand? Let him deliver your gold. Once his debt is discharged, all obligations are finished, no? Then we shall see."

Mobile's dedicated governor listened absentmindedly to his wife's heartfelt complaint that a colony in Louisiana was, first, the ultimate insult to her breeding and position; second, the most humiliating and debasing assignment to which anyone could possibly be posted; and third, no place to raise a daughter of Angelique's beauty, birth and character. The governor shook his head in accord with each bitterly delivered statement. True, Mobile was but a tenuous foothold in the rim of a vast frontier, in no way comparable to Paris. True, with the exception of Colonel Guilbert and his wife, they comprised the only aristocracy for untold miles and were forced to content themselves with oafs and louts and an occasional ship's captain or visiting dignitary. True, there were no eligible suitors for a grown daughter who was, yes, scandalously, still single. He failed to point out the winter climate was much more amenable than Paris's for fear she would recollect the recent summer and the swarms of mosquitoes which had plagued them.

At last the tirade ended. His waistcoat was too tight, Bienville noted, sipping the sherry placed before him by Marmont. "Perhaps this spring," he murmurred noncommittally, striving to placate the imposing woman who sat at the other end of the table and was mercifully half-hidden by the candelabra.

Madame Bienville tossed her napkin to the table. "You've said that a hundred times, monsieur," she declared, piqued at her husband's insincere acquiescence. Her chair scraped back from the table before Marmont could put down the sherry. In a huff, she paused at the door for the final word. "Perhaps this spring, monsieur, the ocean will dry up and I shall be able to ride to Paris in a carriage. Alone, most probably." The door slammed and angry footsteps faded quickly down the hall.

To his right—there was no need to hide *her* behind a blaze of candles—Angelique tilted her head to one side, lifted the glass to obtain a crimson view of the world. "Mother hates it when you don't take her seriously." Bienville sighed. "I like it here," she continued. "Paris is dull and contrived in comparison. I would rather be in Mobile."

Her father scratched beneath his wig. A wife's problems could be ignored, but a daughter's could not. Her preferences elicited dire fears. Angelique was beautiful but willful. Overly so. A tempting flower surrounded by a wilderness garden of hearty male appetites. Recalling the afternoon's confrontation with Gregory and the subsequent discussion with Law, he was forced to rinse the bad taste from his mouth. Brand was a troublemaker in more ways than one. A pirate and a rogue, he had monopolized Angelique's attention when Law had brought him up the bluff to the governor's elegant chateau. Of course she liked it in Mobile. Where else would she find a dashing Scottish pirate? At her most bewitching, it was only through his earnest but subtle intervention that she was never left alone with him.

"Father?"

Bienville started. "Yes?"

"I'm going to join mother. Will you play cards with us later?"

"Of course. Console your mother. I will be in shortly." He accepted her moist, petal-soft kiss, inhaled the heavy fragrance of her perfume. The momentary light pressure of her breasts against his shoulder lingered as he sat alone, aware that the servants were anxious for him to leave so they could begin to clear away the dinner clutter. Well, let them wait, he thought sourly. That's what they were for. Didn't have anything else to do, anyway.

He sipped his sherry—damned English wine, but the only decent thing left until the next supply ship arrived—and tried to clear his mind of all the pressing matters so crucial to the settlement's survival. Law's headstrong aggressiveness, Gregory's threats, the never-ending problems of trade, health, Indians and a thousand other responsibilities, not to mention his wife's ever increasing disaffection and his daughter's capriciousness, muddled about without focus. He poured another glass and wondered if his nose was red, which always happened when he drank to excess or lied.

Marmont waited uneasily to one side of the room, hoping beyond hope that the table could be cleared by nine. Such were the thoughts that occupied *his* mind. His master, Jean Baptiste le Moyne, sieur de Bienville, Governor of Mobile, a colony of His Majesty's Louisiana territory, eased back in his chair and sipped his sherry, trying not to admit his envy of a servant's lot.

Foul weather was their friend. For a week, a winter storm battered Mystéré and kept everyone save the skeleton crews assigned to the ships indoors and under cover. The crews spent their time eating, drinking, gaming and sleeping, with a occasional fling at one of the half-score available women, not counting Hope, who had taken up with Forlicar. After a lifetime of promiscuity, she was content with one man.

For Marie, the week was one of absolute, unadulterated bliss. She was happy for the first time since her abduction from Mysteré. Nights were spent in Jason's arms. Years of humiliation and deprivation were shed in the fullness of caresses and sweet words, of languid lovemaking that left them both pleasantly exhausted. Mornings, she awoke to the sound of rain, the cool vista through the open windows and the security of the man she loved at her side. All she had done for the past year seemed, in retrospect, to have led to this one point in time, no greater than the tiny dot Mysteré made on the face of the Caribbean. Hours and minutes lost their meaning, and laughter, gay and bubbling or calm and serene, filled her heart.

The sun signaled the end of the holidays. Rested and ready to leach the alcohol and laziness from their bones and muscles, the combined crews set to work. Inspection had showed that a heavy layer of barnacles covered the hulls of both ships: they would have to be careened, scraped and calked. Nearly a hundred men, both crews supplemented by some of the islanders, began the backbreaking labor of removing all the guns and stores in order to lighten the ships.

The captains and their mates spent most of their time deep in discussion in the main room at the house on the hill. No point was too trivial to consider, and Jason, backed by Forlicar and Ramahd's superior knowledge of the sea, emerged a decisive and dominant leader. Both ships would be modified. Sixteen cannon would be removed from the *Ravener,* which would make her ride high enough in the water to negotiate the shallow waters of the islands. She would also be rerigged as a bark to make her less recognizable as the old *Sword of Cornwall.* The *Banshee* would take on six of the *Ravener*'s guns and the other ten would be mounted at the entrance to Voûte Paix in case the English or Spanish came to call. In short, the ex-slaver *Banshee* would be stronger, the *Ravener* weaker but more efficient.

The three-day process was more harrowing than Marie cared to admit. She should have been stronger, she knew, but found the effort beyond her means. After all, the changes in the *Ravener* were for the best. They would lose sixteen guns, but any crew she could muster wouldn't be able to effectively man the twenty-four they retained. None of the crew had experience with a bark, but the fore and main masts would still be square-rigged, and learning how to handle the single gaff-rigged sail on the mizzenmast couldn't be that difficult. Besides, Behan's lessons were still fresh in her mind. She, too, would learn quickly.

Next to her and across the table, Tom and Ned looked on with puzzled, glum looks. The bold and questing Raven was changing before their very eyes. And so she was, for Jason had overwhelmed her with logic and reason as, earlier, he had with his body. With each hour she realized she loved him more and more, and that she must not push too hard for her own views lest she alienate him. He had, after all, left her once and might do so again.

Letting him have his way with the *Ravener* was a small price. She would have preferred he give up the whole idea of the coming raids, but it was obvious he was determined to go, and equally obvious she must accompany him. But how much happier she would be if they just forgot piracy and settled down on Mysteré. Her father had done well enough as a planter. There were fortunes to be made on land too. And at less cost. The dreams she had dreamed as a child returned to haunt her. The plantation house, sun streaming through the windows. Her lover—husband—at her side. Children running about and growing healthy in love. They needn't roam again. Not ever . . .

But Jason had the wildness in him. He longed for action, for revenge on the world in general and the English in particular. If she loved him, must she not follow him? Must she not commit her efforts to the furtherance

340

of his? Could she keep him any other way? Looking back wistfully, she remembered the Raven who had taken the *Sword of Cornwall*, who had sailed to Isla Orchilla and listened to the ocean and the wind. But that Raven was gone, buried in a past as distant as her childhood. More important now was Jason, and what he wanted. The last rapturous week in his arms had taught her that.

Captains and mates now aboard with the crews, the tempo increased. On the beach, those handy with mallet, chisel, marlinspike and the hundred other tools required to keep a wooden sailing ship seaworthy, labored as hard as the sweating, tar-streaked men on the ships. Within a whirlwind two weeks, both vessels had been refloated. The next morning Marie found herself relegated to shore, for Jason deemed the rerigging too dangerous and the job of remounting the guns too difficult for a woman.

Marie's throat tightened as she turned away and started for home, skirting the settlement proper. Home? Was it really? she wondered. Or was it just four walls and a roof, the house where she happened to be at the moment? *But that's silly. I am here on Mysteré. This is home. I have found Jason.*

Jason. She could see him without looking: stripped to the waist and bathed with sweat, his powerful figure glowed in the late afternoon light. He was a bronzed god of war, happy with his ships and cannons, completely content, at ease and in his element. Too much so, perhaps, she couldn't help thinking. As the work had progressed, he had changed from a considerate, tempestuous lover to a demanding, uncooperative and aggressive overseer preoccupied with the job at hand. The ships, in short, had become more important to him than she was, and the old fears and doubts had returned.

Thinking back, each moment of restlessness during the first week became an omen. He'd been with her, but only because of the weather. They'd made love, but

341

hadn't he seemed detached? A little distracted and absentminded? There was no other woman, she knew. Armide had left in a huff two weeks earlier with Paolo, the captain of the *Crab,* and hadn't been seen since.

The path took a corner and she could see the house. As always, the sight calmed her. Whatever else had or would happen, this place would be here. Thus cheered, the world looked a little less bleak. Things could be worse. The *Ravener* and its crew were still hers. They would be at sea in another three weeks, and there Jason's influence would be minimal. Perhaps, she thought, brightening, that was the way to ensure his love. He appreciated strength and competence: she would show him the same. And seamanship, too, she determined. He'd learn Marie Ravenne didn't surrender completely. Nothing could be further from the truth. Her love was not to be taken lightly.

And then they would return and Jason would be ready to settle down, sell the ships and live in peace. She could see it all in her mind's eye. Laden with gold—and hopefully sheets of glass for the bedroom windows—the *Banshee* and *Ravener* would sail into Voûte Paix and drop anchor. There'd be a huge party, of course, but later, arm in arm, they'd walk up this same path. The house would be waiting, silent and empty.

Empty? A shape flitted across an open window like the blinking of an eye. Curious, she hurried to the front door and quietly entered the broad, sun-washed main room. "Hope?"

No answer. Empty. Yet someone had been inside. Poised, ready to fight or flee, she listened. To the left was her bedroom, directly across the hall from the kitchen. Tiptoeing, she stole into the kitchen and glanced around. The fire in the hearth had died down. A few scraps left on the huge table in the middle of the room were the only indication anyone had been there recently.

The main room was still empty. Careful of the loose board near the great armchair, she crept to Hope and

Forlicar's room and put her ear to the door. A slight rustling sound . . .

"Hope? Forlicar?"

The rapier leapt to her hand, cold steel whispering. Planting a foot against the door, she kicked it open.

A clatter. A shape lunging from the ceiling. A flash of green and yellow. Marie stifled a scream and leaped out of the way, recovering at the last minute as a swooping shadow flew past her face. The parrot fluttered to his perch on the back of a chair and eyed her sharply. "Petruchio!" Marie scolded. "You almost frightened me to death."

Petruchio squawked once and began to preen himself. Marie shrugged off the dismissal, preferring it to one of the many obscenities she was trying to teach him to forget. Laughing, she rummaged around in the tin box kept on the table and found a thin cake made from cassava root flour. Petruchio wrapped one foot around the treat and began to nibble unconcernedly, imperiously accepting the gift as homage and little more than his due.

Relaxing, Marie entered her own room and froze in the doorway. There was the intruder, partway out of the window. One of the island's mestizos! Three strides and she was behind him, the tip of her rapier touching the vulnerable soft spot below his ribs. "You may step back in. Slowly." With a strained sound like a whispered croak, the intruder turned awkwardly. "Tomás!"

The mestizo stared, eyes bugging out with fright. Marie scolded herself. In the furor of return, she had forgotten that night of recognition when Tomás had faced her from the doorway. Moving to where he could plainly see, she sheathed the rapier. "Don't run away again, please. It's Marie. See? I'm no ghost."

Tomás grunted and wriggled back into the room. Marie smiled, trying to soothe his fears. He did seem a little more relaxed, but had yet to speak. Then she saw why. A horrid smear of scar tissue crossed his throat and pulled his head forward. Paling, she remembered tales of Spanish cruelty, of torture, of slow and agonizing deaths. A red hot iron had been pressed to his throat. Amazingly, Tomás had lived through the ordeal.

But how had he been captured? The answer followed immediately. Perhaps the mestizo had not fled into the safety of the hills. Perhaps he had overcome the panic that sent him howling from Marie and returned to follow the young, frightened girl down to the beach. How many times had Tomás kept her from danger, protected her in Jean Ravenne's absence?

"Tomás," she said gently, holding out her hand for him to touch. "Can you forgive me, Tomás? You didn't have to go back. Not to be hurt so badly."

Trembling violently, torn between fleeing and remaining where he was, Tomás stretched out a hand toward the woman, touched her and gradually relaxed. "This is your house too, Tomás," Marie went on, barely restraining the tears. "Don't run away again, please? You belong here. Will you stay?"

Slowly, a broken smile covered the mestizo's face and he nodded vigorously, bobbing the whole of his torso up and down, for his neck wouldn't move. The only sound he could make was a macabre wheezing in the back of his throat. Marie tugged at his hand. "Come. You look hungry. Come with me and eat." Again the awkward head shaking, this time from side to side. "No? What, then?" The mestizo pointed toward a table against the wall. Puzzled, Marie let him lead her across the room to the desk where lay a heavily wrapped packet he seemed determined that she open. Marie untied the vines and eased back the folds of boar hide to reveal a stack of water-spotted papers bearing a recognizable scrawl. "Oh, my God!" she cried, stunned at the discovery. "His journal!" Many a night she had interrupted her father as he sat near a glowing tallow, dipping a quill into an inky extract of bark. A link with the past. One that Tomás had found and protected for almost six years. An entry leaped from the page.

Today my dearest Pia will have been asleep a year. It is difficult to think of her without pain. At times I think I catch a glimpse of my own sweet dearest dancing in

344

the laughter of Marie's lovely eyes. This child of love, my daughter . . .

Here the ink was splotched and she could read no further. Marie fought to control the welling sobs. Tomás, though unable to read, had sensed the importance of the papers and saved them from the burning house. "Tomás. You buried my father, didn't you."

The mestizo nodded vigorously and pointed toward the hillside.

"Yes. I found it. That was very kind of you." She wiped her eyes with the back of a hand, sniffed, managed to regain her composure. "But you must be starved. God knows where you've been hiding. Hope boiled some beef last night. There should be some left." The half-breed held back, still hesitating. "No," Marie said, taking him by the hand again. "Don't be afraid, Tomás. You're home now."

A late afternoon storm put an end to the work for the day and drove the crews ashore and indoors. Hope and Forlicar remained in town to carouse with the others in the tavern, but Jason continued on up the hill to the house. Soaked to the skin and in a foul mood, he listened impatiently while Marie recounted the tale of Tomás's return. Whether or not the mestizo remained was one and the same with him. Armide had kept him because he could cook. If Marie wanted him, too, there was no reason why she shouldn't have him. Marie bristled at the mention of Armide but spoke no further on the matter.

After a few awkward attempts at conversation, they ate in silence. Only after the meal did Jason seem to slough off his preoccupation. He even came around the table, kneaded her shoulders and brusquely kissed her on the forehead in a poor attempt to repay her for his inattention. Two minutes later the worried frown reappeared and he took to the porch with his pipe to inspect the lowering clouds obliterating the stars. January was a week old, and rain or no, they would have to continue work the next day.

Dispirited, Marie left the cleaning up to Tomás and went to the bedroom to read her father's journal. A half-hour later Jason came back in. Bare feet padding on the floor, he moved behind her and started to read over her shoulder.

"No."

"Why not?"

Sleek and naked in the candlelight, Marie spun to face him. "Because they are mine."

"And you . . ." Jason bent to kiss her breasts, then led her to the bed. Marie resisted but a moment. Then he was inside her with quick, urgent thrusts, driving to frenzied consummation. ". . . are mine," he completed, teeth clenched.

She felt his jaw relax against her cheek. His hardness hadn't diminished and he started to move again slowly, from side to side. She wanted him to stop, feared the excruciating pleasure and the price of surrender. "You are mine," he had said. Love? Or the haughty pride of possession and subjugation? Then it was too late to worry, lost as she was in the starflung realm of climax.

Exhausted, Jason slept. Marie lay on her side, wanting to touch him but not daring to lest he wake. Outside, beads of rain dropped from the palm frond eaves. Globules of cool moisture exploded on the fragile greenery. Moving cautiously, she slipped from the bed, went to the window and stuck out her hand. A pool of water formed in her palm. Sweeping down from the mountain, the soft, whispered laughter of the wind, the dry parchment voice of her father, rustled the leaves.

Lonely laughter, to greet the moon as it emerged from behind the scudding clouds. The world was simultaneously outlined in silver and hidden in shadow. In her hand, a tiny sea of shimmering opal reflected the larger world. She drew her cupped hands to her mouth and drank. The water was sweet, but the vision was gone. Disturbed, she sank back on the bed and found release in troubled sleep.

Chapter XVIII

Toward the end of Marie's father's journal, the pages were covered with erratically scribbled thoughts, jumbled in context. References to Pia and fears for Marie gradually gave way to abstract phrases, meaningless without the tortured moments that framed them. With youth's near total lack of perception, Marie had seen her father as a dear, befuddled, overly protective eccentric. Only now did she realize the depth of his despair. Hindsight was bitter wisdom.

The shrill, enthusiastic cackling of Diana Caron and Hope interrupted the despondent train of thought. Marie looked up and smiled at the two women. Now that Hope had settled down with Forlicar and found a kindred soul in the round, bubbling wife of the tavern keeper, she had become domesticated. The tavern itself, half put together again and cool in the afternoon sun, was empty except for the surgeon, Giuseppe, who sat staring into a tepid brew. Though he continued to prescribe ointments and tinctures, and sew up cuts or let blood when necessary, all overtures of friendship had failed miserably. Despite his recalcitrance, Marie had to admit the man had proved useful. At the same time, there was something both comic and tragic in the way he hunched over the table, peering into his mug of palm wine and clutching the black, grimy links of chain with which he refused to part. He seemed more pathetic than earlier, when she had seen him walking along the beach, the shackles dangling over his shoulder, clanking together with each step and attracting a flock of curious seagulls.

Hope slid into the opposite chair and placed an egg-shaped fruit—though much larger than an egg—on the table. "Kind of ugly, bless its soul," she muttered, brushing her fingers across the smooth gold rind mottled with rusty brown and dragging Marie's attention away from the surgeon.

"A paw-paw," Marie said. "They're good."

"Paw-paw. That's it. Don't make sense, but that's what they call it." She eyed Marie shrewdly. "Still at them old papers, eh? I'd be cautioning myself against such as that."

"Why?"

"Ha. A fair question. Just to look at you answers the same. I seen you here, face all knotted and hurt lookin'. Ain't no history worth that."

"This is from my father. It's as if . . . Oh, never mind."

"What's past is past, Tulip, says I. You've a tot of rum when you need it and a fine brawny lad to lie with. There's little more a woman could want."

Marie listened to the distant cries of the men as they struggled to bring the last of the guns aboard the *Banshee* before dark. Unable to confront the brooding silence of the plantation house, she had followed Hope down to the tavern. Bringing her father's journal had been a mistake. She should have left it at the house. Rum, food and a bold stallion to take abed. There lay Hope's satisfaction. There were the easy pleasures that led to happiness. "I envy you, Hope. You've found what you want."

The harlot shrugged, halved the paw-paw, scooped out a section of the coral-colored meat with her knife and plopped it in her mouth. She chewed twice and swallowed. Her eyes closed in ecstasy. "You remind me of my sister, darlin'," she began, apropos of nothing.

Marie's eyebrows rose. "I didn't know you had a sister."

"Well, I did. Thou Shalt Not Commit Adultery was her name. When mother died, Father sent us to live in the home of a friend, a goat-footed old Roundhead who kept to his lodgings out in the bloody country. Squire Parr was his name. A widower with three burly sons." She scowled, took another bite of the paw-paw. "Me

348

bein' a mite young, everyone of them took a liking to Thou Shalt Not. Well, my sister couldn't make up her mind. As soon as she picked one, she'd find arguments against him and go on to the next. First one, then another, and then the next, and then around the lot again."

She scooped out another bite and held out the knife for Marie. "Try some," she mumbled, chewing. " 'S good. Anyways, Thou Shalt Not was so busy worryin' she never thought to test out a single one of 'em in the heather, if you get my meaning. And what happened? Why, all three up an' left one day. Taken to war or curious to see what lay beyond the next hill, which they hadn't never seen. My sister never saw a one of 'em again. Awful sad."

Marie waited for the rest of the story, but Hope was occupied with the paw-paw. "Well?" she finally asked. "How am I like your sister?"

Hope wiped off the knife, stuck it in the table. "You think too much." The older woman pushed herself away from the table. "I'm goin' to watch 'em load the ship. Maybe hurry 'em along. Tonight's the last night Forlicar and me will have a proper bed." Eyes twinkling mischievously, she chuckled and started for the door.

Marie stared at the journal, then started to gather the loose papers. A question suddenly formed. "What happened to your sister?"

Hope turned in the doorway, her features contorted in distaste. "She married the squire. See what all that wonderin' got her?"

Evening before departure. The sun had barely fallen below the horizon. Only a few minutes of their last day on Mysteré remained. The beach was crowded and a dozen torches thrust upright in the sand conversed with the warm wind in fiery tongues. Marie gratefully recognized her own crew mingling with Jason's. Six weeks of hard labor had taught them how to work together. Behind her, the island's permanent inhabitants watched from doorways and windows. When they woke the next morning, the harbor would be empty and those left behind would return to the more mundane affairs of eking out a living: working the soil, bartering for contraband and performing a host of services for the next rowdy lot that called.

Strange, how a capricious world worked. She had never foreseen piracy. Studying with Behan had been an amusing way to fill untold hours of tedium. Taking the *Sword of Cornwall* was an act of desperation, assaulting the *Niño Muñez* one of survival. Now, there was little choice in the matter. She was beyond the law of all civilized nations. Other than Mysteré, there was nowhere to go. There was nothing else to do: she and her men were forced to steal and plunder, to wrench from hostile, unwilling hands the very life that had been stolen from them.

And yet, how readily she would have given it all up if she could be sure Jason would return. She shaded her eyes against the orange glare and peered across the darkening expanse to where the ships rocked in restless silhouette. How dangerous they looked. *Ravener* and *Banshee*. The names alone were fearful: how much more so when the sleek hulls were filled with the fearless adventurers who manned them. The crew of the *Ravener*. How could she abandon the men to whom she owed so much? After this expedition they could sail alone, but for now they needed her. She stared down at them. There was Tom Gunn, towering above everyone else. Ned Sly had taken to wearing a red bandana about his head. Stalwart Poole claimed his helmsmans's post and had spent the last six weeks learning as much navigation as he could from Ramahd. There was Spanish Jesse, standing alone, calm and unemotional. Young Shelby strutted and cheered enthusiastically on cue. Age would temper him, but for now the buccaneer's life was the grandest sort of adventure. The Poacher skulked on the edge of the throng: he disliked crowds and kept to himself. Ben Tremain likewise held back, assuming the role of wise patriarch.

These seven she could count on in any situation. As

for the rest, the crew had changed somewhat. Seven of the original mutineers had chosen to stay on Mysteré, and she had picked up twenty islanders, making the ship's complement fifty-three. How the new men would react, she had no idea.

Jason stood atop an overturned longboat, explaining in exciting tones the nature of their voyage, the necessity of traveling to Mobile in order to maintain an open port in the New World, then a wide-ranging expedition through the Gulf and into the Caribbean to beard Murcia in his den, strike close to Barranquilla and relieve the don of a few treasure ships. Talk of Murcia only served to depress Marie, and she retreated down the beach, halting in alarm when a figure loomed out of the darkness. Her fingers crept toward the pistol tucked into the sash at her waist.

"No need, *kadın*," Ramahd said, stepping forward.

"Why were you watching me?" Marie asked curtly, irritated by his casual approach.

"I could not help but be intrigued. A raven watching over her flock. A symbol of terrible mystery and demise. For our enemies, of course," he added quickly.

"We have plenty of those."

"It is the way," Ramahd shrugged, squatting in the sand. His olive brown features blended with the deepening dusk into an inscrutable mask. "The last two," he said cryptically.

"The last two what?"

"When you came to Mysteré, there were four ships in the harbor. Three have gone. The harbor will be empty when we leave. No one will be left."

"Those who live here will remain," Marie replied.

"They do not count," Ramahd said, clipping off the words. It took a second before he realized her silence was a refutation. "You mean you want to stay?" he finally asked.

Marie shrugged, tried to assume a careless attitude and failed. "To stay would be to root deep, take hold, build a home and life."

"What? We are not alive?"

Marie met his stare. "We are but chaff in the wind, passing from emptiness to emptiness. I thought returning here would be the answer to everything. I found only more questions."

Ramahd nodded, staring at her with new respect. "I like you, Raven," he said simply. Marie turned uncomfortably to look back down the beach at Jason. The flaring torches cast an ominous glow which transmuted him into a shimmering copper statue planted in the sand. *Jason Brand. How fitting.* A fresh surge of passion swept through her and she wanted desperately to be alone with him, to bask in his heat, to be consumed.

"Morning will come, *kadın,* The voyage begins soon." Ramahd rose effortlessly and brushed the sand from his breeches. "I hope you find your home," he added softly.

"And you? Do you not want the same?" she asked, turning to face him.

The Turk grinned and his eyes became shaded with latent violence. He held out his hands to reveal the cruel throwing knives scabbarded at his wrists. In that instant, Marie saw him not as a confidant and companion, but as a figure of merciless wrath, a nerveless, amoral hunter, like the hawks she had watched at Penscott. The fearful leather-masked forms waited aperch on their master's arms, permeating the air with an aura of menace. When the hoods were torn away, the hunters shot into the sky in a whirring blur of brown feathers. Seconds later, while the watchers held their breath in awe, the living missiles plummeted silently, wings folded, from the sky, to strike their terrified prey with a dull thud of flesh against flesh. The bite of cruel talons brought instant, unfeeling death. Death with neither blink nor thought. Ramahd chuckled mirthlessly. "I am home, *kadın,*" he said so softly she could barely hear. "Everywhere I go, I am home." Without another word, he vanished down the beach.

Marie shuddered at the frightening dichotomy the man projected. Aesthetic slayer. Philosophical killer. Forlicar's simple, straightforward braggadocio was preferable by far in its open, unconvoluted predictability. Ramahd had said he liked her. Whatever the motive, she was grateful. Such a man could be more dangerous than Murcia. To have him on your side was a blessing.

Troubled and irrationally afraid, Marie hurried back down the beach and halted at the tiny knoll from which she had first watched as Jason addressed the crews. Jason was still talking. She prayed for him to finish, needing the tender fury of his love as balm for the frightening premonitions that assailed her.

The embers pulsed like quiet, crimson souls trapped in a purgatory of charred and blackened wood. Jason reached out, thrust a forked twig into the campfire.

"No. Let it smolder," Marie said, rolling onto her side. Jason complied, stretched his naked torso next to hers. Comfortable in the privacy of their secret glen, they had given themselves to desire, sharing their passion on this last night on Mysteré.

Absorbed in the blood-red hue, Jason stared at the glowing ashes. The images he had hoped to disperse by coaxing the flame to life reappeared. A woman's face. His wife's, shifting and unclear around the edges. It had been an arranged marriage, but he had grown to love her, if not with great passion, at least warmly and fondly. Her image faded and another—brighter, clearer—took its place. *My son!* A smiling, happy, serious child. Bold little Douglas, lost in the flames of a burning manor. Lost in the embers of an island campfire.

"Jason?" Marie whispered. The look of pain on his contorted face frightened her.

He blinked, rubbed an ash-streaked wrist across his brow, regained his composure and manufactured a wan smile. One hand slid down Marie's spine and felt her hip tense beneath his palm. Suddenly he reached down, snared a fistful of moist earth and hurled it onto the coals, smothering that accusing eye. Not speaking, he rose and walked to the edge of the silent, cold water.

Tiny wavelets spreading from the waterfall lapped about his ankles.

"Soon enough," he muttered. In a few hours the ships would unfurl their sails to steal from the wind the gift of motion.

"Why don't we just stay here, Jason?"

Her voice came from the darkness behind him. He tensed. "What do you mean?"

"We could sell the ships. Forlicar or Ramahd, Tom or Ned. I'd trust them to come back and pay us. We could do what father did. Settle down, plant, buy and sell. She paused, hardly daring mention the word. "Even raise a family. What's to stop us from doing that, Jason?"

Her question lingered on the night air, trapped under the canopy of leaves, mingling with the susurrant, flattened rush of their breathing.

"Gold," Jason finally answered. "I've promised the men a taste of gold, and they expect me to lead them."

"They're capable enough. With either Ramahd or Forlicar helping on the *Ravener,* they'd do well. You could accomplish so much more by staying here."

He didn't answer for a long while, instead came back to her side and worked on the fire to get it blazing again. When the first bright flames rose to dispel the night, he settled back on his heels. "I've promised myself as well."

Dark anger burned in Marie's breast. "So we set a course of looting and killing, watching our friends numbered in death with no thought or care save for gold? What kind of life is that? Swilling ourselves into a stupor and trying to forget, or grappling in the dark and calling it—" Marie caught herself, spun about. Her black hair stung Jason's neck.

"What do you want of me?" he rasped, catching her arm and roughly pulling her back.

"Something more. A real life. Peace," she said, retreating to the edge of the pool.

Jason scowled, his features clouded as memories swept over him. "My father was . . . a gentle man. A scholar. But more than that. He married a Highland girl, in spite of advice and warnings. God, but her father was furious—and you've not seen a tempest till you've seen a Highland lord in anger. My father, with the help of those men that lived on his holdings, built the great hall where I was raised. Built it of massive timbers and huge stones. When it was finished, father sent an invitation to McGlahan, my mother's sire. He didn't want to come—had disowned her, as a matter of pride—but the news of a grandchild was more than he could hold out against.

"That fierce old man arrived with two score of his men, all armed, not a one of them that wasn't as tough and unyielding as the hills they came from. Father met him outside the gate and, with a grand gesture, welcomed him to his home. But McGlahan was not to be so easily softened. 'Even worms build homes,' he taunted, to the laughter of his men.

"That did it. Alone in front of those twenty warriors, father dragged him from his horse and thrashed him soundly. Then he dumped water on him, revived him and thrashed him again. When McGlahan recovered, he embraced father, rejoicing to learn his son-in-law was a man after all. In return father unveiled a stone table hung over the entrance. On it was inscribed *In Pax Locae*.

"Little we knew of peace, though. Four years later the English accused father of treason and hauled him off to rot in the Tower. He lived a year. No more. And I grew to manhood in an empty, cheerless hall." He paused, eyes closed, reliving the wasted days.

"An outlaw through Penscott's influence, I rode for home when news reached me that the English were crossing the Tweed, and arrived in time to bury the charred corpses of my son, my wife, my mother and all our servants. Our home had been destroyed, torn to earth, razed. Even the stone gate was leveled. I don't remember reaching down to pick up the broken tablet from the wreckage, but later, in the hills, I discovered it tucked inside my belt. 'Pax' it said. And I laughed and thought it the funniest word imaginable. Pax. Blessed, bloody peace. No. I've had enough of peace, thank you. I prefer war, gold and revenge."

Marie could envision him, alone among the hills, a crazed, grief-stricken figure smashing the stone into powder and flinging it to the wind. No wonder he spoke so little of his family. Only once, while still a prisoner in Penscott's chateau, had he mentioned them. Never had he told the story of the stone tablet. Her choice of words had been unfortunate. It would take time and effort to erase those hateful memories.

Merely recounting the story had helped. Jason felt washed out, drained of strength and emotion. Morning would be a relief. The thousand tasks and decisions involved in setting sail would fill the void, fill his hours with activity. Wind and salt spray and water and sun would purify him, make him a new man again. Action was the answer to introspection and despondency.

Marie watched as he crossed back to the fire, stretched out by the soot-blackened circle and closed his eyes. From her place by the water, she stared up at the leaf-broken, starflung expanse, fearing whatever fate lay before them and apprehensive about the journey's final outcome. Jason had changed, and not for the better. She thought of Armide, how he had cast off the mulatto without so much as a good-bye or a twinge of conscience. Was that all she meant to him, too? No. She was more—had to be more. Could not, now once committed, settle for less. The night in the glen, his caresses and whispered endearments could not go for nought. She wanted him to stay, true, wanted to hold him in her arms and bear his children. But he had suffered cruelly, she now understood, and must leach the hatred and bitterness from his soul before he would be hers and hers alone. If she truly wanted him, would she not accompany him on his quest?

"Very well," she whispered. "You shall have your war, my love. For a while." Her mind made up, she returned to her lover's side.

Armide had stolen the candle from the carpenter, sneaking out before he returned to find her there. The cooper unknowingly supplied a tiny flame. Now, two decks below the maindeck, she slid from stack to stack, past looming supplies, back to the corner of the orlop where she'd been commanded to stay. Absence, if discovered, meant the flaying of the pretty skin on her back. Armide would never lightly suffer pain or disfigurement.

Seventy-four guns, Paolo had said. Never before had she seen such a huge ship. In the pitch dark below the waterline, the candle barely lighting the corner where she knelt, she stuck the taper to the deck and tried to blot out the ever-present din that permeated a ship under way. Gradually though, the present blurred into a formless haze. Soon new images would coalesce in the process that would snatch her from the past and fling her into the wider world of that which could be seen only by those with the gift.

There was the beach of Mysteré, receding into the dawn. There was the coast of Mexico, where they'd raided and run. A storm swirled through the wisp of smoke and she relived the *Crab*'s poor attempts to keep afloat. Before it was over, the sloop was nothing more than a floating, bobbing, useless hulk on the face of the sea. But Paolo was a better seaman than lover. Somehow they made land, fitted a new mast and put to sea again without being caught. Poor Paolo. How valiantly he'd tried to satisfy her. She had pretended he did, of course, for to do otherwise would have been a grave insult, and she was at his mercy until they put into a respectable port where she could find another man.

Time shifted and she fell deeper into the single flame, let it suck her in, draw her toward the center. Motion speeded up. The *Crab* danced across the water and the sun and stars wheeled at dizzying speeds. Suddenly, sails appeared. The thin pop of cannon in the rarefied atmosphere of her dream sounded like the infinitesimal crackling of the candle wick. Another second and they were nestling at the side of the big ship.

Ah, Paolo! How sad he looked, how angry and forlorn. They'd hung him without ceremony from the yard,
where, naked, he'd spurted out one last pathetic attempt
to seed the world with his own image. The sharks were
the only ones who cared, and care, in their primitive
brains, extended to no more than a momentary stilling
of the eternal hunger that drove them from carcass to
carcass.

Faster and faster she went, spinning across the last
two days. The candle had become the sun, around
which she orbited. Hunger—they'd given her little to
eat. Thirst—who lived who wasn't always thirsty at sea?
Hunger and thirst fed trances. Deep inside, she could
feel the last vestiges of time, of present, slipping as the
candle flung her into the void. Sightless eyes staring into
the receding pinpoint of light, she began the soft, me-
lodic chant.

> "Y'bo le-le
>   Ca onpo te pou-moin y'bo . . ."

Over and over she repeated the verse, her voice husky
and tinged with dark expectancy. "Y'bo, the hour has
come. What do you bring me, Y'bo?"

Eyes close to swirling shadows. Flames flicker.
Hands clench a worn leather bag containing a feather,
three beads, a dried and yellowed bone. "Conjure bag,
Y'bo, conjure to call you." The walls receded, melted
away to reveal an azure sky.

A gull, a zephyr, a cloud, borne on an eternal sea,
from whose height is seen two ships, two tiny specks on
a green-blue expanse. Closer. Yes, ships. And without
seeing, she moans, for Jason is there. She can feel him,
feel his heat bathing her from the inside. Jason—and
the cursed white-skinned *putain,* Raven. "Go no closer,
Y'bo. No closer . . ."

But the spell will not be broken. Once set into motion, the wheel must complete the turn before it stops.
Nearness is agony. Visions of wind-filled sails. Men
casting eyes to northward. Faces remembered. One
above all others. There, scrambling to the rigging, a

bronze god dancing recklessly on spars, his sun-gleaming eyes alive with adventure.

"Linger near him, Y'bo. Nearer." Day into night. Into day. Into night. "No, Y'bo!" The dark-haired Raven is in his arms! Her sleek ivory flesh lies the length of his! Her ecstasy should be mine! Mine! Mine!

The tormented scream flails the dream, but the vision is not over. See how he mounts her, how they move in opposition, the tempo rising as they near the envied peak. Hear how they cry out as love's wildest flames lap over and consume them!

"Y'bo!"

"Y'bo! No!"

A hand struck her across the face. A calloused, bare foot stamped out the candle. "That'll be enough of that, whore," the odorous master's mate growled. His teeth bared and he aimed another kick at the mulatto, who managed to roll out of the way. Her eyes clouded as if sensing one last image, then it was gone and she was glaring at the man standing over her. "There is one who calls you," he said harshly. "While he waits, you're down here practicing deviltry. I should throw you to the sharks. Up with you."

Armide scrambled to her feet. The hooded lantern he carried left the sailor in shadow. "I am not an animal to be herded about," she hissed.

"Hah! Don't tell me what you are. I can see well enough. And don't make an evil eye at me, either." He thumped his chest, where hung a bag similar to hers. "I've been around these islands long enough to know better, and have protection from your blasphemy."

He held up the lantern to light the way. Armide preceded him through the orlop, past the gun deck, onto the maindeck and aft to the quarterdeck. The marines guarding the entrance to the great cabin stared ahead without expression. They had given up hope of finding such a woman for themselves a long, long time ago. Forcing the last vestiges of the dream from her mind, Armide tried to straighten the thin dress. Whatever else had happened, she desperately needed to make a good impression on this new captain if she didn't want to entertain the animals below decks.

The door opened and she stumbled and stopped in the center of the cabin. A tall, thin, angular figure, hands clasped behind his back, stood gazing out the windows. Armide waited in silence. He would speak when he pleased. When he did, she would be ready, confident of her beauty and the power she could wield over men.

Finally, he turned and strolled across the room to more closely inspect his prize. She did not tremble when he passed behind her, nor when his hand touched her breast and slid down to her stomach. "You're very beautiful, my dear," he finally said.

Armide met his gaze without flinching. The scar on his cheek gave him a satanic look, one of unabashed arrogance and power. She held back her shoulders, knew her breasts were straining against the light cotton blouse. "I'm glad you think so," she answered boldly, at the same time letting her eyes travel down his body, then return to his. "I am Armide."

The captain laughed. "You are very saucy, Armide." He jerked his head in the direction of the bed. "Saucy women are the spice of life."

"As are bold captains. When their names are known."

The captain laughed outright. She pleased him more and more already. "Then you shall have mine," he said, advancing and untying her blouse. Melon-ripe breasts spilled from the fabric and his eyes narrowed in anticipation. "Gregory," he whispered huskily, guiding her hand to the swelling member between his legs. "Captain James Gregory."

Chapter XIX

The precarious settlement of Mobile lay on the southern edge of the great land mass of the New World. To the north, the interior was a dark expanse of forest filled with hostile Indians, poisonous reptiles and a thousand other unknown dangers. To the south lay the no less dangerous Caribbean, largely controlled by English and Spanish navies. The French, in Gallic stubbornness, clung tenaciously to the center, which would become, it was fervently hoped, the gateway to a new empire whose existence, in concert with the enormously lucrative and successful Canadian colony, might squeeze the English from the middle ground.

Marie Ravenne—Raven, she still had to remind herself from time to time—watched from the quarterdeck as the *Ravener* followed the *Banshee* up the bay to Mobile. Both ships tacked against a north wind, lurched across the muddy water and anchored a calculated chain's length outside the most extreme range of Fort Charlotte's lethal batteries. Relationships once warm and friendly had been known to deteriorate, and such a precaution was inexpensive and easily taken.

An hour to sunset. Marie trained her spyglass on a white blur that proved to be an estate enthroned on a bluff. According to Jason's information, that would be the governor's home, made all the more grandiose by contrast with the conglomeration of humble and lumpy dwellings spread out below and comprising the remainder of the settlement. Beyond them both and disappearing into the distance, a great carpet of evergreens broken by blotches of deciduous brown covered the undulating plain and marched in relentless procession to the horizon. The sight was as breathtaking as the open sea and brought to mind the tantalizing glimpses of the east coast near Charleston. Was this the same forest? Save for the obvious changes wrought by winter, it appeared so to the untrained eye.

"Signal flag from the *Banshee*," Shelby called from the rigging. "Captain Brand wants you to join him."

"Jesse, see to the boat," Marie shouted.

"Aye, Cap'n Raven."

"Tom?" The *Ravener*'s "lieutenant" was standing right behind her. "Oh, Tom. Stay aboard and take charge here while I'm gone. I'll send word from the *Banshee* if and when it's safe to let anyone ashore. When they go, let no more than half off, including some of the ones Jason picked on Mysteré. I don't want too many of them aboard with a reduced crew. Not until we know and trust them better."

"You'll be with Brand?" the giant asked, obviously disapproving.

"Yes."

Gunn frowned but nodded in acquiescence. "And if there's trouble?"

"Get out while you can," she ordered soberly. "Don't wait, don't take any chances." She indicated the fort, bristling with cannon. "You'd need far more than sixty men to make a dent in that." Tom took the glass and waited while Marie tied on her cloak. As always, her smile restored his confidence. "But don't worry. There'll be no trouble. We've friends here."

Tom's unhappiness was painfully evident, but Marie felt no obligation to assuage his doubts. Jason had bought the *Banshee* here and claimed to have an agreement with the governor. In any case, they should be safe until the gold had been transferred. Without further ado, she hurried to the railing and was over the side and into the jolly boat. Tom watched the small craft unfurl its little triangle of canvas. A moment later Raven was out of sight as the sail caught the wind and the jolly boat leaned over.

"I don't like it," grumbled Ben Tremain, suddenly at hand.

Tom tried to ignore him, but knew he was right.

362

Raven hadn't been like herself those last few weeks on shore, and the voyage had done her good. Got the Scot out of her mind, it had, so she was more like the Raven they'd named on the night they took the *Niño Muñez* and become pirates. That was the only trouble with her. Or any woman, probably. Let her fall for a man and she became nigh useless. But these last four weeks— that had been another story. The first week they'd made good time, getting used to the ship and all. Everyone was glad to be back to sea. The storm was a help too, especially since it had separated them from the *Banshee*. By the time they met again off the western end of Cuba, Raven had gotten her sea legs back the way she should have had all along. The run up to Mobile had been easy and profitable. He grinned in spite of himself. That old, luggerly galleon hadn't had a chance, boxed as it was between the two faster, more maneuverable ships. There was gold enough for all of them now.

"Just don't feel right, is all."

Tom grunted. "It's a fair-looking land."

"That's not what I mean and you know it. It's Raven. She's goin' to see him again, and he'll twist her head all sideways."

"Best keep your notions to yourself, Ben," Tom said, the anger showing through.

"Don't threaten me, Tom Gunn. Ned, Shelby, Poole and the others all feel the same. And you do too."

Gunn scowled. He watched the jolly boat slide along the side of the *Banshee*. Raven climbed up the rope ladder and over the rail. Jason Brand was waiting, and she flew into his arms. Tom turned away, worried. What Ben Tremain said was true, he reflected. But damn if he'd admit it!

The chill breath of February whipped the purple cloak about Marie's high leather boots. She pulled the cowl forward, further shielding her features. Jason, similarly attired though in brown, cursed as a strong gust of the cold north wind tore open the front of his cloak and whipped across his chest. "Been in the islands too long," he grumbled, gesturing to the cutter sailing out to meet them. "Look at that. Hardly clothed. Damn, but I'd hate to see what a Highland winter would do to me now. Probably catch my death if I ever returned. You ready?"

Marie squeezed his arm in assent. The feelings eroded by separation were flooding back and she had to fight to retain her sense of independence. Luckily, there was little time to think, for a thud against the side of the *Banshee* announced the arrival of the boat from shore. A moment later, a head showed over the railing. Dreams of privacy faded quickly as Jason detached himself from her and hurried to greet the visitor. "John. Good to see you again."

A gruff, humorless-looking individual whose eyes seemed to glare at the world with a mixture of suspicion and contempt shook Jason's hand. "Welcome to Mobile. Again."

"Then I *am* welcome. Good. I'm sorry to make you come so far out"—He gestured apologetically to the fort—"but one never knows. Times change, and it pays to be cautious."

"No offense at all. One can rarely be too careful. He glanced over Jason's shoulder to Marie, raised a questioning eyebrow. "I didn't expect two ships."

Jason grinned. "Neither did I. Come. I'll introduce you to Captain Raven," he said, steering his companion across the deck to Marie. "John Law, Marie Ravenne. Known as Raven."

"Jason has told me about you at length, Mr. Law."

A tight smile creased Law's face. Marie Ravenne! The woman Gregory sought. Now that was intriguing. She looked pretty enough, from what he could see. He wondered what her relationship to Jason was, toyed briefly with the idea of taking her for himself. "Favorably, I trust."

Marie laughed. "Very much so."

"Good. Few do." Light blue eyes that had seen some mischief in their day glinted, quickly traveled down and back up her body, trying to guess what lay beneath the

364

cloak. The smile warmed slightly and Marie saw that the stiff exterior was a calculated defense. He and Jason had much in common. "I hope we will be friends," he continued smoothly.

"I'm sure we shall." Jason hid a frown. He still didn't completely trust either Law or Bienville, and wasn't at all sure he liked the way the financier held Marie's hand. "Oh, yes," he broke in jovially, at the same time clapping Law on the shoulder. "I've instructed Ramahd and Forlicar to ferry ashore a most urgent shipment once we're settled in. You might want to make suitable arrangements for them to be escorted."

At last he let go her hand. For the first time, a real smile lit his face. "Good. I'm a great welcomer of urgent shipments. And now that business is behind us, I'm sure you've had enough of the sea. If you'd be so kind as to accompany me? All newly arriving captains are requested to visit the governor directly. A pure formality, I assure you." Without waiting, he turned and strode to the rail, leaving Jason and Marie to follow as best they might.

Close-hauled and with gunwales underwater half the time, the cutter had to tack twice before reaching the tiny dock. Law remained silent, as did Jason and Marie, until all three stood on the slivered cedar planking. The dock seemed deserted, but as they walked toward shore—how strange the solid footing felt—faces appeared in doorways and windows, from around corners of buildings and stacks of boxed goods waiting for a ship to carry them back to France.

A carriage waited at the end of the dock. Law helped Marie in, then sat across from her and rapped on the ceiling as soon as Jason was seated. With a crack of the whip the vehicle jolted into motion and began the tortured journey along the path the residents of Mobile called, in all seriousness, a street.

The men talked, but Marie ignored the conversation, so intrigued was she with the passing scene. Mobile itself was young, a mere infant of a town more concerned with survival than niceties or cosmetics. Raised stretches of oyster-shell-covered mud served as streets. Huts made of hand-cut planks offered primitive shelter against the elements. The boards were so warped and sprung out of shape they left one with the impression that the buildings had a life of their own, beyond the means of men to tame. Of color there was little—pine green and mud black predominated—but a riot of odors made up for the lack. Fetid tidal flats, a tannery, reeking piles of fish offal, smoke from a dozen smoldering fires, all mingled in unlikely consort with the perfume of the mighty forest of pine which enclosed the enclave hacked from the fertile earth.

"It is not much, madame." Law's apology brought her back to her companions.

"Oh, but you're wrong," Marie protested. "There's spirit here, and enthusiasm. This isn't a refuge or haven. Men are putting their roots deep into the earth. They have come to build lives, not just to hide." Law looked closely at her and she could feel Jason at her side as the movement of the carriage tossed them against each other. Suddenly the carriage felt stuffy. Marie pulled back the cowl of her cloak to afford a better view. Delicate obsidian strands of hair fell forward to drape luxuriously down her breasts.

"Ah!" Law sighed. "Now I understand." Where, he wondered, had Brand found such a beauty? She was far too good for a pirate. No wonder Gregory wanted her back. They'd have to see about that. "The name Raven is most appropriate." He smiled wolfishly, his appreciation overcoming the plainness of his features. Marie could imagine he had many conquests among the women of Mobile.

"Look there," Jason said, changing the subject. They were emerging from the last of the settlement proper and beginning to climb the gradually ascending road leading to the top of the bluff. A trio of garishly painted savages sauntered along the path and stared with dour amusement at the carriage.

"Alabamos," Law explained casually. "Probably on

366

their way from Bienville's." The warriors were clad in tanned hides. Their skulls were shaven and necklaces of beads, quills and claws decorated their muscular chests, bared to the cold air. The carriage rolled past and they were out of sight around a bend. "Madame de Bienville will be furious," Law went on. "She is entertaining the commandant of Fort Charlotte, Colonel Guilbert, and his wife, Liane. The savages—she detests them and the governor is required to listen to them—have no sense of timing and always manage to interrupt at the most inappropriate times. You'll do well to pay her as little attention as possible. Beyond a few flattering remarks, of course. She's striving to create an atmosphere of elegance for the Guilberts and his two lieutenants, Dubois and Clement, both of whom are attracted to Angelique. I am sure you've not forgotten Angelique?"

Jason ignored Marie's inquisitive stare and tried not to grimace as the carriage shot him toward the ceiling. "Perhaps we'd better choose another time to pay our respects to the governor," he suggested lamely.

"No, no. Monsieur the Governor has expressly requested to see you immediately on your arrival. Immediately. Now, about those lieutenants. They're from good families, and all you need do is be civil with them. They hold no real power and are quite weak-willed."

His voice droned on, but Marie paid little attention. An Angelique had been mentioned, and Jason's reaction had been obvious, at least to her. Quite suddenly she found herself very, very interested in meeting this young lady. Whoever she was.

The sitting room was by far the largest and most lavishly appointed room in the governor's house. Great double windows, doors really, to a charming lawn spotted with giant oaks hung with gray Spanish moss, were framed by royal purple drapes. Magnificently wrought brass candlesticks jutted from the walls, eight candles to a cluster. Between these, a pedestal held a priceless Grecian urn, the treasure of the household. A parqueted flooring of oak and pecan hexagrams shone around the edges of brightly colored Persian rugs, Madame de Bienville's only but cherished possessions from the East. The straight-backed chairs, carved walnut with cushions of heavy maroon silk, were a wedding gift from a relieved father. A blond harpsichord to one side dominated the room. Imported from Antwerp, the double keyboard allowed for the widest possible range of sound and style.

Louise de Bienville boldly if erratically attacked the final bars of the sonata. Her pudgy fingers stumbled disastrously across the harpsichord's ebony keys, transforming the notes that wandered sprightly over the paper into a manic dance until she found her way again and beamed with success. An admiring, sycophantic audience applauded enthusiastically. In a land of bone rattles and Indian drums, the aristocracy of a harpsichord, no matter how badly played, was occasion for applause. Especially when the virtuosa was none other than the governor's wife.

"Bravo, Mamá," Angelique called. The handsome lieutenants to either side echoed her sentiments. The colonel and his wife beamed appreciatively. Jean Baptiste reentered and Louise breathed a sigh of relief that he was unaccompanied by the savages that Marmont had reported at their back door.

"Ah, Jean Baptiste, you missed a most laudable performance," Guilbert boomed, at the same time raising an eyebrow.

Bienville nodded discreetly, signaling that all was well. "I listened from the hall. Well played, my dear."

Louise inclined her head in a gracious bow of acceptance. Seated at the harpsichord, the tight confines of her gown limited the movement of her corpulent figure. Liane Guilbert, a woman of similar proportions as her hostess, though plainer in features and younger in years, took her husband's arm. "We must simply have a similar instrument brought over, Richard," she cooed in a affected Parisian accent which still bore traces of her Brittany heritage. "I am certain Captain Honore would make room if you so requested."

Despite a deep affection for Madame Guilbert, Louise felt a heartwarming twinge of satisfaction. "Oh, but Liane, you may amuse yourself with mine whenever you wish," she exclaimed solicitously.

Liane's pinched smile spoke volumes of dark rhetoric bred of envy. Only a master could have detected the anguish in her voice. "I know, dear, and you're very gracious," she answered, with a sharp glance toward her husband. "I will. Until Captain Honore brings us ours."

Guilbert had become immune to such pointed hints and nodded, only half listening, for Jean Baptiste was gesturing toward the dining room and the sumptuously laden table within. Despite his position of authority at the fort, monetary recompense was ever slow in arriving, and in truth the colonel could never afford to be so munificent as either the governor or other commanders in European posts. However, without a war to support France's vast military, and with his family's fortunes at an ebb, he was lucky enough to have Fort Charlotte.

Jean Baptiste maintained the illusion of calm and watched as Dubois and Clement dutifully escorted Angelique to the table. His daughter, in a pale yellow silk gown, was the epitome of innocence save for the startling decolletage that afforded her young admirers a most appealing view. Somehow, the gown had seemed less revealing earlier in the evening. He wondered whether the wisp of strategically placed silk tucked into the bodice when she'd come downstairs had been placed there for the benefit of a suspicious father, and subject to removal when in the company of would-be suitors. Dubois leaned close and whispered some remark that Angelique found most amusing. Clement scowled. The jest had been at his expense.

But Jean Baptiste had more to worry about than his daughter. An orderly had reported the arrival of two ships. The *Banshee* he recognized, but the other was a complete stranger. No telling what had happened. The *Banshee* could have captured the other, or vice versa. Pirates lost their ships and lives with a rapidity astonishing to contemplate. Law knew by this time, of course, but was taking his own sweet time, and in the process committing the inexcusable mistake of being tardy. If it was Brand . . . Damn! Was that who the low-cut gown was for? Angelique had overheard their discussion, he was certain. Did she intend to show herself off for that damnable pirate?

His thoughts were interrupted by the chatter at the table. A fresh kidney pie was thrust beneath his nose. "I've taken the liberty of broaching the crust, and found it well worth the attack," Colonel Guilbert exclaimed from Louise's right, at the other end of the table.

"Then you will the better enjoy a sally against the roast," Bienville suggested, indicating the platter of browned meat Marmont was carving for the women. "This morning it was the haunch of a fat young doe. Tonight she graces our table. But eat lightly, for Marmont has promised me a surprise." He stopped and sniffed the air. "Aha! This must be it."

A second servant entered, carrying a pair of ducks braised in orange sauce. "My favorite," Bienville sighed. "And stuffed with mincemeat liberally laced with chestnuts. If there's a bread pudding to accompany it . . ." Marmont glanced up from the roast and nodded. ". . . we shall have a veritable symphony of taste, indeed," he said, sighing with anticipation and picking up the knife. The duck he would carve himself.

"Madame," Philip Dubois broke in to fill the gap in the conversation, "you must play again after dinner. Your daughter promised me her hand . . ." he paused just long enough to elicit blatant expressions of surprise, ". . . for the first dance."

Angelique lowered her head, spilling a wealth of honey-gold curls forward to hide an amused smile. Everyone else pretended not to have been caught off guard, but Jean Clement, to Angelique's left, was in no mood for childish badinage. He glowered at the boiled potatoes and onions adrift in a buttery lagoon. Until Philip Dubois had arrived to replace another officer who had succumbed to an undiagnosed and macabre malignancy, Jean Clement had felt assured that the governor's ravishing daughter would one day be his. Passingly handsome, he flattered himself, and the only potential suitor of a worthy station in the settlement, his confidence had waxed. And then Dubois had arrived. Dubois came from a better family and was Clement's superior by virtue of seniority. His head jerked to the side as Angelique placed her fingers on the heavy blue fabric of his sleeve. He looked into a teasing smile that fired his ardor and bolstered his resolve.

"And perhaps monsieur will escort me to the Heights, later on. I do so love to watch the stars reflected in the bay," Angelique said demurely.

"I will be most highly honored, mademoiselle," Clement replied, casting a look of victory in Philip's direction.

Clement's rival spun his head so abruptly a vague cloud of powder drifted from his wig. Angelique chided herself for being so outrageously aggravating, but she simply could not help playing off their affections, one against the other. From the lofty summit of seventeen years, the lieutenants seemed mere boys, though in truth they were older than she. But then, everyone who came to call paled in comparison to the man who had arrived that afternoon and might be on his way to the mansion at the very moment. A reckless longing filled Angelique and she sighed softly, remembering an afternoon only months ago when they had walked on the Heights. She had come close to letting him take her. One kiss had led to another. The longing his rough strength had instilled weakened her resolve almost to the breaking point. And now he had returned to claim the prize once denied him. Or so she hoped, and dared to dream.

Marmont entered, bent low and whispered in her father's ear. Angelique watched her mother out of the corner of her eye, noticed a frown spread over her face as the governor rose from his chair. He tapped a crystal goblet with a thin silver spoon. "My friends. We've some newly arrived guests. If you will excuse me one moment?"

Could that be him? Angelique made herself smile at

her companions and act as if nothing out of the way had happened. At the end of the table, Mama began to chatter nervously, recounting the halcyon days in Paris. Jean Baptiste le Moyne and his new bride had dined with marquis, been entertained by chevaliers, enjoyed the uncertain, hectic subterfuge and regal pomp of Louis XIV's court. The younger folks had so much to look forward to. There was a new king, of course, and even though he was still a child, things would be different.

Lighter, gayer, more brittle than it should have been, her voice droned on. Another corner of her mind catalogued the dreadful possibilities. The last intruders had been those filthy savages. And the next? She'd seen those ships, knew only that they weren't French. An apprehensive smile hid the sinking feeling that the newly arrived guests could only besmirch her lovely, lovely little party.

"Ah, Captain Brand—" Bienville halted in mid sentence at the sight of Marie.

"And Captain Raven," Law interjected helpfully, enjoying the governor's startled reaction.

"Enchanted, Madame Raven." He bowed to kiss the hand she extended. No wonder she'd managed to steal a ship. Bewitched the crew, no doubt. Astonishing, how beautiful she was. Madame would be insanely jealous Raven—Ravenne. The alias was ridiculously naive, if she was in fact the one Gregory sought. But unless he missed his guess, two valuable prizes had fallen into his lap at once. If he wanted them, of course. For the moment, though, there was no need to create unnecessary suspicion. "I trust you had a good journey?" he inquired in stilted, noncommittal English.

"Long, but a fair wind on the whole," Jason answered.

"One that left you hungry, I trust? Of course, if you've eaten . . ."

"I'm afraid I rushed them away, Governor."

"Ah, yes. 'Twas my pleasure that kept you from ta-

372

ble. I trust you'll allow my table to be your pleasure in return. If you'll step this way?"

Marie followed, trying the while to shake off a sense of déjà vu. As they left the corridor and entered what was meant to pass for the room of state, it came to her. The statuary and rich tapestry-adorned walls were similar to those at Penscott Hall, and though the interior was more rustic, the effect was as if she had stepped back in time.

A butler let them into the dining room. Introductions were made and Marie scrutinized each individual seated around the table. Madame de Bienville's mask of ceruse did little to hide the abject look of disapproval at the arrival of such ill-dressed guests. Imagine, Marie could almost hear the thought, a woman in man's clothing. How gauche! Colonel Guilbert, the very epitome of authority, rumbled an uncomfortable introduction to his frowning, dumpy spouse. Lieutenants Philip Dubois and Jean Clement bowed stiffly, their faces a mixture of arrogance and curiosity. Angelique, all soft and heather sweetness, managed at last to tear her eyes from Jason and take the opportunity to round the table and parade her queenly attire with a low curtsey. Marie stiffened. The display was blatantly designed for his benefit. So this was Angelique. No wonder Jason had changed the subject so quickly. Had he tasted of her lithe, young body on his previous trip? Worse, did he expect to again? She would have to watch them both very closely.

"I am delighted to meet you again, Monsieur Brand," Angelique purred. Her smile flattened dangerously as she turned to Marie. "Madame." The lightning-fast, sweeping glance indicated contempt for a woman who would wear men's boots. Unseen were the pangs of jealousy that stabbed at her heart.

Full ready to play the game, Marie shrugged aside the folds of her cape and tossed the garment to Marmont. An electric shock raced through the room. Louise and Liane gasped in mortification at the unseemly display of skin-tight breeches. No decent woman—no woman at all!—could possibly dress so outrageously.

373

The governor felt a slow flush creep across his face and forced himself to focus on the obsidian locks that spilled around her shoulders. The haughty lieutenants stiffened, their eyes wide in appreciation of the proud breasts swelling under the shirt. Colonel Guilbert could be heard to gulp and stifle a choking cough.

It was Bienville who shattered the tableau with the hasty summons for three extra chairs, sets of plates and tableware. Suddenly everyone was bustling about, pretending nothing out of the ordinary was occurring. Bright chatter flew around the table, everyone reverting to French save Jason, who couldn't follow the rapidly flowing jests and overly flowery language.

The strain was evident, and the new arrivals ate hastily. Equally hastily, Bienville rose the second the last knife had clattered to the last empty plate and explained that Marmont would serve cordials and confections in the main room, and if Louise would be so kind as to liven the air with a rendition on the harpsichord, he was sure the entire company would be most grateful. Everyone dutifully followed him from the table.

"I see you've charmed the entire household," the brawny Scot whispered as Louise began to play.

"Hush!" Marie snapped. The strain of being near yet not allowed to touch him was beginning to show. She needed sympathy, not sarcasm.

Jean Clement, anxious for promotion, bowed before Liane Guilbert and led her to the floor. The colonel slumped in a chair to one side where he could keep an eye on Marie. Looking for all the world like a stern tutor facing a class of unruly boys, Bienville stationed himself at the corner of the harpsichord and glowered at the wall in front of him. Philip Dubois had claimed the first dance with Angelique, as promised, but wasn't enjoying it. Clement had outfoxed him. If he was too prosaic, Angelique would be sure to pout. If he was too graceful, the colonel's wife would take offense. Law had disappeared for the moment. He was the only one with the temerity to excuse himself from one of Madame's performances.

Jason and Marie sat side by side, neither knowing exactly what protocol demanded. Marie recalled the great glittering affairs at Penscott where lords and ladies posed and bowed like graceful birds absorbed in the delicate machinations of the dance, or chatted gaily to one side, throwing quips and conceits about like brightly colored confetti. When the music stopped, she turned to speak, suddenly realized Angelique was at Jason's side.

"Jason," the girl coyly spoke in English, extending the second syllable, "I must be bold, no?"

Reading her intentions, Jason rose and bowed, took her pale ivory fingers in his hardened hand. Though he had been at sea a long time, the lessons of etiquette taught a young Scottish lord were not easily forgotten. By the end of the first *motif,* he had recalled the sure, floating movements, and moved as confidently as the girl.

"Raven. An unusual name," Bienville remarked, handing Marie a glass of wine. Now the first selection was over, he could leave the harpsichord.

Jason seemed to be enjoying himself. *Why does he smile so?* "It was given me by others," she answered in French, at the same time silently cursing Angelique for being so blatantly tempting.

"Ah. I see." Interrogating such a beauty—especially one with steel-gray eyes that touched a man's soul—was an onerous duty. "Then do you think me inconsiderate if I ask . . ."

There! That laugh! And see how he holds her hand . . . "Marie Ravenne is my true name." *And now she curtsies to titillate him further. See how his eyes devour her? Tart! Bitch!*

"Ravenne? Then you are French." Worse and worse, Bienville thought. Compelled to arrest a Frenchwoman at the command of an Englishman? The tight fit of her breeches was disconcerting. Pirate she may have been, but she was most obviously a woman first. "I should have known. Few English speak our language as well as you."

375

Oh, damn him for a rogue! Dance with her like that!
"You flatter me, sir. My father was French, my mother
Spanish." *He's doing it to annoy me, I know.*

"I see," Bienville muttered thoughtfully. "But how
does a young lady like yourself, how shall I say, find
herself at the head of a . . . a . . ." He couldn't quite
bring himself to utter the word, groped for another with
a dissimulating chuckle. ". . . company of outcasts?"

*They're laughing again. She makes a fool of him. Of
me! I'll scratch out her eyes. But no. That's too lady-
like. I'll shoot her!* Marie grimaced at the thought.

". . . madame?" Bienville repeated with a concerned look. The woman hadn't heard a word he'd said.
A discerning, a sensitive man could see she was no
common mutineer. Here was a troubled soul of great
depth, whose nobility was untouched by apparel or the
circumstances into which the English had forced her.
He bowed low. "My question was in bad taste, madame. Will you accept the humble apology of one who
has become an admirer?"

"Monsieur," Marie murmured, for the first time
really noticing the man. He seemed sincere, and not unsympathetic. What *was* she doing at the head of a company of outcasts? Strange, she hadn't thought of the
Ravener's crew in that way. Yet the world surely did.
"What simple answer suffices for so complex a question, monsieur?" she asked in return. "Yesterday's noble is today's exile. Who can adequately explain these
ironies?"

Bienville nodded sagely to hide a surge of conflicting
emotions. The proof of guilt came from her own lips.
Raven and Marie Ravenne were one and the same.
Brand and Ravenne in one fell swoop! The Englishman
would be pleased and Mobile's safety and continuance
assured. But what of the girl? What of her safety? Having met and listened to Gregory, the answer was obvious—and profoundly disturbing.

The coach jostled its occupants unmercifully as the
horses careened down the slope and managed to find

every chuckhole and rock that littered the road. Road, indeed, Marie reflected, groaning as a particularly violent jolt wrenched her back. The paths traveled by the wild boars on Mysteré were smoother. The next lunge knocked her into Jason. She drew away as if burned and shunned Law's half-drunken stare.

The ride wasn't helping ease her anger. Their first night together in six weeks had fallen into a miserable shambles. For more than two hours she had endured Louise and Liane's demeaning glances, hypocritical smiles, snide remarks and innuendoes designed to inform her of their utter contempt. Colonel Guilbert had studiously ignored her, following a surreptitious elbow to the ribs by a jealous wife. Law had disappeared for much of the evening, appearing only for the last half-hour. She might have listened more intently to Dubois or Clement, were it not for their simpering foppishness and half-hearted, veiled propositions. As for the governor, each passing minute and glass of wine emboldened him further. She would have struck him had it not been for the spectacle of Jason's preoccupation with a laughing, cooing Angelique. How could he tease her so? And now, traitor that he was, he sat casting a wry smile in her direction, trying to act as if he he hadn't been an absolute beast.

The road finally flattened out. Marie gazed at the squat, functional shapes of homes that comprised the bulk of Mobile and wondered about the families who lived there. *Do they sense the excitement? Or sleep contentedly in the knowledge that they are taming a wilderness while we who pass the the night leave nothing to celebrate our passage save ruts in the earth.*

The carriage slowed to a halt. Jason opened the door and a gust of frigid north wind riding a cloud of dust slammed it against the side. Marie shivered, pulled tight her cloak and followed Jason up the shell drive. Behind them, Law called a slurred goodnight and promised to see them in the morning as the carriage lurched away.

The Inn of the Sparrow perched on the perimeter of the waterfront. Less than a hundred yards away, the closest of Mobile's half-dozen waterfront taverns rocked to the sound of sailors at play. "Wait for me here," Jason instructed, his first words since they had left the governor's mansion. "I had Ramahd take us a room."

"And you?" Marie asked tightly. Though Angelique had driven a wedge between them, she was anxious—even eager—to mend the rift.

"I'll . . . be along."

"Really? Perhaps I should accompany you," Marie said, sudden anger making her forget the cold wind. Without waiting, she stared past him.

"No!" Jason caught her arm, held her back. "I must go alone. There are those who will talk to me and none other. They won't speak openly if another is at my side."

"I think I understand—" Marie began frostily.

"Something bothers me about Bienville and Law," Jason went on, gazing up to the bluff. "It's hard to put my finger on it, and I have to find out before it's too late."

"A worthy lie," Marie spat, overcome with frustration and anger. "But no less so than your performance tonight."

"What's that supposed to mean?"

"Angelique." The sound of her laughter was gay, but Jason could see her face was contorted in pain. "No doubt you've a rendezvous with her."

"Quiet, you little fool."

"I will not!" she yelled into the wind. "Well? Go on! What's stopping you? No doubt the sheets are already warm. Maybe *she'll* tell you what her father has in mind."

Jason threw up his arms in disgust, spun away and strode off into the dark. Marie watched him go, trying to think of a final, vindictive indictment to hurl at his back. But jealousy and suspicion had made a turmoil of her emotions and all she could do was stand and stare, the wind forcing tears from her eyes. When the door to the tavern opened and closed, she could stand still no longer. Reaching to the ground, she picked up an oyster shell and hurled it with all her strength. "I wish . . . I wish . . . Oh!" she cried, in a very frustrated fashion.

A figure slid from the shadows and materialized a few feet away. "A strange way for a fierce pirate captain to behave," Ramahd said, obviously amused.

"Go to hell," Marie snarled, in a voice as cutting as the wind. Not caring in the least if that was the way the Turk thought a captain ought to behave, she stalked into the Sparrow.

The dimly lit cavern was peopled with snoring shadows sprawled on the heavy oaken tables. The stench of stale beer and rum mingled with grease and tallow candles. Marie wrinkled her nose: the smell of the open sea was vastly preferable. No innkeeper stood by to help, so she started up the stairs to the broad-beamed balcony overlooking the main room. Five dark, rectangular patches along the wall and one facing her from the end proved to be doors, one of which would be her room. She tried the closest, found it bolted from within. A few moments of examination revealed the door at the end of the hall led to the only unoccupied room, inside of which a lighted candle revealed two broken chairs, a rickety table and a crude, bulky bed that looked larger than it was because the room was so small. At least the bed looked comfortable. Best of all, a small fire glowed with inviting warmth.

"Pssst."

Marie turned, startled. Hope Deferred, swaddled in a blanket and nothing else, stepped into the room. "I built yer a fire, case you come in late."

"Thank you, Hope," Marie said, relieved it was her, yet wishing at the same time Jason had reconsidered and returned.

"And some hot rum there, on the table. If it's still warm."

"Thank you," Marie repeated, slumping wearily on the bed.

"It's mighty good rum. Forlicar bought it. We're on the other side of the wall." She paused and licked her lips. "Tasty rum, I must admit. We drunk up ours already. Them clay bottles are thick and don't hold near as much as they look to."

"You may have mine."

"Oh, I wouldn't," Hope protested, a little too quickly.

"Take it."

The harlot nodded happily and hurried to the bottle. She paused, studying Marie, then stepped across the room and sat on the edge of the bed. As the older woman watched, a tear glimmered and spilled down Marie's cheek. "Tulip?"

"Leave me alone."

"But dear . . ."

"Please, Hope. Now."

Hope sighed, guessing the cause of Marie's unhappiness and knowing from experience there was nothing anyone could say to help. She put her arm around Marie in a motherly embrace, kissed her on the forehead and quietly stole from the room.

"Vagabonds. Thieves. Savages. Harlots!"

"Heavens, Louise." Bienville said in mock alarm. "There were only two of them."

"Two encompassing all the vices. How could you? I just know Liane will spin the most terrible lies about me."

Bienville scowled, slipped the turban over a head whose hair was but a dimly remembered memory. He glanced at the swollen figure of his wife, her expanse unleashed and freed from the gown's confines, and felt again the ignominious encroachment of time. As usual when such thoughts crept in, he was constrained to remember that Jean Baptiste de Moyne, sieur de Bienville, was a governor, a man of staunch and stalwart duty. Duty, fah. What did that English player write? "There's the rub." Yes. Duty demanded Mobile's welfare be given every consideration. But was there never a time when one might bend at the edges? Marie Ravenne had been portrayed as an ogress, but once met, proved to be the most lovely, charming creature he'd encountered since his departure from France.

So what, then, did a rational man do? Arrest her as Gregory had demanded? Did Mobile's security really hinge on the capture of a beautiful woman? And could not a case be made for remaining on friendly terms with the pirates? Who could predict what news the next ships from France would bring? For all he knew, England and France were at war again.

Damn the English captain, then, he thought, deciding on the spur of the moment. The man's overbearing attitude had tried Bienville's patience and chafed his pride. Let him threaten and posture, let him try to cut off Mobile. No Frenchman worth his name would dream of submitting to such intolerable behavior.

A soft knock sounded. *"Mon dieu!"* Louise's voice drifted from beneath the summit of covers under which Bienville had watched her disappear.

"It's Marmont," the governor explained. "Go to sleep. I'll return shortly."

Outside, the wind began a restless dirge. The acoustics in the hall imparted a sinister quality to Marmont's equine countenance as he bowed to his master. "Monsieur Law, as you requested, m'lord. I brought him into the study."

"Very good," Bienville replied wearily, glancing over his shoulder. "And my daughter?"

"In her room, sir. The gentlemen sought to outlast one another and a walk was considered, but I suggested the weather was much too inclement for Mademoiselle to be outside, and that her father would be displeased." Marmont grinned, enjoying the spoiler's role. "The lieutenants left together."

Bienville chuckled and led the way to the study. "All for the best, Marmont. Even if they are from good families, I doubt the sincerity of their intentions. You did well."

John Law was the picture of brooding self-concern. Slumped in one of the two great leather-covered armchairs that flanked the fireplace, he sipped at a glass of hot buttered rum and pointedly remained seated as Bienville entered. When in private and without the need for show, he admitted inferiority to no man. That attitude had seen him exiled from England and a trio of other courts, and though the governor decried it privately, he was forced to be tolerant for the man was invaluable. Iconoclasm and stubborn independence opened avenues of action otherwise closed to a representative of the king.

"I left them at the inn," Law said, not deigning to look up. The trace of drunkenness had disappeared from his voice.

Bienville nodded, waved away a steaming cup of rum and excused Marmont. "Colonel Guilbert knows nothing as yet, as you requested, though I question the wisdom—"

"Guilbert is a gentleman," Law interrupted, "but at times lacks a necessary sense of subterfuge. It is enough that he act quickly when told to."

"If we act at all."

Law grunted, emptied the last of the still-steaming brew. "So you have reconsidered?"

"I had never decided," Bienville protested.

"But now you have. They shall not be harmed." Law forbore a smile. As usual, the governor had swayed in the right direction. "It's just as well. I didn't like Captain Gregory."

"Must you always anticipate my thoughts?" Bienville asked, obviously peeved.

"Anticipation is a great virtue—or art, as the case may be. I have employed it judiciously, and it has served me well. How else have I escaped garrot, noose and headsman's axe?"

Bienville tried to decide if Law was laughing at him, but finally gave up. "Well, since you know, I shall return to bed," he snapped unhappily. "I suppose I could have saved you a trip had I been more aware of your shrewdness. Marmont will show you out. Good night, monsieur."

"Do not be too distressed with me, my friend," Law said, accompanying Bienville from the room. "I only guessed you would not imprison Brand and the lovely Raven. But only you, Jean Baptiste, know why."

Bienville ignored the twinkle in those ofttimes humorless eyes and left his confidant at the stairs. He paused on the landing, heard Marmont bid the departing Law good-night and listened as the servant began the nightly ritual of extinguishing the tallow lamps. Step by step, darkness approached. Outside, the north wind spilled swiftly into the sea like the rush of raven's wings.

Chapter XX

There was little time to lose. Law had told Jason the night before about Gregory's visit. No one knew when the English captain and heavily armed *Breston* would return. Consequently, haste was of the essence, for if the pirate ships were caught in Mobile Bay, they'd be blown out of the water. A morning departure wouldn't be any too soon.

"There's no need to drive the men so. Law can wait for his gold," Ramahd counseled. Jason shrugged, bellowed an order to a second work party loading the *Banshee*'s jolly boat with casks of fresh water and cursed them for their slowness. Tom Gunn straightened from his labors to glare malevolently in Jason's direction. The other men of the *Ravener* paused as well. Jason defied them with an imperious stance. Grumbling, the men at last returned to the task at hand.

"What is it, my friend?"

Jason turned angry eyes on the man at his side. "I don't know what you mean."

"For three days you have kept to yourself. Now the sun has driven the winter clouds away, yet the storm remains. In you."

"You talk too much." Jason started for a mare tethered nearby. A breeze, refreshingly warm after the cold northern wind, tugged at the folds of his shirt.

Ramahd would not be vexed. "And you listen too little," he countered easily.

"Do not provoke me, Ramahd," Jason snapped. He swung onto the mare and dug booted heels into the animal's flanks. Hooves drumming on the packed sand, the startled beast bolted down the beach, past the settlement and Law's warehouse, into the solitude of the empty strand. The salt sea air stung Jason's lungs as he breathed deeply, head back and golden hair rippling in the wind. Mobile fell astern of a blunt point before he reined the mare to a halt at the base of a jumbled fortress of uprooted trees torn from the high bluff behind him. Jagged roots thrust into the air and mingled with shattered trunks, mute evidence of nature's awesome forces at work.

Jason dismounted and secured the animal. The pale brown sand underfoot reflected the warmth of the afternoon sun and served a little to alleviate his dark mood. Alone with the wind and the sea, the Scottish exile-turned-pirate leaning against the gnarled timber battlement made a forlorn figure. Here he could relax a little and, free of the constraint required of a leader in front of his men, sift through and grapple with the contradictory emotions that raged in his breast.

They had been in Mobile for three full days now. Activity in the settlement had come to a near standstill while the winter storm raged and huffed and at last blew itself out. In that time, Marie and Jason had shared naught but passionless, silent nights. Angry because he'd danced with Angelique once too often at the party, she refused to acknowledge his very real concern over their reception and his doubts about Bienville and Law's intentions. By the time he joined her in their room at the Sparrow, she had turned sour and cold, and answered his every overture with silence. As a result, they lay motionless and in fear of disturbing one another, like strangers forced to share the same bed.

So why this torment? She had instigated the whole row, and now her intransigence and strident accusations had driven him away. But that was only part of the reason. His own disquiet must be taken into account if he was to be truthful. Something had been born in the recesses of his soul that first moment in the forest beyond Penscott Hall—and been rekindled on Mysteré. Something he had fought and resisted, an emotion contrary to all the violent discord that had rent his life thus far. Love? Dared he call it love?

"To hell with love," he suddenly shouted to the

385

waves. And why not? What had love brought him other than anguish and grief? That's why he hadn't gone back and taken her from Penscott Hall. That's why he had turned surly and mean on Mysteré and flaunted Angelique's infatuation in Mobile. To drive *her* away.

But damn it, why should he worry? "I need no one," he growled to the gnarled roots. "There's no place for such rubbish. Not in this world of butchers—of Penscotts and Gregorys." The painful image of the crumbled ruins of his estate and the broken, smoldering corpses of his family, danced miragelike over the gulf. Overhead a gull cried and, gliding on the seabreeze, emulated the unheeding passage of time, the turning earth oblivious to men and their petty problems. Jason dug a hand into a pocket on the inside of his cloak and withdrew a crinkled bit of parchment to which the odor of lilacs still clung. The missive had arrived that morning, brought by a nameless servant in the governor's employ. Only the note was not in the governor's blocky handwriting, but in the fluid, delicate penmanship of his daughter, who suggested a rendezvous and entreated him to be "faithful to the request of one who pines for a moment alone with you" before he vanished once again from her side.

And so he had complied. Was "faithful." A sense of betrayal had hounded him the morning long and turned brooding irritability and melancholy to fits of uncontrollable anger. It galled him to think of this as betrayal. Whom, after all, was he betraying? Was he not a man? Did he not enjoy the freedom to do as he pleased? Marie was a passionate wench, right enough, and their relationship offered certain advantages. But bound to her? Hardly. Jason Brand would have who he damned well pleased, and be bound to no one.

Still, anger and insidious guilt lingered. Jason kicked viciously at the sand and tried to transfer the blame to Marie. Robbing him of his manhood, she was. Served her right. Pirate, she called herself. Ha! If the lass had become so dependent as to rely on him, it was her own fault. She needed to learn to rely on no one, for to care

386

was to be hurt, was to be at the mercy of a vicious world. Later, she'd thank him for the lesson, by God. They'd be friends, of course, but that was all.

The distant sound of a horse approaching cut through the whisper of the surf. By the gods but she was beautiful. Wanted him, too. He could tell that the moment they met at her father's house. If the flashing eyes weren't invitation enough, the deep, revealing curtsies were. Those breasts had virtually pleaded to be caressed. Jason Brand was just the man to do their bidding. She was riding sidesaddle, of course, and the wind pressed the skirts against her legs. One finely shaped calf was exposed above her slipper. Higher up, the outline of her thighs fired the imagination. She'd make good sport, this one, with those fine, long legs.

The mount skidded to a stop and Angelique, breathing heavily from the swift ride, looked down at him. The bonnet she'd worn had blown off her head and hung by its string down her back. Honey curls, windtossed, framed a face devoid of makeup. Dark brown eyes, rose-petal lips, a tiny dimple in her chin. She smiled teasingly as his hands encircled her waist and he lifted her down.

She wished the gown had been stripped away, that they both stood naked, caressed by the wind and serenaded by the sea. Perhaps he would take her as his own, to sail the seas in a pirate ship. He'd soon forget the brazen, dark-haired one. "You're here. I rode like the wind."

"I expected a carriage."

"Perhaps I have more in common with your Captain Raven than you think." Jason released her, turned away and leaned on an outthrust root which sprung from the base of a tree like a massive horn. "You do not want to speak of her?" In the face of his silence, she straightened her gown and tugged at the bodice which so well displayed her figure. Out in the bay a seagull streaked down from a circling vigil, snared an unsuspecting fish and lofted into the air again. A trio of his envious cohorts screeched in protest, tried to steal the prize, then gave up. "Very well then. I shall not speak of her. But who then? My father? He would be most displeased were he to learn I am with the notorious Jason Brand. Mother? No. Not of her. She's a loveless creature, really." A mischievous twinkle lit her eyes. "Ah, yes! My lieutenants."

Angelique drew close until her breasts touched Jason's back. His hair reminded her of a golden-red sunset at the end of a perfect day, and she couldn't forbear touching one trailing curl. "Clement bores me really. He talks of bright success, and marriage if I would allow it. And dear Philip. Handsome enough, but a boy. Angelique's needs cannot be filled by a boy. Angelique prefers a man." She giggled. "He does carry on, though. So pawing and anxious."

Jason spun about, gripped her so savagely his fingers left crimson welts on her arms. His kiss was brutal, powerful, like nothing she had ever experienced, and made all the romance she had known in a young life tepid by comparison. Suddenly her bodice was open and her breasts free. Alarmed, she stepped back and tried to cover herself. "Jason?"

His eyes glinted like moonlight on the water and his stare seemed to cut through her fear. Without speaking, he pulled her hands aside and sighed with pleasure. At this sign of approval, Angelique straightened unconsciously, aware of a growing pride in her body.

Jason's eyes slitted. Young breasts, not full but pert and crowned with long, pointed nipples. He reached and touched one, then the other, found them distended and hard as he rolled them between his fingertips, bent to kiss one, roll his tongue around the other and softly pressed it against his teeth.

Weak from wanting him, Angelique sank to her knees and watched in silent, breathless awe as he peeled off his shirt and boots. Below his waist, a long mound bulged against the fabric. Hardly knowing she did so, she reached and touched, shuddered as he undid his belt and let free the swelling flesh. Fascinated, she watched him harden, watched as his maleness rose and stood proudly erect. As in a dream, she reached for him. Trembling fingertips explored the thick brown forest of hair. One delicate hand cupped the roiling sphere, then moved to join the other and gently encircle his manhood.

The breath whistled in Jason's throat. He kneeled by her side, spread her cloak on the sand and forced her back. Aroused now, all thoughts of Marie forgotten, he lifted her hips and pulled up her skirts. God, but she was beautiful. The dark blonde, almost brown, tawny hair was thick and luxuriant, soft to the touch, moistening as he stroked the warm cleft.

Light, darkness, a world of misted shadow, cliff, beach, gulf, sky. All disappeared before their rising passion. Nothing existed save the brown eyes boring into Angelique's and the enticing hand which led to delights unguessed. But this wasn't all, she knew. One final step remained. She was frightened. Of him and his flesh, which would enter hers. Caught between desire and fear, she whimpered, tried to draw away. She couldn't let him. It would hurt, would tear her.

"No," she whispered, terrified.

But there was no game-playing now. The time for teasing ploys was far past, lost in dim, flirtatious yesterdays. He was over her, his knees between her spread legs. Dangerously close, the pulsing scepter touched her, parted the unwilling lips . . .

"No!" She tried to free herself but he pushed her back down. She could feel him enter, glanced down to see the hard flesh piercing her. "No . . . Please . . ."

"Yes," he said, the word guttural, forced from between clenched teeth. His eyes gleamed maniacally and a demonic grin contorted his lips.

"You can't . . ." Why were her arms around him? Why did she ache so with desire? She wanted him. Was afraid. Despised him for this subjugation. But wanted, damn him, more than anything. "You wouldn't dare!"

"I would dare anything," he whispered. "Anything!"

Suddenly liquid fire spread between her legs as he drove into her, rending asunder the delicate maiden's veil. Angelique cried out, but a gust of wind tore the sound from her lips. When he pulled back, she was afraid he would leave her empty, but his weight descended and again she was filled with his length. Not thinking, her legs rose to clasp him and her thighs closed round to hold him fast. As her moan of pain turned to ecstasy, he covered her mouth with his.

The dress was of the sheerest pale blue silk, like a waterfall captured in time. Marie eased it from the trunk taken from the galleon captured on their way from Mysteré. Marie couldn't resist hauling off the inlaid trunk, destined for a Spanish contessa, no doubt, after discovering it in the Spanish captain's cabin while the crews were transferring the gold and precious stones. Now, staring at the sylphlike finery, she couldn't help musing about the practicality of impulse. At least sometimes. Without the gown she'd have nothing but men's clothing. Images of courtly ladies, arm in arm with noble lords, danced through a lazy daydream. Was that what Jason wanted? Was that what Angelique offered? Feminine beauty instead of capability? Perhaps fire would have to be fought with fire. The decision made, she stripped off shirt, boots and breeches, doused herself with cologne and began the complicated process of climbing into the silken puzzle of bows and laces. As a serving girl she had often assisted Lady Gwendolyn into her elaborate garments, and had always thought it was ridiculous to need someone to help you dress. Now she saw why: donning one alone was a beastly impossibility.

"Tulip."

Marie looked up to see Hope in the doorway. "Don't just stand there and stare," she snapped. "Come and help me."

Hope's brown furrowed. She'd never been a servant and didn't plan to start. But the sight of the hopelessly struggling young woman, ill at ease in the lavish entanglement, won the harlot over. "Very well, love," she said, and closed the door behind her.

390

A half-hour later the crew of the *Ravener,* those taking their nooning in the Sparrow, stared awe-struck at the barely recognizable figure of their captain as she descended the stairway. Joints of beef paused midway to mouths. Tankards of ale hung suspended in calloused fists. Marie attempted to ignore them, a difficult task at best with so many familiar faces. Spanish Jesse, Ned, Poole and the others turned in her direction. Obsidian curls spilled across creamy white shoulders emerging from a gown of spun daybreak whose crafted bodice barely concealed the treasures of Marie's exquisite breasts. At the hem, a careful watcher might have caught a brief glimpse of white-jeweled slippers, incongruous against the warped, splintered stairs down which she seemed to glide.

Tom Gunn entered from outside and came to an abrupt halt. A clay tankard slipped from his grasp and crashed to the floor in a shower of slivers and foam. "My God, but look at her!"

Marie glared at him with such vehemence her giant friend lowered his eyes. As if daring a one of them to speak, she picked up her skirts and strode haughtily through the uncomfortable quiet marred only by the scraping of one misguided chair and a subdued chorus of muffled coughs. "Where's the carriage?" she asked as imperiously as possible.

"I sent Shelby for it," Tom answered. His head was cocked to one side and he was trying his best not to stare. "It ought to be here."

At that moment Forlicar chose to enter, his bulky frame scraping the sides of the door. His features broadened into a grin. "Well, tar my hull and set me afloat!"

"Out of the way, bilge guts!" Hope bellowed from behind. "Make way for a lady."

"Oh, by all means!" Forlicar bowed low, swept his great floppy hat through the air and across his chest. "And it's a good day I trust you're havin', your ladyship," he chuckled.

Marie glowered at him, then realized even that was

paying too much attention to the lout and walked past him with all the dignity she could muster. It was some satisfaction to hear his bawdy laughter cut short with a guttural oomph. Hope had come to the rescue, clapping something hard into something soft.

The carriage arrived as Marie went out the door. Older and more dilapidated than the one that had carried them up to Bienville's mansion, this was a simpler affair open to the elements and designed for two travelers. The strain of a frontier existence showed in patched canvas and pitted sideboards and hubs. To Marie's surprise, Law himself was driving.

She hesitated before stepping in. "When monsieur offered to put a carriage at my disposal, I did not know it included himself as well. I didn't mean to impose."

"Ah, but no, madame. An imposition? Not in the slightest. Say a most pleasing distraction from tedious duty." He extended his hand. "If you please?"

There was no other way to find Jason unless she wished to tramp the muddy streets on foot. Law beamed as she accepted his hand and joined him. Her attire intrigued him—even in his wildest dreams he hadn't expected this. Now, by the side of this beautiful and enigmatic creature gowned in the finery of an empress, he felt a great pressure in his chest. His tongue, for the first time in years, felt much too incompetent to dare further speech. And she was with *him*. Oh, but Bienville would be jealous. He had read the governor's interest that first night and had secretly laughed. But somehow, in his self-imposed solitude during the storm, the image of the pirate queen kept recurring, forcing itself into such importance that when at last he summoned his carriage, he set a subordinate in charge of the transfer of booty from the ships to his warehouse and sent his driver elsewhere.

"Monsieur?"

"Oh!" The trance was broken. Law vigorously applied the whip to the gelding's flanks and urged him into a rapid trot. A half-mile down the beach, a handful of men struggled to shove a longboat into the water. Jason was not among them.

"Where is Captain Brand?" Marie called as the carriage pulled up beside them. Loupe, in charge of the party, shrugged. Then he recognized Marie. His mouth dropped open and he stared. "Well?"

Loupe managed to mumble something about the warehouse. "No. He's not there," Law said. "Only the Easterner, Ramahd."

"Well, I seen him ride off," Loupe finally muttered. The man frowned dully. "Maybe up there?" He pointed a grimy finger toward the governor's mansion.

Marie nodded. "That is puzzling. Monsieur Bienville was to see us all tonight."

"Perhaps something has come up," Law broke in, a little worried. He wheeled the carriage around. Moist sand clutched at the iron rims on the wheels, but once the grip was broken, the gelding raced along the beach and onto the road leading to the bluff.

Marmont greeted them at the door. Usually unflappable, his eyebrows rose a minute fraction of an inch as Marie preceded Law into the hall. "We would like to see Monsieur Bienville and Captain Brand," Law instructed curtly. He'd spent far too short a time in Marie's company to cherish finding Brand too quickly.

Marmont looked puzzled. "Ah, but Captain Brand is not—"

A trill of feminine laughter from the next room interrupted him. Marie's face turned white and she swept past the servant, driven by jealousy to the sitting room. Three women sat about a gaming table. Two were playing at cards, the third looking on. All three stared in surprise at the unannounced intruder. Madame Bienville's cards dropped, face up, on the table. Liane Guilbert's mouth opened and closed. The third woman, a few years older than the others, rose from the table and crossed to Marie. "Why Louise, you've been keeping a secret. Someone new to join our little get-togethers," she cried, her eyes shrewdly appraising the newcomer.

393

"Yes. Ah, yes!" Louise stammered. "Newly arrived—"

"I am Marie Ravenne." Embarrassed by her conduct and more than a little confused, Marie introduced herself and curtsied awkwardly.

"And I, Ophelia Dumarest," the older woman answered. Smiling graciously, she touched the silken elaboration of Marie's finery. "Spanish, I would surmise. Ah, but there was a time . . . But come. Join us. Such a beautiful gown, is it not, Liane."

The commandant's wife managed an answer of sorts. "Madame Ravenne is . . . is . . . accompanying an English merchant." Her voice faded and the sentence ended with an undescriptive gesture. A great effort produced a facsimile of a smile. "Won't you have some wine with us?" she asked heroically, hastily filling a goblet and carrying it to Marie.

Liane admirably took her cue and followed suit. "The smoked fish is wonderful," she cooed, the very picture of sudden conviviality, "and Madame Dumarest has brought a most marvelous cheese from her plantation."

Marie tasted the wine, found it palatable. "Plantation?" she asked, enjoying her hostess's discomfort and playing her new role to the hilt. Ophelia Dumarest appeared more a gracious court favorite than a wilderness matriarch.

"Yes. My husband, rest his soul, was an adventurer of sorts and chose to make a house in the wilderness. There wasn't even a settlement then, but Antone won the friendship of the Mississipys—they're quite marvelous people once you get to know them—" she added parenthetically for Louise's benefit, "and was allowed to stay. At any rate, when he returned for me, circumstances in France compelled an immediate and hasty departure. With a pair of reluctant household servants and what we could load aboard a rather creaky ship, we sailed back across the water to the New World."

Her bright laugh filled the room. "Come, come, Louise. Don't look so mournful. Antone died bravely, and would be appalled if I passed my days lugubriously mooning about." She turned back to Marie. "Louise hates it here, but I am quite content. My home and holdings are pleasing in their own way, and though I admit an occasional longing for Paris, still, I am most certainly happy. And not at all as alone as I feared. You see, I have discovered a marvelous occupation. Work."

"Ophelia, really," Louise reprimanded, though not harshly. It was obvious she and Liane held this older woman in high esteem.

Marie, too, found the woman immensely likable. Ophelia Dumarest represented a refreshing change from the cloying civility of Louise and Liane. Marie might have enjoyed the interlude more, but John Law's sudden intrusion reminded her of the reason for their visit. "Ah, Madame Dumarest! I thought I recognized your voice," he said, bowing courteously and kissing her hand.

"Monsieur Law. A welcome face indeed. I had planned a visit with you later in the day."

"By all means, madame. I have just received many worthy objects from—" He glanced at Marie. The other side of the wall wasn't that far away, and he'd heard every word exchanged. Louise fell victim to a coughing spasm. ". . . from a friend," he concluded, without losing a beat. Wisely choosing to avoid Madame Bienville's displeasure, Law hurried on. "Monsieur Bienville is away from the house and Captain Brand has not been here at all today. Shall we search elsewhere?"

Louise positively beamed at the suggestion. "Oh, but Marie has just now joined us," Madame Dumarest protested.

"Still, if you must go . . ." Liane added. Tiring of the charade, Marie returned the conspiratorial smiles.

Ophelia took Marie's hand. "Well, I am certain you are a welcome addition to our little society. I'm afraid being the only eligible mademoiselle has made Angelique a bit conceited. Her reaction to such enchanting competition should be a most amusing divertissement."

"Madame is too kind," Marie murmured, curtseying again, this time more gracefully, as she had learned in Penscott Hall. Now she really had to make an escape. Louise and Liane would be furious. "But now, if you'll forgive me?"

Ophelia Dumarest followed Marie and her escort to the door. "You simply must tell me, dear. I'm certain I recognize that gown's workmanship. Where on earth did you come by it? Was it made for you?"

Marie paused. "No. Not really. In fact"—She looked past Ophelia to the two women frozen in place by the table. —"I stole it. Good day, Madame Dumarest. Dear friends. Good day."

The carriage wound along the path above the bluff, dipped away from the panoramic view of the Gulf and into the sun-splintered recesses of the forested countryside. The afternoon was surprisingly warm for a winter's day, and Marie shunned Law's offer of a cloak. In England, the winter months seemed a constant, blustering cold. Mysteré, except for bouts of rain, was continually warm. Here in the New World, the weather mirrored the land's unpredictability, an aspect that pleased Marie. Their conversation had been desultory at best, broken by long stretches of silence, behind which stretched the rhythmic refrain of hooves, harness and creaking carriage. Enchanted, Marie drank in the sights and ignored Law's sidelong stares.

A tug on the reins and the gelding obediently stopped. Ahead, a grove of willows indicated a spring-fed pool. She had never seen trees quite like them. Brown flowing tendrils swayed invitingly and she tried to imagine what they must look like when covered with leaves. "What kind of trees are those?"

"Willows. They're beautiful, but attract mosquitoes when the weather is warmer."

"A lovely place, monsieur."

Law raised his fingers to his lips, signaling silence. "Listen," he whispered.

She did. At first there was only stillness, but as a

minute passed, the subtle sounds of life became distinguishable. The horse's tail swished. A far bird whistled a truncated melody. A breeze soughed in the tall pines. Gradually a heavier sound intruded: the muted, whispering roar of the sea, forever contending with the face of the continent.

"I didn't know where to find your Captain Brand, so I will show you my world instead, yes?"

"Your world?"

Law faced her, his expression most determined. "Yes. One I would gladly share with you. In many ways." He reached out and gripped her shoulders. Marie tensed, then relaxed. Why not? Jason was obviously avoiding her, had been cool and distant since the night at the governor's. It would serve him right. As for Law, he was turning out to be an intriguing man with an air of ambition and accomplishment that more than piqued her curiosity. His sharp blue eyes bored into hers and she could feel the heat of his hands as he pulled her to him. Softly, she brushed her lips against his, allowed him to enfold her in an embrace.

The contact sent a tiny shock wave through her. She felt giddy and confused. His lips were warm and moist, imparting a pleasant taste to which she felt herself responding. Alone with another man! As a child who tastes forbidden fruit, she found the idea exciting. If Jason were to find them like this . . . She pushed away, eyes still promising.

Law stared at her a moment, then began to chuckle.

"What is so funny?"

"I have never kissed a pirate before." His face turned serious. "I'm afraid you've made an enemy of Madame Bienville. She is so terribly worried about prestige, especially around Madame Dumarest. Not that Ophelia—we are close friends, by the way—would care. She has enough secrets of her own without being vexed by your declaration."

"I don't understand," Marie said, not paying very close attention.

"Dumarest is not her real name. Nor for that matter,

397

in all probability, will John Law remain mine. Should the necessity arise, it will be changed immediately, and none the wiser. There are many here with reason to fear Spanish, French or English justice. Many a man or woman has come to this New World and taken a new name to accompany a new life."

"A new life," Marie echoed. "How inviting." *But I forget myself. I am not here to reverie. Oh, I shall punish Jason.*

Smiling provocatively, she leaned forward and struck a demure pose that Law read as an invitation. His eyes glinted and he pulled her to him, kissing her cheek and throat, then seeking her lips again. "Marie Ravenne. My little Raven," he whispered huskily. "You are a beautiful woman." The voice fell silent and he leaned forward to kiss her eyes, first one, then the other, fleetingly. His hand, rising to her chin, brushed her breasts.

That touch, light though it was, shocked her into awareness. She had attempted to continue the dalliance and submerge the feelings of guilt that lurked in her breast. Now that guilt rose and she tensed, uncomfortable and secretly embarrassed by her behavior.

Law's fingers played along her neck. Deft in love's wicked contest, his leg pressed against hers and he whispered words of endearment. Despite her efforts, Marie could not reciprocate, even falsely. Struggling for breath, she extricated herself from his grasp.

"What is it?" Law asked, confused by her sudden withdrawal.

Marie shook her head, not knowing how to explain. What had he said? A new life? Perhaps that was the phrase. A life without pretense in a land where two people—she and Jason—might truly find a home and a beginning. She could not desecrate that dream with a childish charade in which she didn't believe. "Would you mind if I went for a walk?"

"But of course not," Law said, moving to rise and help her from the carriage.

Marie touched his arm, restraining him. "Alone."

Law stared at her, sighed and sat back. She was not

398

as easy a conquest as he had hoped. "Alone," he responded in reluctant agreement. If he was upset by her rejection, or was in any way angry, it did not show. He gestured toward the south. "Go, my beautiful friend, and walk among the trees. Perhaps you will like this land. Perhaps it will whisper a new name to you. I will wait."

The grass was cool and damp. Marie pulled her skirts up to her ankles and headed for the willows. Below them lay a wet, marshy circle whose center bubbled with the sluggish energies of rising water. Lily pads choked the shallow pond. From them, as she approached, a score of frogs dived into the thick water. One old turtle, mossy back green and shiny, rested on a half-sunken tree trunk and dragonflies darted about, deluded by the false spring day. Beyond, the bluff beckoned.

A strange land. Spring in winter. Savages and tranquillity. A land where old lives and past names could be discarded. A place to start anew and build from a dream. What would Jason say to such a notion? The cruel irony of the tablet marked "Pax" still shaped his life, made him not so much the master of his fate as he might suppose. Could he abandon the buccaneer's life and, more difficult, forget the hatred and vengeance that motivated him?

The forest ended abruptly at a sudden precipice. Far to the south, a line of clouds split the twin blues of sky and gulf. As she approached the edge, the tan and sandy shoreline swam into view, stretching a precarious barrier against the onslaught of ever-rolling waters.

A fulcrum between the majestic wilderness and restless ocean, Marie stood statue still. It was not often the world offered two so contradictory faces in such dramatic fashion, and would have been beautiful were she not riveted in place, staring down at an unexpected, awful tableau through a haze of tears.

The wind tugged at her gown. The pulsing sea echoed the thunder of her heart. Paradise had become a mockery, and in her mind a voice rose to a shrieking crescendo till it blotted all thought and tore the fibres of her being. *Nooooo!!*

Back from the rim of earth. Back through brush that lifted impeding claws to rip the exquisitely stitched hem and silken skirt. Trying not to run, yet hounded by the vision. Trying not to weep, yet shocked beyond mere anguish. Across the brief meadow toward the carriage. Hurry. Reveal nothing. Let no one know the searing agony. Hurry away.

"Take me back," she whispered.

"But mademoiselle—"

"Do as I say, damn you," Marie rasped. Law blanched and hurriedly did as he was told. Wheeling the carriage, he guided the horse onto the path back to town and urged the animal into a brisk pace.

Marie stared straight ahead, heeded not a single word. Somehow she maintained her composure. Somehow she did not break down. They shot past the governor's mansion and down the pocked road from the bluff, careened through the settlement and finally came to a jolting halt before the tavern. Marie reeled through the doors and past the tables, up the heaving stairs and down the nightmare hallway to her room, where the engulfing combination of rage and stunned sorrow gave vent to scalding tears. She saw herself mirrored in her mind, an overdressed bedraggled fool attempting to be that which she was not. For him. For him!

Clawing fingers shredded the gown, furiously tore away the layers of hypocritical silk. Naked and breathless, her legs buckled and she collapsed to the floor. There she huddled, wracked by silent sobs as the image she had fought to deny burst the bounds of restraint and overpowered her with uncontrollable waves of misery and unspeakable pain.

Tumbled battlements of wood. A man and a woman naked, entwined in passionate frenzy. Lies and betrayal. Jason and Angelique . . . together.

"What is it?" Angelique of the tousled coiffure sat

400

upright, her pert bosom not quite so awe-inspiring without the assistance of the whalebone support.

The man standing over her failed to acknowledge the question, instead stared out across the rising combers that swept the shore. Appearances were deceiving though, for he had heard and had asked the same of himself after leaving the heated flesh so recently violated. Doubt assailed him. Dissatisfaction and guilt dragged him to his feet and a tentative step away from the girl who lay on the sand. Guilt? Yes. It was said. Guilt. He had sworn to purge himself of Marie and vowed not to care for another. Caring was weakness. Vulnerability. And so had taken Angelique at, virtually, her own request. They had rutted lustily.

He stared at the bloated sun, a glaring, molten furnace halfway down the western sky.

"Jason?" Angelique purred, touching his ankle with her toes. "Father's dinner is not 'til nine. We have all afternoon." She stood and touched his manhood, hoping it would rise again to give her pleasure. The light sea breeze was too cool for comfort and she stepped close to him for warmth. Even to touch him, now, created excitement almost too great to bear. She swayed from side to side, drawing his still-damp maleness across her stomach. "I learn quickly. You could teach me . . ."

Jason pushed her away, spun her around and gave her a playful but emphatic slap on the bottom. "You're a rapacious lass for a beginner. A sweet bit for any man. All the same, there's work to do. I'll be missed."

Angelique looked at him, not sure what to say. "But I love you."

"Don't use that word!" he snapped more harshly than he'd intended. "Now, into your clothes and be off with you," he added more gently.

"You can't mean that. I mean, you—"

"I know what I've done better than you. We've had our romp."

"Romp?" Angelique whirled on him, her eyes flashing. "Is that what you call it? Of all the unmitigated

401

nerve." Words failed her and she sputtered ineffectually. "Pig! Vagabond! Pirate!"

"And you my brief consort," Jason added, the sadness in his voice lost on her.

Angelique's gown muffled her reply. Only as her head emerged did he hear, ". . . and I hate you! Oh, I'll hate you for all time!" Fumbling awkwardly, she managed to arrange her clothes well enough to ride, and climbed onto the quickfooted mare. Before Jason could protest, she had freed his mount as well, struck it on the flank and sent it galloping down the beach.

"Hey! Wait!" he shouted, starting after her.

"Walk!" Angelique shouted in return, and set the mare at a run. By the time Jason slipped into his breeches and shirt, the girl was nowhere to be seen.

Fully dressed, he trudged back toward town, finally stopping to sit on a bleached piece of driftwood and stare into the watery distance. Oddly unhappy, he was dimly aware of a growing resolution. He would go to Marie and try to say the things he at last felt capable of admitting. If he could find the right words. For those, he need only search his growing shame.

Evening. Over the jagged steeples of distant pines, the scarlet wound of daylight slowly faded, leaving a vast blackness awash with heavenly lanterns twinkling in the silent firmament. The muddy world of men followed suit: candles and flickering lamplight filtered through shuttered windows, spilled from quickly opened and closed doorways as men hurried inside. Spring ended with sunset, and a growing chill returned with its passing.

A crewman from the *Ravener* was guarding the boats and rose as Jason approached. "Even', Captain. Little late for a walk."

"We can't all ride," Jason answered shortly.

The man stiffened imperceptibly. "No offense, Captain," he said in a flat tone, " 'less you want to take it."

Jason laughed. "Hell, no." He sniffed the air. "Wind's shifting. What do the natives say?"

"Backin' to the north again. Should kick us out of here in fine style."

"If we're ready," Jason amended, not wanting to allude outright to his disappearance for the whole afternoon.

"We're ready," the seaman answered. If Brand wanted to go daisy picking while there was work to do, it was fine with him. Still, if he'd been where a captain should have been, Brand would have known they were ready. "Finished just before sundown."

"Good. Good! Well, I suppose I'd better get back." Inwardly, Jason groaned with embarrassment. It was evident the men resented his absence, and the word would have spread. Somehow he'd have to convince Marie he'd been alone and needed time to think.

What had not seemed such a long ride was indeed a lengthy walk. Jason paused before the Sparrow, wondering whether he should go immediately to their room and find Marie or see to a change of clothes elsewhere. Enthusiasm won out. He wanted to hold her in his arms and appease the bitter emptiness that lingered from his afternoon encounter with Angelique. He was a fool to have kept their rendezvous and knew it now. He shoved open the front doors, recognized a few of Marie's crew, ignored the hostile glance of Ned Sly and hurriedly ascended the stairs, bounded down the hall and burst through the door at the end. "Marie!"

Hope spun around, her painted mouth forming a soundless "Oh." Jason froze in confusion. In that instant, something wickedly hard exploded against his skull. Without so much as a moan, the buccaneer crumpled to the floor even as Marie stepped around him.

"Tulip?"

"He betrayed me twice. Once in England, and now here. But never again. Help me tie him up."

Ned swilled the last of his ale, glared at the youth sitting across the table. "So you've but a single night to serve a pair of wenches who just happen to be pining away for the juice of your wine sacks. Poor lad."

Shelby grinned good-naturedly. "Can I help it if the doxies find me more to their taste than you?" he asked. "Now, if you'd just blow out the lamps before they catch sight of your crooked pole. Or maybe it's your age, Ned. They fear you'd collapse with the quinseys and not complete what was started. With me, they know I've got what it takes to give them a belly full of pleasure."

"Age is it? Ha!" Ned snorted. "Hell, I got more left at my age than you'll ever have!" He stopped and stared. "Damn my eyes!"

Shelby turned in his chair, saw the reason for his companion's outburst. Marie, dressed in black breeches and dark blue cape, descended the stairs two at a time. A brace of pistols jutted from the sash at her waist and the silver hilt of her rapier gleamed at her side. She strode to the table and leaned forward. Ned held his breath. Was it merely the reflection of candlelight that made her slate-gray eyes gleam like a cat's? No, Ned thought. He'd seen that look before. And liked it.

"Where are the others? Tom, Ben, Poole? The old hands we trust?"

"Tom and Poole are aboard with a half-dozen others and five of Jason's pick from Mysteré. Ben and Poacher are on the beach. I could find them if need be."

"Do so, but don't arouse suspicion and don't tell any of the men from Mysteré. We'll need at least a dozen, and a longboat. Bring them to Law's warehouse as soon as you can. I will wait for you there in the bushes in front of the main door."

"But what—"

Marie's face was grim. "You know enough for now. Go quietly and let no man know your intentions."

"Aye, Raven."

Shelby shoved himself away from the table and started to leave. "Shelby, you fetch your gear and get to the *Ravener* quick as you can. Tell Tom to lock up the men he doesn't trust and make ready to sail. We won't be coming back here. Ned, make sure your men are armed. Now hurry."

The pirate flashed a wolfish grin. This was more like it. What had instigated the metamorphosis in Raven, he cared not. If she intended mischief, he was her man. "Get my stuff too, Shel," he said quietly. "I'll meet you aboard. Be sure you bring an armful of them," he added, pointing to a row of rum jugs. "Never know when there'll be reason for celebration."

Ned had no sooner gotten out the door than Hope waddled down the steps. Clutching a cloak about her dress, and carrying a bundle of clothes, it was obvious Marie had already told her the plans for the next hour. "Hope, you wait here." Marie gestured to the room where Jason lay unconscious, bound and gagged. "If he gets loose, or if he's discovered, get to the warehouse and tell me. If it's still quiet a half-hour from now, come to the warehouse anyway. Quickly, now."

Luckily, the tavern had yet to fill up and the innkeeper was laboring in the kitchen, struggling to prepare the prodigious amounts of food destined to be consumed an hour later. Marie pulled her cloak tight, shooed Shelby out the door and followed into the falling night. Alone, and emotions in check, she strode through town, choosing less traveled avenues between hovels and ignoring the mongrel pups that challenged her from the darkened doorways. A brisk pace brought her to Law's warehouse where an anxious twenty minute wait seemed like an eternity. At last a whispered call signaled the approach of her men. A patch of shadow materializing at her side proved to be Ned, followed by Poacher, Spanish Jesse and Ben. "I got fifteen," Ned whispered. "Belaying pins, cutlass and pistols."

"Well done," Marie replied.

"What's the plan, Captain Raven?"

"Why're we here?"

"Is there trouble?"

"'Vast the chatter, blast your tongues," Ned hissed. "Raven'll be tellin' us if you give her half a chance." Marie could sense his glee at the thought of going back

405

into action. She wished she could share his good humor, but a foreboding madness raged in her soul. Now would come the action to seal her off forever from Jason Brand, turn the beauty and tenderness they had shared into implacable hatred and never-ending contention. He had lied to her, bent her to his will and played her for a fool, no better or worse than any other woman. She had accepted the role assigned her, attended to his wants without question, cultivated a supple spine and entrusted love, soul and freedom to his heartless grasp. No more, though. He had forsaken her twice, but would never be given a third opportunity. Nor would anyone else.

The warehouse was a large barnlike structure with an ornate second floor housing Law's private quarters. Built partly over the water, a longboat or cutter could be sailed into a concealed slip for easy and discreet loading and unloading. The glow of a lantern from an upstairs window indicated Law might still be in his apartment. But not for long. He was expected at the governor's and would have to leave soon. Even as she turned to order the men into the warehouse, a coach rumbled up the path and rolled to a halt before the main door. A guard stepped from the shadows and greeted the servant perched above the team.

"Ned. Poacher."

Reading her mind, both men nodded and sneaked off into the shadows behind the coach. "Come when I call," she ordered the rest of the men.

Marie stood up and stepped into view. At first no one noticed her. Law emerged from his warehouse, paused to leave final instructions with the guard and then climbed into the coach. At that moment the driver spotted Marie and called a warning to the sentry who rounded the team, musket in hand. Law peered from one of the side windows and recognized Marie as she stepped into the circle of pale amber light surrounding the carriage. The driver unhooked one of the carriage lanterns and held it up.

"My dear, this is a surprise," Law said.

"I wanted to see you," Marie answered.

Law chuckled. "You are truly a creature of many moods. But then I should expect as much." Gallantly refraining from remarking on her return to breeches, he pushed open the door and offered her his hand.

Marie stepped inside, the cloak concealing the flint-lock pistol until she was seated at Law's side. Outside, there was a sound of scuffling and a quick grunt of pain following the slap of a belaying pin against someone's skull. Alarmed, Law called to his men, then immediately quieted as the chill maw of Marie's pistol touched his throat. The door opened and Poacher thrust his pockmarked face into the coach. "All clear, Raven."

Realization, horrible in its enormity, slowly spread across Law's face. "Get out!" Marie hissed. "Go to the door and bid your men inside to allow us entrance."

"No."

Marie forced back his head until it bumped the wooden panel. Law's eyes bulged as he peered down at her finger tightening on the trigger. "All right. All right. I'll do as you say."

Marie relaxed her grip. Law swallowed. Perspiration beaded his brow with icy droplets. "A woman of too many moods," he muttered sourly. "Why?"

"Does it matter?" Marie asked, grinning devilishly. "I'm afraid you're about to miss dinner. Move."

Law scrambled outside and found himself surrounded by the men of the *Ravener*. Marie jumped down, nudged him in the small of the back. Dutifully, her captive strode to the main door, rapped twice, then twice more. A panel slid open. "Let me back in."

The panel closed and a bolt screeched against metal retaining rings. When the door opened a crack, Marie shoved Law. The guard, taken by surprise, fell back and then to the floor as fifteen grim, determined seamen surged into the warehouse. Success was immediate. The five guards on duty surrendered quickly and lay down their weapons. Within minutes, the doors opening on the interior dock had been opened and Marie's men were busy loading two cutters with gold that had been delivered from the *Banshee* only the day before. While the men worked, Marie led Law about and, in lieu of having every crate broken open, had him point out the valuable ones. A half hour later, a trunk full of rich silks, a crate of finely crafted muskets invaluable for trading, a small chest containing a dozen jeweled goblets and another with silver ingots lay in the bottom of one of the cutters.

The task completed, Marie instructed her men to bind securely Law's men and warned them not to alert the fort until their employer was back with them. Hope had arrived a few minutes earlier and was standing on the dock, staring down into the loaded cutters. When the coach driver had been brought inside and the front doors locked, they were ready to go. The men, with Spanish Jesse guarding Law, jumped into the boats. Hope vacillated. "Hope?"

The harlot stepped back from the edge of the dock. Marie leaped and caught her arm. "What's wrong?"

"I'll not be going, Marie." The older woman turned a tear-streaked face to her friend. "Look at me, would you? Last time I cried I was still a virgin, and that was so many years ago I can't remember."

"I don't understand—"

"Sweet Tulip. If an old bag of guts like me could have had a daughter . . . Oh, the hell with it," she sighed, leaving the thought unfinished.

"But why?" Marie asked, her heart a leaden pressure in her breast.

"I ain't much," Hope began, faltering, "and never had a man to call mine no longer than it took for his root to sprout. A tumble were all a man meant to me, and all I meant to anyone. Exceptin' now. Forlicar's a blustery braggart and has him a troublesome temper and the like, but we have a special care for one another. I can't be leavin' him, dearie. I just can't."

Marie embraced the woman, hugged her long and close. "Hope Deferred Maketh the Heart Sick. Goodbye, dearest friend," she finally whispered, then jumped into the waiting boat. At her cry, the lines were cast off

408

and the men dug their oars into the water. They were on their way. Marie faced resolutely forward. She was capable of a great deal, but not looking back to see Hope standing on the dock and waving.

One more problem remained. The *Banshee*. There was no way in the world the *Ravener* would be able to depart unseen. Marie stared into the darkness, wrestling for a solution. She knew Forlicar had the duty and would be on board. Whatever else happened, he must not be hurt. And yet, they must not be followed for at least a day. The *Banshee* would have to be disabled. Luckily, they would arrive at the *Ravener* without being seen from Jason's ship.

Everything was ready. The five new crew members had been trussed and left below decks where they could cause no trouble. The sails were ready to drop at a moment's notice and the anchor pulled in until the line was nearly straight up and down. "What's happening?" Tom asked as he helped Marie aboard.

"We're leaving."

"But—" He stopped and stared, thunderstruck, as Law, bound and gagged, was shoved over the rail.

"Rig lines to get some contraband aboard."

"I don't understand."

"I've taken the gold Jason paid him," she said, nudging her prisoner with her foot. "That and a few other bundles we can use. Get the men to work and join me in my cabin. Poacher, you come too."

Tom hesitated for a fraction of a second, then jumped as a hand touched his elbow. Sly and the others were pouring over the railing. "I'll see to getting the stuff aboard. You'd best go with her," Sly counseled. "I haven't seen her like this, ever. I don't know what Brand did, but she's hurtin' bad and mad as a hornet. We'll have Brand, Law and the whole damn French navy after us when this is over." A low laugh welled from his chest. "I feel better'n I have for weeks." With a clap on his giant friend's shoulder, he started rounding

409

up the men and prepared to haul aboard their newly won treasure.

There was no doubt Poacher was the man for the job. Silently, he and Tom and Marie had gone over the side and into the dinghy. Silently they'd rowed the three hundred yards separating the two ships. Tom had tried to make Marie stay on the *Ravener,* but she refused to be dissuaded and insisted on taking part. She owed Jason Brand a debt, and wanted to help repay it in person.

They shipped oars as the hulk of the *Banshee* loomed overhead. Not a soul was stirring on deck. Only a couple of wedges of light leaked from the gunports. The men left aboard would be sleeping, playing dice or otherwise whiling away the boring hours. With luck, they'd never know what had happened until their ship put to sea.

Tom reached out and grabbed the anchor line. Quiet as a snake, Poacher was off the seat and skinning up the rope. Marie held her breath. She'd wanted to go aboard and help with the dirty work, but at this Tom had drawn the line, daring to deny her. Within a minute a soft whisper drifted down from above. By looking closely, they could see their man edging along the outside of the rail. Tom dipped the oars in the water and followed Poacher from below, stopping amidships and holding the dinghy steady. Another minute and the silent figure moved again. The dinghy kept pace.

The whole job took no more than a quarter-hour, but by the time Poacher slipped down the anchor line and into the small boat, Marie felt as if she'd just spent a week. "Well?"

Poacher slipped the knife into its sheath. "All done," he said calmly, as if the escapade were no more than a walk to market. "Every load-bearing line has been cut half-through, and where they can't see it. She'll be fine until they put on sail." He shook his head in wonder. "Won't that be a sight to see, though. Lines'll be poppin' all over the place, sails and masts tumblin' . . ."

410

"Good job," Marie said, relaxing a little herself. There would be no stopping them now. By the time Jason got free, assembled his crew, set to sea and then spent a day or two repairing every piece of standing rigging on the *Banshee,* the *Ravener* would be far away. Jason Brand would rue the day he betrayed Marie Ravenne.

The *Ravener* was ready to go upon Marie's return. All the chests had been carried below and stowed, one of the cutters shoved adrift and the other put in tow should they need it later. Marie toured the deck, checking every detail before they made sail, aroused the crew of the *Banshee* and possibly drew their fire. Making her way back to the quarterdeck, she gave the order. "All right, Tom. The wind's backed far enough. You may get under way."

Hushed voices called to the men in the yards. The mainsail dropped and the sheets were hauled tight. They didn't have enough men to pull in the anchor, so a single blow with the axe parted the line. As the gaff-rigged mizzen was pulled into place, a gust of wind caught and swung them around and toward the open Gulf. So far, not a word came from across the water. The *Ravener*'s departure would go unnoticed. The second they were out of range of the *Banshee,* Marie went to the mainmast where Law was tied. Unsheathing her knife, she cut his gag and the rope binding his hands.

Law stood straight, regaining control of his temper only with great effort. "Do I remain your prisoner forever, madame?" he asked in a voice quivering with anger.

"No. We're trading you one of your cutters for our jolly boat. When we reach the mouth of the Bay you'll be set free. You should be able to land on Dauphin Island without any trouble."

Law looked perplexed. "Then I am not to be killed?"

"Monsieur Law. We are thieves, not murderers. Thank you for your hospitality. And your gold." She gestured to the rail, where one of the hands stood by a rope ladder. "And now, if you please, adieu."

411

Law bowed. "Knowing you has cost me a great deal, Madame Raven. I wish I could say it had been worth it, and shall console myself with one thought. We will meet again."

"Adieu, monsieur," Marie repeated emphatically. Without waiting to watch him escorted over the side, she turned and strode aft to the poop, giving orders for the five of Jason's pick to be put to work when the ship was well out to sea. At last she stood alone, hands on the carved railing. Astern, their wake was a phosphorescent trail on which, after a few moments, the jolly boat rose and fell like a chip in a tub. Further away, Mobile had become nothing more than a glimmering patch of light against the obsidian expanse of the continent.

She had bested him. Repaid Jason in kind for his heartless use of her. Triumph. That's what it was. A sound triumph.

If that was so, why did a heavy shadow darken her soul? "A special care," Hope had said. Foolish woman. Special care led to deceit and treachery and deception. Kisses, caresses, sweet words and lovemaking meant nothing. Not Jason's. *Well, I have won, Jason Brand. It is ended now, and little need have I for your love. Not ruthless enough? A pirate, you scoffed, and treated me like a simpering brat. But who has your treasure? Who bested you at your own game? Who has, after all, the final laugh?*

Then why the doubts, Marie wondered. Why the bitter yearning, the terrible, lonely sense of loss? She'd gained a treasure. And a victory. Wasn't that enough? Only perhaps. For though she could not bear to admit it, the victory was hollow, and the more precious treasure left behind.

Not even the north wind could make her cry. There was nothing left to cry over. Dry-eyed, she stood alone until a concerned Tom Gunn led her to the great cabin, laid her down on the bed and covered her with a warm quilt. Much later sleep finally came to her heavy heart. And restless dreams. She had won. Marie had surely . . . won . . .

Chapter XXI

Dreamhaunt. Yesterday's vanished spirit-child, recognizably the same and known by name. Her name. Dark on a storm-tossed sea, nightmares breed unseen under the cover of darkness, under the coverlet covering the tears. There are hours yet to go. Hours during which to ponder that which was within grasp but is now lost forever.

Marie remembered everything: faces, laughter, love, the intense longing that greeted each new day, the breathtaking, bold exuberance of a thousand dreams. Now father and home were lost. She had been carried to a distant, cold country, incarcerated in an unfriendly home, made to serve those she hated. Through it all, the dreams lived, doggedly continued in the face of despair.

And then she had met Jason. Jason Brand, the embodiment of love and the fulfillment of all the dreams. No one had told her, though, nothing prepared her for the dangers hidden by love's deceitful promises. When she waked to reality, the dream lay dying, pierced by the wicked tangle of roots on which his clothes hung, smothered by the blonde tresses of the vulpine beauty who writhed underneath him, poisoned by the very air that dried the perspiration from their heated bodies and blasted up the face of the bluff. The knight errant of love lay transformed before her eyes, had become the henchman of cold passion, a robber tyrant running amok in the gentle fields of trust and faithfulness.

The never-ending catalogue of things she must learn to get along without reeled on. She had weathered the loss of everything else dear to her. Why not love? Shouldn't she be grateful to Jason for showing her the mocking reality at the core of those once-wished-for truths? In spite of life's ugliness and constant warnings, she had remained convinced of a dearer, honest, loving possibility. Now she knew such notions were illusions, that the wonders of the heart consisted of endless demands and continual contests in which self-preservation was the only prize. Caustic laughter born of cynicism welled from her breast: Marie Ravenne had survived, and was the wiser. Nothing could touch her now, for she was beyond pain. Only prosperity remained, and toward prosperity she turned determinedly.

Images of Jason, golden in his hard warmth, of the two of them born again to wrest their destiny from a fertile wilderness, faded, spun into fragile strands light as spider silk, then shimmered into nothingness in the furnace of her heart's vengeful tempest.

The storm subsided. The *Ravener* sailed on, carrying treasure and a weary crew captained by a woman who, in denying herself, was more alone than ever before. At last, a cloud on the horizon spread. Below it, a mote grew to an irregular emerald fastened in an azure setting. Colors, vague pastel sheens born of mist-filtered sunlight, transformed their destination into a portrait of fairy finery. Marie pictured the face on the cliff, hidden on the far side of the island. Soon she would see it, for perhaps the last time.

Shelby, who preferred the lofty heights of the masts to the more secure purchase of the deck, skinned down the rigging, a spyglass caught at his belt. "Nary a ship in sight, Raven. In fact, can't see hardly anyone stirring," he said, joining Marie on the quarterdeck.

"Well, it's morning," grumbled Ned, off to one side. He leaned back against the railing, elbows bearing most of his weight. "Chances are what's there is sprawled beneath old Caron's tables—which I figure to be before nightfall."

"And I," echoed Poole from the helm. "A keg of rum and one of Mistress Diana's roast pigs should set us straight."

"We'll need to find us some more men so's we can work the ship proper, too."

414

"If we can in a hurry," Marie answered. "We'll not be here long."

Ned stood upright. Poole groaned. "What?"

"A day, two at the most. Long enough to get some of the cannons and a few other things," she said, not wanting to specify her father's journal and Tomás.

"But Raven—" Shelby began.

"I'll hear no more. Do you think we have seen the last of the *Banshee*?" Marie asked. "Or Brand, for that matter?"

"We can handle Brand," Ned exclaimed, glowering.

"With what, Ned? We've few enough men as it is, barely enough to handle the *Ravener* without having to worry about a fight. The *Banshee* will be carrying twice as many men, with those we left behind in Mobile."

"I don't like the idea of running from him."

"As soon as we can muster a full crew, we shall have no need to run from any man."

"We might find some new ones here in Mysteré," Shelby suggested. "With them and the cannons on shore, we should be able to hold him off."

"Who and how many we take is a decision I'll make after we're provisioned," Marie declared flatly. "There are too many in town who are loyal to Brand. We'll be better off looking elsewhere."

"Where do we go if not here?" Ned asked. "Hell. Name me a better place."

"I have one in mind," Marie snapped.

"Well, then?"

"You'll find it out when we're on our way." So saying, she whirled and disappeared into her cabin. The last thing she wanted to leak out was their destination: Isla Orchilla. Jason would hear and follow before it suited her to meet him again. If he wanted to try anything, let him wait until she'd found and trained new men. Marie smiled. It would be a pleasure.

Tom Gunn stood at the forecastle, his great bulk perched above the running waves. Approaching from the northwest, they were sailing with the wind a point aft

415

of their port beam. In another few minutes they'd be reaching as close to the wind as possible on the first of two tacks that would send the *Ravener* into Voûte Paix and anchor. It would be good to touch solid ground again. The seafaring business was full of adventure from time to time, but he couldn't forget his carpenter shop and the family that had probably given up waiting for his return.

The time for daydreaming came to an abrupt halt. Gunn peered closely at the shore and brought the spyglass to his eye in time to catch a puff of smoke belching from one of the cannon they'd left behind. He looked back over his shoulder at the anxious, jostling activity that infected every crew when they neared land. Poacher was close at hand. "Damn fools to waste powder in a salute," the big man growled. "A body might think we was the bloody English navy droppin' anchor in the Pool."

Poacher ran a dirty paw through his scraggly hair, then yelped in pain. "Damn!" he said, shaking his hand. The end of his ring finger had been caught in the bight of a rope and pinched off and he kept forgetting how tender it could be. "Lemme see." He reached out for the spyglass, took it and searched the shore in time to see a second puff. "Nine-pounders, all right. Don't see no shot landin'."

"A welcoming," Tom groaned, rubbing his aching back muscles. They'd come from Mobile without firing a shot and the lack of exercise had done him no good.

"Powerful long for a welcome," Poacher grunted, handing back the glass.

Tom focused on the shore again as another battery opened fire. Like gray blossom, clouds of dark, chalky haze drifted sluggishly across the bay. Poacher was right. It *was* a powerful long welcome. And a disturbing one, too. Such a silly expenditure of precious gunpowder deserved a healthy clout over somebody's pate. When they tied up, there'd be a few heads knocked together.

But maybe it wasn't a salute at all. Maybe it was a

warning! Suddenly alarmed, Tom's veins grew icy. He swept the glass across the village. Not a soul was stirring. All the more unsettling. The single eye raked the turned fields on the sloping hills, ranged the island rim, following it to either side down to the water's edge. Nothing seemed out of place. Pristine sand and solitude, squat, water-carved boulders, towering palms, and behind them the barren spires of . . .

Trees, hell! Jutting like a spike behind the slope of the southern shoreline, a second questing trunk angled into view and suddenly sprouted wings—great, white, snowy wings of canvas. For a stunned second, Tom gawked silently. Behind him, Poacher's eyes widened, round and swollen like eggs as he stared in horror.

"Sail ho!!" Tom's voice rolled over the unsuspecting crew. "Visitors to starboard. Look lively, lads!"

Faces looked up, surprised and suddenly afraid. Marie raced out of her cabin, ran to the quarterdeck railing and stared in horror as a mighty vessel rounded the tip of Mysteré. A ship of the line, she was. Well over fifty guns and flying English colors. A terrible hunter come to roust the wolves from their den. "Damn me. Damn my eyes," Ned swore. "It's the *Breston!*"

Recognizing the ship in the same instant, Marie paled and a horrible certainty filled her soul. Law had told them Gregory had come to Mobile and had assumed command of the *Breston* after the captain had received an incapacitating injury at the hands of the mutinous crew of the *Sword of Cornwall.* But how had Gregory discovered Mysteré? By accident? A sixth sense told her no.

The warship was running downwind, now angling to cut them off. "Gregory? How?" Shelby asked, his face brave but his voice cracking.

Marie ignored him, rushed to the helm without answering. A plan, she needed a plan. The crew turned, expecting orders—a miracle, anything. Damning her silence, Marie forced herself to take time, to assess the situation. They were going too slow, beating upwind. If they fell off too far the *Ravener* would sail right for the

Breston which, turning at the last moment, would engulf them in multiple broadsides. If she tried to wear about, there was no doubt they'd end up beam to beam, with identical results. Coming about would lose time, but at least put them upwind of the enemy—and prove entirely useless, for there was an island in the way and they were in the lee.

Only one possibility remained, and that was to escape with their lives. Some of them. "Hold to course," she shouted to Poole. "Ned! Tom!" The men were at her side already. "We can go closer to shore than the *Breston,* for she draws more than we do. Gregory will get in one broadside, but that we'll have to chance. Once we've weathered that, we fall off the wind and run. Get every man ready on the sails, for there'll be no time to spare."

"What about our guns? We might get in a shot or two, make her—"

"We can't afford to take the chance. Keep everyone low until I give the orders, then to the ropes and pulleys quick as they can. It's our only chance."

The men split up, Tom taking the fore and main masts and Ned remaining aft. With their shouts, the crew burst into action. Even the five men Jason had picked hurried to their posts, for they'd find no welcome on board an English ship and knew it. "We're done for," a nearby voice croaked. Old Ben Tremain, haggard and showing his age for the first time, slumped beside a barrel, ready for the end. "They'll bring us back to England. We'll hang at Tyburn for sure."

"Ha! Cheer up," Spanish Jesse chided, all the while coiling the line he'd been assigned. "We've had us a grand time so far. Ain't going to be the end of nothin'."

Marie took her post on the quarterdeck. Tom strode down the deck, cutlass gleaming in his fist and a look of wild excitement in his eyes. The odds were long against them yet he exuded an aura of confidence born of a roughhouse life and a love for a good brawl. Behind her, Ned finished assigning positions and duties and came forward. She was glad to have them close at hand.

Tom Gunn and Ned Sly, one on either side of her. Come what may, no captain in the world could boast better comrades at arms.

Sly cast an anxious glance toward the southwestern shore of Mysteré, then at the leading edges of the sails. They were pointed as far into the wind as they could. By the time the *Ravener* passed the *Breston* and wore about to run to the open sea, they'd be lucky to miss the hard rocks and shake free of the island. "We just better hope we don't end up on shore," he said. "It'll be close as my beard."

Marie calculated swiftly. The *Breston* was coming along slower than expected, was spilling some of her wind in order to force the *Ravener* closer to shore before committing herself. Worse and worse. The further into the lee they sailed, the less reliable was the wind. Their situation was more desperate with each passing second. The only hope, then, would be to alter course the instant the two ships came bow to bow, and steer for the *Breston*'s stern. That way, at least, they'd be a narrow and shifting target. Every ball that missed would strengthen their odds.

"We're going to change course earlier than expected, Tom," she said. "You'd better warn your men. Ned, you too."

Tom lumbered forward. Ned hesitated. A smile split his features. "Friends to the end, Captain?"

Marie's face lit up with the memory of their former animosity, the duel they'd fought and how it had ended. So long ago. "Friends," she said, almost shyly, then impulsively leaned forward and kissed him on the cheek. Ned blushed furiously and retreated aft.

The *Breston* plunged on, the snowy summits of her bulging sails beautiful were they not part of a machine of war bent on destruction. The *Ravener* stood straight and tall, clawing furiously toward shore. Marie drew herself erect and refused to consider the results of the coming bombardment. In any case, the hail of fire and death would last no longer than a few seconds.

The ugly snouts of cannon poked from gilt gunports

and a great bitterness welled in Marie's breast. How had Gregory discovered Mysteré? Perhaps it *was* by accident. Perhaps the same fate that had saved her from death and given her command of the *Ravener* had also decreed this inevitable souring of fortune. Anger against the English and Gregory specifically threatened reason and she considered ordering a collision course. There would be no small satisfaction in delivering a mortal blow to a ship of the line. But what would that prove? She shook herself. *Defeat. Why am I thinking of defeat? We have a chance, we'll take it. A week from now we'll all be bragging about how brave we were, about how we weren't afraid.*

Time for one last look around. The men were ready, were standing steady. A warm feeling of peace stole through her. By God, but they were a crew! Landsmen but a few months past, they'd become as fine a bunch of sailors as a captain could want. She laughed inwardly. *I wanted only one man, would have traded all the rest for him.* On impulse, Marie scanned the horizon. Foolish thought! Jason and the *Banshee* were miles away. She herself had seen to that. There would be no help.

The gap narrowed. Two hundred yards apart, the *Ravener* and *Breston* would pass on almost parallel courses. A dreadful silence linked the two ships like a chain of iron. Destroyer and prey, the pair were inextricably entwined in fate's web.

"God, why don't they fire?" Poacher muttered, his eyes wide with the crushing tension.

"Why don't the bloody bastards fire?" Tom echoed.

"Look to the shore," cried Shelby. Eyes turned. Faint, tiny gray-white blossoms sprouted along the beach near La Cachette. Musket fire! A line of redcoats vainly tried to stem the tide of inhabitants fleeing into the forested hills.

Marie forgot the shore, kept an eye on the *Breston*. Only a few yards and their bows would slide past one another. "Ready to wear ship!" she called. The men turned to their tasks. Muscles tensed, ready for the cru-

420

cial acts that would swing the sails about and point the *Ravener* toward the *Breston*'s stern. The second the maneuver was completed, the crew would go to the pumps and fire buckets. If she could only return their fire, Marie thought, as quickly forcing the wish to the back of her mind and concentrating on an imaginary line drawn from bowsprit to bowsprit. The instant it was straight between them, she would give the order. The *Breston*'s gunners would be cocky, her officers overconfident. Precious seconds would be lost correcting their aim.

"Damn them!"

"Damn their souls."

"Why don't they fire?"

"Why?"

"Wear ship! Wear ship!" Marie's voice whipped the men into a frenzy of action. Lines were let loose, hauled tight. Poole swung the wheel violently. The wind filled the foresail, bellied out the gaff-rigged mizzensail. The *Ravener* lurched like a man struck. Lurched and began to turn toward the *Breston,* whose momentum would carry it beyond them.

At the same instant, the whole length of the ship of the line erupted with a thunderous explosion of belching flames and brimstone vapors. Marie's maneuver had come too late, or was anticipated and countered with an early firing. The *Ravener* shuddered, leaped in the water and knocked everyone off their feet. Eighteen-and twenty-four-pound cannonballs ripped through the frail timbers and filled the air with a deadly hail of splinters. One ball shattered the mainmast just above the mainsail. Rigging gave way, the taut lines popping and snapping like maddened snakes. The very fiber of the ship groaned.

Pandemonium. A chorus of screams rent the smoke-filled air. The great jagged spears of split wood had done their work. Stunned, half-deaf, Marie staggered to her feet. The *Ravener* lurched to one side as the top half of the mainmast slid over the side. The port side standing rigging held on for long enough to slow the

Ravener, then gave way with a loud crack as the splintered railing sawed through the lines.

"I'll see to the pumps," a voice roared out of the buzzing mist that filled Marie's skull. Tom Gunn, driving a half-dozen men before him, staggered to the hatch leading below. Somehow they were still afloat. Those on deck grabbed knives and axes and began to hack at broken spars and confused, tangled lines. Marie looked to the helm. Poole, miraculously untouched, waved a triumphant hand. Someone caught her arm.

"He's bringing her into the wind and will soon have another broadside." Ned pointed a grimy finger covered with blood. "We'll not make it. Tell Poole we've got to try for shore. It's our only chance now!"

It was true. The *Ravener* had lost nearly all headway, and was close enough to shore for the waves to try to push her the rest of the way. Astern, the *Breston* turned upwind and would soon bring her guns to bear and revenge her ignominious defeat at St. Kitts. Land *was* their only hope, and that before the English marines could march the mile and a half from La Cachette to the southern tip of the island. Marie turned and screamed at Poole. "Quick!" She pointed toward shore. "Beach us if you can!"

The mainsail flopped about uselessly. Only the gaff-rigged mizzen could help them now. Slowly, the *Ravener* answered the helm and pointed toward the rock-strewn beach. "Tie her down and follow us, Poole! We'll have to swim for it!"

Impossible! All her hopes and dreams were disintegrating. She'd wanted peace and freedom, now found herself surrounded by carnage and presiding over the demise of the *Ravener*. The men had depended on her, and because of her overriding anger with Jason, she had let them down. Retribution beyond bearing, to watch them die so vainly!

Mind numb with shock, Marie jumped from the quarterdeck, slipped and fell on the blood-drenched planks. Several bodies, mutilated beyond recognition, lay strewn amid the wreckage. Spanish Jesse, torn almost in two, lay sprawled among them. Horror-stricken, Marie wiped the blood from her hands. The hatch was open but covered with a spar. She tried to pull it away and yelled into the depths of the ship. "Tom! We're going aground. Forget the pumps! Get out! Get out!" How he heard she couldn't imagine, but the frantic clank of the pumps stopped. Seconds later, the first head showed in the gloom.

Tom, white-faced with shock and bleeding from a huge gash on his arm, helped the first man out, grabbed another and shoved him through the hatch. "What—" His question was lost in the following explosion, for the *Breston* had come to bear and was firing at their stern. A pair of cannon balls tore the length of the deck. Three of the men from Jason's command were struggling with a tortured mound of wood and canvas and rope beneath which an arm wriggled like an insect pinned hopelessly to a board. The balls plowed through the three, crushing two and shearing a leg from the last. Iron death careened toward Marie, missed her by a hair's breadth, shattered the railing and dropped into the sea.

The *Ravener* was wallowing badly now, plunging into the waves thrown up by the rapidly rising seabed. The sails were completely useless in the lee of the island, and only momentum and the force of the waves drove them toward shore. Marie stumbled, almost fell. Ned appeared from nowhere, gripped her arm and helped her toward the jagged wood that had been the bow. "'Sblood," Ned croaked. "We're on fire!"

Even as Marie turned to look, Tom Gunn staggered onto deck. Smoke followed him through the hatch. Marie could imagine the scene below decks. Cannons blasted loose would be rolling back and forth unchecked. Weighing over a ton and a half apiece, they would be deadly missiles, wreaking havoc on every piece of timber they hit, crushing any unfortunate seaman who chanced to cross their path, and at last smashing through the outside bulkheads and into the sea. Several already had, leaving the *Ravener* seriously holed, but lighter.

Marie paused on the remains of the forecastle, looked back over the ravaged deck. Miraculously, they still rode stern first to the *Breston,* which gave them a few extra minutes. Had they swung sideways, the heavy iron balls surely would have sunk them already. Tears welled in her eyes as she realized Poole was no longer standing, had somehow managed to thrust his arms through the spokes and catch them in the wheel to prevent it from turning. How pathetically noble. If he'd had time to tie off the wheel as ordered he'd be with her now. The homely lout who had once tried to harm her had now saved her life and given them all a last chance with his dying effort.

Marie heard her name. Tom was shouting at her, tugging her arm. But she couldn't go yet. Where was Shelby? And Ben? Ugly, capable Poacher? The *Ravener* was burning fiercely. She pictured the lapping tongues of orange devouring timbers and canvas, eating an inexorable path to the magazine. No wonder the *Breston* was falling back, trying to put as much distance as possible between herself and the imminent explosion.

"What the hell are you doing on board?" Ned yelled, running toward Tom and Marie.

Marie stared in shock. There was treasure below. The *Ravener* was burning. All was lost. "Oh, Ned. We've lost . . . everything."

"Get off!"

"She's froze," Tom shouted. "Give me a hand."

A massive jolt shook the battered craft and the *Ravener* ground to a halt, mortally skewered by a fang of jutting stone. Off balance, Tom was thrown over the side and disappeared under the roiling waters. Ned took a quick look. If Raven wouldn't move . . . He grabbed her around the waist and flung her off bodily, then followed as quickly as possible.

Marie gulped seawater, flailed to the surface. The shore was fifty yards away, but the ship might explode at any moment. The cold water restored her senses and

424

she chanced a look back. The jolt had toppled the remaining masts and the *Ravener* was completely wrecked. Flames sprang along the main deck. Marie thought of the men still trapped and squirming in pain beneath the wreckage, shuddered at the horrible death they faced. Even now their screams of agony rose in terrible crescendo. Dazed, she slowly began to paw the water.

Forty yards. A hopeless distance. A rough hand on her arm gave her courage. Ned was with her. Somehow she kept her head above water, feebly kicked her legs. Mind reeling. Dizzy. Water, fire, death. The shore, so far ahead. So far . . .

Her toes dug into sand and she realized the water was no more than knee deep. Through a mist, she watched Ned stumble upright, catch her arm and haul her onto the beach, then fall, coughing and spitting water. Marie gulped the sweet air, tried to get up. *Got to get to the hills. Got to hide.*

"Down!" More a sound than a word. Ned surged to his knees, knocked Marie to the side and fell on her. At the same time, an explosion behind them ruptured the very fabric of the air. A hot blast roared off the water, followed by a screaming storm of wood splinters, whipping pieces of rope, bright gold and pieces of iron. A party of English marines hurrying toward them fell in a mewling windrow, casualties of the killing blast.

The earth spun crazily on its mad axis. Spun and steadied. Marie found the strength to wriggle out from beneath Ned's inert form. "Ned," she gasped, "English soldiers!"

More marines emerged from the protective vegetation, hurried toward them across the beach. "We've got to run, Ned. The trees . . . safety . . ."

Ned rolled onto his side and opened his eyes. A two-foot-long sliver of jagged wood from the *Ravener* jutted from his back. A tiny crimson point poked from his chest. As if embarrassed, Ned covered the trickle of blood on his chest with one hand. When Marie pressed the other, he grinned at her and died.

Across the water, the pitiful remains of the *Ravener* burned and crackled. Chunks of wood fell hissing into the sea. Marie couldn't stand the sight, looked down to Ned, whose death-clouded eyes stared back at her. Tenderly, devoid of fear now, she closed the lids so he wouldn't have to see, and could rest in peace.

Was she the only one to survive? Bitter waves of self-recrimination engulfed her. *My fault. Mine alone. So many dead.*

More English soldiers were closing in. With cunning and determination, she could still lose herself among the forested paths, could hide out for as long as necessary, then escape.

Run! Run to the trees!

But why? Why bother? Weeping, she cradled poor bleeding Ned, loyal Ned Sly. Friend.

Chapter XXII

Marie awoke to the smell of wood smoke, the crackle of
fire and the creak of gallows rope. Her eyes adjusted
slowly to bleak sunlight, a pale yellow disc swimming in
a billowing soot-gray cloud that rose from La Cachette.
Once again the town had been ravaged. The view shimmered into focus and she turned her head from the sight
of the burning buildings to the horrible gallows burden
close at hand. Three ragged souls, inhabitants of Mysteré,
dangled at the ends of coarsely corded rope. The
corpses rocked back and forth, set to motion by the
light afternoon sea breeze flowing in to offset the rising
heat from the fires. Marie started to lose consciousness
when a hand caught her, lifted her head and tilted a cup
of water to her lips. She looked into Giuseppe's face
and tried to thank him, but a marine thrust a musket
butt against the surgeon's chest and shoved him back on
his haunches. "Here now. When we want to give her
water, we will. It ain't for you to do."

"What's the matter, Sergeant?"

The frowning soldier stepped aside to make way for
an officer. Marie thought she recognized him, but could
not be certain until he came closer. Pulham! she remembered.

The lieutenant bent at the waist and peered closely at
her. Whatever concern he might have felt was masked
by an officious facade put on, Marie hoped, to impress
the guards. "So you *are* alive. Good." His glance drove
back the enlisted men. "Unfortunately, there is no way I
can help you. I trust you understand," he whispered
quickly.

It was difficult to concentrate. Wincing, Marie
touched the bruise on her forehead. "Am I to join

427

them?" Her eyes rolled feebly, indicating the three dead men.

Pulham sniffed. The sight of hanging rubbish always turned his stomach. "No. Captain Gregory expressly wishes you be kept alive." He paused, recalling the night they'd spent together. It was almost inconceivable that the woman who had made love so passionately was a mutineer, murderess and pirate. He shuddered. "There's a small matter of Newgate and Tyburn waiting after you've been dragged through the courts and made an example of. Publicly, I'll have to concur. Privately . . ."

His voice faded as Marie's gaze met his.

"I'm glad you weren't aboard," she said, incapable of anger.

Pulham straightened at the sound of footsteps. "Sergeant, see the rest of the men are brought in, if you please. We'll be leaving as soon as everyone is aboard, which, I trust you'll see, is within the half-hour."

"Aye, sir." The marine saluted briskly and hurried off.

"Surgeon," Pulham continued, "you may continue with your ministrations. And see she doesn't get out of hand or your health will forfeit."

Giuseppe knuckled his forehead to the departing lieutenant. His face had turned pale and his hands shook. Marie noticed he was at least free, so the ruse with the shackles had proved successful and saved him from the hangman's noose after all.

"I'm sorry, Raven," he muttered. "You were always kind to me and didn't laugh like some others I could name. I wish I could let you go, but—"

"I don't think I could run very far anyway, Giuseppe. Everything is spinning so." She sipped gratefully at the water he offered. "What happened? Is everyone dead?"

The surgeon shook his head. "Oh, no. Fled into the hills. Only those three behind you were caught, that I know of. Some from the *Ravener* made it ashore, but what's happened to them I can't say. One was killed, but some others escaped. Anyway, Pulham has seen to the burning of the town, in revenge for the marines killed last night and today when the lobsterbacks chased Caron's men into the hills."

Marie sighed in relief. "Then perhaps they will not raze the entire island."

"Oh, no," Giuseppe chuckled. "You were the one they wanted. Oh. Excuse me. But it's true. I heard them. They're satisfied now that they have you. Taking you back to be hung, they say." A doleful look crossed his face. "I'm sorry."

"I expected no less," Marie said, sinking back and glancing at the three already hung and as quickly turning from the sickening sight of leathery tongues protruding from cracked lips, "though I think I'd rather get it over with more quickly."

"I've heard them talk. Gregory is smug as a pig full of truffles. He's going to see you well cared for until you hear the tolling of the bells in London. It's the only way he can redeem himself, what with the grief you've caused him." A file of marines emerged from between the burning buildings. "Here comes another contingent now. See, they carry four . . . five lads brought down from the hills."

Marie looked to where he pointed. Her eyes swam out of focus, cleared. As the marines passed, she saw among them a handful of bound men, all from the village of La Cachette. Farmers and fishermen, they were. Men who had forsaken the freebooter's life long ago. Now the past had risen like a rancorous beast to confront them. Their chains clattered with each hopeless step of bare feet thudding in the sand. One of them paused and met Giuseppe's gaze. The little surgeon instantly looked away in embarrassment. A marine shoved the ragged captive, who stumbled, managed to retain his footing and staggered onward.

Rough fingers suddenly dug into Marie's shoulders and hauled her to her feet. A half-dozen redcoats clustered around, gaping at her shapely form clad in tattered blouse and breeches. Lust showed plainly in the leering faces. "We'll see to her now, sawbones," one swarthy private muttered.

429

"But I was told—"

"Get to the boat or be left behind," a sallow-cheeked corporal barked.

Giuseppe, utterly cowed, scurried off. Marie wavered, unsteady yet determined not to display weakness before these louts. "Well, missy. A pirate indeed. Now there's a laugh. What have ye to say for yourself?"

"Aye. She's a pretty crack that'd take some fillin', I warrant," another cackled.

Marie slapped aside a questing paw and shoved another man back on his heels, only to suffer the indignities of a third who sent her leaping into the center of a closing circle, her buttock bruised from a vicious pinch. "It's common knowledge," Marie hissed, "that the poorest material on any king's ship can be found among the lubbards and sloppers such as yourselves."

The corporal, incensed, slapped her across the face. Marie's cheek stung from the force of the blow and an angry buzzing filled her head, but she refused to fall. The corporal raised his hand again.

"Corporal!" Pulham shouted. He couldn't do much for her, but of this he was certain: when she was in his charge, the riffraff would not harm her.

The marines snapped to attention, spine-straight and muskets at arms. "I'll have your name."

"Guinness, sir! Robert." The marine's chin quivered, so tightly did he hold himself. "Corporal in His Majesty's—"

"That will do. It is not, to my knowledge, your place to administer punishment."

"Yes, sir," the corporal barked. His companions remained dutifully silent, each grateful beyond words not to have been considered a culprit. Once a man's name was taken, there was no telling what was in store for him where Captain Gregory was involved.

"Boats, ho!" The shout prompted a flurry of activity along the perimeter established around the landing place. Marie swiveled her head and saw the sergeant returning with a squad of red-coated marines, their white belts and leathers soiled from the day's exercise.

430

They no sooner passed her than Pulham ordered her bound and taken to the waiting longboat, then drew his sword and waved it over his head.

In answer, the *Breston* belched smoke. A second later the thunder of her large guns split the air and the keening whistle of balls passing overhead could be heard. As in a nightmare, Marie found herself dragged across the sand and roughly tumbled into the smaller craft. Resistance was impossible. The landing party was withdrawing under the protection of the *Breston*'s own guns. On the sergeant's command the men assumed their assigned places in the boats, with Pulham the last to come aboard. He paused at the edge of the water, dramatically drew his pistol and fired one last symbolic ball of defiance toward the distant palms. Satisfied, he turned to climb aboard, then suddenly jerked, clasped a hand over his left arm and toppled into the boat. "By bloody damn!" the young officer swore, before fainting dead away. The shot had come from close by in town, but from where no one knew, for the drifting smoke concealed the unknown assailant's hiding place. Blood spurted onto the trouser legs of those at the oars. No one needed to tell the marines and accompanying sailors to pull for the *Breston*. Giuseppe picked a path through the straining men in order to help the lieutenant. The sergeant stood and bawled useless orders to the rowers. Already the longboats had crawled fifty yards out from the shore.

Marie stared at Mysteré. Tiny figures could be seen scurrying down from the hills to salvage what they could of La Cachette. All hope fled. No one could help her. She would be hauled aboard the *Breston* and taken to Gregory. Gregory! How he must hate her. What scorn and derision must have been heaped on him for allowing a woman to parade him naked before his crew and then steal his ship from under his feet! He would not miss his chance to repay the outrage. Her humiliation would be complete.

Marie shrank from the thought. Death was preferable to whatever Gregory might have in mind. If only things had gone differently. With Jason at her side, life would have been so beautiful. But there was no time for wishing. She had to act now, for the boat was reaching the *Breston*. Without hesitation or warning, she lunged for the side.

She almost made it. One startled crew member ducked in surprise, but the boat pitched a peculiar way and the gunwale rose to catch her across the waist. Guinness lunged and grabbed her legs at the same time her torso twisted into the water. Despite his diminutive stature, he possessed enough leathery strength to haul her back into the boat.

Sputtering and gasping for breath, kicking, scratching and squirming, Marie fought desperately. Enraged, Guinness lost his temper. He swung one practiced fist, quickly and without mercy. Pain exploded in Marie's jaw and her head slammed against the gunwale with a dull thud that dimmed her senses. Vainly she tried to sit upright, but the world had gone awry. A spiraling vortex emanated from the center of Guinness's fist, spun counterclockwise and, in widening circles, engulfed her. Contact with reality became tenuous and dimmed until nothing remained. Only a stygian emptiness through which she continued to plummet.

Bouyant in a shadowy realm. Floating past fluid, bloodless, pale columns that undulated slowly, the tempo increasing until they writhed like giant worms or fearful serpents. Now into gray coolness where dark patches stained the liquid ether with black aureoles, holes through which the very depths of space yawned and beckoned. The blackness expanded, to be replaced with an all-consuming orange glow, the remnants of an oozing, shapeless, sunlit landscape.

Marie awoke. Blurred faces around her shifted into focus. One was more familiar than the rest. Powder could not conceal the furrowed cheek beneath his left eye nor the triumphant expression of malevolent glee. "So good to see you again," Gregory said in dulcet snake-tones.

Marie shivered. Her torn clothes were still damp. Bedraggled and unkempt, she felt like a rag doll that had been used for a game of catch and throw by a half-score of spiteful children. Every muscle and bone ached terribly. Gingerly she prodded her bruised jaw with questing fingertips. She was lying flat on her back on a floor. Gregory stood at her feet, his head towering high above her. Marie glanced up. A young marine stood directly behind her, his feet almost touching her head. "Help me up!"

Without thinking, the youth responded immediately. Only when she was on her feet did the realization strike that the woman was a prisoner and had no business ordering him to do anything. Blushing furiously, he returned to his place by the door.

Marie inspected the sumptuously decorated cabin, far more spacious than the *Ravener*'s. No expense had been spared to ensure the comfort of the captain. Gilt abounded, outlining the carved paneling. In the center of the room a massive table was dressed with a damask cloth and held a formal silver tea service. Heavy armchairs covered with light, brushed leather sat bolted to the floor. A half-dozen brass lanterns had been polished to such brightness they gave the impression they could dispel the deepest night without being lit. To one side, a mammoth japanned wardrobe filled one corner. Another was taken up by the captain's bed, curtained with yard upon yard of fine linen, into which had been woven, in dark blue, the crest of the *Breston*'s disabled captain.

Gregory—she vowed not to cringe before him—had affected an imperious stance, one hand resting on the hilt of a new rapier. "You will forgive me, Captain, if I do not return your sword and dueling pistols," Marie said in a voice heavily tinged with sarcasm. "I fear they were left behind in my ship." The possessive "my" was emphasized slightly.

The slur struck home. Gregory stiffened and his supercilious smile disappeared. Suddenly the door to his cabin flew open and a dusky girl in voluminous gypsy

433

skirts whirled into the room. Armide stopped dead in her tracks. The fires of hatred flashed in her eyes at the sight of Marie, who stepped back in shock, taken totally by surprise. She must have told Gregory about Mysteré. But how had he found her? "She lives!" hissed the mulatto. Three quick strides took her to Gregory's side. "Why does she live? You said she would hang."

Gregory reached for and caught the solid copper bracelet around Armide's wrist and twisted. The girl bent at the waist and tried to escape the biting metal but the Englishman jerked roughly, pulled her arm around behind her back and her wrist up between her shoulder blades. Armide cried out in pain and stood on tiptoes. "I've told you under what circumstances you may enter my cabin," Gregory said pleasantly enough. He pushed her away and Armide reeled against the bulkhead. "In the future, please remember."

Not one to be slowed by a mere arm-twisting, Armide bounced back and lunged for Marie, her outstretched talons clawing the air. Exhausted by her ordeal, Marie could only defend herself. The two women grappled and fell against the marine by the door, whom Gregory dismissed with a sharp command. When the door closed, he turned to the women who, on hands and knees, faced each other across a bare three feet of polished teak flooring. "And now, ladies," he said with a tight smile of anticipation, "would you like to continue."

"No," Marie began. "I have nothing—"

Once again, Armide attacked. Marie scrambled back until she could go no farther and then, at bay, lunged and grabbed Armide's hair and flung her to one side. Hissing, Armide rolled to her feet and kicked at Marie's head. Marie caught her attacker's skirt and jerked. The skirt ripped all the way to the waist. The kick missed.

Gregory had taken a seat. "Bravo!" he called, laughing.

"Make her stop!" Marie pleaded, rolling away from another kick and managing to stand.

"You're the one who likes to fight, my dear." His

434

face was ugly, twisted with hatred. "You make her stop."

Marie was dizzy with exhaustion. She tried to hold off Armide, but the mulatto was too strong. One hand flashed out and a fingernail raked a groove down Marie's cheek, went on to catch in her blouse and rip open the front. Marie managed only one blow in return, then found herself caught from behind. Armide's forearm was against her throat and choking her. Like a wild animal she struggled, but to no avail. She was simply too tired. The cabin became hazy, spun madly. She thought she could hear the roar of the ocean.

"Enough!" Gregory stepped forward and struck Armide with a fierce blow that made her lose her grip. She stumbled, ran into the table and slumped on its surface, gasping for breath.

Panting, barely able to remain on her feet, Marie watched as Gregory's face came closer. His eyes were hooded and a sardonic grin split his face. "I always did say you had beautiful breasts," he laughed, touching first one and then the other.

Marie recoiled from him, stood braced against the bulkhead. Tears ran down her face and she tried to cover her breasts with her hands. Her legs were weak and trembling and she was sure she would faint.

Armide heaved off the table and started for her again. "Enough!" Gregory commanded sharply, freezing her in place. To press the volatile Englishman too far would be a dangerous venture. Armide pouted and Gregory, as was predictable, mellowed. "She will be punished. Never fear that. But later, and in England."

He turned to Marie and she suffered him to touch the damp, untamed tresses curling wildly across her shoulders. "You have cost me much discomfort, girl. I have been ridiculed, my career has been placed in jeopardy. And all because of a single impertinent, impudent wench who doesn't know her place in the world." He paused and his hand tightened, twisting her hair and pulling her head to one side. His eyes gleamed and the scar on his cheek turned red under the makeup. "You listen now, bitch, for the truth. No punishment is too great. No humiliation adequate enough. There are six hundred men aboard this ship. Shall I let each have you in turn? I wonder how many it would take before you were howling for mercy? How many? What a fitting demise for a market slut like yourself!"

He chuckled, let go the grip on her hair and shoved her upright before crossing to the massive desk near the transom windows. Light spilled through the glass and played on his shoulders in beatific irony. Gregory poured himself a glass of Madeira and took exquisite pleasure in the first, slow sip. Armide glowed with satisfaction, then scowled in disgust as he continued. "However, there is more at stake here than revenge. Caution and further-reaching considerations must override immediate gratification. To that end, I've arranged a suitable compartment for you directly 'neath the bow. Two men will guard you at all times. You will be fed regularly, and will exercise each day under the watchful eyes of your guards." He leaned toward her and a twisted smile creased his face. "I trust those conditions meet with your approval."

"I—"

"Silence! I didn't give you permission to speak." The smile was gone. "You will be interested to learn, perhaps, that it is now my turn to use you. In England. When you have served your purpose, I personally shall escort you to the gallows and watch you hang, until dead." His eyes closed and he straightened, under a spell of his own devising. For over a minute, no one spoke. Finally, Gregory shook himself and called for the guard. "Get me Corporal Guinness."

The marine at the door saluted and hurried from the room. Armide had slunk off to the bed. Her full coffee-colored breasts bulged upward over tightly folded arms. Not one to long contain rage, it seemed only a matter of seconds before she burst into action and attacked Marie again, but Guinness reentered before she could act.

"Ah, Corporal," the captain smiled without a trace of

436

warmth. "I am placing you in charge of this prisoner."
The corporal of marines stiffened with pride and hid a
smirk: how lucky could a man get, to have his own bed-
warmer across the cold Atlantic. "You will escort her to
the brig in the bow and, with others of your own choosing, post a perpetual two-man guard outside her door."

"Aye aye, Captain."

"And hear this, Mr. Guinness. I intend to bring her
to London in the best of health. To that end, she will be
fed, exercised and unmolested. I want her hale and
hearty, that she might find ample opportunity to reflect
upon her sins and experience to the fullest the ordeal of
imprisonment and the hangman's noose. Should anything interfere with my intentions, you will take her
place. Is that understood?"

The glitter of anticipation faded as the promise of a
sexual feast dissolved. The unfortunate corporal silently
cursed his luck. Bed-warmer, hell. More like a millstone
around his neck, and him balanced on the edge of a
cliff. Few things in life were sure, but this one he did
not doubt: Captain Gregory was just the man to see
him swing at Tyburn. "Come along with you, then," he
ordered gruffly, nudging Marie toward the door.

"A pleasant voyage, *Captain* Raven," Gregory smiled,
bowing ever so slightly.

Marie was too benumbed to respond. The passing
minutes had taken on the aspect of a nightmare, utterly
phantasmagorical. Surely she would awake, surely find
herself in Jason's arms. Secure. Safe. No! There was
treachery there. Everywhere.

She was led into the blood-red illumination of a setting sun, past the interested stares of the crewmen on
deck who craned to see their prestigious captive. Many
had been on board the *Breston* that day in Anguilla
when the *Sword of Cornwall* had surprised them with a
withering broadside. They'd lost comrades, suffered
wounds and the derision of the fleet for being taken so
unawares. Worse, their disabled captain had been replaced with Gregory, a man for whom not a one of

them had a jot of admiration or affection, and the girl was to blame.

They could stare until their eyeballs fell out as far as Marie was concerned. Of greater moment was the hatch into which she was led. Once again the dusk below decks yawned, ready to swallow her. At Guinness's command, she halted in front of the entrance to a sparsely furnished compartment. Reluctant to enter her new jail, she hesitated. A shove from behind sent her stumbling inside to fall against the opposite wall. Then the door slammed. She was alone at last.

So weary. Marie searched the dimly lit room, discovered a thin, vermin-infested pallet left in a corner and fell on it full length. Cracks in the wall were defined by the fading light. While she watched they gradually dimmed, leaving blank darkness in which she lay unmoving.

Mysteré. They would be well gone from the island now. She had not caught a glimpse of land while on deck. The dead . . . No. She couldn't bear to think of them, for they were her fault. Their souls lay heavily on hers, and with the dark, weighted her beyond grief.

If she could only cry! *Oh, God! My eyes are empty.* The gesture of prayer was cut off by the sound of laughter. Her own, she finally realized, for the mad humor of the day had struck home. She was being taken from her home again. As a young girl, and now. Full circle. Trickster fate had brought her to this pass, even provided new ghosts to lurk in the emptiness and watch the progression of life denied them in their shadowy realm.

I'll join you soon enough, dear friends. Father . . . Did he hear? Or was her voice as the passage of clouds before the moon, soundless and without substance?

Father?

In her weary depths, she wanted to call to Jason, but pride muted longing and love. There was no Jason to cry out to. Not anymore.

Again, I am alone.

In the darkness, she could not tell whether her eyes were open or closed. In truth, it hardly mattered.

438

He'd been a fool, and was paying for it. The episode with Angelique had ignited a chain of events no one could have foreseen. He'd awakened in the back room of the inn, sick as a dog and confused. Confusion gave way to rage when the tale of Law's abduction and the theft of the gold was discovered. Assuming she'd taken Law with her, he rounded up his crew and set sail. The rigging went before they got out of the bay.

Morning revealed the extent of the damage, and it was a chagrined Jason who hailed a forlorn Law who rowed in from Dauphin Island. During the four days it took to rerig the *Banshee,* Jason worked like a madman and drove the crew as hard. Marie's perfidy grew until it became a monster raging in his breast. So he'd had a fling with Angelique. That was no reason to negate all that had passed between them. She hadn't even given him a chance to explain! The bitch had coshed him over the head, wrecked his ship and run.

Sputtering to himself, sweat pouring down his body in spite of the north wind, he changed tack and placed the blame on himself. To jeopardize his relationship with Marie had been the act of a madman. Their reunion in the glen. The week of bliss together. Her kisses had driven him mad with lust and love.

Each league closer to Mysteré took forever, during which time he swung between rage and self-pity. When they tacked into Voûte Paix and saw the wreck of La Cachette, self-pity disappeared. The bitch hadn't had to do that! He'd see the *Ravener* sunk and mistress . . . what? No punishment would be too cruel. Damn her. Damn her beauty, her kisses and lies.

Once landed, he had learned the truth. Now, Jason squatted on his haunches and listened patiently to the finale of Franco Caron's sad tale of the English attack, the *Ravener*'s fate and Marie's capture. The *Breston* had sailed into port the day before Marie's arrival, sent a token broadside screaming into La Cachette and off-loaded the marines. The islanders had been at work in the fields, and by the time anyone could even try to organize resistance, it was too late. The *Breston*'s mission became apparent when the seventy-four-gunner slipped out of harbor and took up watch on the far side of the island, out of view to anyone arriving from the north. During the night three or four men slipped away from the guards with enough powder to fire the hidden harbor guns. The rest waited silently, unable to affect the outcome of the coming fray should the *Ravener* and *Banshee* return. The next morning, the imprisoned islanders watched in horror as the *Ravener* neared, then they broke en masse for the hills when the marines deserted the town in order to pick up the survivors of the quickly defeated pirate ship.

"There was nothing we could do, Captain Brand," Caron apologetically finished. "Absolutely nothing but defend ourselves as best we could once in the hills. We managed to rescue some of Raven's shipmates, but beyond that . . ." The tavernkeeper shrugged and cast a curious glance at the bronzed freebooter. Once ashore, Brand had ordered the survivors of Marie's crew placed under guard. As yet none of the islanders knew why and were, consequently, a bit hesitant around him. Caron sniffed an aroma of roasting pig in the warm air and rubbed his growling belly. "Ahhh. Someone has made a good catch. I hope Diana is nearby and secures a bit for my supper."

Jason's gaze was penetrating, and though Caron wanted to escape, he felt constrained to keep on talking. He cast about for a suitable subject, settled on the mestizo servants slowly building a new tavern over the ruins of the old one. "I talked the others into staying. Some was for finding another place now the English have found Mystéré. Told them they was damned fools, that we just have to watch more careful in the future. Watch and make do the best we can."

Jason nodded absently, his attention no longer with the tavernkeeper, who grabbed the chance to scurry off in the direction of the suckling pig. Six days had gone by since La Cachette had fallen to Gregory's torches, and now that he'd arrived and heard the story, he needed time alone to think. The incoming waters of the

440

Caribbean played tag with his footprints as he walked down the beach. So Marie wasn't at fault, which had been his original premise, reasonable enough in light of her treachery in Mobile. The actions of a madwoman they were, to turn on one's friend, steal his gold and disable his ship. Law had been furious, of course, and mollified only with great difficulty. Luckily he'd sensed her wrath when she came away from the bluff overlooking the beach. Jason cursed silently. If Law hadn't been so all-fired anxious to get Marie alone, none of this would have happened.

Footsteps from behind distracted his attention. Forlicar and Ramahd had finished their inspection of the damage and were hurrying to report. "Well? What is it?" Jason asked.

"Nothing different than what you know already. They tumbled two or three cannons, but the rest is as was. Hope Deferred says she's feedin' the prisoners and if the captain don't like it he can——"

"Never mind," Jason interrupted, grinning. He'd already been the target of Hope's tongue when he voiced the opinion Marie herself might have fired the town as part of her mad rampage. "I can well imagine what Hope suggests. It's impossible. Let them eat."

Forlicar nodded in relief. "It was for the best, Jason. I had no wish to try the woman's temper further. She already threatened to cook my parrot."

"'Twould be poor eating," Ramahd replied drily, "but worth the quiet." Forlicar scowled, but Ramahd paid him no mind. "We've fresh water aboard. Another day and we'll have fruit and meat and be ready to weigh anchor."

"Weigh anchor?" Forlicar grunted. "What for? Where are we going to go?"

"To sea," Jason answered shortly. "Where else? I've got to replace Law's gold or he'll see that the whole damned coast is closed to us."

"No easy task," Forlicar said.

"No more difficult than convincing him we'd naught to do with the raid."

441

Ramahd couldn't help smiling. "Still, a clever bit of thievery," he said wistfully, perhaps wishing he'd thought of it himself. Used to the temper that had made his captain all but unbearable these past days at sea, he met Jason's stare for a long moment before dropping his eyes. As well as any man, he knew better then to press the Scot too far.

Jason relaxed, turned to more immediate matters. "Forlicar, you'd best see to a close watch on the harbor guns. I don't know how Gregory found this place, nor who else knows. I'll not have the *Banshee* play hapless hare to English hounds."

"Aye, Captain." The mate turned, leaving Jason and Ramahd behind.

Day was raveling out. A purple sky tinted the weathered, watchful face above Voûte Paix. "They did not burn the house," Ramahd finally said.

"What?"

"I followed the path to the plantation. The house is untouched. Her mestizo waits in silent patience for her return."

"Damn her mestizo servant. Why do you bother me with this?" Jason asked, the anger growing anew.

"I tell you because you care."

"You are a fool. Leave me alone."

Strangely, Ramahd did not take offense. "I have done many things in my life, Jason Brand. Good, bad . . . many things. But I always knew why I did them."

"So?"

Ramahd gave no more than a last, lingering look in reply, then turned away and followed Forlicar's deep footprints up the beach.

"Insubordinate devil," Jason fumed. "Never should have thrown in with a Turk. Fanatics, they are, always proclaiming the rhyme or reason of someone else's life. I wonder if they truly believe their own obscure mouthings. Bah!"

Alone now at last, he followed the path among the gnarled mancanillas overhanging the water, then rose with the land and disappeared in a maze of windbent palms. "I know exactly why," he said aloud, startling himself with the sound of his voice. "I'm here because she betrayed me. I came for vengeance, only to find justice has preceded me. The English have already seen to an unpleasant task. So be it. Who am I to argue with fate? She wronged me, humiliated me before my crew and the French. No one does that. Not to Jason Brand."

Muttering angrily, unconcerned where his steps might lead, Jason ascended the steepening slope, marking each misstep with a curse. At last he reached the summit and descended the other side in spite of the growing darkness and the hazards of the dense vegetation. The last vestige of daylight eased into twilight and his thoughts, muted by the gloom, churned wildly in the cauldron of his mind. Reliving moments, now. No matter that somehow, someway, she had discovered his liaison with Angelique. Damn but he'd been a fool! Women! Curse their spiteful—

He stepped from the trees and froze in place, staring into the clearing surrounded by the broad heavy silhouettes of ycao trees which covered the obsidian pool. "Damn. What manner of madness has led me here?" he whispered, held powerless by the memory of emotions he dared not admit.

Someone with him . . . He spun around, gazed into a featureless stone wall. Yet not alone. Was that laughter? He turned again. "Marie?"

He entered the clearing as cautiously as a wizard his pentagram, for who knew what dark secrets lay at the threshold of night. Laughter again. Night's breath among the branches? There . . . two lovers entwined—or roots writhing upward from the loam?

Run! Silent dialogue, torment arguing with anguish.

No. Why are you afraid?

It was her fault. Her fault . . .

Whose?

Marie's. There. Say it again. Marie. The reason . . . she is gone from my life . . .

It is ended. Here we made our fire, and here joined our bodies, our love melting into passion, into oneness.

"Ended? Gone from my life?" No echo. The trees sucked up words as a dry sponge water.

It is ended. Forget her.

"No!" His knees struck the rich carpet of earth once warmed by their love-making. "I never loved her. Only . . ." His mind searched for the right words, but words no longer made sense, fell apart, fractured into incoherence by rising grief.

"Marie's fault, damn it. She deserved . . . she . . .

Did nothing, came the refutation from his churning soul. *Who used her, played with her love to effect his escape? And did so again in this very glade? Who denied what he knew to be true and when faced with his cowardice, vainly attempted to prove his independence in the arms of another woman?*

Forced to face the truth. The pain and loss, Jason realized, differed not a jot from that he had inflicted on Marie, whom he had cherished above all others in spite of the blind arrogance which drove him from her. Nightglade and sorrow. *I loved her, yes. Admit it freely. Still love her, but too late.* If only her ghost would leave him alone. Sorrow tore his throat with great heaving sobs.

Irretrievably lost! By my own hand driven away. He dug his fingers into the earth to brace against the overwhelming despair until the inner core of strength, so long encrusted with cynicism and bitterness, lay bare and sprang to counter defeat.

Irretrievably? Not while he lived. Slowly, his fierce coppery features became transformed with cunning radiance. Gregory would take her to England to be imprisoned and hung as the courts would certainly decree. To England. A man would have to be mad to follow, mad to even think of snatching her from them. Mad . . . or in love.

Tom Gunn's jaws clamped on a steaming chunk of muscle still attached to the porkbone and tore it off in a great spattering of grease. He fixed red-rimmed eyes on Loupe, who recognized a threat when he saw one and leveled his musket at the giant carpenter-turned-pirate. Poacher spat into the flames and ignored them both. Shelby, the only other survivor of the *Ravener,* placed a calming hand on Gunn's shoulder. "Easy, Tom. The cowardly likes of him would like nothin' better'n to puncture your hide."

"Aye. If he'd do me the honor of puttin' down the ord'nance, I'd see to poppin' his neck twixt my thumb and forefinger." Loupe shuffled back a few steps just to be on the safe side.

"More belly-timber?" Hope asked, stepping past the sentry and breaking into a circle. She carried a stew kettle which she plopped down on the ground in front of the prisoners.

"I'll take some more," Poacher said, holding out a bowl. Hope bent to ladle out meat and broth.

"What do you think he intends to do?" Shelby whispered.

Hope shook her head. "Don't look good. Forlicar says Brand was off walkin' by hisself. In a terrible temper, too. He's a dark, moody man with an anger buildin' inside him."

"I curse the luck that brought me under his guns," Tom grumbled. "But I'll warrant you this. Brand will not be havin' his way with me. Not so long as I've a breath left in me."

"The same's for me," Shelby added bravely in a feeble attempt to bolster his sagging spirits. Poacher smirked. Heroics be damned, he thought. Gunn and Shelby could blow out the fire with all their bluster, and die in the process. He meant to live. With Raven gone, the only person he owed loyalty was himself. The circumstances called for stealth and cunning.

"Damn my eyes." Gunn paused, remembering how often Ned had used those same words. "Damn me!" he added fiercely. "Here he comes now." Hope straightened and stepped to one side. Ramahd and Forlicar, aware something was afoot, flanked their captain.

Jason had chosen his time well. Many of those who might have been interested in the unfolding drama lay

445

snoring, either in a drunken stupor or exhausted slumber. A few inhabitants and crew members did rise from their places along the beach and watch the Scottish rogue. Gunn, Shelby and Dearam the Poacher stood and faced their captor, for it was obvious Brand had made a decision. The moment of their fate was at hand. Loupe braced himself, musket at the ready.

The trio strode up to the prisoners. Tom's fists clenched and his head lowered bull-like, ready for battle. Jason met his stare, read the hatred in those eyes, accepted it and looked past him to Shelby and Poacher. "I've come to offer you your lives," he said, "if you'll sail with me."

"We owe no allegiance to you, Jason Brand," Tom said belligerently. "Raven was our captain, and still is as far as I'm concerned."

"Fair enough," Jason replied. "I'll let you prove your loyalty. The *Breston* is taking her to England. They've had a head start, but the *Banshee* can outrun her. With luck, we'll arrive at the same time. Maybe sooner."

"My God, Captain, what are you saying?" Forlicar blurted.

"I'm for England to free a caged Raven." Hope jumped as if burned, almost dropped the kettle in her surprise. Jason grinned at her then looked back to Tom. "Are you with me?"

Tom frowned, confused by this unexpected change and convinced Jason had gone mad. Go to England? They'd be caught and killed for sure. Poacher lowered his head and stared at his stew. Heroics. That's what they were talking about. Bound to end badly. A fool's errand, and one he'd take no part in.

Shelby stepped forward. His face was white, his features drawn. "I'd rather die tomorrow," he said in a hoarse, choked whisper, "than live another hundred years with the thought I'd let them hang her. Tom would too, only he's too damned obstinate to admit it."

Tom colored. He hadn't thought about that. "I guess I'd be seein' those eyes and that hair every night of my life," he admitted. "I'm with you."

446

Poacher looked around the circle of faces staring at him and waiting. Suddenly, his face split into a huge grin. Three damned fool heroes deserved a fourth. "You think I have time to finish my stew before we leave?" he asked laconically.

Shelby whooped and clapped him on the shoulder, then froze when he saw Loupe's musket pointed at Jason. "The crew'll have something to say about you takin' the ship," the Frenchman snarled. He had no desire to spend the next months cooped up on Mysteré, less to sail to England and a certain death. "Hugo, wake the others," he called into the dark. "Now. Not a one of you—"

Hope dumped the steaming contents of the stew kettle on Loupe's hands. The pirate dropped his weapon and yelped in pain. Jason stepped close and slammed a fist against the burned man's chin. Loupe collapsed, knocked senseless. A grumbling rose from the darkness around them as men woke and tried to figure out what was happening. Jason turned to Forlicar and Ramahd. "I'll not ask you to come, for it's a fool's errand I'm on, and we'll probably end up in Newgate ourselves. But I have to try."

"No need to ask," Ramahd replied softly. "I've not played the fool for a great while. It's high time."

"Yer daft," Forlicar cried. "Why, you got as much chance of savin' the life of that lass as my parrot's got of growing teats."

"Oh, hush up, you bag of guts and come on," Hope scolded.

Forlicar looked offended. "Hmmmph. I just wanted to make sure we all understood, is all."

For a brief second, no one moved or spoke. A voice from the beach called out angrily, wondering what the hell the ruckus was about. Suddenly, all seven broke out in huge grins and, as one, ran for the *Banshee*'s jolly boat, a scant hundred yards down the beach. One group of pirates who'd finally figured out what was happening rose from the dark and tried to stop them, but the seven, with the advantage of speed and purpose, ran through the still half-asleep men without even slowing. Panting, they shoved the boat into the water and pulled across Voûte Paix with swift, sure strokes. By the time they reached the *Banshee,* a full-fledged commotion had risen on shore.

Expecting trouble from the watch, all were surprised when they managed to board without being challenged. The reason was even more perplexing: both sentinels lay unconscious, bound and gagged. Jason and Forlicar loosed their pistols when a shape flitted down from the mainmast and landed on the deck. It was Tomás, eyes wide with a mixture of fear and determination.

"Hoho! It would seem another has the same idea as us," Forlicar bellowed.

The mestizo brandished a brace of pistols, looked uncomprehendingly at this unexpected array of people. "She's a sweet craft to sail, Tomás," Jason said, "but more than two hands are needed."

Gunn's towering form loomed out of the darkness. "Tomás, we're going to go get Marie." The half-breed glanced at each in turn. Gunn nodded reassuringly. "All of us. You come too, no?"

When Tomás grinned and lowered his weapons, Jason quickly took command. "Forlicar, cut the anchor. Tom, take these two and lower them into the jollyboat. The rest of you, into the rigging."

Hope glanced up in horror toward the spars overhead. Jason couldn't help but laugh. "Hope, you make a list of our provisions. We'll need to know how much we have, how much we can spare for each day."

"I can't write."

"Well, then use your memory, woman!"

"All right. All right. You needn't shout." The buxom harlot hurried toward the nearest hatch.

Jason checked the progress above. Already, Shelby, Ramahd and Gunn were untying the lines holding the sails. He glanced toward shore. Fires had sprung up and a longboat was being pulled into the water. Obviously, the *Banshee*'s crew disagreed violently with Jason's plans and had decided to replace him with someone more amenable to their desire for gold. Forlicar hacked the anchor cable in two, laughed aloud and roared a thunderous, good-natured curse. The longboat skimmed across the water, impervious to his insults until he hauled the three-pounder bow gun around and touched it off with a piece of smoldering punk lit from a nearby lantern. The iron shot skipped across the water and came close enough to give those aboard the longboat second thoughts about coming any closer.

With a yell from the rigging, the mainsail dropped. Forlicar rushed back and hauled on the sheet. The sail bellied out, swollen with wind and shining with an eerie blue-gray sheen. Jason ran from the port sheet tie-down and took his position behind the wheel. The *Banshee* heeled over slightly and angled out of the bay.

A half-hour later they cleared Mysteré and set their course on the first long tack destined to take them to the windward passage, then on to England and Marie. Jason looked to the east, knowing full well the odds decreed defeat. Withal, a wild recklessness infused his spirit. At long last, he knew why.

And he was happy.

Chapter XXIII

Like an animal that senses the footfall of the hunter and is roused from sleep on the instant, so did Marie awaken and lay motionless on the pallet. An intruder? Guinness? No. Only once had he tried to molest her, and received a bloodied nose for his trouble. To reinforce the lesson, she had feigned an attempt on her own life, a ploy that caused drastic changes in the guard's attitude. Through the simple and successful suicidal action of a mad woman, he might find himself in her stead.

And so, the final seven weeks of the tortuous passage passed in uneasy truce. Marie was a model prisoner and Guinness an exemplary jailer, both concealing malice with conciliatory good manners that, no matter how false, served their mutual benefit and advantage. In truth, any other arrangement would have been too enervating, for the journey was difficult enough. The *Breston* wallowed through the high spring seas of the North Atlantic, which delayed the journey for a good two weeks. One storm-tossed week saw the ship nearly capsized. The two packet boats following in her wake were sent on with the news of the *Breston*'s captives and hopefully imminent arrival while repairs were made in midocean. During that same week, Marie had saved Guinness's life when she snatched him from the path of a loose barrel of salt pork which had broken loose and threatened to crush him. No, it was not Guinness who had interrupted her slumber.

Listening. Slowly, her eyes adjusted to the dim light in the cubicle. The room was empty. Then who? Even as her mind began to search, icy fingers coursed her spine. The *Breston* was at anchor! Was it possible they'd reached London already? Impossible. The night before they'd been lying to in the Channel, waiting for the winds to shift. She ran toward the door, which swung open the second she beat on it with her fists.

" 'Ere, now," Guinness muttered, rubbing the sleep from his eyes. "Hey!" he blurted, instantly awake, as she ran past him and up the ladder.

He caught her at the rail. Though she had not tried to escape, he clamped firm fingers around her arm. Marie ignored him and stared across the smoothly flowing Thames to the wooded hillsides of England. Where was the bustling water traffic that clogged the great Pool of London? Where were the teeming streets, the sooty air and grimy shops? No tower thrust its terrible battlements to heaven. No great bridge. Why had they dropped anchor here in the middle of the countryside?

"My God!" she exclaimed, so strongly that Guinness, fearing an attack, let her go and grasped his musket. When none came, he cocked a wary eye on his prisoner, who gripped the railing with such force that her knuckles whitened and blue veins stood out.

Armide swaggered forward, threw a cocky glance at the corporal. "She should not be out here. You let her escape, my captain will tickle your back with the cat."

"Take your witchery elsewhere," Guinness snarled. "This bird's my charge and I'll see she don't escape. Nor come to harm from the likes of you."

Armide looked past the soldier. "Raven . . . Raven," she taunted. "My English captain will put me up in a great big house. I will have many fine clothes and jewels. Maybe I watch them hang you, eh?" Her eyes filled with tears. "Because I hate you, Raven. You hear me? I hate you!"

Guinness shoved her away with his musket. The mulatto stumbled backward, tripped and fell. He skirt bunched at the waist to reveal dark coffee-colored thighs joined at their apex by a darker triangle. "Your captain," he sneered. "You ain't got no captain anymore and we all know it." The word had spread about the ship, how a week earlier Gregory had ordered the mulatto wench to pleasure Lieutenant Pulham to keep him from grieving over the loss of his arm, which had been mangled beyond repair during the early hours of the storm. Whatever else

451

the half-breed wench had, Guinness knew, it wasn't the captain, and he needn't fear angering her. "Now leave," he ordered gruffly, forcing his eyes from the dark nest where only officers were allowed to cavort.

Armide struggled to her feet. "I'll—"

"You'll do nothin' missy. I told you once. Leave." Armide scowled and turned aft, still holding her head high. "And you," Guinness barked, turning to Marie. "I've had enough of your high-handed ways. Get below where you belong, damn it. You're my prisoner. Are ye deaf?"

So striking was her trance that Guinness finally stared toward shore, trying to figure out what she was looking at. Nothing was out of the ordinary. A manor, a signal flag at a small landing dock. "Damn your eyes. What're you lookin' at?" he asked, getting a little nervous. "Tell me!" he repeated savagely.

Marie slowly faced the marine, then with all the strength she could muster, walked past him and disappeared down the hatch. On her way, she whispered a name in passing. The corporal scratched his head, looked toward the shore and repeated the unfamiliar name as if it should mean something.

"Penscott Hall?"

Captain James Gregory paced his cabin and struggled to maintain his composure, then gave up the task as too arduous. A semblance of calm would manifest itself when the need arose. Of course he was anxious, and rightly so. The message he'd received from the packet boat in the channel had indicated the *Breston* and its prisoner could arrive none too soon. He should have been proceeding upriver to make anchorage in the Pool of London by nightfall. How galling to be delayed. Still, when the Duke of Brentlynn summoned, a lowly captain had best obey. Damn! If only he had Brand in tow! Then he would gladly stop and flaunt the capture. As it was, it would have been better to pass Penscott Hall under cover of darkness. Then no signal would have been visible and he could not be faulted for sailing past, oblivious to Lord Penscott's anxious wishes. No help for it now, though. He jammed a blue tricorn with traces of glittering stitching on his head and ventured on deck to greet the emissary coming from shore in the cutter. To his surprise, a complete stranger climbed over the side and strode across the deck to meet him.

"Ah, Captain Gregory?" The officer's broad Germanic face brightened with recognition as he approached.

"I'm afraid I do not have the honor," Gregory replied stiffly, unsure of his guest.

"No, we haven't met. But I recognize authority. I am Colonel Heri Goff, assigned to Lord Penscott by my liege and countryman, and your monarch."

A Hanoverian, Gregory mused. His thoughts were interrupted by a squad of four soldiers climbing over the rail. Less resplendent than their officer, they still cut very sharp figures for enlisted men.

"And what need has the Duke of Brentlynn with a Hanoverian escort?"

"Why, as a matter of esteem." Gregory digested that and tried to discern if it was the truth. Nothing in the officer's eyes betrayed any less. "My Lord Penscott is one of His Majesty's most trusted servants, and I am consequently a symbol of the love and trust our Majesty bears Lord Penscott."

"Then you are most welcome aboard the *Breston*, Colonel." His mind racing, Gregory bowed. The language had been a little flowery and the slight emphasis on "trust" was a clue not to be overlooked. Had Goff been sent to keep watch on the old man? It could well be. A year was a long time and from what little he'd learned through gossip around the fleet, there had been subtle but important rearrangements in the structure of power surrounding the king. "I can offer you a pleasant journey to London. If you have not yet sailed aboard an English vessel of war, you might find the experience enlightening."

"You misinterpret, sir, though I do thank you." He smiled thinly and drew a letter from his coat. "My mission is more prosaic. I have a letter for you from Lord Penscott. Will you receive it in your cabin?"

453

"Of course," Gregory agreed. Stranger and stranger. He spun on his heels and led the way to the captain's quarters, not liking this Hanoverian in the slightest, even if they were, as appeared likely, unknowing colleagues. Once inside the cabin, Gregory took the letter, pointedly declined to offer his guest any refreshment and stood to one side to break the seal. As he read, his features underwent a metamorphosis and became a veritable portraiture of rage. "This . . . this cannot be," he sputtered.

Goff pulled at his broad, square chin. His frown might have expressed sympathy, but Gregory couldn't be sure. "M'lord explained the nature of his request before my departure," the Hanoverian said as diplomatically as possible. "He stressed, as I am sure he does in his letter, that according to standing orders, he wields authority over all captured freebooters. He wishes, furthermore, that I tell you this authority has been confirmed not less than a month ago."

Not much more needed be said. Gregory kept his face expressionless, tossed the letter onto his desk and shouted for his orderly. A towheaded young seaman entered, knuckling his forehead. "Find Corporal Guinness. Tell him he is to release the woman prisoner to the custody of Colonel Goff." The youth sped out the door.

Goff saluted. "I am certain Lord Penscott will be most pleased with the speedy manner in which you have complied with his request."

Gregory searched the man's face for a hint of mockery. Finding none, he bowed slightly in dismissal. "Always a pleasure to be of use to the duke. You may tell him that."

The colonel nodded. "Of course. Now, if you will excuse me, I will see to my prisoner. Good-day, Captain Gregory. So nice to have made your acquaintance." The Hanoverian bowed crisply and left the room, his boots rapping the wooden planks in a precise cadence.

The door closed and Gregory slumped into the chair behind his desk. His stomach seethed with nausea. He reread the single page of handsome script directing him to relinquish Marie into Goff's hands, explaining that she was to be sequestered at Penscott Hall until further notice. Damn! If he only hadn't sent ahead that packet! What in the world had induced the old man to such an action? For a second Gregory had considered ordering the stuffy colonel off his ship, but such a move might damage his career irrevocably, even if he were vindicated at a later date. No doubt he had chosen the wisest course: comply for the moment, then proceed as quickly as possible to London to secure a reversal of Penscott's instructions. One way or another, he'd get the bitch back.

The door opened and he felt another presence in the room. Armide had entered and stood just inside the door. "Get out," he said, his voice like the hush before a terrible storm. "Get out and stay out." When he glanced again, she was gone, almost as if she had never been there at all.

The cutter listed to starboard as a southeasterly breeze filled the canvas triangles. Marie huddled in the cloak given her by Colonel Goff, drew the cowl over her face and shrank into the heavy folds as if she sought to escape reality within the confines of the russet fabric. No one spoke to her, a fact for which she was grateful. Overwhelmed by this totally unforeseen development, she watched the approaching shore with a mixture of numbness and quiet acceptance. The stone facade of Penscott Hall loomed beyond the trees. To her left she could see the formal gardens, delineated by cleanly cut hedges. The south wing came into view. Was he watching her even now? That would be his bedroom there to the left. Lord Roger Penscott, a figure of vengeful caprice and unpredictable whims. Gregory knew only brutal cruelty, but the Lord of Penscott Hall had a thousand ways to subjugate a captive guest. The memory of imprisonment in the chateau with the gallows outside the window was as fresh in her mind as if it had been yesterday.

The boat scraped against the dock where two white uniformed soldiers dutifully waited to help the colonel who, in turn, extended a hand which Marie refused.

Ahead, the path to the chateau stretched into the woods, but when she started up it, a firm hand caught her arm in a tight grip. "Please follow me," Goff said, and started toward a waiting carriage.

"Where are we going?"

"The answer to that, mistress, you will learn in good time." Without further ado, she was handed into the coach, then jolted against the wall as the horses were urged into a brisk pace. Moments later they left the river road and pulled up the long drive that swelled into a circular court before the great manor. The colonel offered his assistance again, and this time Marie accepted without thinking. Still clutching the cloak closely about her, she allowed him to escort her up the steps to the massive doors, which yawned open as they approached. A bony-cheeked butler greeted them. His face seemed to sweep back from a jutting nose and the coat that he wore flared at the waist and fluttered as he walked on the stick-thin legs. Thrush!

"This way, please," the master servant said, his tone curt and almost feminine. He seemed not to recognize her and Marie, thankful for the cowl, made no effort to reveal herself.

Nothing had changed. The massive balustrade rose along the sweep of marble stairs. Sculpted faces of Greek and Roman gods stared in mute amusement at the foolish antics of passing mankind. Only little more than a year ago, Marie had toiled here, polishing the richly burnished wood plaques and dusting cobwebs from the marble pantheon. Only a little over a year: that serving girl seemed a stranger now. Lost in a raveling cocoon of rediscovery, Marie paid no attention to where they were going until Thrush led them into a spacious bedroom comprising the whole end of the northwest wing. "Someone will be assigned her," the master servant informed the colonel.

The cowl slipped away from Marie's features as she stared in open wonderment at the bedroom that had once been Gwendolyn's—Lady Penscott's. "My God!" Thrush blurted out. Marie turned toward the outburst. Open-mouthed, Thrush staggered backward through the

456

door. Marie found herself smiling in spite of her predicament. That the butler hadn't been told was a stroke worthy of Lord Penscott.

"You will remain here until summoned," Colonel Goff said, obviously as perplexed as Thrush yet unprepared to admit he didn't know what was happening. "A girl will be along shortly. Two men are stationed outside your door." He paused as if to say something else, something to appease his growing curiosity, then bowed gratefully and left as abruptly as Thrush.

Marie stood in the center of stillness. Glass windows at the west end opened onto a porch. A wind caught the silk-fringed drapes and sucked them outward like diaphanous wings trying to fly to freedom. Curious. If she could only fathom his will. Why ever had she been brought to Lady Gwendolyn's room? The mistress hated her and she couldn't imagine Penscott turning her over to his wife. It didn't make any sense. Uncertain and confused, she stood awkwardly, waiting, and trying not to admit her growing anxiety.

Dimly remembered conversations formed a chorus of the past. Her mistress's robust beauty beset by advancing age. Her outraged monologues against inexorable time and, in compensation, the heated couplings with young and eager stallions who lingered on the periphery of her husband's machinations. A raven-haired serving maid who shyly helped the lady of the house at her toilette. "Then it's true you've never known a man." Had Lady Gwendolyn said that? Yes. And more . . .

"We must forget about husbands and lovers."

"Did you see the Scot? Now there's a secret worth discovering . . ."

"To one's own grief," Marie whispered. "Yes, I saw the Scott." The room didn't answer, and the ghosts to whom she spoke drifted beyond the veil of her mind's muddy discourse.

Suddenly she started, cursing herself for such unconscionable self-pity. So absorbed in her own strange misfortune, she had completely forgotten the one true companion yet remaining her, and close by at that. Behan. She must see him. Quickly, she scrambled to the door and opened it, only to find crossed muskets barring the path. "Let me through."

"Not hardly, miss," one of the soldiers said.

She recognized him as one of the rowdy young men Penscott had employed as a groundsman. How gangly he looked in his ill-becoming tight whitecoat and breeches. "Johnny, let me pass. Please. Escort me if you must."

The lout grinned, displaying uneven rows of stumpy, blackened teeth. "The colonel gives us orders, and don't take light to privates that forgets them."

"It's only to see Behan, Johnny." The grin disappeared and the soldier's face hardened. "Look at you," Marie continued. "A year ago you hated soldiers and would have done anything to help one of your own."

"An' a year ago I didn't have this fine uniform that the kitchen lasses like so much. Reuben an' the others can grub in the fields all they want. Me and Terrell here ain't fixin' to bend our backs to no hoe ever again. Of course, we'd not be a'verse to matchin' a favor for a favor sometime."

Marie slapped away his hand as he tried to touch a pale revelation of shoulder beneath her tattered blouse. She slammed the door in the face of their laughter and stalked into the room, there to sit and wait for whatever happened next.

She woke to sun shining into her face from the west windows. A good share of the day had passed. Yawning, she rose and paced the room, wondering why Gwendolyn hadn't appeared. The glint of sun on steel gleaming over the hearth directly opposite the windows caught her eye. Against a swath of magenta silk, two rapiers crossed cruel edges in downward cuts. They proved to be blades of fine Spanish workmanship, she noted on closer inspection. Why leave two obvious weapons in here? But of course. This was a lady's bedroom. Of what use were rapiers to one whose weapons ought to be beauty and clever grace? Marie smiled. Lord Roger Penscott, Duke of Brentlynn, was not infallible after all. It gave her hope.

The doors opened and Marie stepped away from the wall and peered toward the shallow vestibule where a young girl waited nervously, her pert features tight with apprehension. Dimpled cheeks and lively eyes were terribly sober beneath a lace cap. "M . . . m'lady," she stuttered. "Mistress Ravenne?"

Was I like that once? Poor dear. "Who are you?" Marie asked, smiling and trying to put the girl at ease.

The soothing voice helped. "I am called Rachel," she said, staring at Marie's torn and threadbare clothes.

"What do you want? Why are you here?"

In response the girl crossed the room to thick velvet curtains. When she drew them apart, Marie recalled the sumptuous bath she filled from time to time for Lady Gwendolyn. "I filled it while you were asleep."

Hot water! Only once before in her life had she had a real bath in a tub full of hot water. Weak with anticipation, Marie stripped away the soiled garments and stood in front of the mirror. Eight weeks aboard the *Breston* had left her a trifle thinner. She turned sideways. All the bruises from the sinking of the *Ravener* and her capture had disappeared.

It took little imagination to think oneself a great lady, here in this room full of lace curtains, dainty furniture, a great mirror and a tub of steaming water. She posed, shoulders thrown back, breasts thrust forward and hands on hips. Not provocative enough, she thought, rearranging her hair to half-conceal one breast.

Rachel entered with a pile of towels and placed them on the same chair Gwendolyn used to sit on after her bath. Marie stepped away from the mirror and into the water. It was hot. Slowly, she eased herself down, sighing with pleasure as the water crept past her thighs and waist. "I'll do your back, mistress, if you please," Rachel said.

"Mmmm. That would be nice." Marie leaned forward as the girl knelt by the tub and dipped a huge sponge into the water, soaped it and began to wash her back. The soft sponge, slippery with soap, running up and down her back, scrubbing until her skin felt tingly and warm, was a luxury unrivaled.

"Rinse, mistress?"

"Yes, please." Marie sat up and Rachel emptied a dipper over her shoulders. The warm water ran down her back and breasts, felt like very soft hands caressing her. Jason had done the same, when they bathed the morning after their reunion in the glen. How she had thrilled, then, to his touch. Suddenly, tears of longing welled in her eyes. "Perhaps you'd better leave now, Rachel," she said quietly. "I think I need to be alone a little while."

Alone. She'd been alone for so long. Weeping softly, she sat back in the warm water and concentrated on trying to forget Jason. Sooner or later the pain, the hollow feeling that left her aching for him, would go away. Gradually, the water soothed and relaxed her and she had to fight to keep her eyes open. The last thing she remembered before the calming water sent her to sleep again was the way Jason's eyes glinted when they made love, and the way he whispered her name even as she called his.

When she woke again the water was tepid and the room aglow with a combination of brilliant sunset and at least a dozen flickering candles. Scrubbing quickly, Marie rose from the water to find Rachel close at hand with a soft towel. Dried, she was led to the great bed where a gown of satin the color of pale amethyst waited. Marie paused—what had happened to Gwendolyn? Where was she that a prisoner should be given her room? But Rachel insisted the gown was for her. A half-hour later, she stood in front of the mirror and stared in awed astonishment at the bewitching creature framed in gilt. The daring light green bodice revealed the soft mounds of her breasts. Graceful paniers stitched with silver and gold thread cascaded teasing folds of increasingly darker purple silk to the parqueted floor. Around her waist an amythyst-studded stomacher reflected the candles with a thousand points of pulsing light.

Rachel placed a row of scented powders close at hand. Next to them, ceruse and other ointments for her face stood open and ready. "No. I'll have none of those," Marie decided.

"But mistress—" Rachel, whose concept of beauty was molded by the current mode, rebelled at the very notion that a lady should appear in public without the usual masque and elaborately constructed coiffure.

"Take it away," Marie ordered, a trifle more curtly. "We'll spend the time brushing my hair instead." The girl nervously obeyed, and for the next half-hour stood behind her strange new mistress and brushed the dazzling raven-black hair until the rich locks glowed with the lustrous highlights in the candlelight, until the long curls fell in artfully contrived waves about her shoulders.

Marie examined her reflection once again. She had not worn such finery since that day in Mobile when she had gone to look for Jason and discovered him . . . the memory was too painful. She reeled dizzily, steadied herself by leaning on a throne-backed chair. Rachel was already at the door, waiting. "Mistress?" the girl asked, concerned. "Are you all right?"

"I'm fine," Marie said, straightening and taking a deep breath. This was no time for silliness. Something was about to happen and she would need all the wit she could muster. The door was open and Johnny and his soldier companion made no move to halt her progress as she and Rachel moved into the hall. She could conceal her curiosity no longer. "Where are you taking me, child?"

Rachel looked surprised that Marie did not know. "Why, mistress, you are to dine with the duke. Lord Penscott is waiting for you even now."

Thrush materialized from the shadows and opened the doors to the upstairs dining room. Marie paused to peer into his face, but the master servant had recovered from his earlier shock. Only a single, barely noticeable twitch in his right eye betrayed the forced air of indifference. Inside, a smaller replica of the oak table in the spacious great hall dominated the center of the room. It was covered by a cloth of intricately knotted lace, and held, evenly spaced down the center, a trio of matched candelabra, each holding at least a dozen blazing candles. Stately armchairs sat at either end, and in one of these sat Lord Roger Penscott.

"Do sit down, my dear. Ringe's pork pies must be eaten fresh from the fires or not at all."

Marie forced herself to stand straight. The years at Penscott flooded back. The master querying her in the library, assigning her to Behan, watching her from afar for what purpose she had guessed only much later. And that last scene. His hand had shook and he leaned on his cane as, voice trembling, he had given her to Gregory. The intervening months had been unkind. How old he looked, she thought, in his great waved periwig with its sheen of blue-white powder. Inside the cloud of white curls, his face had hardened and darkened until it appeared a leathery, seamed map of emotions beyond her ken. One aspect, though, remained as she remembered: his light blue, disturbing eyes snapped like live coals as he stared back at her.

Thrush held the chair and Marie sat, still unable to take her eyes off the apparition beyond the candelabra. Almost magically, the master servant appeared at Penscott's side and began to carve a slab of breast from the roast duck placed before him. Marie looked down at her own plate, a disk of pounded gold bordered with pearls, on whose mirror-bright surface Thrust ladled portions of duck, pork pie and mounds of vegetables. Whatever Penscott had in mind for her was suddenly of no importance. Fed on salt pork, pease soup and weevily bisquits for the past eight weeks, and nothing at all since the night before, Marie was faint with hunger. The temptation to refuse his food faded quickly. When one didn't know where the next meal was to come from, it was wiser to eat.

Penscott's keen eyes never left her for a minute. At last he chuckled, scooped a final morsel of pie into his mouth and shoved away the plate. Marie's was already empty, and on the master's signal, the platters were removed and replaced with clean goblets and small dishes of fruits and cheeses. "Fill our glasses and get out," Penscott said with a curt wave of his hand.

"Yes, m'lord," Thrush murmured respectfully, speedily obeying. Moments later Marie was left alone with the man who had saved her from drowning, kept her as a servant and then banished her. What he had in mind next, only he knew. Fed and full, she sat back to await developments.

Penscott ruminated for a long, silent moment before he struggled to his feet, and, leaning on an ornate cane of carved maple, limped toward her. His movements slowed by age, he kept a steadying hand on the edge of the table. A lesser spirit might have quailed before those agate-blue, predatory eyes, but Marie sat peacefully. The last year had been filled with far more danger than even this old and powerful man could bring to bear.

"You were hungry," he finally said.

Marie smiled graciously. Behan had always said not to commit oneself too soon. She would know when the niceties were done with. "Very. I hadn't realized, before, how exceptional Master Chef Ringe was." She frowned slightly. "He is, of course, still here?"

"Yes, yes. Gwendolyn, toward the last, fancied his fare too well, I'm afraid. Had hips as large as Darlington's paniers. I sent her away just this spring. But enough of that. Come with me and sit by the window. I want to watch the lighting of the torches."

So he'd sent her off. A smile seemed out of place so Marie kept her face neutral and followed the duke through patterns of candlelight across the room. A low, cushioned bench ran the length of the broad west window looking out to the circular drive where a number of tall brass braziers ringed the stone surface. Each burst into flame as a runner rounded the court, thrusting a torch into the bowls. Soon the entire space was aglow, and the drive leading down to the river road as well. "Curse the night!" Penscott muttered as the last brazier flared up, then settled down to burn evenly.

The spectacle might have been lovely, were there fewer fires. More widely spaced, they would have sparkled like flaring stars plucked from the heavens and brought to earth to serve mankind. As it was, the display was a garish attempt to hold back the darkness, the inevitable end of day. Yes, she thought, a year had wrought a deep and disturbing change in Lord Roger Penscott. Surely something had happened. Or was it merely age? Did a year make that much difference?

He must have been reading her thoughts. "You haven't asked me why," he said, his voice dry and flat, perhaps tinged with disappointment. "Why you are here dressed in finery and surrounded by luxury. Why you are feted like a queen when you were, after all, responsible for the escape of my son's murderer. Surely, it's a puzzlement, hmmm?"

"And as surely you will tell me when you see fit, my lord."

Penscott nodded approvingly. "Better and better." He moved away from the window and crossed back to the table where there was more light. "Curse that servant! I'll have more candles in this room, or his hide," he grumbled, picking up his goblet. "This particular vintage was given me by Sunderland."

Marie remained seated, a figure of composure. Behind a calm veneer, her mind raced with the possibilities of this confrontation. A strange course of events was in progress, a terrible rushing tide in which only the wary would survive. Penscott was a very real puzzle indeed. Changing the subject with each sentence, he was hard to keep track of, harder to predict. She could only wait.

"You have blossomed into a beautiful woman, my dear," he said, sipping the wine and continuing with the rambling, one-sided conversation. "Damned fool, Sunderland. Won't listen to reason. I have suggested the necessity for a cautious contact with the prince, for when the father falls, the son will have his due. Granted it's risky. One hand learning what the other is doing could bring disaster. Power is a terrible burden, my dear. Frightfully difficult when so many would gladly see me torn down. Clamor for my blood, in truth. One tries to take precautions. One even drinks chocolate with Tories—surreptitiously, of course—and still, one never knows. Not for sure. Those summoned to insure our safety have a nasty habit of turning on us, attacking through the door to the rear that was supposed to be closely guarded."

He paused and peered up at the portrait of his predecessor. The patriarchal face appeared to be constantly changing expression in the flickering light. "I should imagine Captain Gregory to be most distressed at your release."

"I did not see him."

"His father has become a bore as well as a turncoat. Gregory himself—yes, news does travel across the ocean, even if slowly—is no better. I had thought he was serving me, but am left with strong reservations. The young fool of an upstart! To think he can . . ." His voice trailed off. The old man finished off the wine and turned, a benign look on his face. "But that's of little import here, eh? The question is, what shall I do with you? You've become quite notorious, you know." He tried to suppress a laugh and was forced to choke back a cough. "By God! So that's what Behan was doing back there. Teaching you how to be a pirate. Who'd have thought it!" The laughter stopped and he stared at her with piercing eyes. "You didn't answer me. What shall I do with you?"

The reference to Behan had passed before she could ask about him. Now there was no time, for she sensed the question was of great importance. "Does what I want really matter?" she asked, tossing her long curls and crossing the room to stand directly before him. "You'll do with me as you please and we both know it."

"Spunk."

"M'lord?"

"Spunk, damn it. Spunk. You've heard the word." He pounded the tip of his cane on the floor in emphasis. "If you'd shown more of it earlier, things would have turned out differently. Now they want your neck. What do you think about that?"

Marie stiffened. "I think it's to be expected, m'lord."

"Of course it is." He stopped. Leaning toward her, he gazed directly into her eyes, one, then the other, as if searching for something. Marie stood without moving and returned the stare openly and easily, aware he was making up his mind, yet strangely calm. What would happen would happen.

"Sit down and listen to me," he finally said, leading her to her chair, then beginning to pace awkwardly through the pools of light. "I'm an old man. Grown older in the last year than in the dozen before that. I know it. Everyone else knows it too. I'm saddled with a damned spy, sent with the king's blessing to keep an eye on me, even if it isn't me who needs be kept watch of." He paused and leaned on the table. "Do you know what they want with you?"

"No."

"It's very simple. You'll rot in Newgate until you testify that the French and Spanish are out to wreck the Alliance. You'll be promised freedom but you won't get it. When they've got what they want, you'll hang."

Marie leaned back in the chair. There were a great many unanswered questions, but the overall pattern was clear. Gregory was a man who hated inordinately well. For whatever reason, he had added Lord Penscott to his list. The reasons for or against the Quadruple Alliance were beyond her, but the sides, as far as she could see them, were clear: Penscott wanted it to continue in effect, Gregory and his fellow conspirators were eager for it to fail. Marie Ravenne was the pawn to be used by both parties. "But what good am I to you here?" she finally asked.

"Call it a whim. Call it boredom or whatever you want. I'll not be taken for a fool. Right now Gregory is in London, meeting with those who would see me fall. Goff's messenger will join them tomorrow with intelligence from our illustrious colonel. My colleagues are aware of that, of course, and are preparing for the next few days. A week, two weeks from now, and it will be over with." He stopped to rest, then went on. "Whether you stay or go, the battle is met and will go on until I either win or lose. If I win, a certain amount of power is still mine, including the power to spare your life. If I lose . . ." He shuddered, seemed to shrink. "You will

466

certainly die, and I'll be left with nothing more than a stipend and these grounds. It's not a great deal."

Suddenly intent, he leaned forward and brushed a leathery hand against her cheek. "I am a fair man, Marie. I give you your choice. Say the word and I will have Colonel Goff bring you to London and the Admiralty's justice. Or remain here under my protection for at least a while. If it goes badly? You'll have had a few weeks, and perhaps, because I'm old and eccentric, I can help you in other ways." He chuckled. "Others have escaped from Penscott. You wouldn't be the first, as you know. If it goes well? There are worse ways to live than as the companion of the Duke of Brentlynn. Well, what is your answer?"

Marie hesitated, wondering what he was offering in full truth. To be his vassal? To allow him to use her for his own gain? *But I am alive. And in life is hope.* Perhaps the good Duke of Brentlynn wouldn't find her as malleable as he thought.

"Come girl. Your answer. Mistress of Penscott Hall, or reunion with the vaunted James Gregory."

She would rather have been mistress of a small plantation on an unknown island far from civilization, but was given little choice in the matter. The alternative was to hang. The mistress of Penscott Hall would enjoy no small amount of power. Properly wielded, she might return to the Caribbean one day.

A sly smile curved Marie's lips, concealed as she leaned forward to rise and curtsey. "My lord," she whispered in acquiescence and a voice sweet enough for treachery.

"Good. Good! It pleases me to know you've some sense." His eyes lit with pleasure and he brought his lips to her neck and bare shoulder. Marie fought down intense revulsion, allowed his papery kisses to linger a moment more, then stepped back. "I trust my lord will forgive me, but I am weary. This morning imprisoned aboard the *Breston,* and now . . ."

"Hmmm. Yes. I suppose so," he chuckled. "I shall see you on the morrow when we break our fast in the garden. Ten o'clock sharp, eh? I'll have Thrush see to it.

And we'll have a game of chess. You haven't forgotten, I trust? I insisted you be taught."

"Of course, m'lord. I remember well." Once again the opportunity rose to ask about Behan. This time she couldn't let it pass. "But you always played with Behan. I should hate to—"

"Behan is dead."

The words struck her dumb, with such severity that she gasped. "Gone to the dark," Penscott continued. "A week after the first frost last fall."

Marie shuddered. Behan was dead. "Did he . . . did he suffer?"

"What?"

"Did he suffer?" Penscott was looking at her strangely. "I loved him, m'lord. He was my teacher, and my friend."

"And mine," the duke said, sinking to his own chair. "No. Not overly. I had his cottage boarded up. He is buried in the tenants' plot, in a place of honor." His head sank to his chest. For the first time he was not looking at her. "So you see, I have not played chess in some time."

A door opened. He looked up, glimpsed Marie's departing figure in the hall. For a moment he considered becoming upset, then decided against it and started for his own bedroom, where he paused in the doorway. "Not enough light in here. More candles!" he bellowed. "Thrush, curse you. There isn't enough light!!"

Chapter XXIV

Bright-eyed men watched as Armide moved her dusky form about the tavern. Brass finger cymbals provided the only accompaniment to her motion.

Ting. Ting. Ting.

Armide is dancing. Desire her.

Ting. Ting.

Armide is passion. Lust embodied. Smell of sweat. Sight of glistening trails across dark flesh.

Ting . . .

Hands—dull yeomen hands that had never known the caress of such exquisiteness—groped to touch her legs or belly and the room rocked to the sound of cruel guffaws, stamping feet, fists and mugs pounding on tables. "Let me go, damn you!" Armide hissed. "Or by the teeth of Y'bo, I'll—"

Two jokesters grabbed her wrists and hauled her to a boisterous drunkard who was obviously aroused. His powerful hands slipped under the mulatto's skirt, gripped her thighs and pulled her down to straddle the horrible length. Everyone cheered the first and successive thrusts. Armide gasped, strove to lift herself free of the coupling. One of his great hairy arms pinned both hers and the other was clasped about her waist, lifting her up and down, up and down. She could not extricate herself from the torment.

At least not by force. A look of sly pleasure clouded her face and her lips opened in an inviting pout, wet by a flickering tongue. Harry turned his grizzled jowls toward the onlookers. "'E's got her now," someone cheered.

"She's comin' around, Hurry. Don't stop now!"

"Give us a kiss, love," Harry groaned, pulling her close.

"Ah, yes . . ." Armide moaned, bending back and then forward in feigned spasms of pleasure. "". . .

love . . . yes . . ." she whispered. Avoiding his ugly mouth, she fastened her teeth firmly on his nose and bit down.

Harry shrieked in agony and leaped from the chair, hurling Armide across the room where she landed in the crowd. From somewhere on the fringe, a lantern shot across the room to explode in the midst of the tables. Pandemonium ensued as the patrons shrieked and clawed and shoved their way toward the door and windows, trying to escape the spreading flames. Armide struggled upright, spat out a distasteful gobbet of flesh and joined the rush for the door and fresh air. Behind her, the tavern's owners were already battling the flames and bringing them under control. Armide thought grimly of her few belongings upstairs but, not relishing a confrontation with Harry or his friends, slunk through the gaping spectators and into the night.

"Well done," a gravelly voice at her side said. Armide walked faster but the stranger kept pace. "Whipjacks and rufflers. A woman like you deserves better'n that scum. Why'n't you come with me, dearie?"

Armide stopped. The alley was dark and though she couldn't see the stranger, the voice was vaguely familiar. "Who are you?" the mulatto asked. A week in London had taught her to be careful.

"Don't matter. I got me two fine gentlemen for the night, and can only be with one. The other one likes 'em fiery. After what you did to 'Arry, I 'spect you'd do."

"Two *gentlemen*?" Armide asked, a little suspicious. Would real gentlemen be in this part of town? She didn't know, but from what she'd seen of London during her short stay, anything was possible. In any case, she needed someone with power to champion her. Someone worthy of the spell she could weave. If this was the only way she could meet them, it would have to do.

"Well, you willin'?" the unseen harlot asked. "If you do him good, there's a pound or more in it for you."

Armide nodded and followed the buxom figure through a maze of alleys and sooty vapors. They wound their way between crooked and sagging buildings whose inspired irregularity gave mute testimony to the efforts of some mad constructionist. Eventually they came to a squat, two-story hostel of mortared brick and stone. A roof of overlapping shingles framed the facade like thick eyebrows on a frowning face. "It's all shuttered," the girl observed.

"'Course it is, dearie. These gentlemen appreciates their private go-forths an' don't like bein' interrupted." She hurried to the door, rapped twice, then three more times. The door creaked open. "They still here?"

"Upstairs," a voice replied.

"Got the money?"

"In their purses. I seen it."

"Better'n better. Come along dearie, lest they get tired of waitin'."

Armide nodded and entered into near total darkness. The door shut behind her with disturbing finality. She suppressed a moment's panic when a hand—the older woman's she hoped—caught her arm and guided her across the room. Keeping close to her newfound companion, she ascended a staircase and paused before a door at the top of the landing. An amber glow filtered from around its edges. "Yours is in there, sweet."

Armide smoothed her dress and pushed against the door. She hoped he was handsome, but as long as he had money she'd be happy. Hips swaying and face molded into a promise of countless delights, she entered and looked around, then froze, unable to move. A bronze, golden-haired ghost stepped from the snare of shadows and placed a restraining palm against the door.

A thousand questions whirled through her mind. What was Jason doing there? How had he found her? He must have found out about the bitch, Raven, and followed her. She had to be careful. Only one way, and that she must take. "Jason," she purred, ignoring the hand that kept her from fleeing. Gliding, she pressed her full breasts against him, let her thighs meet his. Her nipples tightened and she knew her breasts were swelling with desire. He would remember, would take her.

They would be together again and he would forget the black-haired one.

"Well met, little one," Jason said, accepting her embrace, brushing his lips across hers then melding them in a feverish kiss. Armide undulated against him, demanding closeness, demanding his body. How good they had been together! She tugged at his breeches, caressed the growing length between his legs. Jason suddenly laughed, swept her into his arms and carried her to the bed. Armide purred, settled onto the mattress. Her skirt slid up and her legs parted, ready for him.

"Jason . . . hurry . . ." she panted as his hands slid over her shoulders and stroked her breasts.

"Armide," he whispered.

"Hurry."

"Listen to me. Where is she?"

For a fleeting instant she thought she had misunderstood him, but the truth struck her numb. She'd been trapped! The harlot disguised by gloomy night was the hag who'd been on Mysteré. Raven's friend! Her reaction was instantaneous. "Bastard!" Flailing hands reached to rake his face and eyes.

Forced to let go her throat, he caught her wrists. "Where is she, damn it! Where——"

Armide squirmed sideways, managed to twist free and rush for the door. It slammed back on its hinges and she fled into the hall and down the stairs. How had he known? How had he found her? Lost, confused, frightened and angry, she paused at the foot of the stairs. The room she had passed through in darkness now shimmered in candlelight and she recognized three men from Marie's crew and, as she had guessed, Hope. Forlicar was there, too, and Ramahd, his eyes sadly watching her. At a table in their midst, a half-drunken Giuseppe pointedly avoided her stare.

"You" she spat. "You told them." She spun around. Jason was descending the stairs.

"I . . . I was below decks when they took her off," the surgeon stammered, "and just as surprised as anyone when I learned she weren't aboard no more."

Armide leaped the last step and ran toward the door.

472

Tom Gunn intercepted her. She pummeled his muscular chest. "Let me pass. Whoreson—"

Her cry was cut short as his huge fingers tightened about her windpipe. "My house was empty. My shop a home for beggars and whores," Tom said, his voice choking. "My wife and boys was gone. Gone! There's nothing for me here. Nothing but to find the girl and see her free."

"That's enough, Tom," Jason shouted.

"No. She will tell us."

"Let her go!"

"No."

Jason slammed his pistol against the giant's arm. Tom howled and loosed his grip. Armide sank to the floor, gagging for breath. The huge man glared at Jason and started for him but Shelby intervened. "He's right. Tom. She can't tell us if you break her neck."

For a tense second or two it looked as if Gunn would hurl Shelby out of the way, but at last he backed away from his companions, slumped down on a bench at a far table and said no more.

Jason looked down at Armide and nudged her with his toe. "Where did they take her?"

"Leave me alone."

Jason knelt. His thick gold mane glowed with a crimson light borrowed from the candles. "You've some dark deeds to answer for, Armide. Now, I'll not torment you or be your judge, but you must tell me what Gregory did with Marie. She's not in Newgate, if I can trust my spies, and none of the poor wretches carried off from Mysteré are alive, so I can't ask them."

He paused, took her hand and helped her sit up. "I'm sorry, Armide," he continued gently, "for the wrongs I did you. But now time is short. You must speak. I—all of us—have come a long way to find her and won't leave disappointed."

"Captain Gregory will—"

"Gregory won't do anything to you. That I promise. He won't even know you talked to me."

"You'll let me leave here?" she asked warily.

"Yes."

A sneer crossed her face. "How can I trust you?"

"I shall see to it, *kadın*," Ramahd said in an ominous voice. She might find Jason a faithless lover, but Ramahd would never contradict himself.

Armide nodded. She looked around the room. Each face was a study in intensity. In the candid, quiet reaches of her soul, she suddenly confronted the inescapable reality of the woman called Raven, the woman who had taken her man. Her man? No. Jason was no more her man than the one before him or the one after him. Since childhood there had been men, but none of them hers. Instead, she had been theirs; each had used and discarded her, dropped her by the wayside for another. These men—and the woman—had sailed thousands of perilous miles to the heart of the enemy's country. Their very lives were in danger. They'd come of their own free will. And for another as unlike her as day was unlike night.

For another. Who had ever done anything for Armide? So much love. Never would she taste of it. Such love was reserved for others. Never for Armide. An unbearable sadness overwhelmed her and her hate for Raven dissolved, to be replaced by a curious, gentle envy. She would wander the filthy streets of London, so different from the blue waters and white sands of the Caribbean. Men would violate and use her, but it wouldn't matter, for it was too late. Surrounded by others no better treated, she would have but one consolation: somewhere amidst the squalor and dirt, the ugliness and depravity, there existed at least one who was loved.

"I do not know the name of the place," she said quietly, looking into the flame of a candle. A tear, untouched, ran down her cheek, but her voice was strong. "The captain halted partway up the big river leading here. Strange soldiers came. Soldiers like those in the streets. White coats and breeches—"

"Hanoverians," Forlicar grumbled distastefully. "Go on."

"They take her."

"But where?" Jason insisted.

Armide shrugged. "There was a great house and beautiful gardens. Very beautiful. I think they bring—"

"Penscott Hall!" Jason blurted. "Of course. That wily devil!"

In the excited talk that followed, none paid attention as she rose and started to the door. She was almost away when Poacher caught her arm. "Hold. We'll tell you when you can leave."

"Let her go," Ramahd cautioned, stepping near.

Poacher's ugly scowl defined how he felt about that. "Many a good man is dead because of her," he growled.

"I gave my word, Dearam," Jason said, trying to defuse the situation.

Poacher remained steadfast a moment more, then shrugged and stepped aside. Ramahd led Armide outside and paused to peer down the alley. "Do not fear for me," Armide said calmly. "I don't need it."

Ramahd smiled sadly. "Poor little one—"

"Nor do I wish your pity," the mulatto hissed, and stalked off into the gloom without looking back.

"Or my heart," Ramahd added quietly so she would not hear.

Inside, Armide already forgotten, the talk went on. "Who is this Penscott?" Forlicar was asking.

"Even I have heard of him," Giuseppe moaned. "A very powerful lord. Duke of Brentlynn. It is said Penscott Hall is a magnificent mansion. I have never known of anyone escaping from there, and I've heard he keeps a gallows for unwanted or unwilling visitors. There is nothing you can do for Raven if she is there."

"I have been to Penscott Hall as a guest and as a prisoner," Jason said. Gunn looked closely at him and Poacher's eyebrows raised in disbelief. "Forlicar and Ramahd know this is so. There is a way to take her from them, but we must act quickly."

"Aye. The quicker the better," Hope said, speaking for the first time.

"No English ship will chance upon Dunston's Cove," Jason said reassuringly. "I used it many a night before our paths ever crossed. As for Tomás, he'd die for Marie and will keep a close watch on the ship. The fishermen are Jacobites and have no love for the king or any of his men. Our worry is not with them, but with the task at hand." He turned to Dearam. "We'll need a fishing cutter."

"Said and done," Poacher said from near the door. His eyes glittered with the prospect of action.

"I'll help," Shelby added eagerly.

"Good," Jason said. "Find what you can and send Shelby back here so we'll know where you are. We'll meet you sometime around three in the morning, which will give us time to get past the tower before daybreak. Meanwhile, where's Ramahd?"

"Here," the Turk answered, entering.

"You'd better come with me. We'll need provisions. Forlicar, why don't you wait here and make sure no one steals Giuseppe's bottle."

Giuseppe's hand fluttered to his cheek in consternation. "I don't feel like drinkin' no more. You don't owe me anything."

"True enough," Jason grinned, looming over the pathetic Italian. "But you just might tell someone else you told us, might you?"

"No!" Giuseppe said quickly. "No. Of course not."

"I know. You'll be asleep." He straightened, checked the room. Tom Gunn continued to slump dejectedly at a far table and Jason waved Hope toward him.

Hope nodded in understanding and, as Jason and Ramahd slipped into the night, waddled over to Tom and sat across from him.

Gunn stiffened, rubbed his sore arm and glowered at her. "We'll be havin' need of you in the long nights to come, Tom. Come. Have a tankard of ale with me."

Tom stared into the candle. Wife and sons gone. Shop gutted. A man wasn't given much choice. Without friends he was doomed to hate alone and probably die alone. At least he had friends. Together, they might make a new life. There was naught to do but say goodbye to the past, painful as it was. With a long, slow sigh, the tension gradually eased and the knotted muscles in his broad shoulders relaxed. "One," he said, shaking his head up and down. "One."

The threatening, beefy-red countenance of Kitchen Master Ringe softened affectionately as Marie entered his room of hearths. He mopped a cloth across his balding pate and dragged his immense bulk step by step toward Marie. A half-dozen servants busy with the morning meal at a table in the corner grew quiet as the woman who had once been as lowly as they passed through. Hushed whispers raced around the table.

"Aye, used to scrub floors, she did."

"You wouldn't think to look at her now that she'd tasted Thrush's cane."

"Slept in the room next to mine, she did, until that Scot took to givin' it to her. Helped him escape, she did."

"Henry says she been a pirate. Killed a dozen men or more."

"And now she's the grand lady of the house? Kill a few myself, for that."

"You'd have to swive the old man, to boot."

Marie ignored their mumbled tittering. "You're kitchen smells as good as ever, Master Ringe."

Ringe touched his forehead. "Thank'e Miss. Pleasure to see you here," he said, glancing about uncomfortably.

"Now, Jonathan," Marie laughed lightly to cover her own nervousness, for she felt strangely out of place and somewhat impertinent for calling him by his first name. "And quit touching your forehead. I'm the same old Marie with a new dress on, is all. I'll not have the man who kept me alive treat me like the grand lady I'm not."

Ringe grinned self-consciously. "Still and all, miss, the new dress does wonders. And if his lordship says you're the lady of the house, it's good enough for me."

"Good enough to make me some of that plum pudding?"

"Plum pudding? I've three of them. There's the—"

"The one you brought me just before they took me away."

Ringe beamed with delight. "I remember. Tonight you'll have a plum pudding the likes of which you've never seen."

Marie smiled, briefly held his hand. "Old friends of mine have a habit of coming to a bad end. I wouldn't like to be the cause of your misfortune, Jonathan."

A girlish voice tittered. Ringe swung around and glared. An awkward silence fell on the table and all the servants decided they'd eaten their fill. Within a minute they'd shoved aside half-finished plates of food and scurried from the room.

"They meant no harm," Marie said, still glad to see them go.

"Poisonous tongues always mean harm, miss. Always have and always will."

"Yes. I suppose so—"

A great hiss of steam interrupted her. Ringe started, stared in horror at the big fireplace where a huge kettle of water was boiling over and threatening to douse the flames. He was off like a shot, shouting for help to the kitchen boy who had fallen asleep in the corner.

Marie hurried across the room and left by the rear door. No sooner had she started down the path than she caught sight of Colonel Goff watching her from the rear of the manor. "Never fear," she muttered to the white-uniformed officer, though he was beyond hearing. "I don't seek my freedom. Where do you think I'd flee to? At least this is a familiar prison." Ignoring him, she swept up the hem of her gown and headed across the garden.

The path to the cottage was ill-tended, for with Behan's death there was no one to travel that way to carry his meals. She slowed as she approached. With the exception of one window which was open to the elements, the shutters were closed tight. It had taken her almost two weeks to venture this far. Now her love for the venerable old tutor conflicted with apprehension at actually visiting this earthly reminder of their friendship and the hours they had spent together.

The door resisted at first, then gave way as if it sensed a familiar hand. Early morning sunlight probed the dusty interior, alive with dancing motes thrown into the air by the suction of the opening door. Timidly, Marie stepped across the threshold. Dust lay in drenching thickness on everything. Books, some opened, lay in scattered profusion on table, hearth and workbench. An overpowering sense of the past engulfed her, drew her further into the room. A puff of air stirred the debris at her feet. Leaves, brittle blossoms, a wisp of cloth, a broken bit of mast from a carefully modeled ship: the signs of his presence—and passing.

Eyes misting, Marie stopped by Behan's chair. Was it possible she heard him speak? The bones of their conversations rattled in the thin air. Shared kindnesses lingered, bittersweet as the remains of the cup of chocolate on the table where his arm always rested. Even now there was comfort in the old room. Peace, too. She brushed cobwebs from the hard-backed chair opposite Behan's and sat carefully. The chair creaked, but only through disuse, for it was as solid as ever.

Here she had sat and listened to tales of the Brotherhood, learned the intricacies of sailing ships and tactics in the unceasing war between those born to power and those who fought to obtain and keep the freedom that was as important to them as the air they breathed and the water they drank. Here she had watched rooks, knights, bishops and queens go down to defeat, until one day she had finally won her first game on the dusty chessboard that still rested on the table. There in the center of the floor she had mastered the rapier, practiced until her legs and right arm were a mass of screaming, tortured muscles. Here, too, she had whispered of her love to the only one of Penscott's subjects who would understand and keep it secret. Here she had plotted to free Jason and planned their flight.

Jason. Always Jason. Why couldn't she banish him from memory? He was far away in every sense, didn't love her and never had. Better to concentrate on Behan, he who had never been unfaithful to her, who had shared kindnesses and given comfort. She started, painfully aware of his absence. What a short time he'd been gone! A half a year? Less? It didn't matter. She could still picture him, irascible when she didn't immediately grasp a point, pleased when she bested him. What had blind Louveteau called him? Behan Blackheart? She laughed silently. If only every man and woman in the world had so black a heart!

Suddenly Marie yelped in surprise as a furry gray creature leaped from around an overturned globe and into her lap. The animal meowed plaintively. "Fair Weather! It is you, isn't it?" she exclaimed, hugging the cat and brushing her cheek against its soft pelt.

A rasping purr of satisfaction was her answer. "Dear Fair Weather. You've remained faithful to the last, waiting for your friend." Fair Weather licked the back of her hand. His tongue felt like a rough ribbon stroking her flesh. It was evident the cat had been living alone in the little cottage, coming and going through the broken shutter. Unused to fending for himself, he looked thin and drawn. And lonely.

Lonely. Marie held him tight and scratched his neck. The new day was warm enough but a chill crept over her and she peered apprehensively about the room, feeling terrible for its disarray. How pitifully small it seemed now, how inexpressibly cramped. Behan, who had sailed the open sea and lived under the infinity of sky, had been reduced to this tiny space no larger than one of Penscott's drawing rooms. Somehow he had acclimated himself to it, packed it with a universe of his own. But could she, even with all of Penscott Hall at her disposal? Dark forebodings filled her soul and she huddled, trapped, alone and afraid, in the chair. Was there no escape? None?

Fair Weather stiffened in her arms. Marie looked around, frightened. The cat bounded to the floor and disappeared under a table as Colonel Goff appeared in the doorway.

"A most inappropriate place for the lady of Penscott Hall," he commented drily, dabbing at his nose with a silk kerchief. "I should think . . ." his face screwed up. ". . . should think . . ." A sneeze racked his frame, then another.

"The dust bothers you, Colonel?" Marie asked with the amused smile she was careful to maintain in his presence.

"It does not you?"

"My spirit, perhaps."

The Hanoverian looked distastefully. Two inquisitive steps had ruined the shining, polished surface of his boots and consequently his expansive mood. He grimaced. Marie's laugh was light as the lilting music of a spring morn. "Do you think I plot mischief, Colonel?"

"A beautiful woman should be seen in sunlight," he remarked sarcastically. "Come. I will escort you. In my country—"

"We are not in your country, Colonel. However, neither are we in mine." She placed her fingertips on his arm and allowed him to lead her from the realm of sheltered memories into the glaring present.

Their path took them first toward the Hall, then veered off to the right and toward the landscaped woods and glades between the chateau and the river. The day was one of those incomparable English early summer days when the ugliness of winter has long since vanished and the dusty hot weather has yet to get a grip on the countryside. At first, Marie paid little attention, merely followed where she was led. Then, as the silence between them stretched on, she became aware of a growing tension. Her mind began to spin with a thousand possibilities which she assessed coldly and dispassionately.

Goff's aloof character had gradually thawed in the two weeks she had been the curious mistress of Penscott Hall. Perhaps she could make use of such a metamorphosis. She took stock. The gown she wore, silk and taffeta the color of a maiden's blush, was almost peasant in cut. While the colonel's attention was distracted by the movement of a hare in the bushes, she hunched her shoulders and settled her decolletage an inch or two lower. Now her breasts, barely confined, swelled above her bodice and invited caress. She had used her body once before to win freedom. Perhaps she could do so again.

The colonel looked back to her, his eyes drawn down, then back up, masking a pleased look. The tension in her arm increased and he led her into a small, sunswept glade. "Now, is this not better than that tomb?"

Marie's heart was beating so loud she thought he must hear. The air smelled clean, washed with the scent of lilacs. Like diminutive cathedrals, fir trees pointed emerald spires toward heaven. A host of chattering birds swooped down to scold. When the man and woman failed to leave, they carried their commotion elsewhere. Her knees weak, Marie sank to a fallen tree whose knobby trunk made a most excellent bench. Goff half-knelt, half-sat beside her, striking a classic pose. So confident was he in his own handsome nobility, so incapable of entertaining the notion that a woman might not seek his favor, the colonel failed to see through Marie's enticing ruse.

"You speak of tombs, Colonel. Of the past." She tightened her arms at her sides and the colonel's breath quickened as her breasts swelled, dangerously close to slipping out of the bodice. "The past doesn't worry me. It is that which clouds my future I find most disturbing."

"You have nothing to fear. Not now, surely. Lady to a powerful personage like Brentlynn, and he decrepit enough to allow you freedom . . ." His words were ripe with meaning. He leaned forward, brought his lips to her hand.

"Freedom, sir? With guards at my door?"

Goff's eyes rested openly on her breasts. His right hand lifted and a scrubbed and manicured finger traced the line of her bodice, lazily slipping into the deep cleft between her breasts then out again. "Even a colonel must obey instructions. Fortunately, he is allowed some discretion. If he were, say, engaged in a *tête-à-tête* with his prisoner, the guards might be removed for such time as he deems necessary."

Marie leaned forward slightly, increasing the pressure of his finger. "And how long," she asked, her voice a husky, sensual purr, "do you think might be necessary?"

Goff wet his lips and his eyes narrowed. "As long

482

as madame wishes, given her cooperation and certain, shall we say, assurances of her good will."

So be it. The means to gain release. No longer the pawn in love's cruel game. To conquer, I have only to yield. Allow his arms to bring me close to him. Let my lips melt beneath his. Lips that have known the taste of Jason's. No! I cannot! No use. His clean, sun-burnished image defied her efforts, held her soul in an unbreakable grasp.

She felt herself lowered to the ground, felt nettles catch in the obsidian cape of her hair. Her breasts were free to his provoking tongue, her skirts raised to her thighs, and then beyond. A horrid chill enveloped her soul as the memory of days and nights with Jason washed over her. No matter his unfaithfulness. She had given herself to him, heart and soul. Her love for him was a blazing candle whose flame still burned. Could she deny it now? Deny the purity of the vision? Love had seared her whole being. Were she to die this moment, enter oblivion alone, that love would still blaze to light the way. She could not betray Jason, even if it meant her life.

Panic-stricken, she began to struggle in his arms. Goff, mistaking her reticence for a game, attempted to force her, one hand sliding her skirt past her waist. Somehow he'd opened his breeches, and pressed the swollen pulsing staff against her naked leg. "Come dearest. Your . . . spirit is . . . unseemly," he grunted, trying to imprison those hands which suddenly threatened his eyes.

"Release me," she hissed.

"Soon, my love. And sweet release, too," he panted, swinging one leg over her.

Without warning, triumph turned to defeat in the form of a well-placed knee driven into his sex-engorged groin. Goff rolled to one side and Marie scrambled to her feet. "You bitch!" he gasped, gulping for air and fighting the pain.

Marie arranged her skirts and bodice, brushed the leaves and nettles from her gown and hair. Gray eyes glinted while she watched Goff try to stand, then fall back into a sitting position against the trunk of the tree. "You've crippled me," he groaned, clutching himself.

"Hardly," Marie scoffed. "Taught you a lesson in manners would be more likely."

"You're as mad as the duke. I gave you your chance, and you've thrown it away like a fool. Mad, I say."

"Perhaps, Colonel Goff. Or perhaps, for the first time, quite sane."

By noon the sky had clouded over. She passed Behan's cottage and started for the manor. Thrush, the wings of his coat furiously flapping as he ran, met her on the path. Beads of moisture streaked his chalk-white face. "M'lord wishes to see you in his garden. I've been looking all over for you."

Marie nodded in dismissal and altered her course to round the south side of the house and pick her way through the maze of hedges. Lord Penscott, his demeanor bleak and foreboding in contrast to the carnival of blossoms surrounding him, sat slumped on his favorite bench, caught in the shadow of a passing cloud. Marie stopped and stood before him, dreading to hear the proof of her sudden premonition.

Penscott's cane lashed out. A silver pot flew from the table and spun through the air, spilling hot chocolate in a wide arc. "Damn Tory drink," he cursed, eyeing the bent and misshapen pot.

"I'm to be brought to London, aren't I?" she said quietly.

"Power. A man is nothing without power." The duke chuckled. "When the lights are out, all cats are gray." He traced a directionless path in the earth with the tip of his cane. "And those that cowered on command now stride the palace halls like Colossi. So it ends."

"I'm to be taken to London for punishment, aren't I? Answer me!"

Penscott looked past her as if she weren't there, looked up at the scudding clouds, reading them as he had learned to do as a midshipman. How many years ago? Too many. "There'll come a storm," he said. "Mark my words. Nor'west by nor', or I miss my guess.

484

Shorten all sail and double-lash the cannons. High seas tonight, lads. High seas."

"M'lord?"

Penscott jerked as if pulled from a dream. He blinked his eyes and looked at Marie in surprise, seeing her for the first time. "My servant has brought the news," he said haltingly. "Gregory is on his way to take you back to London to testify—and be hung in Tyburn Square."

Chapter XXV

A dull gray storm-pall settled over the land as the western horizon became totally blotted by a towering bank of ugly black clouds. A chill wind gusted the curtains and bent the hastily lit candles into sputtering orange streamers. Marie overturned the joined vials of sand. An hour begun anew. Another hour irrevocably lost. Perhaps the rain would slow his coming. But to what profit? An extra day's life? She peered through the distorted glass divided by a steady trickle of sand. Portraits in an hourglass. Time and the world, marked by spilling grains. Rachel crossed to the balcony to close the windows. "Leave them open."

"But the rain—"

"Has yet to begin," Marie completed. "Leave me. Go back to your room if you wish."

"Yes, mum."

The serving girl was more than likely aware of Marie's impending fate. In fact, by now the messenger was certain to have recounted the news to half the household. Those who didn't hear it from him would hear it soon enough from others. By the time the house settled in for the night, the story would have been told and retold, embellished beyond any semblance of reality.

Rachel's startled gasp caught Marie's attention. And then she heard it too: the sound of a cane tapping on the marble floor. Penscott was coming to see her.

The girl stepped between the two sentries at the door, curtsied quickly and hurried off down the hall with a muffled "m'lord." Marie approached the door to greet her visitor, noted with alarm that the guards from Penscott Hall had been replaced with the colonel's own Hanoverians. Apparently Goff no longer trusted the locals, now that Gregory was so close. Their muskets, raised to let Rachel through, snapped crisply into place again. Lord Penscott found his path blocked. "I wish to enter."

Neither guard appeared to have heard. "Surely you speak some English," Penscott snapped. "I wish to enter."

Still the sentries ignored him. "Let me pass, damn you!" the old duke shrieked. Veins like purple lengths of string stood out on his temples.

"Here, here," another, calmer voice said. Colonel Goff stepped from the shadows. "Really, my dear Lord Penscott. Such an outburst is most unseemly from one of your exalted station."

"Damn my station. And yours, too. This is my house."

"And the girl is my prisoner until I've been otherwise informed."

Penscott's eyes narrowed and he straightened, the need for a cane forgotten. Marie could have sworn he grew—or shed years—before her eyes. For the first time she caught a glimpse of his character as a younger man, a glimpse of the strength that had made him a force to reckon with in court circles. "These men will let me pass, Colonel," he said with icy calm. The words were clipped, the accent flat. "If not, I will summon my tenants and have you expelled bodily from these grounds, instructions or no."

Colonel Goff stood his ground for a moment, then sighed in resignation. Obviously, he could restrain the duke, but the danger of injury to the old man was too great and would never do. He nodded to the two sentries, who immediately relaxed their stance. Lord Penscott flashed a single glance of contempt at the colonel and stumped into the room, slamming the door behind him.

"Welcome, my lord."

"Hrmmph. You needn't pretend sweetness with me. Won't get you a thing. I can do nothing to help you." He crossed to the open windows as the first swollen drops dappled the tiled flooring of the balcony. The world was poised at the brink of darkness, the sky a seething maelstrom scudding from the northwest. "Thus comes the darkness to swallow day and leave men in the grip of heinous night. So speak the poets," he said, becoming again an old man and weary.

"The poets are sometimes wrong, m'lord. Night is some hours away," Marie was bold enough to comment.

Penscott cocked his head toward her. Strangely enough, he did not lose his temper. "Your waspish tongue might best be used on others."

"I have little need for courtesy now, my lord."

"True enough," he said, gazing out at the drive. "It will be impossible to keep the lights lit tonight."

"I feel certain Captain Gregory will find his way. Revenge is a very bright beacon."

"Well said." Penscott looked around the room. "A pity."

"M'lord?"

"At my age one is permitted to indulge in fantasy. It's a pity you didn't occupy this room long, long ago."

No matter what had passed between them, Marie was touched by his tone of voice and the certainty that he meant what he said. "You flatter me, m'lord."

"Do I? Unfortunately, I am capable of no more than flattery." He seemed lost in thought for a moment, then repeated, "There is nothing I can do for you."

"I have not asked for anything, m'lord."

"No, you haven't, have you." Leaning heavily on his cane, Lord Roger Penscott, Fourth Duke of Brentlynn, bowed, took Marie's hand and kissed it, then nodded and limped to the door. The sentries allowed him free exit. The hall was ablaze with candles. He was grateful for that.

The cutter kept close to shore. For most of the journey from London it had shot unremarked past larger craft in service to the navy as well as occasional patrols of English soldiery assigned to keep the roads safe from the depredations of those not inclined to honest wages for honest work. But now, with a storm brewing, they could not help but draw attention to themselves, for no legitimate fishing craft would be out in such weather. To make matters worse, Hope, used to a larger vessel, had been felled by the craft's constant heaving motion.

The wind increased and the sky darkened further. If the storm hit while they were on the water, there was real danger of their capsizing. The journey would have to be continued by land, and the switch must be made soon, before an accident soaked their limited supply of powder. Dearam, who knew that part of the country better than Jason, suggested they put ashore on a relatively level beach nestled between two large tree-covered knolls. Ramahd's calm hand on the tiller guided the swerving, leaping boat to safety. Tom leaped into the water, followed by Shelby, Forlicar and Jason. The four held the cutter while Poacher and Ramahd gathered the sail. From there, it was short work to drag the boat onto the beach. Only when everything else was safely unloaded did Hope struggle to her feet, step across the gunwale and out.

Jason thrust a pistol into his belt and motioned for the rest to gather around. The sky was darkened and the clouds lowered ominously until it seemed as if night would fall prematurely. Only by watching closely could they make out the simple map he drew in the moist sand. "Here we are. And here beyond this stretch of trees is the river road. Five or ten miles east is Penscott Hall, where we're heading and where we'll find Marie, if all goes well. Now, there's a tiny cove just barely downriver from the manor. We'll meet there if we get separated."

He paused, looked around the circle of faces. "I think I remember a tavern"—he marked an "X" on the sand—"right about here. Called the Owl, I think. With this weather, no traveler in his right mind will be on the road, so the stable should have horses enough for all of us. That's where we go first."

"Looks simple enough to me," Tom said, speaking for them all.

"Damn! First pirates and now highwaymen," Shelby joked, anxious to be off. "And father wanted me for the clergy."

"Churchmen and thieves. The same thing if you ask

me," Dearam snorted as Jason rose and led the way up from the beach.

"Such terrible things you say," Hope chided. "You're a blasphemous man, Poacher."

"Aye. And known hunger in my gut while those of the church grew fat as the hogs they ate. Don't talk to me of blasphemy." He pulled at his ungainly nose for final emphasis and would say no more.

A hundred yards through the forest brought them to the river road, which was empty of any sign of life. Jason breathed a sigh of relief and struck out toward Penscott Hall, keeping well ahead of the others in order to hide the fear that raged through his mind. For all he knew, Marie might already be dead.

Trees overhung the road and deepened the heavy shadows. Looking back to check, he could see the tension in the faces of his companions. Ironically, Ramahd, usually the most stoic and imperturbable, seemed the most apprehensive. Jason waved him forward and the two men plunged ahead together.

"We will have to feel our way before long," the Eastener complained, stealing a glance upward where broken fragments of black clouds raced the swaying branches of the trees.

"What is it, old friend?" Jason asked. Not wanting to speak, Ramahd shook his head. "Ramahd?"

"There. Listen. Do you hear it?" The wind soughed among the branches and obscured the noise of their passage. Save for that, Jason could hear nothing. "There. Again," Ramahd said, eyes wide.

"But there is nothing."

"There is a voice." Neck hairs bristling, Jason listened intently. "You do not hear the voice?" Ramahd asked, almost pleading.

"Only the wind," Jason said.

The Turk nodded, resigned. He smiled grimly. "It calls my name," he whispered softly. "We must hurry."

"That's it. I was right," Jason exclaimed, relieved that his memory had not failed. The Owl and the Peacock, as the tavern was correctly called, appeared bustling with preparations against the coming storm. Horses were being led into a large stable. A woman was struggling to gather in a load of clothes hung out to dry. In the yard, a wheelwright in a leather apron was busily engaged in fitting a new wheel on a carriage. A nobleman stood behind him, urging him on.

"Looks like that'un ain't fixing to stay long," Forlicar muttered. Jason crept ahead another twenty feet. The would-be rescuers followed his lead. Eyes narrowing, Jason peered into the gloom. The afternoon was so dark the wheelwright had called for a lantern. He thrust a stake into the ground and hung the lantern near the wheel. The nobleman gave one final instruction and turned toward the inn. Flickering light played for an instant on the scarred visage of Captain James Gregory.

Jason clenched his fist and his eyes darkened with hatred. As the English captain neared the Owl and the Peacock, the front door opened and two soldiers stepped out, saluted smartly and received his orders. Immediately, they marched to the carriage, where one stationed himself by the wheelwright. The other continued on to the stable.

"I'll wager there's a sight more of 'em inside," Poacher said.

"And all of them bound for Penscott Hall, or I miss my guess," Jason added.

"At least there's horses," Gunn added, suddenly coming alive.

"Aye. But how many bloody soldiers to take 'em from?" Forlicar asked.

"You don't need to come if you don't want to," Shelby chimed in nervously.

"I'd just like to know how much of a hero I'm about to be," Forlicar shot back, somewhat miffed.

Jason grinned. They were a high-spirited lot, and the prospect of going into action with them at his side allayed his fears. "Well, There's only one way to find out. Let's go."

Bunn of the King's Fourth Mounted couldn't have cared less about the weather. Let it rain. He had a roof over his head, even if it was only a stable. What galled him the most was being separated from a leather jack of ale and the buxom pleasures of Katy, the innkeeper's daughter. Now that bloody bastard Grahamby would have her to himself. Curse all sergeants, especially Grahamby. The other men could mutter all the oaths they wanted behind Gregory's back: he was a sea captain and no concern once they'd fetched Penscott's prisoner and brought her back to London. But Grahamby was always with them and spoiling the fun. Perhaps another mishap with the wagon could be arranged. If it broke down again they'd stay the night for sure. Better still, he might have an accident himself. The thought of spending a day or two recovering in Katy's arms left him invigorated. His wife, Priscilla, might suspect, but Katy's nubile, eager form was reward enough for the dangers he'd face at home.

A tendril of a shadow darted from the wall, became an arm and hand holding a gleaming fang of steel that ripped across Bunn's throat and ended visions of unrepentant pleasures. The dilemma of Katy and shrewish Priscilla became far less important than the immediate problem of staying alive. Gagging, trying to call out, he staggered out the door and tried to run for his companion by the carriage.

He didn't get two steps. A dark form slipped behind him and a sun-darkened hand cupped his chin and jerked backwards. Bunn's musket clattered uselessly to the earth and his fingers spread before him in supplication as the shadow drew him back inside the stable and out of sight. Twice more the horrid fang struck, driving under the ribs and unerringly finding the heart. Soundlessly, Bunn slipped to the ground. He did not feel the knife being wiped clean across his chest, nor see the intent face that peered into his own. Nor hear Ramahd's soft grunt of satisfaction at a job well done.

"Never seen the like a' him," the soldier sympathized in answer to the wheelwright's continuing complaints. A body shouldn't have to be called out to fit a bloody wheel to a carriage when an unholy storm was threatening to break any minute. Hell. Where was anyone going to go anyways? No carriage would be able to make it once the rain started, but he'd have to walk the half-mile to his cottage.

As if in support of his grumbling, thunder rumbled out of the west and washed over the land. The wind rose and trees bent, swaying violently and driving the birds from the air. The soldier and the wheelwright stared up. "Can't tell if it's night or them is just clouds," the private said, shivering.

"It don't matter," the wheelwright replied. "Either way you'll be staying right here 'til morning. Maybe longer. That road east? You ought to see it after a good wettin'. A quagmire, that's what—"

A great booming stilled their conversation as clouds were rent apart and crashed into new formations. Lightning sizzled across the sky. The soldier stepped around the carriage to wave in his companion. "That damn Bunn. Thunder must've scared him inside. Well, let him sleep with the damn horses if that's his wish."

The wheelwright kicked the hub and was about to pronounce the carriage ready for travel again when he saw Hope coming toward them. " 'S'blood! And who might this be?" he wondered aloud.

The soldier swung about, his stance relaxing when he saw it was only a woman. "Hello, sweet," he said, his eyes ranging approvingly over her large breasts.

"Heavens me, a soldier of the king," Hope exclaimed, her voice alive with promise. "And it's thankful I am, too." She loosened her shawl.

"I ain't never seen you about," the workman said, shrewdly observing the new arrival.

"Nor I you," countered Hope. "But that don't mean a lad can't be civil and see a lady has a pint of ale and a warm bed on such a night." The wheelwright snorted and bent to pick up his tools. The soldier stepped close and put an arm around Hope, who nudged him with her hip and flashed a lascivious smile. "I've always said there's nothin' like a fine, brawny soldier boy on a stormy night."

"Ha. Then you're in for a terrible disappointment,

lass," the wheelwright jeered. "I'll warrant these men of the Fourth will be off quick as a flash when I tell the captain his carriage—"

"A few more minutes won't matter," the private said, leading Hope a few steps to the side. "Now, lass, you'd best tell me where you've come from."

"Why, from down the road."

"Where down the road?"

"Hmmm. If you must know, there's a certain noble gentleman who has a fine manor but ugly manners." She dug an elbow in the private's side to emphasize her little joke. "I'd enough of him, in short, and left. And here I am. Walked out on him and all the way."

The private shook his head. "I'm sorry, lass, but I'll have to show you to the captain. Orders."

"But you can't. Please? It will go hard for me if you do."

"Well, there might be a way of changin' my mind," the soldier said slowly, stroking his chin in a semblance of thought.

"*Our* mind," the wheelwright added, catching the drift of the conversation.

Hope looked back and forth between the two, stalling for time. "Maybe I could offer something in the way of payment," she finally admitted.

"Aye. That you could." The workman, eager now, was almost dancing from one foot to the other. He had no stomach for conspiracy, but the prospect of a bit of something new—surely the old lady who was pleased to call herself his wife would never hear of this one—was almost more than he could bear.

Hope smiled, looked around and pointed to the barn. "I'll bet there's some nice soft hay in there."

"You picked it," the soldier said. "But there's another inside to demand payment for a closed mouth. Bunn's his name."

"Never settle for two when you can have three, I always said," Hope laughed, leading the way. With nervous backward glances to the inn, the men followed.

Hope was the first to enter the nearly totally dark interior. The soldier followed and the wheelwright

494

trailed along in the rear. "Bunn?" the private whispered. "Damn you, man. Wake up and show a light. Quickly now. See what I've brung us."

No answer. Groping, he took another tentative step, tripped and landed on something like a pair of legs. "You stupid bast—" His hands, feeling in the dark, encountered the gaping wound in Bunn's throat. "My God!" he blurted, leaping to his feet and knocking into the wheelwright. "My Gaaaaa—"

A huge, bony fist shot out of the darkness and exploded against the side of his skull. The private dropped to the floor. Behind him, the wheelwright struggled in Forlicar's iron grip. A candle suddenly sprang to life and the wheelwright gave up: Jason and his men surrounded him. "No. Please. I didn't do—"

He got no further. "You go to sleep now, no?" Forlicar whispered in his ear. Without waiting for a reply, the pirate spun him around and struck him over the head with a horse pistol.

"Hurry and saddle the horses," Jason ordered.

Hope blanched at the prospect. "I ain't built for ridin'," she complained.

"The hell you say," Forlicar joshed, heading for the nearest stall. "Sure fooled me."

A commotion at the door cut short Hope's reply. A red-coated figure had appeared for the briefest of seconds, then darted from sight. A rolling crash of thunder obliterated his cry of alarm.

"Finish saddling, all of you. I'll stop him before he sounds the alarm."

"But—"

"Damn it!" Jason cursed, and was through the door. He was the nearest to the fleeing guard, and it would be up to him to catch the man. Still he shouted over his shoulder for Ramahd. The English soldier, come to check on the guard and report on the wheelwright's progress, now ran for his life. Jason leaped the carriage hitch and grabbed a dagger from his belt. A pistol shot would surely alarm the tavern and there was no chance of catching the soldier before he got to the door. He held the dagger by the handle as Ramahd had taught

495

him in their too few lessons. The soldier was almost to the door. "Now or never," Jason said to himself, and hurled the knife. The spinning steel gleamed with a life of its own as if flew across the yard and thudded, hilt first, into the soldier's back.

Screaming, sure he was dead, the soldier leaped onto the shallow porch and slammed his fists against the door.

Someone would hear! Someone would open the door and the soldiers come streaming out. There was only one recourse, one final, mad gamble. Jason loosed his rapier and one pistol and ran toward the tavern. The door opened and the soldier fell through, voicing a shrill cry for help. In the same instant, Jason cleared the porch and hurtled into the half-closed door, sending the frightened soldier and the man who'd let him in flying headlong into the broad common room.

A fleeting tableau of flaming hearth, of long, crudely planed tables and red-coated men in various states of disarray. Of clay mugs, pewter and leather tankards, platters of meat, muskets stacked. Jason's momentum propelled him through the room. Off balance, he slammed against one man and rebounded toward the table in front of the hearth. Slashing wildly, he stumbled over a bench. His toe caught a stool and he toppled shoulder-first across heavy oaken planks. In the same motion, he fired his pistol at a red-coated shape lunging toward him. The soldier was blown backward into the hearth. He managed to roll himself from the fire, his heavy coat black and smoldering. The man shuddered once and died.

Another soldier came from the side and Jason ran him through with the rapier, losing it as he fell to the floor. The fall saved his life, for the soldiers had recovered quickly and grabbed their weapons. Lead balls thudded into the heavy oak planks or spattered fragments from the stone chimney. Jason was weaponless, and any second the soldiers would realize it and be over his makeshift barricade. Desperate, he grabbed for the nearest piece of anything he could use for a weapon, a short-hafted iron shovel on the floor of the hearth. At the same time the firing stopped and there was a moment to think.

Voices. They'd decided. Quickly, he slid the shovel into the fire, into the middle of the mound of glowing coals. Timbers dropped, exploding as they rolled onto the hearth. Jason swung the shovel in a mighty arc, timing his movements with the rush of boots as the soldiers charged. Coals, burning chips of wood and ashes flew into their faces. The three leading the attack howled as flames bit at their uniforms. Others collided with one another, blinded by the burning soot. Jason scooped up more coals and sent another shovelful of fire across the table. One soldier penetrated the midst of swirling embers. Jason parried a thrust bayonet and brought the flat of the spade in a ringing blow to the youth's skull. The lad dropped, his torso dangling over the table edge.

The sharp crack of a musket to his left, the searing shock of a lead ball tore through the flesh of his upper arm. Jason staggered and dropped to his knees. The soldier on the stairway shouted to a companion who joined him, realized he had a clean line of fire and raised his musket. Jason, steeled himself for the second shot. He was trapped at last. The soldier grinned, tightened his finger on the trigger.

Without warning, the shuttered window across the room flew inward as a barrel came smashing into the room. At the same time the door burst open, completely torn off its hinges with the full force of Tom Gunn's irresistible force. Behind him, Poacher and Ramahd emptied a brace of pistols each while Forlicar did the same through the gaping hole that had been the window. Drawn by the sound of the unequal battle inside the tavern, the four arrived just in time to save Jason's life, for their explosive entrance so unnerved the soldier on the stairs that his shot went wild.

Jason leaped up, grabbed his rapier from the chest of the youth on the floor and jumped from bench to table to stairs. The first soldier died as he tried to aim his reloaded musket, the second felt himself flung over the railing to land on his back on one of the benches. Jason glanced around. Men swirled about the common room.

Forlicar had gone berserk with battle lust. Soldiers scattered from the path of his cutlass. Others fell, knocked senseless by blows from Tom's mighty fists. Ramahd leaped atop one table, took aim and loosed his daggers slowly but with devastating effect.

It was too much. Where there had been one madman in their midst, now there were five, wielding cutlass, rapier, dagger and fists, and in the process reaping a harvest of blood. The remaining soldiers dropped their weapons and ran into the night or allowed themselves to be bound. A quick check showed Gregory was not among them, nor was his body among the twisted shapes of the dead or wounded. Cursing aloud, Jason raced up the stairs, shouting the English captain's name.

The first two doors he kicked open revealed empty rooms. In the third, a young girl of fourteen or fifteen, naked and clutching the remains of a dress about her chubby frame, glanced from Jason to the open window near the bed. "Damn!" Jason shouted. "Fled! Where?"

The girl could only gape and stutter uselessly. Turning, Jason descended the stairs three at a time, leaped the dead and was through the door on the instant, shouting over his shoulder for Ramahd and Poacher to follow him. The wind was furious now, pressed against his body so he had to lean forward to keep his feet. There was smoke coming from the stable. It was on fire.

"What the hell's that young'un—" Poacher started, the admonishment dying in his throat as he entered behind Jason. A gout of flames sprouted from a pile of straw in the middle of the room. Smoke began to fill the stables. The noise was incredible. The horses, maddened with fear, screamed and whinnied, rolled their eyes, reared and kicked at the slats. Shelby lay sprawled in a heap at the edge of the burning straw. The front of his blouse was crimson with his own life's blood.

"He killed him." The three men jerked around, reached for their weapons. Hope, a livid bruise spreading over the whole left side of her jaw, staggered toward them. Tom and Forlicar appeared in the doorway.

"Shelby's dead. Free the horses!" Jason's harsh voice spurred them from their trance.

Forlicar shook his head. "I'll see to my Hope," he growled in a voice not even the devil would argue with. Jason nodded and joined the others trying to coax horses from their stalls. Only when shirts and blankets were thrown over their heads, and soothing words crooned into their ears, would the crazed beasts respond.

Even then it was a battle that consumed precious time. Jason chose a sturdy gelding, led it outside and returned for a saddle. Hope was sobbing in Forlicar's arms. "Poor little lad. Never had a chance. Gregory came in an' disarmed him, then shot him in cold blood. Shelby just stood there, too proud to run." Suddenly she stiffened, looked at Jason. "He said he'd beat you yet."

Jason nodded, already fearful. "He's gone to Penscott. I'm sure of it. Gone for Marie."

The night flared into phosporescent brilliance as lightning crackled nearby. "Then ride, man! We'll join you," Forlicar yelled above the storm's thunderous barrage. "Poacher can show us the way."

Jason tightened the cinch and swung into the saddle. "Scatter what horses you don't take," he shouted, trying to calm the rearing gelding. "Give me your cutlass!" Forlicar handed him the weapon without question and Jason dropped his own, broken during the fight in the tavern. "The soldiers—"

"Don't worry about them," Tom bellowed. "The tavernkeeper's going through their pockets, taking what he can find as payment for the damage. Besides, they'll have no horses. Ride, man!"

Hope placed a restraining hand on Jason's leg. "You'll save her?"

"I'll do my best. If I fail, or if we get separated, look for me at the cove. If I'm not there, ride for the *Banshee* and get away yourselves!"

"We'll be hard on your heels."

Jason nodded, grim-faced, and turned his horse to the darkening road. Two hours to nightfall. He'd have to ride hard.

It began to rain.

Chapter XXVI

Thunder on the land. Scintillating bolts of electricity stabbed downward in heavenly wrath. Lord Roger Penscott, Duke of Brentlynn, roared in agony like a wounded beast as the latches gave way and the heavy, glassed doors leading to the balcony swung inward. A violent gust of wind extinguished candles and toppled candelabras. Penscott fought his way to the doors, where Thrush materialized at his side and helped shut them. "Light those candles again."

"M'lord, Captain—"

"Damn you, do as I say!" Penscott hobbled from the dark chamber, seeking the comfort of light. Safe in the hall, where flickering tapers lit the portraits, he headed for the stairs, wincing at each thunderous cannonade. He paused at the topmost landing of the broad central stairs, debating whether to venture the descent to the downstairs library and deciding against it. Goff might be there, and the last thing he wanted was to exhibit his irrational fears before the unsympathetic colonel. He toyed with the idea of calling on Marie but rejected it as well, for each visit with her left him more disturbed than the one before. Better to leave well enough alone. Damn the storm. Damn the night!

"Penscott!"

The voice startled him, the speaker even more. Penscott peered down the stairs. Stationed in the middle of the great vestibule, Captain James Gregory stood, wild-eyed and wearing a rain-soaked cloak. He wavered for a moment, then steadied himself and began to climb the stairs. Colonel Goff had heard the commotion and ran into the hall from one of the drawing rooms, straightening his uniform as he came. Two men of his command stationed outside the drawing room door snapped to attention.

"I have come for the little whore you stole from me," Gregory said, not yet at the top of the stairs.

"How dare you enter my house unannounced?"

"I sent your master servant to inform you of my presence, only to be left standing at the door like a common servant. Now, where is the girl? I want her now."

"You've changed your tune since we last met, young man. Then, you swore to bring back a man. Now, like a wet and bedraggled spaniel, you break into my house and demand a woman. You're no better a man than your father, who is not a man at all, but a traitor." Penscott paused, quivering with rage. "But not even a spaniel deserves this weather. Since you are here, I will have Thrush find a room for you. When the storm breaks, you may leave."

"No! We leave immediately."

"What's that?" Penscott asked, incredulous.

"You're not serious," Goff interjected.

"We shan't go far," Gregory continued. "Only to your gallows, Lord Penscott. The woman dies tonight." He reached inside his waistcoat and extracted a waterproof packet which he handed to Goff.

The colonel tore open the packet and read quickly. "He has the authority, m'lord," he announced, handing over the missive.

Penscott read silently, then stared at Gregory. Behind him and leading down the stairs to the main doors, a set of muddy tracks left a clear trail. There was a time when no man would have dared . . . There was a time . . . His face a mask to hide the pain of failure, he leaned on the balustrade and stared blindly into the light below.

Gregory glanced meaningfully at Goff. "Jason Brand is on his way here."

"Brand?" Goff queried. "The pirate Brand? I don't understand. You must be mistaken. Whatever would he be doing in England?"

"It seems he and the woman were lovers. Incredible as it may be, he's evidently come to get her."

"Come, come, Captain. Another man, similar in build—"

"I must beg the colonel's pardon," Gregory said, seething with impatience. "He has confederates, all of whom are armed and dangerous. If I may respectfully suggest you post your men—"

"My men? I have but four." He shrugged eloquently, indicating how little faith he placed in ploughboys changed into soldiers but a month earlier. "And two of them I've recruited from the household. We never expected more would be necessary. I take it you came alone?"

Gregory flushed, unwilling to admit the disastrous affair at the tavern. "Yes."

"But Brand will not," Goff persisted. The English captain was every bit as much of a boor as he had been the first time they'd met on board ship. If he couldn't be polite, he would be humbled.

"There were others with him," Gregory explained, straining to stay civil. "I assume they'll accompany him here, if they're able. Sir, I must beg your speedy indulgence. I—"

"He'll come here, no doubt about it," Penscott chuckled, interrupting him. "But not just for the girl. He'll be looking for me. And you too, Captain Gregory."

"Gladly," Gregory replied softly, not caring whether anyone heard him or not. He would have a fine present waiting for the brigand: Marie Ravenne as gallows bait.

The door to her room flew open and crashed against the wall. Marie jumped from the chair and cast a calculating glance toward the rapiers on the wall. There was still time. After the storm, when they left for London, they would not find her willingly awaiting their pleasure. Gregory strode into the room, followed by the guards. "You expected me?"

"One never expects jackals." Marie flipped the raven hair away from her face. She would not bend before him, nor ask for his mercy. Her look of defiance turned to puzzlement as Johnny and Terrell passed Gregory and stationed themselves on either side of her. Before she knew what was happening, her arms were seized and bound behind her back.

*My God! He's taking me tonight. Tonight! The rapiers
. . . Too late . . .*

Gregory pulled forward the cowl on his cloak to protect the ceruse and powder that had already begun to
streak despite efforts to keep his face dry during his
hectic ride. "Follow me," he ordered curtly. "Hurry."

Two more white-clad soldiers were waiting below.
Colonel Goff made no move to join the party. Gregory
shot him a quizzical look.

"I shall remain behind and await any visitors who
come to the front door," the colonel explained. Hiding
the unspoken humiliation in the woods that morning, he
allowed a faint smile to cross his face as he looked at
Marie, then bowed curtly to the captain and returned
the letter of authorization to his pocket.

Marie averted her eyes, unwilling to allow the Hanoverian a final, mocking stare. Goff gestured to the
great hall. "This way, Captain Gregory. You will find it
a drier path."

Gregory nodded. "Bring her along," he ordered,
leading the way. Gripping her arms with unrelenting
insistence, Johnny and Terrell pushed Marie forward
until she shrugged free of their hold and continued of
her own volition. A host of unanswered questions left
her confused and frightened. Where was Lord Penscott?
What was happening? Why were they rushing so? The
journey through the manor became a macabre odyssey.
Servants paused in curious appraisal to watch her pass.
Thrush stepped from a side gallery, his arms full of candles destined for Penscott's room. His drooping nose
dipped and he wagged his head in dismay at Gregory's
watery tracks. As for Marie? She wasn't his concern.

The unceasing fury of the storm underscored their
passage. Into the scullery now, where raging hearths
combated the unseasonable chill. Young boys carried
wood to feed the fires. Girls labored over a dozen
dishes, not nearly so many as for a banquet, but enough
to satisfy their lord's delicate tastes. A mammoth shape
loomed to one side. Marie attempted a wan smile but
Ringe's grief-contorted face eroded her confidence. *They
all know! If they only dared help!*

503

The rear door opened onto slate-gray sheets of water. Marie recoiled but was dragged forward. The chill rain struck her bare cheeks and shoulders like a plague of needles. She bowed her head, but the luxuriant luster of her hair was already transformed into inky, cloying strands. At times she lost sight of the world, save for the muddy path underfoot and the undeniable presence of her escort. She moved in a landscape of downpour, of piercing blue-white lightning and deafening crash of thunder. The smell of ozone permeated the air. She wanted to call out to the caped and cowled figure hunched forward and leading the way, but pride refused to permit him the satisfaction. And then the ultimate question was answered. Looming out of the drenching grayness was the gallows of Penscott Hall.

Lord Roger Penscott, Duke of Brentlynn, loaded the dueling pistol. Once, ages past it now seemed, he had presented this very weapon to James Gregory and instructed him to kill Jason Brand. How ironical! He rammed the powder charge down the heavy octagonal barrel, gave it an extra tap with the ramrod, then picked the most perfectly round lead ball and jammed it into place. Flashes of lightning brightened the curtains. Mad gods were at play beyond the walls of Penscott Hall.

Within them, too.

Convinced at last that Brand was coming, Goff extinguished the candles on the balustrade lining the great stairs, checked the four loaded pistols at his side and took a position behind one of the pedestals on which rested a long dead Roman emperor hewed from marble. Like the Roman, Goff was a soldier with a soldier's instincts and training. This Brand, if he were a clever fellow, would chance capturing Brentlynn and use his prestigious hostage to secure the release of the girl. Better that than to try to take the woman directly and so risk blundering into an unknown number of guards. He dabbed at his upper lip, then tucked the silk kerchief back into his sleeve. He checked the priming in the pistols and adjusted the flints. If Gregory was right, he wouldn't have long to wait.

Jason guided the gelding off the river road and onto the cobblestone drive leading up to the huge, blackened silhouette of Penscott Hall. Heedless of danger, cutlass in hand and vengeance in his heart, he urged the steed up the stone steps and dismounted at the top, tethering the animal to a loop of iron on one door. The other swung open at his touch.

Head ducked and cutlass ready, he charged through the door and dove for cover behind a heavy japanned table. The foyer looked empty. Ahead, the central stairway swept upward into quiet darkness. Below, candelabra filled the hall with a soft glow. There were shadows everywhere, too many shadows. Warily, he crossed the hall at a run, ducked behind a chair placed another dozen steps closer to the staircase. Beyond that lay open territory. There was nothing for it but to run, keep low to the floor and hope for the best. Zigzagging, he left the protection of the chair, then froze as the sharp bellow of a pistol reverberated through the hall.

The echoes made it impossible to tell from which direction the shot had come. Jason glanced about, expecting attack from a dozen different doors and hiding places. There was no time to regret the brashness of his entrance. Above him in the shadows at the top of the staircase, a pale figure leaned into the amber light. A Hanoverian, by his uniform, pistol in hand, aimed at Jason.

The Scot crouched, ready to leap to the side on the instant he saw the telltale puff of smoke from the pan. To his surprise, the pistol appeared to waver and grow ominously heavy despite the efforts of the soldier, who reached out to steady himself. Straightening, Jason glimpsed a streak of crimson welling from the officer's lips, then watched as he fell face forward and slid down the stairs. Cautiously, Jason checked the corpse. A stranger, never seen before. But who had shot him?

"I did not do it for you," a voice said.

Jason stepped around the body and bounded up the

stairs. Lord Penscott stood in the hall, scant yards from where his victim had waited for Jason. A wisp of smoke trailed from the barrel and firing pan of the dueling pistol he held. "Nor the woman," Penscott added.

"Where is she? Take me to Marie."

"Let us call it a matter of honor."

"Damn it, man! Marie! Where is she?"

Penscott shook his head as if to clear away the remnants of a dream. When he spoke, his voice was clear, almost uncaring. "Marie? Why, Gregory has taken her to the gallows, of course."

The thunder and lightning had abated, and while the rain continued to fall, it lacked the ferocity earlier displayed. The scaffold steps were slick, the wood exuding an oily substance that made ascent tricky. Johnny and Terrell steadied Marie. From their faces one could tell they dreaded the task at hand. Playing the soldier's role and guarding a helpless woman was one thing, but hanging one was entirely different.

"Hurry, curse your souls!" Gregory shrieked, already at the lever which would open the trap. "Bring her to the noose. Be quick."

The captain's voice overrode their misgivings. Gregory's wrath was a very real threat. In that light, it was far better to hang the girl than be hung later by the man. Stepping carefully, they pushed her across the platform.

The cruel length of rope filled Marie with abject horror. Courage completely failed her for the first time and she cringed, drawing back from the yoke of death. Her action elicited a gleeful outcry from Gregory. "Not so proud now, eh little bitch? Not nearly so proud. Come on, damn you, get her over there! Come on deck, m'lady. We'll see you mutiny your way out of this one. I've—"

"Gregory!"

The voice stilled him. Johnny and Terrell halted before the noose, both men terror-stricken and rooted in place. Not daring to believe, Marie sought the voice and saw Jason through the mantle of rain. Had he followed her, then? He had! Beyond hope, he had followed her!

506

He was there! She knew the sun-struck hair and glorious, high-born features, radiant despite the dark shroud of the storm. Her heart swelled and she knew the giddiness of jubilation almost beyond bearing. He was there! He had followed her! Unwilled, his name welled in her throat.

"Jason!!"

Jason saw her. She was still alive. Marie was alive, and through the intervening yards, her heart reached out to touch his! He drove booted heels into the gelding's flanks. The willing animal plunged across the treacherous ground.

"Stop him!" Gregory roared to the two guards below. He turned to shout a command to Johnny and Terrell, saw them leap from the scaffold, chancing broken bones, shame and punishment rather than face the war god bearing down on them.

A wild, Highland battle cry split the gloom. Marie tried in vain to avoid Gregory's outstretched arms, but he caught her in two steps and wrestled her to the center of the platform. Bound, she could not stop him from slipping the abrasive noose over her head.

Jason reined his charging mount through the pair of Hanoverian soldiers who had the temerity to try to stop him. One fell, trampled under the horse's hooves. The other spun away, half unconscious from a well-placed kick to the jaw. "Marie!" The gallows! The gallows were so far away!

Marie winced as Gregory tightened the noose about her throat. *Jason, my love! My faithful love . . .* She could not take her eyes from him. In those brief seconds, time crawled to a standstill. Gregory, hurrying to trip the lever . . . Jason, leaning forward in the saddle, his eyes never leaving the woman he had loved and lost and found, captured in his heart . . . Marie, knowing he could not reach her in time, knowing only that her last dying thought had to be of Jason, that she loved him, would always be with him, in death as she had hoped to be in life.

Gregory gripped the stout oaken lever to release the trap door and yanked. The doors underfoot dropped away. Marie stiffened, braced herself as she plummeted, steeling herself for the horrible snap that would wrench her from the world. Her rump struck the soft earth beneath the scaffold with an undignified jolt. Above her, Gregory stared in disbelief as the last of the rope trailed over the end of the crossbeam and disappeared down through the trap hole. And with it, visions assailed him. Of the ignominy of being marched naked onto the quarterdeck of his own ship. Of hatred, implacable save through Marie Ravenne's death. Of Penscott's mock hangings to break a prisoner's resolve. Of the time he had led Brand to this same spot and laughed at the Scot's astonishment at finding himself still alive.

How devilishly amusing. What a fine, sardonic jest. A jest!

The rope! He had never thought to check . . .

"Nooooo!!" Eyes wide and colorless, brain reeling. Mad with failure, his last failure as he turned to the sound of pounding hooves. Paralyzed, he watched as the horse skidded to a halt and Jason Brand, the man he had sworn to kill, reared in the saddle and drove the cutlass upward through the rain.

Agony. More than Gregory had ever thought possible. He stared down at the basket hilt sprouting from his belly, felt the metal grate against his back. Blood welled through the rent in his cape and dropped, undiluted, to the floor of the gallows, where it spattered on the soaked planks. Lifeblood draining, he took one straight-legged step forward, slipped in the watery scarlet puddle underfoot and tumbled head over heels, striking the rump of the gelding and landing face down in the mud which smothered his final dying plea for a mercy he had never shown in life.

Marie. Marie!

Trembling, Jason tore the rope from around her neck. He brushed the clinging strands of hair away from her pale cheeks. Cradling her in his arms, he kissed her forehead, eyes and lips. "Marie," he whispered. "Marie."

508

Her eyes opened. Gray eyes as soft and timeless as the ocean mist. "Jason. I didn't dare hope—"

"Shhh. I'm here. I'm here."

Mud spattered. Her drenched gown clung to the inviting curvature of her breasts and delineated her legs and thighs and stomach, gently rising with each breath. Unspeakable desire. Untamable longing. Love, thought lost forever, had been found again. Not the same love, but one tested as few loves ever have been. A love as fresh as the wind-driven, perfumed days of spring. A love as pure as a snow-fed mountain stream or the limpid, throaty piping of meadowlarks. Love, full and forever.

"I love you."

A smile. They had spoken the words at the same time. In gentle unison, as one. Sometime during the infinity of their first kiss, the rain ceased. And thus their friends found them. Like hands joined in prayer, Jason and Marie pressed close, one to the other, unable to speak, only wanting, needing, never to be apart again.

Epilog

Our departure from Penscott Hall was part joy, part sorrow. In a way, I knew I should miss Lord Penscott. Though he had used me ill and for his own gain often enough, yet I could not forget that he had pulled me from the sea, that it was he who was responsible for Behan's tutelage. Most of all, were it not for this aged duke, I might never have met Jason, nor lived to see him again, for surely Brentlynn may be credited with delaying my execution and, as fate would have it, once again saving my life. For all his evilness, I could not bring myself to hate him.

Our journey to the cove where the Banshee lay at anchor, though promising peril, for the most part went remarkably well. This was, I believe, wholly the work of divine providence, as if heaven itself had decided we'd enough of plaguing misfortune. There at Dunston Cove we bid farewell to Ramahd, our Eastern friend, whose strange ways and fierce devotion had contributed to our success. As to his destination, he would only reply, "London." Why he returned to London we never knew, for he was a very private man. I have thought of him often through the years, and hope he found that which he sought.

Tomás welcomed me with open arms. Later, I rejoiced to discover he had saved Father's journal and brought it with him. Today the words are faded but still legible in places, and I keep it carefully wrapped against the light. When this, my journal, is finished, it will take its place with Jean Ravenne's so our sons and daughters, and theirs, will be able to read of whence they come.

With sails unfurled like the blossoms of spring and the motions of the waves like the promise of rebirth, the Banshee set out. Tom and Poacher, Tomás, Forlicar *and Hope Deferred, and Jason and myself—all of us prayerful that we had seen the last of strife—were kept busy keeping our craft before the wind.*

How blissful those days seem now. In the quiet of the diamond-hung nights, Jason and I quenched the thirst of our passion while the ship sailed on between the sea and the stars. Many a night, lying in the warmth of our bed, our thoughts reached back to those friends we had lost, and ahead to the New World where life would begin anew.

Mobile was closed to us, as Jason laughingly enjoyed repeating to my endless consternation. Oh, I would hate him then, 'til he took me in his arms and his lips traced endearments upon my breasts. Then I would open to him as a flower her petals to the honeybee. Forced to an English port, we resolved to change our names, for those of Brand and Ravenne would surely have brought us grief. Rather than risk the loss of our common dream, we chose a name to share in common, and vowed to seal it before a man of God. An appropriate name was a monumental problem which all on board tried to solve, until I remembered Jason's account of his father's wish for peace expressed on the inscribed plaque, trampled in the ruins of . . .

Like her father's, Marie's journal is no longer complete. Though there are many more pages, practically all have been disfigured by time and the elements. What is known of her later life with Jason is mostly hearsay and cannot be verified, as in the case of her Raven years, by the subject's own words. But parts of the story have been passed from generation to generation, much as the remnants of her journal were handed down.

Most agree she and Jason, and their friends, renamed the *Banshee* the *Fair Weather* and sold it in what is now Charleston, South Carolina. From there they traveled inland to a broad, fertile valley where the ruins of what must have been a magnificent plantation can still be seen. The property continues under family ownership, though not one living relative has attempted to disturb the serenity of the original homestead.

What few words remain legible on the end page of her journal serve not only as proof of the origin of the family name, but, ironically, as perfect summation of this extraordinary character, this remarkable woman whose story I have gleaned from the brittle pages of yesterday. What can be read is as follows:

. . . *are these, my days.*

September 22, 1760
Marie Ravenne Paxton
. . . to live for love.

Shana Carrol
Dallas, Texas